"*Bitterwood* is thrilling, full of plot twists, fabulous coincidences and reversals of fortune that drag the reader towards a neat, affirming conclusion."

—*The Guardian*

"In this imaginative new novel, dragons are refreshingly portrayed as the antithesis to the stereo typically fearsome, scaled beasts of old, and are instead intelligent, poetry loving, social creatures, who smell slightly of fish and are capable of love, hope, despair and daydreams... Bitterwood himself is a classic hero—and like the best of them, is often stomach-churningy gruesome in his exploits as the would-be saviour of humanity."

—*SciFiNow Magazine*

JAMES MAXEY

DRAGONFORGE

SOLARIS

First published 2008 by Solaris
an imprint of BL Publishing
Games Workshop Ltd
Willow Road
Nottingham
NG7 2WS
UK

www.solarisbooks.com

ISBN-13: 978-1-84416-644-2
ISBN-10: 1-84416-644-9

Cover art by Michael Komarck

10 9 8 7 6 5 4 3 2 1

A CIP catalogue record for this book is available from the
British Library.

Designed & typeset by BL Publishing.
Printed and bound in the UK.

For Laura Herrmann

Behold, I have created the blacksmith
who fans the coals into flame
and forges the weapons of destruction.
I have created the waster to destroy.

Isaiah 54:16

CHAPTER ONE

THE SUBTLE ART OF FALLING

1100 D.A. (Dragon Age), the 1st Year of the Reign of Shandrazel

GRAXEN SKIMMED ALONG the winding river, the tips of his wings teasing the water with each downbeat. The sunrise at his back cast a shadow dragon before him, a phantom companion that swooped and darted across the rippling current. The elms and maples along the riverbank had shed their leaves, papering the earth with rust and gold. In the crisp morning air, Graxen's breath billowed out in clouds that rushed back along his scaled body, forming a wispy trail.

As Graxen journeyed west, the river grew rockier, with patches of white water. He welcomed a rare mirror-smooth stretch of river. He opened his toothy jaws and scooped up a quick gulp to refresh himself. He glided upward as he savored the icy drink, gazing down at the pink-white sky reflected on the still water. Graxen was a gray blur against this pastel backdrop. Unlike other sky-dragons, he lacked even a single blue scale. Some trick of birth had robbed his hide of the azure hue that other members of his species wore with pride. Graxen's body and wings were painted by nature in a palette drawn from storm clouds.

Graxen knew the area below him only from his study of maps. The river he followed meandered in a serpentine path among low mountains. Soon he would arrive at the dam, an imposing structure dating from ancient times. Beyond this, a body of water known as Talon Lake filled long, twisting valleys. His destination was the Nest, an island fortress just beyond the dam. Sometimes, on the edge of sleep, Graxen could see himself as a fledgling perched on the Nest's rocky shores. His earliest memory was of watching small fish dart about in a shallow pool as he waited for the biologians to take him away.

As an adult male sky-dragon, he was forbidden to return to the Nest. Only a select handful of males were invited to those hallowed shores. Graxen was forever excluded from those ranks by the color of his scales. Under other circumstances, he would have no chance of admittance. However, the world had changed in recent days. Graxen had a satchel slung over his shoulders, the long strap allowing the bag to hang near his hips. The contents of this satchel gave Graxen the courage to journey to a place where only his imagination had been allowed to travel.

As he tilted his wings to follow the river north toward the dam, his sharp eyes spotted dark shapes flitting high above. Valkyries, three of them. The dam was hidden by one more turn of the river, but

Graxen calculated that the valkyries were circling above the structure. He wondered if they'd spotted him. His drab color against the stony river might provide some camouflage.

He negotiated the final bend and closed in on the dam, barely a mile distant. The dark shapes suddenly wheeled toward him. The valkyries were the guardians of the island, female sky-dragons trained from birth in the warrior's art. Save for his first year of life, Graxen had never seen a living female of his own species. He knew them only from books and sculpture. Now, they seemed like creatures of myth as they hurtled toward him, their silver helmets gleaming in the sun. The polished steel points of the long spears in their hind-talons twinkled like stars in the morning sky.

Graxen spotted a dry rock rising in the midst of the river, barely large enough for him to land on. A few other rocks jutted nearby, natural landing spots for this trio of guards. He could see a strategic advantage to having this encounter take place on land. He tilted his hind-claws forward and lifted his wings to drift to a landing. He raised his face toward the valkyries and held his empty fore-talons open to show he carried no weapon.

The valkyries closed fast. It didn't look as if they intended to land. Graxen held his ground. He was breaking no law by standing on this rock. The land outside the lake was the property of the sun-dragon king. He was as free to stand upon this stone as he was to stand by the fountains at the College of Spires.

He studied the lead valkyrie as she raced toward him. At first glance, the differences between a male and a female sky-dragon were trivial. Some primal layer of Graxen's brain, however, was busily cataloguing the subtleties that identified the valkyrie as a member of the opposite sex. Sky-dragons had heads that resembled goat skulls covered in scales, with a fringe of long feather-scales rising from the scalp and trailing down the neck. The leader's helmet concealed some of these scales, but those that showed were a deep sea-blue, with tips that trailed off into a pale white, a pattern unique to females. The leader was also slightly larger than a typical male. Male sky-dragons had wingspans averaging eighteen feet; the leader's wings easily stretched twenty. Her torso was chiseled from life in the sky, while most male sky-dragons possessed the softer bodies of scholars.

The valkyries unleashed powerful war cries, fierce primal shrieks that tightened Graxen's intestines. The leader aimed her spear to drive it into Graxen's chest. Graxen stood still as stone. He noticed that the leader had a large silver bell attached to her belt, the clapper covered with a leather hood. An alarm device to call reinforcements, no doubt. Five yards away, she lifted her neck and beat her wings. She zoomed over Graxen's head, the tip of her spear missing his face by no more than a foot. The wind of her wake washed across his cheek. He could smell a faint aura of blackberries.

The second valkyrie darted past, then the third, close enough that he could see his gray eyes reflected in the large silvered plates that studded her leather breast armor. A pair of iron manacles dangling from her thick belt threatened to clip his cheek. He tilted his head a fraction of an inch, allowing the chains to pass without touching. Graxen possessed a keen mind for spaces and vectors. In contests of speed and reflexes he had no peer. Yet was he known as Graxen the Swift? Graxen the Nimble?

"Graxen the Gray!" the lead valkyrie shouted as she circled, coming to rest on the stone that jutted from the river before him. "Your kind has no business here! Begone!"

"I am a representative of the king," said Graxen, half-surprised she recognized him, half-fatalistically accepting it. As the only gray-scaled sky-dragon ever to survive birth, he had little hope of anonymity. "I come as a courier of important news. I'm charged with delivering this message to the matriarch herself."

A second valkyrie landed to his right. "We care nothing of your mission," she growled. "The king's domain ends at the lake's edge." Graxen noted this valkyrie was younger than her companions, perhaps still a teen. Despite the normal female advantage of size, Graxen judged himself taller.

"Fortunately, I haven't reached the lake's edge," said Graxen. "I ask that you read the scroll I carry before you judge the importance of my mission."

The third valkyrie, the one with the manacles on her belt, landed to his left. She was larger than her two companions and, to his eyes, more relaxed. The other two stood in stances that indicated they were prepared to defend themselves from a sudden attack by Graxen. This last valkyrie didn't look concerned.

He turned his attention back to the leader as she spoke once more. "If the message is important, give us the scroll and be gone. We will see it reaches the matriarch."

"The king would be disappointed if I failed to speak to her personally."

"Would the king be disappointed if your body was discovered on the rocks downriver?" the young valkyrie to his right asked. "Perhaps he could take comfort in knowing that we found your satchel and delivered the scroll without you."

A silence fell as the valkyries allowed the implied threat to settle into Graxen's mind. Graxen studied the youngest valkyrie. Her eyes were full of scorn, with perhaps a touch of fear. She looked ready to run him through with the long spear she carried in her fore-talons. He turned back to the leader. Her face was a cool mask, impossible to read.

He tilted his head to study the final valkyrie. Her eyes were cold little slivers of copper. Graxen caught his breath as he noticed a slight discoloration against her cheek. A single scale of gray, the color of fresh-cut granite, sat below her left eye like a tear. The rest of her hide was flawless; she seemed sculpted from sapphire, her lean and well-muscled body sporting graceful lines and symmetry that rivaled the statues that adorned the College of Spires. This valkyrie continued to regard him with a look that approached boredom.

With one guard showing uninterest and another looking prepared to run him through, Graxen knew his best course of action was to win the leader over to his cause. He said, "As a commander, you are obviously a dragon of proven judgment. Perhaps you should examine the scroll yourself." Graxen reached into his satchel and produced the scroll. He stretched his wing across the watery gap to offer the message to the leader. Her fore-talon brushed his as she took the rolled parchment. This brief touch was his first adult contact with a female. He found the experience… unsatisfying.

The leader unrolled the scroll. She tilted her head and furrowed her brow, attempting to decipher its jagged calligraphy. The message had been scribed by Shandrazel, a sun-dragon. With talons twice the thickness of a sky-dragon's nimble digits, sun-dragons seldom earned praise for their penmanship.

"What does it say, Arifiel?" the youngest valkyrie asked, impatient.

"Quiet, Sparrow," said the dragon with the teardrop scale. Graxen guessed that Sparrow was a nickname. It was rare to encounter a dragon whose name corresponded to something in the physical world. All sky-dragons' names were drawn from the *Ballad of Belpantheron*. The two-thousand-page poem was the oldest document verified to have been drafted by a dragon. Unfortunately, it was also a document that had defied ten centuries of scholarly attempts to decipher its mysterious language. Tradition held that it told the story of how the young race of dragons slew the older race of angels. Less poetically inclined scholars speculated that the work was schizophrenic babble granted sacred status by the passage of time.

"It does say he is to be given safe passage," Arifiel said, rotating the scroll to a thirty-degree angle as she puzzled out the script, "but, this isn't Albekizan's mark."

"Albekizan is no longer king," said Graxen. "He died at the hands of Bitterwood following an uprising of humans in the Free City. His scion, Shandrazel, charged me with this mission."

Arifiel tilted the scroll in the counterclockwise direction. "I guess that could be an 's.' That's probably an 'h' and an 'a.' Shandrazel is... plausible. However, all that's here is the order of safe passage. I see no further message."

Graxen raised his fore-talon to tap his brow. "I have the message up here. It's too important to be entrusted to mere parchment. This is why you should provide me with an escort for the rest of the journey."

"I see," said Arifiel.

"Shall we grant him passage then?" asked the teardrop valkyrie, still relaxed.

"No," said Arifiel. "Last I heard, Shandrazel was banished."

"Who cares if Shandrazel is king now?" Sparrow growled, directing her words toward Arifiel. "Male law ends at the lake's edge. Whatever transpires in the outside world is of no concern to us."

"True," said Arifiel, rolling the scroll back up. She eyed Graxen even more skeptically than before. "My gut tells me this is a trick. Desperate males try far more clever schemes to reach the Nest in the hope of mating."

"This is no scheme," said Graxen. "I'm marked by birth as one who will never breed. No female would ever submit to my touch."

"Desperate dragons will attempt to breed by force," said Arifiel.

"If I were here to resort to violence, why would I wish to journey into the heart of the Nest?" Graxen asked. "Wouldn't a desperate dragon attempt to ambush valkyries on patrol, away from the safety of the fortress?"

"Perhaps that's your plan," said Sparrow. "Perhaps you didn't expect to be outnumbered."

Graxen found Sparrow's tone grating. He felt that if she would only be quiet, he might have hope of convincing Arifiel. He said, "Arifiel, do you always allow the dragons in your command to abuse guests so?"

He expected Arifiel to order Sparrow to silence herself. He didn't expect Sparrow's face to suddenly twist into a mask of rage as her muscles tensed, ready to strike with her spear.

"Abuse is all a freak like you deserves!" Sparrow shouted.

"Sparrow, halt!" barked Arifiel.

It was too late. Sparrow lunged. Graxen shifted his weight back on the rock, swinging his tail around for balance as he pulled his shoulders back. The spear pierced the air before him. The weapon was twice Sparrow's height. Graxen calculated that avoiding the thrust might lead to tragedy. Sparrow was off balance, falling forward. If she toppled, her spear would reach all the way to the valkyrie with the teardrop scale. Perhaps her armor would deflect the blow, but could he take that chance?

Graxen grabbed the shaft of the spear, using the full weight of his body to halt its forward path. He jerked the spear backward. Sparrow let go, her hind-talons skittering on the wet rock. Before she could spread her wings to steady herself, Graxen jabbed the butt of the spear between her legs, tripping her. She landed in the water with an angry shriek.

Arifiel, perhaps mistaking his act of protection for an attack, released the scroll and readied her own weapon. Graxen dropped the spear, crouched, and then sprung into the air, whipping his tail forward to knock the falling letter upward before it hit the water. He grabbed the document in his hind-claws as he beat his wings, climbing into the sky with all his might.

"Stop!" Arifiel shouted, drawing back to throw her spear.

"Stop me," Graxen called back, climbing higher.

Arifiel grunted, hurling her weapon, but Graxen didn't bother to look down. The weapon had been designed for a thrusting attack, not for throwing. He was practically straight over her, fifty feet up. The anatomy of a sky-dragon's wings simply wouldn't allow the weapon to reach him. Seconds later, he heard the spear clatter against the rocks. He kept flapping, turning the fifty-foot gap into a hundred feet, two hundred, more.

He glanced down to see Arifiel and the dragon he thought of as Teardrop chasing after him. Teardrop proved as strong as she looked, and was leading Arifiel by several body lengths. Indeed, if she weren't slowed by her leather breastplate and heavy spear, Graxen had every reason to think she might have gotten close to him. After a minute, Graxen judged he was over a hundred yards above her, and half that distance again above Arifiel. Graxen grimaced as he saw that Arifiel was no longer chasing him. Instead she was drifting in a circle as she used a hind-talon to free the hood on her alarm bell.

Graxen folded his wings back and held his body straight, plunging toward Teardrop. It was time to show these valkyries what he knew of the subtle art of falling. Teardrop looked up, her eyes wide as he shot toward her. She drew her body back, raising the spear she carried in her hind-talons to catch Graxen.

As Graxen hurtled down, the wind felt like water. His feather-scales were a thousand tiny paddles with which he pushed the current, controlling the angle of his fall. At the last second, Graxen curved his tail in a gentle arc, steering away from a collision. Her spear point flashed past his eyes. For a lightning instant he glimpsed the valkyrie's face with its single scale of gray, then her long serpentine neck flickered past, then her armored torso, and then there was her belt. In his right hind-talon he held Shandrazel's letter of passage. With his left, he snatched the manacles, ripping free the metal hook that held them. The sudden jolt threw Teardrop into a spin. As she flapped her wings for balance,

Graxen shifted his tail once more to delicately adjust his fall. Off to his side, on a parallel course, a bright gleam caught his eye—a spear point. Teardrop had dropped her weapon. The spear now fell toward Arifiel on a path that would run her through. He kicked out with the manacles and clipped the tip of the spear, knocking it into a path that would do no damage.

By now Graxen had reached terminal velocity, words that possessed a double meaning. He could fall no faster, but if he collided with Arifiel at this speed, it would kill them both. He opened his wings into twin parachutes, tilting his hind-talons down. He dropped the scroll and craned his neck to catch it in his teeth as it flew upward. In the space of a heartbeat the distance between Arifiel and himself vanished as his hind-talons reached her left wing.

Graxen grabbed Arifiel's fore-talon, the three-clawed hand that sat at the middle joint of her wing. In a fluid motion, he snapped the first cuff of the manacle around her talon. The impact caused his body to flip, as his legs tarried at her wing while his head snaked downward. He reached out his fore-talons and grabbed her left hind-talon. She tried to kick him free.

Arifiel's sharp teeth sank into Graxen's thigh, but the awkward angle of her bite kept her from doing real damage. She growled and shook her head as they tumbled, free-falling a hundred feet in a blur of gray and blue. She opened her jaws, perhaps in search of a more vital body part. Graxen spread his wings and darted away, leaving Arifiel with her left wing manacled to her left leg.

For a sun-dragon, this would have been a death sentence. Fortunately, sky-dragons were masters of the air. Arifiel spread her free wing to its maximum capacity and pulled her body into a tight ball. She became a blue whirligig, descending toward the forest in a dizzying spiral. Her landing wouldn't be delicate, but she'd survive.

Graxen tossed away the bell he'd stolen from her belt, the leather hood once more covering the clapper. From the time he'd started his dive to the time he'd shackled Arifiel, no more than ten seconds had passed.

Something fell past him, barely glimpsed from the corner of his eye. At first, he had difficulty identifying it as it tumbled. Then a silver disk flashed as it caught the sun. It was a valkyrie's empty breast plate. He looked over his shoulder to find Teardrop barely ten yards behind him. She'd shed her armor, even her helmet, leaving her groomed for speed. Her breast muscles moved like mighty machinery beneath her scales. Graxen's heart beat joyously. He always enjoyed a good race.

Graxen turned away from his pursuer and dove once more, aiming for the river. He pulled from his dive to skim along the surface. The spray from the whitewater moistened his face in welcome relief. If not for the letter in his teeth, he would have risked a quick drink. He banked toward the forest, the jagged tree trunks looming before him like a maze. Beating his wings for a further burst of speed he plunged into the woods. Flying above the treetops was one thing. Flying amid the branches of an unfamiliar forest was a feat most dragons would regard as suicide. His eyes tracked every limb and shadow as momentum carried him forward. He beat his wings to stay aloft in the gaps between the trees. The tips of his wings knocked away twigs and vines. A whirlwind of dry leaves followed in his wake.

Ahead, he spotted a bright patch on the forest floor—a clearing—three times his body length. With a sharp, hard burst of energy he zoomed heavenward, flitting back above the trees. Only now did he allow himself to glance over his shoulder. He was certain the valkyrie had been stubborn enough to follow, even though her longer wings would have made the feat impossible. He hoped she hadn't injured herself too badly when she snared in the branches.

To his astonishment, she was still in flight, now many yards behind, about to reach the clearing. He watched, slack-jawed, as she found the open space and rose back over the treetops, her gaze still fixed upon him.

Very well. If he couldn't outfly her, he'd have to cheat.

He banked in a sharp arc as he reached up with his hind-claws to the leather satchel. With a violent grunt, he yanked the bag so hard its strap snapped, freeing it. He darted back toward Teardrop with all the speed he could manage. His eyes locked on hers. Their paths would intersect in seconds. She showed no fear as the space between them closed.

Then, at the last possible instant, Teardrop lowered her head to dodge, passing beneath his body. Graxen snapped the bag in his hind-talons, opening the satchel wide. With a satisfying shudder, the leather ripped from his claws as the makeshift hood slipped over her head.

He bent his whole body in the air, heading once more for the dam. He glanced back to find Teardrop whipping her head, trying to free the hood, obviously disoriented. Instinctively, she was climbing slowly, as any temporarily blinded dragon would do. Graxen was relieved she showed no sign of injury. The high-speed hooding had carried the risk of snapping her neck.

Leaving his last opponent far behind, Graxen raced toward the dam, rising quickly over its massive stone wall. He found himself over the deep silver-blue waters of the mountain lake. The Nest, an impressive fortress of stone and steel, jutted from the waters like a racial memory. He knew this place in his blood. He'd been born within its walls. The air smelled like dreams as he breathed in great heaves through his nostrils.

There were dark shapes dashing all over the sky now. A dozen valkyries had spotted him. None were closer than half a mile. Unless there was another among them as swift as Teardrop, none could intercept him before he reached his goal. He darted upward as he reached the outer wall of the fortress, rising above the iron spikes that edged it. The Nest would be a bad place to fall. Every surface was covered with sharp metal shafts pointed skyward to discourage any males who might wish to land. Ahead, the central bell tower began to clang out an alarm. He heard a command shouted somewhere below: "Get clear! The gates are closing!" A rumble came from deep beneath the island as ancient gears slipped into service.

He aimed for the tallest spire of the fortress and a balcony that jutted from it. As he rose above the lip of the balcony, he saw the open door to the chamber beyond. A metal grate was sliding down to seal the room, like the jagged teeth of some great beast. He hoped that the marble floor beyond was as smooth as it looked. He flattened his body, slipping beneath the teeth. He slammed against the marble, sliding forward. He snaked his tail into the room as the grate clanged shut. He spun and pivoted as he slid, spreading his wings to lift himself back to his hind-talons, his sharp claws splayed out, desperate to halt his forward slide. He skidded to rest inches from the opposite wall.

He opened his jaw and let the scroll drop. He caught it with his fore-talon as he spun around. The scroll was damp with spittle. He held his wings in a gesture of surrender as countless valkyries rushed into the room, spears pointed toward him.

"Greetings," he said, in as calm a voice as he could muster. "I have a message from the king."

The valkyries drew into a half circle around him as he pressed his back against the cold stone wall.

"Your kind is forbidden here!" one growled.

"We should gut you where you stand!" snapped another.

"We should," said a firm voice at the back of the room. "But not yet."

Graxen looked over the wall of valkyries to see an aged sky-dragon, the weight of her body supported by a gnarled cane. Her body was stooped but her eyes were bright. Her face was lined with an aura of dignity that made her instantly recognizable. The matriarch!

"He's made it this far with his precious message," she said, her voice raspy with age, yet still firm with authority. "We shall allow him his say."

"Thank you, Matriarch," Graxen said. He cast his gaze over the guards. "I've been ordered to speak to you privately. Would you dismiss your attendants?"

"Do you think we'll fall for this trickery?" a valkyrie snarled, jabbing her spear to within a whisker of Graxen's ribs.

"Lower your spears!" the matriarch commanded, drawing closer, studying Graxen with a cool gaze.

"We've nothing to fear from this pathetic specimen. He's nothing more than an overly large carrier pigeon."

"I prefer to think of myself as an ambassador for the new regime."

"Ah yes, the new regime. Rumors travel more swiftly than you, Graxen. I've already heard of Albekizan's death. Shandrazel is king."

"For now, yes," said Graxen.

"A strange choice of words," said the matriarch.

"An appropriate choice for strange times."

"Explain yourself."

"I shall," he said, looking back over the guards. "If we may have privacy."

The matriarch waited a long moment, her golden eyes fixed on his face. He saw himself reflected in her gaze, a gray dragon against gray stone. He tried to see any emotion in her eyes, any hint of... Of what? What did he wish to see? Remorse? Tenderness? Hatred? Love? He'd not set eyes on the matriarch since infancy. He'd imagined this meeting almost every day, practiced what he would say in his mind, but now that it was happening, he felt utterly unrehearsed and awkward.

The matriarch sighed. "You shall have your private audience. Valkyries, leave us."

Graxen relaxed, lowering his wings. Until this moment, he hadn't known if he'd live through this meeting. The valkyries were notoriously unmerciful toward interlopers. He hadn't known if he would be treated any differently. There was every possibility he could have been treated worse, given his family history.

"I was worried you would hate me," Graxen said to the matriarch as the last valkyrie left the room.

The guard closed the door with a final glance back, her eyes full of murder.

"I hate you with all my blood," the matriarch said, shaking her head sorrowfully. "You're my greatest mistake, Graxen. I curse the decision not to snap your neck as an infant. It gives me nothing but pain to see you again."

Graxen nodded, no longer feeling awkward. These were also words he'd heard many times in his imagination. He was a freak of nature, a mockery of the careful breeding and birth lines the sky-dragons had labored for centuries to maintain. Of course the matriarch, whose sole duty was to protect the integrity of those lines, would despise him.

"I... I'm sorry," he said.

"Of what use is your sorrow?" spat the matriarch. She shook her head, and sighed. "Your sorrow cannot mend my grief. I gave birth to four daughters, and two fine sons. Their offspring should number in the dozens by now. Yet fate snatched them all in their youth, one by one, through disease and accident and treachery. All dead... all save the accursed seventh born."

Graxen lowered his head, unable to find the words that might ease her pain. Part of him felt pity for the aged dragon, part of him shared her grief. Yet, underneath it all, he bristled at the injustice of her scorn. It wasn't his fault that he'd been spared the misfortunes of his siblings. How was he to blame for having been her only surviving child?

CHAPTER TWO

FRAYED THREADS

GRAXEN FOLLOWED THE matriarch down a winding staircase, leaving the tower far behind as she led him to the heart of her domain, the fabled Thread Room. The enormous round chamber, nearly a hundred yards in diameter, was like an interior forest filled with thick granite columns supporting the fortress above. Elaborate, colorful tapestries covered the walls of the room, depicting in glorious detail scenes from the *Ballad of Belpantheron*. Bright crimson sun-dragons savaged golden-winged angels in their bloody jaws at the climax of a battle that raged for decades.

The valkyries were masterful engineers; while the chamber sat beneath the surface of the lake, the room showed no traces of leaking or flooding. Mirrored shafts were set in the ceiling twenty-five feet overhead, funneling sunlight into the room. Despite the radiance, the room was still beset with a cave-like chill and dankness. The cloying incense that rose in wispy tendrils from silver sconces lining the room couldn't quite hide the underlying scent of mildew.

The matriarch walked through the chamber without looking back at Graxen. The only sound in the room was the tap of her cane as she hobbled across the tiled floor. She had not spoken, or even glanced at Graxen, since they'd left the tower. Graxen wanted to speak but feared disturbing the sacred air of this place. The tapestries of the Thread Room were priceless. Underlying the visible representation of battle, the threads themselves were woven in an elaborate code. For the matriarch and others initiated in their lore, each thread of these tapestries told a story. Thicker lines represented the lives of individual sky-dragons, every one born in the Nest through the centuries. Thinner threads ran parallel, representing desired genetic traits. The web of lines intersected in elaborate patterns as every mating, every birth, every death of a sky-dragon were recorded in minute detail.

Centuries earlier, it had been decided that the genetic destiny of the sky-dragon race was too important to be left to mere chance. Males and females were not allowed to mingle or mix according to whim or desire. Each mating represented a careful decision made by the matriarch and her predecessors. Many pairings were planned generations in advance. Others would arise after a sky-dragon demonstrated a novel trait—superior intelligence, for example, or a well-documented resistance to disease—and it was the matriarch's duty to capture these desirable mutations through careful interweaving with a receptive bloodline.

On the far side of the room a black section of the wall stood devoid of tapestries. The matriarch moved toward this area, a single smooth slab of slate, twelve feet high and four times that length, covered with lines of colored chalk and countless scribbled notes. The matriarch paused, studying the board, as if she had forgotten Graxen's presence and resumed her normal duties of steering the fate of the species. She leaned her cane against the board as she lifted a thick finger of chalk in her fore-talon.

As often happened in older dragons, the colors of the matriarch's scales had faded, tinting white the frill of long scales that ran down her neck and along her spine. The once jewel-like sheen of her scales had dulled, as if muted beneath a lifetime of dust.

Graxen cringed as the matriarch brought the chalk to the slate and drew a long, screeching line from top to bottom. To the left, hundreds of scribbled notes in a rainbow of colors were surrounded by circles, with lines and arrows connecting them. He didn't recognize any of the names save one. In a large yellow oval, surrounded by pink question marks, in thick, capital letters was the name VENDEVOREX. There were no lines connecting his circle to any other.

To the right of the line she had drawn, the board was fresh and black. She wrote in neat, balanced letters despite her trembling talon: "World order, post Albekizan."

Without facing Graxen, the matriarch asked, "Is it true the so-called wizard is dead?"

"Yes," said Graxen. "His funeral pyre is to be lit tonight."

The matriarch drew a bold white "x" across Vendevorex's name. "The 'master of the invisible' has been a burr under my scales for fifteen years," she grumbled. "He was bloodless, a beast without history. I never learned where he came from. I'm happy to know he's gone. Ash in an urn is the only appropriate fate for an... *aberration.*"

The way she said "aberration" gave the word mass, making it a solid thing that struck Graxen in the chest.

She did not give him time to dwell upon the blow. "Shandrazel now wears the crown. He fancies himself a scholar. Metron will control him with ease."

"Shandrazel is a free thinker," said Graxen. "He won't be anyone's puppet. He definitely won't be a pawn of Metron."

"Metron was able to control Albekizan," said the matriarch. "The High Biologian will be more than a match for his son."

"Your informants have failed you," said Graxen. "Metron is no longer High Biologian."

"What?" She jerked her head around to fix her eyes on Graxen for the first time. She quickly turned her gaze away, looking distraught over this news. "Is he dead?"

"Banished," said Graxen. "Metron allied himself with Blasphet. Androkom is the new High Biologian."

"No!" The matriarch looked as if the news caused her physical pain. She walked along the tapestries, her fingers tracing from thread to thread. "Androkom is a dreadful choice. His bloodline is one of genius, yes, but also carries a risk of madness. Look here!" She pointed her gnarled talon at a dark red scale on the cheek of a sun-dragon. "Shangon, his second seed removed—"

"Second seed removed?"

"What the less educated might call a grandfather," she grumbled, sounding angry at the interruption. "Shangon was a brilliant scholar. At the age of thirty he earned the right to breed.

Unfortunately, as sometimes happens, the experience shattered him. He went insane and tried to return to the Nest. The valkyries were forced to end him. Until five generations have passed, members of Androkom's bloodline must be kept from positions of authority. To make him High Biologian is an absurd risk!"

"It's a risk Shandrazel is willing to take," said Graxen. "He appreciates Androkom's boldness of thought, his willingness to value reason over tradition."

The matriarch traced black threads from the second seed removed to another red scale that represented Androkom. No black lines radiated out from it. Androkom was relatively young, not yet eligible for breeding. The matriarch hooked a needle-sharp talon into the tapestry and tore at the threads that formed the scale, fraying them.

"No further," she said, her voice cold. "I cannot undo his past, but I have just undone his future."

Graxen shuddered as he understood the harshness of her judgment. "Androkom may become the greatest High Biologian known to history," he protested. "You would end his bloodline now, in a moment of anger? How can you know what the future holds?"

The matriarch's eyes narrowed. "I do not know the future," she said, coolly. "I create it."

"But—"

"Save your breath, Graxen. You cannot understand the burden I bear, the responsibility of ensuring the strength of our race for eons to come. You haven't the capacity to judge me."

"Why not?" asked Graxen. "Presumably, as your child, I was designed to inherit your intelligence."

He studied the tapestry that bore Androkom's bloodlines. Was the thread of his own life marked somewhere upon this canvas? "What's more, I presume my father must have possessed many desirable traits to have been chosen as your mate."

"You are so transparent, Graxen," the matriarch said. "You will not learn your father's name from me."

"Why?" Graxen asked. "Other sky-dragons know their heritage. Why has the identity of my father been kept secret from me?"

"His bloodline ended with the production of an unfavorable aberration. His identity is no longer of any importance. You are his only offspring. When you pass from this world, the danger he represented will be at an end."

"I could have passed from this world at my birth," said Graxen. "Other aberrations have been drowned in the lake. Why was I allowed to live?"

The matriarch lifted her fore-talon in a dismissive gesture. "What a pointless question. You are alive now; you have a purpose in life, however menial, of messenger to the king. So far, you have shown an appalling lack of competence in carrying out your duties. What was Shandrazel's message?"

"I bring an invitation. Shandrazel is convening a summit in three days. He wishes to invite leaders from throughout the kingdom to discuss the end of the era of kings, and to help design a new era of equality and justice for all races."

The matriarch released a barking noise that Graxen at first took as a cough, but then realized was a laugh. "Equality? There is no equality in this world and never will be. The Earth has produced four intelligent species, it is true, but it is self-evidently absurd to think they are equal."

"Shandrazel feels differently. When you hear him speak on the matter, I believe you will find his arguments compelling."

"I hope you find it compelling when humans are marching with dragon heads atop their pikes," the matriarch grumbled. "They are merely tall and talkative monkeys, with baser urges unchecked by reason. Their animalistic breeding practices mean they outnumber us by a thousand to one. Granting them freedom is dangerously irresponsible."

"I've had little experience with humans. If they're truly as primitive as you say, what threat can they pose?"

The matriarch shook her head at Graxen's ignorance. She sighed. "This is only one more crisis to be managed. Fly back to Shandrazel. Tell him I will send an envoy to his summit. There must be someone there to serve as the voice of reason."

"Thank you," said Graxen.

"You've delivered your message," the matriarch said, turning her back to him once more. "Now take your leave."

"I've had a long journey," said Graxen. "Isn't it customary to offer a messenger of the king time to rest, to partake of food and water?"

"You have said Shandrazel doesn't respect custom," said the matriarch. "He could have sent a member of his aerial guard. Why send you, if not as deliberate taunt?"

"Shandrazel has no interest in the bloodlines of sky-dragons. I don't believe he knows I am your son."

"I am to believe it is only coincidence he chose you?"

"No. When Shandrazel was banished by Albekizan, he sought shelter at the College of Spires. Chapelion sent him away. But I felt pity for Shandrazel and followed him. I served as his messenger in exile. Now, I serve him openly. Still, you are correct. My presence here isn't chance. I asked for this mission. It was my one chance to ask… to ask…"

"Don't stammer," she snapped.

Graxen felt as if the simplest words were almost impossible to utter. He stared at the frayed threads that had been Androkom, and suddenly grew aware of hundreds of similar threads representing the conclusions of bloodlines. He knew he was one of them.

"I want to mate," said Graxen. "It grieves me to think that your thread ends with me. The color of my hide is only a superficial flaw. In every other way, I believe I am an excellent candidate to carry on your bloodline. I'm strong, I'm studious, I'm—"

"Get out," she said.

"But, if you'll—"

"Valkyries!" she shouted.

The tapestries on the wall bulged outward. A score of valkyries emerged from hidden passageways, spears readied. Graxen's gut twisted as he realized they must have been listening to his every word. Sky-dragons were supposed to be creatures of intellect, devoid of the lusts that fouled lesser beings. His shameful confession of the desire to breed had no doubt been heard by all these warriors.

"I'll go," he said.

"You arrived with great speed," one of the valkyries growled. "Let your departure match it."

Grinding gears vibrated through the stone walls as Graxen climbed the steps from the Thread Room back toward the tower he'd entered. Arriving at the high chamber, he found the iron bars now raised. Valkyries stood in twin rows, forming a living hallway through which he passed. He lowered his eyes as he walked, unable to bear the icy stares of the females.

As he leapt to the balcony rail and spread his wings, he heard a muttered word from one of the guards behind him: *"Freak."*

He tilted forward, falling toward the spikes below. Rust and moss and damp sand scented the air that rushed across his face. His feather-scales toyed with the air, pulling him out and away from the spikes in a gentle arc, until, an instant before he dashed against the rocky shore, he flapped his wings and shot forward, then up, into a bright winter sun that failed to warm him.

A moment later he passed over the edge of the dam. The sky in all directions was thick with valkyries. He felt a stir of grim pride that he was sufficiently threatening to justify such a force.

He followed the river once more, adhering to its twists and turns, lost in thought. What did it matter that he wouldn't be allowed to breed? There were hundreds of dragons who shared his fate. More, there were male dragons who refused the chance even when offered. Many prominent biologians believed that any mingling of the sexes would muddy the mind; they dared not risk the damage even a single night of passion might cause to their intellect. The fact that Androkom wouldn't be invited to breed would perhaps not bother him at all. Metron, the former High Biologian, had famously refused an invitation to the Nest with the words: "I would rather history judge me by my works rather than the quality of my biological debris."

As he flew, Graxen's musing about breeding slowly gave way to thoughts of food. The king's messengers traveled light, relying on the hospitality of those they were sent to speak to. Fortunately, his next destination wasn't far. The town of Dragon Forge was no more than thirty miles distant.

The terrain changed as Graxen neared the town. The nearly pristine forested mountainsides that surrounded the Nest gave way to rolling hills, many of them stripped of trees. Giant mounds of rusting metal dotted the landscape, and ragged shanty towns sat beside muddy stream banks. Humans in rags trudged along, hauling carts full of twised scraps. These were gleaners, men who made their living by scouring the landscape in search of relics from a previous age, incomprehensible artifacts crafted from steel that had long ago decayed into rust. Yet, even rust had value—the gleaners sold their wares to the foundries of Dragon Forge, where immense furnaces melted down the scraps of metal, freeing the ores, which were then refined and cast into the armor and weapons used by the armies of the dragons. The humans below were fueling the engines of their own oppression.

Three plumes of smoke rose in the distance. Graxen's nose wrinkled as the stench of the foundries reached him. He traced a wide arc around the town, looking for a good landing spot. The earth-dragons below looked like small beetles from this height, as they hurried across the packed-earth streets of their town. Nowhere within the fortress was there any hint of vegetation. The surrounding hills were nothing but rust-colored clutter and weeds, with a few bare and scraggly trees here and there. Earth-dragons weren't known for their appreciation of beauty.

At the far side of his arc, glancing back through the smoke plumes, Graxen caught a glimpse of sparkling light. Continuing in his orbit, he discovered the light was the gleaming helmet of a valkyrie a few miles distant. Was he being pursued this far from the Nest? Or was it mere coincidence? Valkyries must do business with Dragon Forge—all the steel grates and spikes that turned the place into a fortress had to come from somewhere.

He slowed his flight. The valkyrie continued toward him. Was this some messenger from the matriarch? Perhaps she'd changed her mind? The instant he had the thought, he dismissed it, and was embarrassed by his heart's willingness to hold onto hope.

Graxen decided to meet the valkyrie head on. He adjusted his path to match hers and the distance between them rapidly closed. As they drew within a hundred yards of each other, he was struck with recognition. It was Teardrop, the dragon who'd given him such a chase. She'd once more donned her armor, though she wasn't carrying her spear. Was she pursuing him out of some desire for revenge? If so, why come unarmed? She began to glide in an arc and he joined her in a counter path, so that they traced a large circle through the air. They looked at each other across the gap as they glided leisurely in their orbit.

"You dropped your bag," she said, the hint of a smirk showing in her eyes. Graxen noted the leather satchel hooked over her belt where her manacles had once hung. She flicked her tail forward and knocked the sack free. It plummeted earthward, spinning as it fell. Graxen dove and snagged it in his hind-claws. The bag felt heavy—something was inside. He jerked his head up. Had this been a ploy to distract him from a sneak attack? The valkyrie continued in her slow circle, looking toward him with an expression devoid of malice.

"Thank you," he said, flapping his wings to reach her flight level once more.

"I'm sorry Sparrow attacked you. She should never have been allowed on that patrol."

"She was only doing her job."

"Our job is to defend the island, not to abuse innocent messengers."

"I'm used to hostility," said Graxen.

"It's left you with remarkable reflexes," she said.

Graxen wasn't used to compliments. He found himself unsure how to respond. There was a long moment of silence.

Teardrop took his quietness as an invitation for further explanation. "Sparrow only became a valkyrie a year ago. On her first patrol, she and two more experienced guards were ambushed by a band of tatterwings."

"Oh," said Graxen. The only thing lower in the ranks of the sky-dragons than a freak was a tatterwing. These were criminal sky-dragons whose wings had been slashed as punishment. Forever condemned to the ground, tatterwings survived by begging or by banditry. It sounded as if Sparrow had fallen victim to the latter kind.

"The elder valkyries were killed. Sparrow was... abused. She only recently returned to duty. Her attack on you was an attack upon the ghosts that haunt her. And, of course, she is from the lineage of Pachythan. So, she perhaps felt an extra obligation to be tough with you."

Graxen wasn't certain what her lineage had to do with anything. Pachythan was the younger brother of Metron. Was she saying Sparrow was more diligent due to being the niece of such a prominent sky-dragon?

"I didn't want you to think ill of all valkyries. Most would never have attacked you unprovoked."

"I'm glad you don't think of the events that followed as a provocation," Graxen said.

"If you'd been near when I freed myself, I would have gutted you. But, I bear no grudge. You simply outflew me. I won't be such an easy opponent should we meet again."

"Noted," said Graxen. "Although, it seems unlikely we will meet again. The matriarch has vigorously uninvited me from the Nest."

"As is her duty," said Teardrop. "Fly far, Graxen the Gray. Go with the knowledge that you've earned my respect."

"I'm honored," he said. "May I ask your name?"

She banked away, flapping her wings, her body aimed for the Nest. She glanced back, then called out, "Nadala."

Graxen drifted in a slow gyre, watched Nadala grow smaller as she flew away, until she was only a speck, then only a memory.

Graxen returned his attention to Dragon Forge. He dropped down into the city, toward a broad avenue that ran near the central foundries.

In unison, thousands of earth-dragons were filing into the street chanting,

Yo ho ho!
The slow must go!
Yo ho ho!
The slow must go!

The verse lasted all of five seconds, with the "yo ho hos!" rising in tone, and the "slow must goes" falling. The verse was then repeated, and was then repeated, and was then repeated, until Graxen was struck by the intense urgency to complete his mission here and move on. He dropped the bag in his hind-claws just before landing. Coming to rest, he retrieved the satchel and slung it over his shoulder.

He again noticed the weight, but before he could examine it he was nearly run into by an earth-dragon marching straight toward him. Earth-dragons were squat, wingless creatures, resembling the unholy union of a human, a turtle, and an alligator. Most stood little more than five feet high, and were almost as broad due to their powerful musculature. Their green, beaked faces resembled the heads of turtles. As a species they were notoriously nearsighted, which could explain why the one that approached him was only inches away from collision before he stopped, looking befuddled.

Graxen figured this creature was as good a guide as any, and said, "I'm here to see Charkon. Can you tell me where to find him?"

The earth-dragon looked at him dully, as if trying to fathom what Graxen might be saying. Earth-dragons varied a good deal in intelligence. None were as smart, on average, as sky-dragons, but many managed something approximating human intelligence, and most were smart enough to obey commands and hit the things they were told to hit. Still, a fair number weren't smart enough to talk. Graxen wondered if he'd grabbed one of these by mistake, even though the earth-dragon was still tonelessly repeating, "*the slow must go, yo ho ho…*"

Finally something sparked in the dragon's eyes.

"Charkon's our boss," he said.

"Right," said Graxen. "I need to find him. Is he around?"

"It's hatching day," the dragon said.

Graxen was about to give up and try another dragon when this one said, "Follow me." Graxen fell in behind the creature, taking care not to step on the dragon's thick, alligator-like tail as it dragged in the dirt.

Graxen joined a crowd of earth-dragons heading for the center of town. All the human gleaners he'd spotted earlier had vanished. The crush of earth-dragons at the town square was worrisome. Though Graxen stood taller than anyone in the crowd, even the smallest earth-dragon was four times his weight. Graxen had a grim vision of being crushed by these horrid creatures. What were they all here for anyway? And would they never tire of that damn song?

Fortunately, his guide proved to be quite effective at moving through the crowd. The earth-dragon simply pushed ahead, knocking down and trampling those before him, occasionally pausing to bite a particularly slow moving obstacle to encourage it to move more quickly. Graxen mumbled apologies as he hopped over the dragons pushed down by his guide.

Finally, they reached the center. A large mound of red clay was piled here, resembling an ant hill ten feet high and twice as wide at the base. The clay was cracking and crumbling, giving it a surface resembling shattered flowerpots. It looked as if it was being wracked by small earthquakes.

Next to the mound stood a figure that Graxen instantly recognized as Charkon, though they had never met. Charkon was old for an earth-dragon, nearly eighty. Earth-dragons continued to pack on ever denser muscles as they aged, giving Charkon arms and legs thick as tree trunks. But it was his face that identified him. Charkon was a veteran of the southern rebellion, and at one point had found his face on the wrong end of a battle axe. A large jagged chunk of his left beak was gone, and where his eye had been there was now only a nasty bulb of scars. Yet, despite Charkon's hideous visage, his remaining eye gleamed with a savage intelligence, and he stood with a bearing that was as close to noble as an earth-dragon could ever hope to be.

Charkon gave Graxen a nod, then waved him closer.

"You're Graxen the Gray," Charkon said, shouting to be heard above the chanting crowd. "I thought I'd be seeing you."

"Shandrazel has sent me to—"

"I know," said Charkon. "He wants me at the palace. I'll set out tomorrow. The dragons of the Forge have served sun-dragons for centuries. It will be an honor to confer with Shandrazel."

"Oh," said Graxen, leaning in closer so he could better hear over the deafening singing. "I was hardly needed here at all, was I?"

"I've stayed alive this long by listening to the right voices," said Charkon. "Don't feel bad. Gleaners constantly bring me rumors. I have a good instinct at picking which ones are right."

"I see," Graxen shouted back. He cast an eye toward the red clay mound, which was now positively trembling. "What's happening here?"

"It's hatching day!" said Charkon. "I'd take to the sky if I were you. Now!"

Though he didn't understand what was going on, Graxen recognized wise advice when he heard it. He leapt skyward, climbing into the air with sharp, rapid strokes. Below he heard a cracking sound, and the crowd roared: "*The slow must go!*"

He looked down to see the mound disintegrate in a cloud of red dust. Tens of thousands of mouse-sized earth-dragons spilled out of the crumbling clay. Though they looked like turtles, the hatchlings hopped and darted with the speed of rabbits, dashing off in every direction at once. Instantly, the crowd of earth-dragons surged forward, falling to their hands and knees, slapping at the hopping creatures, cramming those they caught into their beaks.

Charkon's beefy fingers reached out and snatched three of the infant beasts, then tilted back his head and opened his disfigured beak wide. He dangled the tiny dragons above his maw, their stubby tails trapped between his digits, before dropping the critters down his gullet one by one.

Despite the crush of bodies, or perhaps because of it, many of the hatchlings escaped between the legs of the assembled dragons, or leapt over the crowd, from head to head, before vanishing into gaps in the walls of nearby buildings, or burrowing into the bins of coal that sat next to the foundry.

Graxen wasn't completely ignorant of earth-dragon biology. He knew that, unlike the winged dragon races, they were egg-layers, and they hatched their young in community mounds. He'd also heard they were unsentimental in winnowing out the weaker members of the hatch. He just hadn't expected them to be so enthusiastic about the process.

Graxen rose up through the foundry smoke and soon found his bearings, locating the Forge Road, which he would follow back to Shandrazel's castle. He flapped away from Dragon Forge, eager to leave behind the foul air and brutish inhabitants, and especially eager to get beyond the range of that damned song. Still, this was twice today he'd delivered a message and not been offered food, drink, or shelter. Messenger of the king was proving to be an unrewarding job.

Once he was out of range of the smoky air and had cleared the barren hillsides where the gleaners lived, Graxen alighted in the upper branches of a tall tree. He was weary from his flight. As he landed, the shifting weight of his satchel reminded him once more of its mysterious contents. He opened it.

Within was a loaf of dark-crusted bread and a ceramic flask of water, sealed with a cork. Four dried trout were wrapped in a sheet of oily parchment, and beneath them sat two apples, red as rose petals.

Graxen drank half the jug, the cool liquid feeling like life as it flowed into his body. He bit into one of the trout and found the flavor smoky and salty. It was a fine meal, fueling his spirit and his body, giving him the strength to fly further. Yet he didn't move from the tree branch for many hours. Instead he looked back in the direction of the Nest, watching the sky, contemplating the restorative power of unexpected kindness.

CHAPTER THREE

MAD IN THE
TIMELESS DARK

THE BURNING GROUNDS lay in the shadow of
Shandrazel's palace. Winged dragons honored
their dead by cremation, releasing the spiritual flames that remained trapped within the body. In
the aftermath of the battle of the Free City, the
pyres of the Burning Grounds had burned every
night from dusk to dawn. Tonight, Vendevorex, the
sky-dragon who had served as Albekizan's wizard
for fifteen years, would be placed upon the flames.

A choir of sky-dragons sang, their eerily high
voices echoing the ephemeral nature of flame. Jandra stood stoically at the base of the pedestal of logs
on which the wizard would be burned. A human
female sixteen years of age, Jandra had been raised
by Vendevorex almost as a daughter. He had
trained her in his arts. She alone knew the secrets of
his powers, although there were many more secrets
he had carried with him into death.

Beside her stood Pet, a human male nearly ten
years older. Jandra didn't welcome his company.

Though Pet was hailed by other humans as the leader of the rebellion in the Free City, Jandra knew that the true Pet was a shallow opportunist. Even now, standing next to her, he was living a lie. Everyone believed Pet to be the legendary dragon-slayer Bitterwood. Pet looked the part of a hero: tall, broad-shouldered, square-jawed, with long golden locks and pale blue eyes. He'd been trained in the theatrical arts, and could deliver inspirational speeches at a moment's notice, summoning grand words from among the countless plays and poems he'd memorized. But behind those lovely words, Pet was, she knew, a coward and a scoundrel.

Pet placed an arm around her shoulders and pulled her near as a band of earth-dragons carried the coffin that held Vendevorex's remains to the Burning Grounds. It was a gesture of tenderness that surprised her. She would have preferred to watch the cremation alone, but, as he gently rubbed her shoulder with his strong hand, she found herself welcoming the consoling touch. Perhaps he was capable of compassion and empathy after all.

"I can only imagine the grief you feel," he whispered.

"I feel numb, mostly," she whispered back. "Everything in my life turned upside-down so fast."

"I know," he said. "Hopefully things will turn again, for the better. Shandrazel genuinely wants to improve the lives of humans. You and I are well positioned to be granted considerable power in his new world order."

Jandra stiffened. "I'd rather not be discussing politics now," she said.

"I understand. Sorry." He gave her shoulder a reassuring squeeze.

The earth-dragons walked up the wooden ramp toward the top of the piled logs.

"I don't want power," she said. "I just want Vendevorex back. I miss him. I wish I hadn't been so mean to him in the weeks before his death."

"I don't think you were mean," said Pet. "Just confused. He gave you good reason to be angry."

"I know," she said. "But I've barely slept since he's been gone. The things I wish I'd told him just keep running through my head. I keep imagining the things he still had left to tell me."

The earth-dragons lowered the coffin onto the pine logs. The new High Biologian, Androkom, climbed onto the platform to deliver his eulogy. Androkom was a young sky-dragon, still in his twenties, the youngest dragon ever to hold the post of High Biologian. He looked weary. Since the fall of the Free City, multiple funerals had been held each night, and all required his presence.

Pet took Jandra's hand as the earth-dragons pried open the lid of the coffin. Many days had passed since Vendevorex had fallen. He'd been placed in the coffin as his body began to decay, but it was customary for a dragon to be cremated with his body exposed to the open sky.

"You know," Pet whispered, leaning closer, "perhaps you shouldn't sleep alone tonight. You could stay with me."

Jandra rolled her eyes. "Are you trying to seduce me at a funeral? Have you no self control at all?"

"I assure you, my self control is legendary," he said, with the hint of a grin. "I was merely trying to comfort you. The fact that you interpreted this as seduction perhaps reveals something about your unspoken desires?"

She would have slapped him, but it wasn't the appropriate setting. At least one human at this ceremony should possess a sense of decorum.

She looked back to the platform. Androkom was staring down into the coffin, looking confused. The earth-dragon pall-bearers scratched their scalps, equally bewildered.

Jandra ran to the platform, up the rough-hewn logs that served as a makeshift ramp.

"Jandra," Androkom said, looking spooked as she approached. "I'm sure there's some logical explanation—"

"What?" she asked, drawing near the coffin. She looked down into the long wooden box, bracing herself for the sight of Vendevorex's mangled body.

Save for a few blood-encrusted feather-scales, their sky-blue hue shining amid the shadows, the coffin was empty.

PET CHASED JANDRA as she bounded up the stairs to the tower. She proved remarkably swift for someone wearing a long black dress more appropriate for mourning than running.

"Jandra, wait!" he called out as she scrambled up the steps. Jandra had grown up in the palace and knew all its shadows. Pet worried that if he lost sight of her he wouldn't find her again.

"Leave me alone!" she shouted as she reached the top of the stairs.

Pet followed her into a star-shaped room. The room was large, built on a scale to accommodate a sun-dragon. The chamber was empty save for a bed, a wardrobe, and a few other pieces of furniture sitting within one of the arms of the star. The human-sized furniture in the midst of the giant open space looked lonely. Jandra ran toward the bed, falling to her knees as she reached it. At the foot of the bed sat a heavy oak chest sealed with an iron lock. Jandra grabbed the lock with trembling hands.

"What's so urgent?" Pet asked as he drew closer. "If Ven was alive enough to get out of his coffin, he's probably still alive now."

"He was dead!" she snapped as the lock clicked open. "We both saw him die!"

"He was magic. He could cure the sick with his touch. He survived a gutting by Zanzeroth! Why is it so hard to believe he came back to life?"

Jandra threw the lid of the chest open. She dug her hands into the carefully folded garments inside, tossing them wildly around the room. The light from the lantern by the bed glinted on something silver. Jandra lifted it from the chest—a skullcap. Pet had seen it before. It was the head gear Vendevorex had always worn.

"Pet," she said, "it's too complicated to explain right now, but Vendevorex and I don't control magic. Vendevorex didn't believe in magic."

"He could set things on fire with his mind," Pet said. "He could turn invisible! *You* turn invisible! How can you say it's not magic?"

"Vendevorex trained me my whole life and I never figured out how to do half the stuff he did," Jandra said. "I can't explain our powers to you in five minutes, or even five hours. Ven used to say that 'magic' would be acts that violated physical laws. We don't have supernatural powers. What we have is possession of an advanced technology that looks like magic to those who don't understand it. Vendevorex controlled that technology with this." She held up the skullcap. It was beaten and bent in the aftermath of Vendevorex's violent end. "If the skullcap had been gone, I might have believed he was still alive. Since it isn't, someone stole his body."

"Why would anyone do that?" Pet asked.

"Maybe they thought he was supernatural and there's some power to be derived from possessing his bones. It was probably humans. They believe the dumbest things."

"Hmm," said Pet. "Might I remind you that you're human?"

"Am I?" Jandra asked, sagging back against her bed, the skullcap resting in her lap. She looked very small in the oversized room. She normally projected a defiant strength that Pet found irresistible. Now, the tragic events of recent weeks had finally caught up with her. She looked like a lost little girl, with no hope of ever finding her way home. Pet wanted to take her hand, but knew she would only see it as another attempt at seduction. Which it could lead to, he supposed. All women succumbed to his charms eventually. She sounded on the verge of tears as she said, "Why am I only comfortable around dragons? Why does every human I meet make my skin crawl?"

"Do I make your skin crawl?" he asked.

"You especially," she said.

These weren't words Pet was used to hearing from young women. "You know, I'm the reason humans won their little uprising in the Free City. They rallied around me. Now I'm going to be standing up for all of humanity in this conference Shandrazel is holding."

"What is your point?" Jandra asked.

"Just that you are proving to be especially difficult to impress."

Jandra sighed. "If you want to impress me, figure out who took Ven. Or help me find the real Bitterwood."

"That crazy old man? What do you want with him?"

"Things happened so fast the last time I saw him," she said. As she spoke, the look of vulnerability faded from her features. Pet noticed that when there was something she wanted to do, she always summoned the strength to do it. "One second, I was trying to help Bitterwood find his lost family. The next, he was shouting at me to go away. I never got the chance to tell him something that he needs to know."

"Which is?"

"Bitterwood thought his family had been killed by dragons. But I think his son, Adam, might be alive. He wasn't listed in Albekizan's slave records. I knew Bitterwood's daughters, and they told me that their grandmother had taken their baby brother when the dragons raided their village. She jumped into the well to hide. They didn't know if Adam survived the raid, but they knew he wasn't taken captive."

"Don't you remember how callously Bitterwood treated us?" Pet asked. "He left us to die. Why do you owe that monster anything?"

"Bitterwood wasn't entirely a monster. There was a little girl with us when we were captured. Her name was Zeeky. He treated her in a kind and fatherly way. And while you take credit for the victory in the Free City—a victory I believe you actually owe to Vendevorex—Bitterwood is the one who really won the war. He's the one who killed Albekizan."

"No one has seen him since," said Pet. "Just because they didn't find his body when they searched the river doesn't mean he's still alive."

"He's alive," she said. "I've asked around. Some of the people in Richmond saw an old man and a little girl riding an ox-dog west along the river. I'm positive it's them."

"Assuming it was, if Bitterwood's lived this long without knowing his son might be alive, he can wait a bit longer. Don't go off chasing some man who doesn't want to see you again. I need you here by my side, Jandra."

"Pet, I'm not going to sleep with you. Just give up."

"No," he knelt in front of her, so she could better see his face. All his life he was acting, but now he wanted the masks he wore to slip away. He tried to project sincerity as he spoke. "I mean, yes, I'll give up trying to seduce you. I want you here because you're smart and you're brave and you're tough. Maybe you don't feel like a human, but you're a better human than me. I need you beside me at the summit."

"Aren't you up to the job?"

Pet took a long, deep breath, then shook his head. "No," he said. "We both know I'm a fraud. You're right—I did nothing to win the battle of the Free City. Two prophets, Ragnar and Kamon, rallied their followers to fight for me; they did all the work. And, you're right about Vendevorex. We would have been slaughtered if he hadn't shown up. My sole contribution to the battle was to stand before the crowd and look heroic."

"Yeah," she said. "You do look the part."

Pet grinned. He couldn't believe she'd finally given him a compliment! He returned to his attempt at sincere confession. "We both know I'm the worst person imaginable to have at that table. I've spent my life trying to please sun-dragons. I'm worse than a slave. I've lived as a sun-dragon's pet."

Jandra shook her head. "I'm no better," she said. "I grew up feeling like the daughter of a dragon.

I've never known any human family. I'm told my parents are dead, but does that mean I'm all alone? What if I have sisters, or a brother, or even grandparents still alive? The horrible thing is, I wouldn't know what to say to them if they found me. Look at my wardrobe. I dress in gowns with fabrics that resemble the scales of dragons. I braid feathers into my hair to look like the neck fringes of sky-dragons."

"A very fetching look, may I say," Pet said. "You grew up in a palace. You can't be expected to dress in burlap sacks."

"I know. But it's my dreams that frighten me. In my dreams, I'm a dragon. I dream constantly of flying."

"Ah," said Pet. He was bonding with Jandra at last, and he did know something about her particular condition. He reached out and took her hand, cupping it gently with his. "Dreams of flying are usually dreamt by women who are still virgins. They're a symptom of sexual frustration. Perhaps—"

"Perhaps if you leave right now I won't slap you," she said, jerking her hand away.

From the look in her eyes, he could tell she meant it. He stood up, stretching his back. "You can't blame me for trying."

"Just leave," she said, looking down once more at the skullcap. "I was actually starting to feel a little sympathy for you. I should have known it was only another seduction ploy."

Pet turned and walked across the vast and empty room. Flattery hadn't worked on Jandra, lies hadn't gotten him anywhere, and now the truth had failed. For a brief instant, a new and strange thought flickered across his mind: perhaps, if he wished to have her by his side, he should be prepared to accept her as a friend. Instead of constant attempts at seduction, he should simply value her for her fine qualities and welcome her into his life as an equal, or even a superior, rather than as just another conquest. He truly did want her to stand beside him at the upcoming summit. He honestly admired her courage and her convictions. He glanced back across the lonely room. She was standing now, studying herself in a full-length mirror. She was beautiful, slender and virginal, and once more had that vulnerable lost look upon her face. He wanted to say something, but couldn't find the words. When he saw her again, he would work on winning her as a friend. Perhaps then she'd be easier to seduce.

As THE DOOR to the star-shaped chamber closed, Jandra looked back over her shoulder. She almost felt like chasing after Pet. He wasn't the best of company, but being alone in this room was painful.

For as long as she could remember, this tower had been her home. Once, its walls had been lined with thick, leather-bound tomes and countless parchment scrolls. The interior had been a forest of tables covered with vials and beakers and magnifying lenses of the finest quality.

"The world thinks of what we do as magic," Vendevorex had told her. "Their ignorance is an important source of our power. We do not manipulate supernatural forces. We move matter and light according to inalterable rules, using tools that must remain invisible to others."

In this room, she'd learned to understand the building blocks of the material world, and the countless ways these blocks could be pulled apart and placed back together. Using her "magic" was an art, a kind of sculpting on the finest scale imaginable.

Of course, all of the tools of teaching were gone now. The king's wicked brother Blasphet had taken command of this tower after he'd been released from the dungeon. He'd turned the room into a torture chamber. Earth-dragons had since cleaned the room. Most of the dried blood had been scrubbed out of the cracks in the floor; with incense lit, the faint hint of rotting gore was nearly undetectable. Jandra's possessions had been returned to their former positions. Now her every step echoed in the vacant chamber. Moonlight seeped through the high windows, painting the marble floors with ghostly shapes. Not that Jandra believed in ghosts. Vendevorex had raised her as a strict materialist, and had always been dismissive of the spiritual world.

"There are indeed realities in this world that cannot be seen," he had said. "We move through a world of fields and forces. We control machines too small for the eyes to discern. We are masters of an unseen world—but the invisible is not the same as the supernatural."

Jandra studied her face in the mirror. In her old life, when she'd looked into this same glass, she'd been staring at the face of a naïve and innocent girl. She'd been through so much since then. She'd nearly died. She'd felt her life slipping between her fingers in warm gushes. What's more, she'd learned to kill. She'd heard the gurgling, gasping breaths of a dragon dying by her hands. She closed her eyes, and all the violence of the recent months washed through her mind. She'd learned to fight when she had no strength to fight. She'd learned to live for days in clothes caked and clotted with blood.

She opened her eyes—and found she was still looking into the face of a girl, but a girl who was no longer innocent. She lifted her chin and studied the thin pale line where her throat had been slit. She looked with sorrow at her shoulder-length hair— once it had hung the full length of her back. She'd been forced to cut it to disguise herself. She brushed away the fringe of hair across her scalp that concealed the metal band she had once worn as a tiara. This was a smaller version of Vendevorex's skullcap, a device that allowed her to communicate with the unseen machines that floated by the millions in the air around her. She'd changed her hair to hide it when she'd been a fugitive.

She removed the tiara and placed it on the table.

There was no longer any need to hide who she was.

Indeed, now it was time to proudly announce to the world her true heritage.

She lifted Vendevorex's skullcap and brought it to her brow. Her eyes were locked on their reflection. They were cool hazel circles, devoid of sorrow or joy or hope or fear. They were the same sorts of eyes through which Vendevorex had looked upon the world. She was the inheritor of Vendevorex's power. And, she hoped, she was the inheritor of his wisdom and strength.

She lowered the skullcap onto her head, willing the metal to drape like cloth over the contours of her scalp. She closed her eyes to concentrate on the way the metal felt as it formed a helmet that matched her head and hers alone. Then, with a thought, she willed the malleable metal once more into solid silver.

She opened her eyes, expecting to find herself transformed. Instead, her mouth fell open as she let out a gasp. Behind her in the mirror, his golden eyes gleaming in the dim light, stood Vendevorex.

BLASPHET, THE MURDER God, woke to the familiar blackness. Since the fiasco of the Free City, Blasphet had been locked in the lowest chamber of the dungeon, his wings, legs, neck, and tail shackled to the bedrock. A dragon with a less vital mind might have been driven mad in the timeless dark. Blasphet philosophically accepted his confinement as an opportunity to contemplate the error of his ways, free from normal distractions.

Unfortunately, Blasphet still had a few abnormal distractions. When Shandrazel had captured him, he'd known of Blasphet's reputation for concealing poisoned needles and small tools among his feather-scales. He'd unceremoniously plucked Blasphet like an oversized chicken. Now his scales were growing back, with an itch he felt was surely unprecedented in all history. To lie in tomblike stillness and be aware of each new feather-scale seeping from its follicle, like a billion tiny insects burrowing from his hide... Was it possible his hatred of Shandrazel was even greater than his hatred of Albekizan?

Albekizan had been the central focus of his hatred for half a century. As those decades passed, Blasphet had enjoyed a thousand enticing visions of how his brother might suffer. Over the years, his schemes had grown in complexity. Once, he'd imagined sawing off his brother's limbs, then hooking his mouth to a tube and force feeding him for months until Albekizan was a bloated blob. Then he would starve his brother, melting off the fat, reducing him to little more than a skeletal torso draped in an enormous sheet of flesh. Finally, he would cut Albekizan open, breaking and rearranging his bones, wiring and pinning them into the shape of a throne. Blasphet would reign over the kingdom from the living throne of his brother, leisurely looking down upon the former king's plaintive eyes, reveling in the despair he would find in them!

He sighed at the memory, and reminded himself that he was here to learn the error of his ways. His biggest error, he knew, was his need to torment his enemies rather than simply kill them.

For Shandrazel, there were no visions of elaborate torture thrones. He would simply close his jaws around the bastard and rip his throat out! The thought filled him with a warmth that defeated the chill of the bedrock.

Above, Blasphet heard the creak of a door. Once a day, guards would come to feed him gruel and muck up the pool of filth that Blasphet had excreted since their last visit. Blasphet hadn't yet killed any of his guards, though he had thought of a dozen possible ways. Perhaps today he would indulge himself. A faint light seeped through the darkness. The acrid odor of an oil lamp reached his nostrils as the guards descended the stairs.

Something was different. Blasphet cocked his head to better to catch the guards' footsteps. The sound was wrong. Whatever approached wasn't as heavy as earth-dragons. Humans? Perhaps coming to take revenge? It seemed so unfair. Human genocide had been Albekizan's vision; Blasphet had taken up the challenge only out of intellectual curiosity. He bore no hatred of mankind, as a whole. Humans had been the only species ever to grant him proper respect. Humans once worshipped him as a god—the Murder God. It hadn't been hard to convince an army of assassins and spies of his divinity. Humans believed in gods with the same obvious certainty with which they believed in weather. It was simply in their nature. At the height of his power, before Albekizan had crushed the cult, Blasphet's worshippers had numbered in the thousands.

Keys rattled in the lock of the iron door. Tendrils of light glowed around the edges of the frame. Slowly the door groaned open, pushed by a half dozen earth-dragons, their legs straining. A single earth-dragon should have been more than strong enough to open the heavy door.

Blasphet tilted his head to watch as the earth-dragons marched into the cell. Four more followed, carrying a man-sized bundle of canvas bound tightly with coils of rope. Silently, the earth-dragons advanced, rings of keys jangling in their fists. The six who had opened the door went to the shackles that held him. Without a word of explanation they crouched, slipped the keys into the locks, and turned them. Iron clattered on the stone floor as they pried the shackles loose, grunting with the effort—in the damp dungeon air, the shackles were already beginning to rust.

Blasphet had been staked to the floor on his back. His limbs felt weak, nearly paralyzed, but through sheer will he rolled to his side. The earth-dragons helped him to his belly, then stood back as Blasphet rose on trembling, unsteady legs. He stretched his wings, shaking them, loosening the damp grime that coated them.

As one, the earth-dragons knelt and lowered their tortoise-like heads until their brows touched the ground, their arms stretched before them in a position of prayer.

"You're humans, aren't you?" Blasphet asked, his voice raspy. His throat felt sore and raw where the shackle had been. "The motions of your bodies betray you."

One guard rose, looking up at Blasphet with dark, cloudy eyes. Certainly, they looked liked earth-dragons, and smelled like them as well, but these eyes weren't natural... They looked more like lifeless glass than a living organ of sight. The earth-dragon placed both hands upon his gray-green head, gave his skull a twist, and lifted it from his shoulders.

A human's face was revealed where the dragon's had been. It was a young woman, her head shaved, a black tattoo of a serpent coiling above her right eye, writhing across her scalp, then snaking down her neck and shoulder. The other earth-dragons stood and removed their heads as well. Ten women, all in their teens, all with shaved scalps. Even their eyebrows were missing.

"We are Sisters of the Serpent," the first one said, bowing her head. She spoke in a soft, reverential tone. "We are your humble servants, O Murder God. I am Colobi, serpent of the first order. Our disguises were never meant to deceive you."

"Of course," said Blasphet, flexing his fore-talons, feeling the blood flowing into them with a pleasant tingle. "What's in the bundle?"

"We knew you would be hungry for proper nourishment," Colobi said. "We kidnapped Valandant, Kanst's youngest."

Blasphet nodded, his eyes wide with admiration. Kanst was dead now, but he had been Blasphet's cousin, so Valandant was his own kin, albeit somewhat removed. Kanst had also been commander of Albekizan's armies. His widow and family would still be well guarded. These Sisters of the Serpents were promising. It pleased him that his worshipers showed such initiative and competence.

They carried the bundle forth. It struggled feebly. Valandant was only two years old, little bigger than the girls who carried him. Of all the dragon races, only sun-dragons formed family units. The death of a fledgling this young, following so soon on the deaths of Kanst and Albekizan, would cause grief of unimaginable sharpness for all his family.

The humans unrolled the canvas. The young dragon struggled but his wings were pinned behind his back by an iron ring that pierced the skin just inside the wrist joint at the fore-talons. His legs were tied together by a thick cord of hemp, and his snout was shut by a similar cord. Valandant whipped his tail wildly, causing the humans to jump back.

"Shhhhh," Blasphet said, leaning over the frightened dragon. In the lamp light, Valandant's red feather-scales glistened like blood. His wide eyes were damp with tears.

Suddenly, thirst ripped Blasphet from snout to belly. He opened his jaws wide, took Valandant's slender neck between his teeth, then clamped down, piercing it. Hot salty gushes spilled across his tongue. The fragrant iron-tinged tang of blood filled his nose. He grabbed the still-struggling dragon and lifted him over his head, upending him like a jug of wine. He drank from the now limp body, blood dribbling down his neck and falling in hot drops upon his belly until his thirst was quenched.

Blasphet tossed the emptied corpse aside. He rubbed in the blood that coated his scales with his fore-claws, luxuriating in its warmth. He looked at his blood-soaked claws. For a moment, the gore made it seem as if they had reverted to their natural red coloring. However, as he licked the blood away, he found his scales had once more grown in clear, leaving the black hide beneath showing through. Once he had speculated that it was lack of sunlight that leached the color from his scales. Now, he wondered if it wasn't some long-term side effect of the poisons he'd ingested over the years. He was pleased with the look of his new scales—they were bristly, even spiky. It made his skin look angry.

The Sisters of the Serpent stared at him in awe. The fresh blood inside him burned like liquid fire in his belly. Murder God, they had called him. It had been too long since he'd heard the words from human lips.

"Your gift pleases me," he said. Then, he randomly pointed to five of the sisters. "You will come with me. We shall go to my temple. I assume you've built a temple?"

"Of course, my lord," said Colobi.

"You five," he said, eying the others. "You won't be coming home. I've hidden poisoned knives throughout the castle. I will tell you where to find them. Then, I want you to charge forth and kill as many creatures as you can, in celebration of my return. Dragons of all species, humans, horses, ox-dogs, rats… if it breathes, make it stop. Kill with no regard for your own safety. Kill until something kills you. If you kill everyone in the castle, kill each other. Do I make myself clear?"

"Yes, O Murder God," the five said in unison, their eyes fixed upon him as if he were the most precious thing in the universe.

CHAPTER FOUR

LAUGHTER
SPITTING BLOOD

"**V**EN!" JANDRA SHOUTED, spinning to face her
mentor. "You're alive!"

"No," Vendevorex said. "I'm almost certainly dead."

Jandra paused, confused. Vendevorex had died in
her arms, it was true, but she couldn't ignore the
plain evidence of her eyes. Vendevorex was alive.
His sky-blue chest expanded and contracted with
each breath. His scales nearly shimmered. From the
strong, sharp lines of his shoulders to the well-
formed legs that held him with such balance and
poise, Vendevorex was the picture of health.

She ran forward to embrace him, throwing her
arms around him, then through him. His body fluttered like smoke.

She jumped back, her voice catching in her throat;
some primitive part of her mind felt certain she was
in the presence of a ghost. Quickly, the more rational part of her brain deduced the truth.

"You're an illusion," she said.

"Correct," Vendevorex answered. "An interactive recording stored within the skullcap. I don't know the circumstances of my demise, Jandra, but you are the only one with the proper training to have triggered my helmet when you donned it. The fact you're seeing me shows that the helmet is functioning. As the device continues to adapt itself to your brain, you will discover it to be a much more powerful tool than your tiara. Unfortunately, this increased power comes with increased risks."

Jandra raised her hands and ran her finger along the rim of the helmet where it rested against her forehead. More powerful? She'd always assumed that Ven's skullcap and her tiara were equally functional. Were different capacities the reason Vendevorex's abilities had seemed so advanced?

"Just as the helmet will adjust itself to better interface with your brain, it will adjust your brain to better interface with it. In the coming days, the helm will expand the range and sensitivity of your senses. You may find this disorienting. In time, you will adapt."

Jandra held her breath, trying to discover if she could hear anything new or different. It didn't seem so.

"The helmet provides an interface between your mind and the outer world, but your true abilities lie in the training and knowledge within you. The helmet will gently restructure your neural pathways to make them more efficient, allow you finer control over your memories. Most of this will happen as you sleep, but there may be some carry over into your waking life. This may result in hallucinations. Be careful... you may injure innocents by attacking threats that exist only in your imagination. Conversely, you may hesitate in the face of genuine danger. This effect will fade after a few years as your brain reaches its most efficient structure."

"A few years?" Jandra said, her heart sinking. Her mind felt adequate already. What could possibly be worth years of not being able to trust her own eyes?

"Finally," said Vendevorex, "I must warn you of the most serious threat. I'm not the creator of the helmet. It is a tool from the hidden city known as Atlantis. You may have wondered why, given my abilities, I took a subservient position in the court of Albekizan, and seldom used my power to truly alter the world."

Jandra *had* often been frustrated by her mentor's reluctance to use his powers more aggressively.

"The helmet wasn't a gift from the Atlanteans. It was stolen. Take care to avoid their attention. You may think that after so many years the Atlanteans are no longer searching for their property. Unfortunately, time is no obstacle to the Atlanteans who are, for all practical purposes, immortals. I have no doubt they will come for the device. It may even be that they were simply waiting for my death to reclaim it. You may be in grave danger. Use utmost caution should you encounter an Atlantean. Their powers will exceed yours by an unimaginable factor. However, this doesn't mean they can't be defeated. Atlanteans possess one flaw that may prove fatal should you choose to exploit it. All Atlanteans—"

Vendevorex's voice was drowned out by a shout from below, a cry of rage that sounded violently torn from the shouter's throat. It was followed by the voice of an earth-dragon screaming, "Stay back!" Though the voices originated several floors beneath her with layers of thick stone to muffle them, the words sounded almost as if they had been spoken in the same room.

As she thought about the voices, images flickered through her mind. The faces of thousands of earth-dragons she'd met flashed before her in an instant. A heartbeat later, the images were gone, and a single face remained in her memory, that of a guard named Ledax. She barely knew him, having only heard him speak once in all the years he carried out his duties around the palace. Yet, she somehow knew it was his voice that had shouted the warning to stay back. She also knew, with equal certainty, that the first shout she had heard had come from the lips of a human woman.

Below, Ledax let out a pained grunt. The woman's gurgling scream transformed into a satis-fied, eerie giggle.

Jandra ran for the steps, slowed somewhat by her heavy funeral gown. She wished it was shorter. As she moved, the gown inched upward to her knees. The fabric pleated into a loose skirt, allowing her legs greater freedom. She leaped down the stairs, taking them three and four at a time. She could hear the chilling laughter growing closer. She burst into the room, freezing as she took in the gory scene. Vendevorex's warning of hallucinations suddenly seemed relevant.

Ledax was splayed limply on the floor, blood ooz-ing from a gash in his shoulder. Crouched over him was a naked girl, younger than Jandra, her breasts and belly painted with blood. Her lips were spread wide in an evil grin. Dark red saliva streamed down her chin as she giggled. Black, serpentine tattoos decorated the skin of her scalp and neck. Similar inkings coiled down her thighs and arms. In her right hand, she held a long dagger, its black blade glistening. The girl's eyes made Jandra hesitate, wondering if she'd slipped into a nightmarish hallucination. The girl's pupils were vacant black circles set in bloodshot pools of pink. Jandra had faced killers before. She'd stared down tatterwings, locked eyes with earth-dragons, and stood defiant in the gaze of sun-dragons. Nothing prepared her for the empty void of the girl's eyes, the hollow, unblinking stare of a fanatic transformed into an instrument of death.

While Jandra was frozen by her doubts, the girl suffered no such paralysis. With a grunt she leapt, swinging her dagger in a high overhead chop aimed at Jandra's face.

Jandra raised her hand to catch the girl's arm. The black blade sank into Jandra's palm, puncturing it. Droplets of blood splashed against her face. Instantly, her hand numbed; with her next heartbeat, her whole arm went limp. The girl drew back, still grinning. A third heartbeat numbed Jandra's entire torso. There was no fourth heartbeat. Her lungs no longer drew breath. In serene silence, her body lifeless as a doll, Jandra crumbled to the cold floor. She tried to blink and couldn't. She could only watch, suffocating, as the girl leapt over her.

In her dying, paralyzed body, Jandra listened helplessly as the girl laughed her way down the hall, in search of more victims.

PET GLUMLY WALKED through the palace, lost in thought. When he'd been the companion of the sun-dragon Chakthalla, he would amuse himself in the evenings by stealing out to visit young women in the nearby village. He'd not been with a woman since he met Jandra, mostly due to spending the majority of his time as Albekizan's prisoner. Still, he was free now. The human town of Richmond wasn't too far away. Yet he found himself unable to imagine the company of anyone but Jandra. What was wrong with him?

He found himself heading to the courtyard with the heated baths. One of Albekizan's ancestors had built giant pools whose waters were warmed by a system of pipes that ran through hidden furnaces. Pet thought it would be comforting to sink into those warm waters and let his worries melt away.

Alas, as he stepped into the brick courtyard, he discovered it was already occupied. Shandrazel was sitting in the main pool. Shandrazel was the heir of Albekizan. The sun-dragon's blood-red scales glistened in the flickering torchlight surrounding the bath. Beside him in the pool was Androkom, the High Biologian, apparently taking a moment to relax in the aftermath of the fiasco of Vendevorex's funeral.

Pet turned to leave, but Shandrazel shouted out, "Ah! Bitterwood. Come join us."

Pet looked around, wondering where Bitterwood was, before remembering that *he* was now Bitterwood. He'd claimed the name as part of a ruse to save the villagers near Chakthalla's castle. As a consequence of his deception, he'd been branded with the identity of Bitterwood by King Albekizan himself before thousands of his fellow humans in the Free City. By all rights, Shandrazel should have treated him as a mortal enemy. Yet, either Shandrazel didn't believe Pet's ruse, or else Shandrazel was completely drunk on his dream of launching a new age of peace and justice, and willing even to forgive a man famous for killing dragons.

Pet gave a charming smile as he approached the pool.

"We were just discussing the upcoming summit," said Shandrazel. "We would love to hear your thoughts."

"Okay," Pet said, loosening his belt. He slipped out of his clothes unselfconsciously. He'd never been embarrassed by his own nudity. He held his breath and leapt into the water. The pool was quite deep, built for the comfort of a sun-dragon, creatures that stood over twice the height of humans. The water was uncomfortably hot, almost scalding. Pet rose to the surface with a gasp. He noticed an oily film on the water. Fish were a major component of the diets of dragons, and the oil coated their scales as they preened themselves. Pet would require a bath after this bath.

"So," he said, bracing himself against the edge of the pool. "What did you want my opinion on?"

It was Androkom who answered. A sky-dragon with vivid blue scales, Androkom looked uncomfortable in the water, since he was forced to cling to the sides of the bath as Pet was. Androkom said, "We were thinking that true reform cannot take place without a change in our vocabulary. For the last half century, the lands from the mountains to the eastern sea have been called the Kingdom of Albekizan."

"I guess that should change now that he's dead," said Pet. "The Kingdom of Shandrazel?"

"No," said Shandrazel. "I am the king who will end the age of kings. I will not rule this land—I will serve it. I make no claim to its wealth. Instead, the land is the common wealth of all, dragons and humans. Which is why I propose we call it the Commonwealth of Albekizan."

"Hmm," said Pet. "I notice the name Albekizan is still in there."

"While I did not approve of my father's tactics, it is pointless to dispute that his conquest of smaller, warring states created one united territory that has largely existed in peace for decades. In a sense, my father created the Commonwealth that we all share. Leaving his name on the land recognizes historical reality and pays tribute to the opportunity for true justice he created."

"I guess that makes sense," Pet said, though it didn't.

Shandrazel's eyes brightened. He looked pleased at Pet's acceptance of the idea.

Pet was familiar with the look. His life had been devoted to making sun-dragons happy. It was his calling in life. As a result, he'd lived a life of comfort other humans couldn't dream of. Perhaps it would be best if he continued doing what he knew how to do well, and simply accepted everything Shandrazel suggested. Shandrazel was kindhearted. Things would work out, wouldn't they?

"Excuse me," Pet said, pinching his nose and sinking beneath the steaming waters. Here, weightless, surrounded by water as warm as a womb, he felt free to think.

What he thought about was that horrible day he'd stood on the platform of the Free City, with Albekizan looming over him, taunting him as the dragon armies swarmed into the square to slaughter the assembled humans. Of course, the king's plans had gone wrong. The humans had fought back. Was he now going to surrender their lives back into the control of dragons? Was this the reward those countless unknown soldiers would pay for his survival?

His lungs at the point of bursting, he popped back above the surface of the oily water.

"No," he said.

"No?" asked Shandrazel.

"No what?" asked Androkom.

"No, I don't like having Albekizan's name appearing on new maps of this land. If we truly wish to form a new government, we should cut ties with the past. Simply call it the Commonwealth and nothing more."

Shandrazel raised a fore-talon to stroke his scaly chin. "There is wisdom in your words," he said. "So much injustice in this world exists as an artifact of history. Grudges and grievances planted centuries ago blossom as today's violence. Very well. The Commonwealth."

"I like its brevity," said Androkom.

"It's bold in its simplicity," Shandrazel mused. "It says that we have closed the book on history, and now take a quill to fresh pages to write the world anew."

Androkom said something in response, but Pet didn't hear it. There was a disturbance in the castle, near the chamber door that led to the bath. It sounded like women screaming, high-pitched shrieks that trailed off into cackling. Pet was something of an expert at deciphering the shouts of women. Despite the laughter, these women sounded out for blood.

Androkom and Shandrazel got out of the pool. The wave created by Shandrazel's sudden motion was enough to lift Pet to the pool's edge. As he stepped out, an earth-dragon attendant came toward him with a big white cotton towel. The towel was meant for a sun-dragon, as big as a bed sheet. Pet draped it over his shoulder to form a toga. He rubbed his hair dry, wrinkling his nose at the fishy odor that clung to him.

"I wonder what the commotion is," Androkom said, sounding nervous.

In answer, an earth-dragon soldier stumbled into the courtyard. He collapsed on the brick, his own spear jutting from his back.

"What—" said Shandrazel. Before he could finish the thought three women burst from the shadowy doorway, leaping over the guard's body.

The women were naked, their pale bodies young and limber, as they charged across the room toward Pet and the dragons. Normally, Pet welcomed the presence of nude young women throwing themselves at him. The fact that these women were soaked with blood and waving long black daggers over their tattooed heads made him think their visit would not be a pleasant one.

"Shandrazel!" Androkom shouted, leaping into the sky. "Save yourself!"

Androkom beat his wings and rose into the air, unsteady. Sky-dragons used their tails for balance in flight; Androkom's tail was little more than a stub after his escape from one of Blasphet's deathtraps.

Shandrazel didn't follow his smaller companion into the air. As the women charged, one of them threw a volley of darts. The darts struck the earth-dragon attendant who stood near Pet. The dragon shivered, then fell to the ground, no longer breathing.

A second woman threw her darts at Shandrazel—the biggest target in the room. Shandrazel responded by sweeping his wings forward, creating a powerful gust that knocked the darts off course. Two of the women continued to charge the sun-dragon while the third picked Pet as her target. An unearthly shriek erupted from her bloody lips. She hacked the air before her with her dagger as if she were stabbing at a swarm of invisible bees.

In the course of a decade of carousing, Pet had bedded, if his math could be trusted, a total of three-hundred seventeen women. Some of the more heartbroken ones had physically expressed their displeasure at his faithlessness. Which is to say, Pet had experience in dealing with young women trying to sink a knife into his chest. He danced aside at the last second, allowing the assassin's blade to slice only air. He kicked out his leg and caught her by the ankle, tripping her, sending her splashing into the hot pool.

He turned to see if Shandrazel needed any help. The sun-dragon seemed to have little to fear from the two girls. He swung his long tail around in a whipping motion, catching the first attacker in the belly, folding her in two. The momentum of the blow sent the girl flying, crashing into one of the marble pillars that decorated the courtyard.

The last woman leapt at Shandrazel, attempting to plant her dagger in his thigh. He caught her in midair, sinking his teeth into her shoulder. She squealed as she thrust the dagger up with both hands, burying it to the hilt in Shandrazel's jaws.

Shandrazel's face went limp. The girl fell to the ground, a vicious row of red puncture wounds dotting her left shoulder. Shandrazel stumbled backward, knocking over a large clay pot filled with shrubs. He clawed at the blade with his foretalon, freeing it. It fell to the bricks with a clatter. Shandrazel lowered his head and stared at the blade with unfocused eyes. He lurched drunkenly then toppled, his tail whipping about as if it had a mind of its own. The wounded girl darted forward and grabbed the blade, then turned toward Pet. The assassin who had smacked into the marble column was also on her feet, limping toward him, her blade held in a trembling hand.

Behind him, he heard the splashes of the first woman climbing from the pool.

"Ladies," he said, raising his hands, backing away, turning in a slow circle. No matter which direction he looked, there was always one just out of sight. "I'm sure we can talk this out."

The women responded with laughter, spitting blood.

JANDRA COULD HEAR her killer in the outer hall. More guards had come in response to the commotion. One by one, their armored bodies crashed heavily to the ground.

If only she could have known the poison they were using, perhaps it wasn't too late to command the microscopic machinery that swam in her blood to form an antidote. At the thought, a single molecule came into focus before her, enormously magnified. The years Vendevorex forced her to study chemistry proved useful. She recognized the molecule as an organic alkaloid. The long chain of atoms was coiled like a serpent about to strike. The poison was made of dozens of carbon and hydrogen atoms, tangled together with a few oxygen and nitrogen atoms. Just two nitrogens, in fact. The molecule would be easy to break at these points. In her mind's eye, one of the tiny machines that swam in her bloodstream darted forward and snapped the molecule in two with its infinitesimal claws. She imagined the action being repeated through her body.

An instant later her heart beat. It was a feeble flutter, faint at first, but it grew stronger. Air gushed back into her lungs. The fingers of her left hand wriggled. Her right hand, which had taken the knife thrust, remained limp and useless. She sat up, woozy, and found herself staring at Ledax's lifeless body.

Or was it lifeless? Was he paralyzed as she had been, slowly suffocating? She saw the puncture wound in his shoulder. She jammed two fingers into the hole. It was as if her fingertips were covered by a million tiny eyes. She found the same poison in his blood, which now lay stagnant inside him. She willed the microscopic machinery within her to leach from her pores to attack the poison inside Ledax. Nothing happened as the seconds ticked by. Her own blood had been full of the devices necessary to fight the poison. The earth-dragon lacked this advantage. She knew she should give up, abandon him, and go in search of the assassin. Yet, there was a look in the earth-dragon's desperate eyes that told her that some spark of life still burned within him. Her heart leapt as those eyes blinked. Ledax gasped as his lungs stirred back to life.

Confident that her devices were working to save Ledax, Jandra struggled to her feet. Her dizziness was fading but her right hand was still limp. She studied the wound. Her eyes focused on such fine detail she felt as if she was examining her hand under a magnifying lens. She could see how each side of the puncture wound fit together, skin cell to skin cell, nerve to nerve, with each torn blood vessel having a perfect mate across the gap. Willing the matched cells to reconnect, the wound closed over in less than a minute, leaving a ragged scar. She wriggled her tingling fingers. She liked this new helmet!

With a killer in the castle, there was no time to dwell on her new-found powers. She chased down the hall, listening for any clue. She found the still bodies of two earth-dragon guards as she turned a corner. There was perhaps still time to save them, but if she tarried, how many more dragons would the assassin reach? Clenching her fists, she made the bitter determination that it was a higher priority to stop the assassin than to heal the dying. She ran faster, her strength fully restored, all traces of the poison gone.

She raced around one more corner and found the assassin surrounded by the bodies of three more guards. It looked as if one had gotten in a blow, for the tattooed girl was bleeding profusely from a gash across her ribs. As Jandra ran toward her the girl looked up, her eyes still full of the same dark hatred. Yet now something new flashed within them: confusion.

"Ah ough ah ill ooo," the girl grumbled.

"You thought you killed me?" Jandra asked, drawing up short, her eyes focused on the deadly blade. Jandra no longer feared the poison, but she wasn't anxious to be stabbed again. It was time to attempt a feat she'd witnessed Vendevorex perform many times. She dipped her fingers into the pouch of silver powder that hung at her side, then flicked her fingers toward the girl. She waited several seconds as she and the girl circled each other, their eyes locked. The girl seemed wary, as if she were facing a ghost.

The microscopic dust settled over the dagger. Vendevorex had been able to command the particles to instantly decay matter. Jandra reached out with her mind, willing the dagger to crumble to rust.

The dagger glowed with an internal fire, then began to crack and crumble. The fire didn't stop at the dagger, however. The girl dropped the weapon and wailed, shaking her hand as if she was in terrible pain. As she shook, the skin of her hand unraveled, the flesh falling away in damp nuggets until she was waving fingers of bone.

Blood gushed from her wrist as Jandra watched in horror. The glow continued up her arm. Jandra reached out, trying to find all the particles with her mind, commanding them to stop. The girl fell to the floor, her right arm now nothing but bone. The flesh of her shoulder bubbled, but the girl had stopped screaming. Jandra finally brought the reaction under control, but it was too late. The girl was dead, with a good portion of her right rib cage exposed. Jandra turned away, sick to her stomach, as the girl's blood pooled across the floor. She slumped against the wall, welcoming the coolness of the stone. The sound of the girl's dying agony still echoed in her ears. Only, as she listened closer, she realized it wasn't the girl's death cry she was hearing. Another girl was screaming, several of them in fact. There was more than one assassin in the castle.

There would be time to feel sick later. Now, she clenched her fists and ran toward the noise.

PET WEIGHED HIS odds. He was confident he could deal with any given girl. It was just a question of how quickly the other two would move to attack when he acted. The two that Shandrazel had fought were wounded. The bitten girl grew paler with each step as her wounds trickled wet red ribbons across her breasts and belly. The other girl was limping after her collision with the column. So, the greatest threat was the girl he'd tripped. He tilted his head to see her movements from the corner of his eye.

She was growing closer... closer... and then, she leapt.

Pet whirled, slapping the knife from his attacker's hand. Before she could react he swung his fist in a roundhouse punch, catching her on the chin, putting his full weight into it. The blow numbed his arm. The girl spun backward, stumbling, her arms flopping limply. He was certain he'd knocked her out. Unfortunately, she stayed on her feet and turned around to face him, her eyes full of hatred. She stood next to one of the decorative marble columns and placed one hand on it to steady herself. She used her other hand to wipe the blood from her mouth. Pet's eyes flickered over the bricks. Where had her knife flown to? If he turned his back on her...

Suddenly, a heavy flower pot dropped parallel to the marble column, crashing into the girl's head, smashing into a hundred fragments. The girl toppled sideways, her legs twitching.

Pet looked up. Androkom perched atop the marble pillar, his eyes wide with fear. "Watch out!" he shouted.

Pet spun to find the limping assassin barely a yard away. Her blade cut the air as Pet jerked away, the tip missing his throat by inches. His feet carried him backward, trying to open some space between him and the girl. Unfortunately, the enormous towel he was wrapped in wound up under his feet and he tripped, falling to his back. The girl loomed over him, raising her blade high.

Then, suddenly, her blade was gone, along with most of her hand. She lowered the stump of her wrist, staring at the blood jetting out with each heartbeat. She grew white as Pet's towel as her eyes fluttered up in her head. As she fell, Pet saw a familiar figure behind her.

"Jandra!" he yelled out. "There's a third one! Be careful!"

"Where?" said Jandra, her eyes scanning the room.

"She's behind that column," Androkom yelled, pointing with his wing.

Jandra crept toward the marble pillar as Pet found his footing. He cinched the towel higher as he, too, approached the column, his eyes alert for any movement.

Rounding the column at a respectful distance, Pet found the final assassin sitting with her back to the marble, her legs splayed before her, her arms hanging limply by her side. She was shivering, and her skin had taken on a bluish cast. She held the black dagger loosely in her right hand.

"Drop the knife," Jandra said.

"She's dying," Pet said.

"I see that," Jandra said, sounding annoyed. Then, to the girl once more, "I can save your life. Just put down the knife."

The girl cocked her head toward Jandra, fixing her vacant, dying gaze upon her. A smile played briefly upon her lips. Her mouth moved as if she was saying something, but no sound came out, only a gush of fresh blood. With a final burst of strength, the girl raised her blade, grasped it with both hands, and plunged it into her left breast, burying it to the hilt.

Her head drooped as her arms fell to her side, a final sigh bubbling from her lips.

"These were servants of the Murder God!" Androkom shouted from his perch. "Suicide assassins! There could be a whole army of them!"

"Let's hope there's just the four," Jandra said, running to Shandrazel. "How long since he was stabbed?"

"Only a few minutes," said Pet. "Four assassins? I counted three."

"I killed one upstairs," she said as she ran her hands over Shandrazel's hide. "Where was he stabbed? I need to touch his blood."

"He was struck in the jaw," Androkom called out.

Jandra ran her hands along the line of his long, crocodilian jaw. "Found it!" she shouted as her fingers wriggled into the stab wound. "He's still alive," she said, seconds later. "I'll need a moment to find all the poison."

Pet stood over her, looking at himself reflected in her silver helmet. "This is a new look for you," he said. "I liked the tiara more. But the skirt does show off your calves."

"Can we discuss my wardrobe another time?"

Pet shrugged, then went back to check on the other two assassins. The girl who'd been hit by the flower pot was obviously dead, the top of her skull dented in. He moved to the second one, kneeling beside her. Blood no longer spurted from her wrist. He placed his fingers on her throat, feeling for a pulse. Nothing. She'd lost too much blood.

"Too bad we didn't take one alive," said Pet. "We could have found out what they're here for."

"Isn't it obvious?" Androkom said. "They're here to free the Murder God! Damn Shandrazel! I told him to kill that monster."

Shandrazel mumbled, his jaws barely moving, "I will… consider your counsel."

There was a commotion in the hall, the heavy slapping sound of earth-dragons running at full speed, their weapons and armor clattering. Two of them burst into the courtyard, shouting, "Sire! Sire!"

Shandrazel raised his head slowly, an effort that seemed to require all his strength. Jandra, her fingers still in his wound, looked almost as if she moved his head like some oversized puppet.

"Hold still," she grumbled.

"Sire," the first guard said, skidding to a halt in front of Shandrazel. "Blasphet is no longer in his cell!"

"I knew it!" Androkom said, vindicated.

"We found these," the second guard said as he reached Shandrazel. He held out his arm and opened his claw. In the palm sat several pale lumps of torn flesh. Pet stepped closer, then recoiled when his eyes finally solved the puzzle of what he was seeing. The dragon was holding severed human tongues.

"They cut out their own tongues so they couldn't talk if they were captured," Androkom said.

Pet looked back at the pale pink lumps in morbid fascination. Many tongues had been in his mouth over the years. He doubted he could ever kiss anyone again without thinking of this. Then he realized that the silent tongues had one more bit of information to confess, as he counted them. "There's one more assassin," he said. "We've killed four, but there are five tongues."

A large shadow fell over the room. Pet looked up to see a sun-dragon descending in the moonlight, his wings spread wide to catch the air as he glided toward the courtyard. Pet didn't recognize this dragon, but he instantly recognized what the beast carried in his hind-talons. A human girl, nude, tattooed... the final assassin.

A foot from the brick, the dragon dropped the girl's limp body. He spread his talons out to land. Once he was firmly on the ground, he placed a talon over the girl's still form, trapping her.

"Hex!" Shandrazel shouted, excited.

"Hex?" Pet asked, looking at Jandra.

Jandra shrugged, not recognizing the name either.

"I heard you were king now," Hex said. He nodded toward the woman he'd pinned. "Looks like our uncle has sent a gift for your coronation. I found her on the roof. I took her alive, in case you wanted to question her."

"That's useless," Androkom said, his eyes darting about the courtyard, searching for more assassins in the shadows. "They've cut out their tongues."

Jandra took her hand from Shandrazel's throat and moved to the earth-dragon who held the tongues. She took one and walked toward Hex and his prisoner. She dropped to her knees and pried open the girl's limp jaw. With a determined look on her face, she put her fingers into the girl's mouth, exploring. A moment later, she shook her head.

"Not hers," she said, tossing aside the tongue. "Hand me the next one. She's going to be in for a surprise when she wakes up."

CHAPTER FIVE

HEX

PET RETRIEVED HIS pants as Jandra stuffed the third tongue into the girl's mouth. His clothes lay near the dagger he'd swatted away from the girl he'd thrown in the pool. After he pulled on his pants and boots, he carefully picked up the dagger. The blade was full of pores, black venom oozing slowly from them. He shook the weapon gently and heard fluid sloshing in the handle. Up close the poison stank, an odor somewhere between sour milk and boiled cabbage.

He jumped as Androkom dropped down beside him, an empty flower pot clasped in his fore-claws.

"Here," Androkom said, motioning for Pet to put the weapon inside. "When Graxen returns, I'll send the blade to the College of Spires. They'll want to catalogue this toxin."

Pet dropped the blade into the pot. He looked back over Androkom's scaly blue shoulder to the newly arrived sun-dragon. Most humans, no doubt, thought all sun-dragons looked alike. All were enormous, with forty-foot wing spans and jaws nearly a yard in length. All were red as a ripe chili pepper, with green eyes and black claws. Pet, however, had lived among undragons long enough that he could spot their individual differences. What had struck him as most unusual about this new dragon were the features he shared with Shandrazel. The dragon was older, a bit heavier, but the shape of his face, the normally unique bumps and ridges along the snout between the eyes and the nostrils, were a close match with Shandrazel.

Leaning closer to Androkom, he asked quietly, "Who's that?"

The new sun-dragon proved to have excellent hearing. He turned his head toward Pet and said, "I am Hexilizan, eldest son of Albekizan."

"Oh," said Pet. "I didn't know Shandrazel had any surviving brothers."

"Hex is the only one alive I know of. The fate of two remain mysteries," said Shandrazel.

"I was bested in the contest of succession nearly thirty years past and have dwelled ever since upon the Isle of Horses in service to the biologian Dacorn," Hex said. "He met an untimely death not long ago, and I've been occupied settling his affairs. I've returned due to rumors I've heard about my brother's plans." Hex turned toward Shandrazel. "Is it true you intend to overthrow centuries of tradition and implement radical new ideas of governance?"

"We live in dark times if concepts such as justice can be defined as radical," said Shandrazel.

"Dark times indeed," said Hex. "As long as we speak of justice, I must ask about the second rumor: Father died at the hands of Bitterwood."

"His true assailant is unknown," said Shandrazel. "Bitterwood was in the Free City at the time, fighting for his life."

It took Pet half a second to remember they were talking about him. He cleared his throat. He searched for words that a fabled dragon-slayer might say about the king's death, something that would be defiant without being provocative. "Albekizan was responsible for the deaths of thousands. It was only a matter of time before someone sought revenge."

"Agreed," said Hexilizan. "Father was a tyrant. I do not mourn his passing."

"Hex!" said Shandrazel.

"Shan," Hexilizan said, coolly. "After my defeat, father treated me as if I were dead. I've spent decades in servitude due to the old ways. If you intend to overthrow all the laws and traditions that have shackled this kingdom for centuries, I applaud you."

"I don't wish to overthrow all laws," Shandrazel said. "Indeed, I want to launch an age where laws are respected as upholding the common good. I intend to draft new laws that treat all sentient beings equally."

"Do as you wish," said Hex. "But I have pondered the matter for many years and now believe all laws to be fundamentally unjust. Laws exist only for the benefit of the strong; they unfailingly justify the oppression of the weak."

"I vigorously disagree," said Shandrazel. "Laws can serve to protect the weak from the strong."

"Under your new government, if a sun-dragon were to murder an earth-dragon, how would your law respond?"

"The sun-dragon would be captured, of course, and punished."

Hex looked smug as he listened to his brother. He said, "Don't you see the act of capturing and punishing another being is an act of force? It's impossible to enforce laws without violence. Some authority always wields the power to arrest, to imprison, and to execute. The sole purpose of law is to provide a moral gloss for the use of violence to bend others to the will of a higher authority."

Shandrazel furrowed his brow, looking uncertain at how to respond to this.

Androkom diplomatically ended the argument by saying, "Hexilizan, you've obviously given a great deal of thought to these matters. Perhaps you should participate in our summit; your ideas will no doubt lead to a more lively debate."

Hex shook his head. "I have been confined to the Isle of Horses for too long. Now that I'm free, I wish to travel and see the world. The thought of sitting for weeks at some summit debating governance holds no appeal. You now know my full opinion on the matter. All law is unjust."

"Without law, there would be anarchy," said Shandrazel.

"Anarchy isn't such a bad thing. There is no law in the forest. There is no law in the sea. Let the world run wild," said Hex. "There is no injustice in nature."

Pet cared little about the philosophical debate, but Hex's scorn for the law suddenly placed a dangerous idea in his head. He walked back toward the two sun-dragons.

"Hexilizan—" he started.

"Call me Hex," the sun-dragon said. "It's what my friends call me."

"Okay, Hex," Pet continued. "Isn't it a little suspicious that you show up talking about the unfairness of imprisonment on the very night that Blasphet escapes? Aren't you his nephew?"

"Yes," said Hex, swinging his head down to Pet's level. He brought his jaws to within inches of Pet's face, then said, calmly, "So's Shan. What's your point?"

Pet's familiarity with sun-dragons meant he wasn't easily intimidated by them. Still, with Hex's carrion-scented breath washing over him, Pet somehow lost his train of thought.

"My brother had nothing to do with Blasphet's escape," Shandrazel said. His tone made it clear there would be no further speculation on this point.

Pet nodded. "Right."

"Of course, it would be the fifth tongue," Jandra muttered. All eyes turned to her as she stood, stretching her back. Jandra, standing next to the captive, said, "I'm going to wake her. I guess we should tie her up first?"

"I'm pretty good at that," Pet said, glad that another of his talents would be of use.

JANDRA CROUCHED NEXT to Pet as he wrapped the slumbering assassin in the oversized towel. She reached out to touch the white nappy fabric, wiping away the blood and saliva that coated her fingers after her molecular surgery on the girl's tongue. She was startled by the texture of the cloth, the way the ridges of her fingers ran against the weave. Suddenly, she was intensely aware of her own skin, of the beads of sweat that coated her face and neck, and of the way her clothes clung to her body. She felt every tiny bump in the bricks beneath her knees. Her every nerve cell became a hundred times more sensitive. What was the helmet doing to her now? She closed her eyes, trying to regain control. Now it felt as if her skin was one giant eye that could see in all directions, but instead of perceiving light it sensed heat. The two sun-dragons at her back glowed like furnaces. Pet emitted a torch-like warmth as his muscular body rolled the assassin in the towel, mummifying her. Jandra opened her eyes as he ripped the loose end of the towel into long strips, then used those strips to tie the assassin in a tidy bundle.

As he worked, she stared at his bare torso. The well-defined muscles in his shoulders clenched and coiled as he worked. Her eyes wandered down his long arms to his perfectly formed hands, the fingers so graceful yet powerful in their movements.

"Done," said Pet. "She won't get out of that."

"You're Vendevorex's apprentice aren't you?" Hex asked. "Jandra, I believe?"

"Yes," Jandra said, standing to face the sun-dragon. Hex bore a family resemblance to Shandrazel, the same vivid red coloring of his scales fading to orange and yellow tips. Hex's eyes were a dark green, almost black, similar in shade to the ivy that covered the castle's rocky walls, while Shandrazel's were a brighter emerald. The deep wrinkles around Hex's eyes made it apparent that he was many years older than Shandrazel.

"I've heard of you," said Hex. "It's rumored you command the same supernatural powers as the wizard."

"I won't claim to be his equal," said Jandra. "Still, I'm improving. I'm flattered you've heard of me. I'm a little embarrassed I hadn't heard of you."

"You aren't the one who should be embarrassed," said Shandrazel, apologetically. "Our father was a strict adherent to the old ways. After Hex lost the contest, my father never spoke of him again. It's my father who deserves the shame here."

Androkom said, "We can discuss family history later. Every second counts if we hope to find Blasphet. Wake the prisoner."

Jandra didn't like the new High Biologian. She found him overly bossy. Still, he was right. There was no point in putting this off.

"How will you wake her?" asked Hex. "With magic? It's said that you command the elements."

"I'll command an element, all right," Jandra said, walking toward the bath. She reached down and picked up a wooden bucket that sat at the edge. It was already full of water. She headed back to the bound girl. "Call it magic if you want."

She upended the bucket, aiming the deluge at the girl's shaved head. The prisoner coughed and sputtered in the aftermath. Her eyes jerked open.

"Where am—" The girl's face went pale, as if she were terrified by the sound of her own voice. She struggled within her cotton cocoon. Her wide eyes darted around the room.

"That's right. You can talk," said Jandra. "Where's Blasphet?"

"I'm a Sister of the Serpent!" the girl screeched, arching her back as she strained against her bonds. "I'll kill you all!"

"Sister," said Jandra, putting her foot on the girl's belly and forcing her back down, "You're not killing anybody tonight. You may as well relax and answer our questions."

The girl grew quiet, glaring at Jandra. She stuck out her tongue defiantly. Then with a sudden jerk of her jaw, she bit an inch from the tip. Tears filled her eyes as she rocked her head back and forth, blood speckling her cheeks.

"Oh for the love of..." Jandra grumbled, picking up the tongue. "I can keep sticking this thing on all night." Although, in truth, she wasn't looking forward to putting her fingers near the girl's mouth with her awake.

"Dissolve her teeth," said Androkom.

"What?" said Jandra. "No!"

"Why is the idea so repellant?" asked Androkom. "This human is willing to maim herself. If you dissolve her teeth she won't bite off her tongue again.

"I know," said Jandra. "But…"

"It would be torture to maim a captured foe," said Pet. Jandra was surprised by his intervention. Pet had his shoulders pulled back and his head held high. He could look like a confident leader when the role demanded it. "Stand your ground, Jandra. I was a victim of Albekizan's torture. The day when helpless humans suffer beneath the talons of dragons must be at an end."

"She wouldn't be suffering beneath the talons of a dragon," said Androkom, frustrated to be explaining the obvious. "Jandra's human."

"It's you who gave the command," said Pet. Jandra wondered why Pet was so willing to talk back to Androkom. Was he trying to impress her?

"No one is giving anyone commands but me," Shandrazel said. "I may wish to be the king who brings an end to kings, but, at this moment, I *am* king. Jandra, I respect your aversion to hurting another. Still, the information this woman possesses is of utmost value. Perhaps losing her teeth will make her more cooperative. Will you reconsider?"

"No!" said Pet.

Jandra was a little annoyed he spoke for her. "No," she said. "I have no qualms about using my powers in self defense, but this is too much to ask."

"This is what I was talking about," Hex said, in a scolding tone directed at Shandrazel. "King for barely a week and already you would issue a command to torture. What degree of physical pain will you need to inflict to break the will of a fanatic who bites off her own tongue?"

"We shouldn't be discussing this with her listening," said Androkom.

"Agreed," said Shandrazel. He nodded toward the small army of guards that had by now gathered in the courtyard. "Take her to the dungeons. Secure her tightly. I'll be down in the morning with... further orders."

Pet leaned close to Jandra. "I'm proud of you," he said.

"I'm a little surprised by you," she whispered. "I didn't expect you to stand up to Shandrazel."

He placed a hand on her shoulder and drew his lips closer to her ear as he whispered back, "I'm a little surprised myself. But, having been on the receiving end of torture, I honestly don't want to see it inflicted on even my worst enemy."

The warmth of his hand seemed to fill her entire body. She found her eyes drawn to his lips, and the pearly white teeth that gleamed behind them. Propelled by instincts she didn't quite understand, she leaned into him. He wrapped his arms around her in a strong hug. Her cheek was pressed against his bare shoulder. He stank of fish, but beneath that was a musky aroma, the smell of his sweat. It took all her power to resist sticking out her tongue to taste him. What was happening to her?

As she thought the question, something in the helmet found the answer. His sweat was full of chemicals, tiny jigsaw pieces that locked into receptors in her nose in a perfect mating process. Was this what lust felt like? She'd never been attracted to a man before. To whom was she supposed to be attracted? The brutish slaves the sun-dragons hunted for sport? The thuggish dockworkers that populated Richmond? Human men had always seemed so animalistic when compared to the refined and mannerly dragons. Now, the idea of being an animal found a certain resonance within her. Her heart raced as she took a long, deep breath of Pet's scent. She closed her eyes, feeling her body melting into his arms.

Was this so bad? What could this lead to?

The helmet suddenly flooded her mind with what it could lead to. She jerked her eyes opened and pushed Pet away.

"Enough hugging," she said. "There's work to be done."

Pet looked a little hurt. She swung around, unable to face him, certain that her lust was written in tall clear letters on her face. She was tempted to remove her helmet. What was the advantage of having sharpened senses if she lost all control of them? But was it so bad to lose control? Eventually, she would experience intimacy with a man, and Pet wasn't such a bad candidate. He brushed his teeth, kept his nails trimmed, and seemed to be fairly experienced. Who better to learn from?

She closed her eyes and clenched her fists, feeling her nails pressing into her palms. This had to stop.

"I'm leaving the castle," she said. "There's too much I need to do."

"What?" asked Pet. "Right now? It's after midnight. The only thing we need to do is get to bed."

She shook her head. "I'm too keyed up after the attacks to sleep. I had planned to leave soon to find Bit… to find Zeeky. She told me she was from a village known as Big Lick. I want to make sure she gets home safely."

"Why is this so urgent?" Pet asked.

"There's just a lot to do. I want to see Zeeky, I want to find out what happened to Ven's body, and now Blasphet's on the loose. The only one I have any real information about is Zeeky. I'll go find her, get that out of the way, and then come back." Hopefully, by the time she returned, her senses would no longer be so erratic.

"I need you here," Pet said. "We both know you're the smart one. I need you at the summit."

"You'll be fine," said Jandra. "You stood up to the dragons just now. You... you're a better man than you think you are."

Hex approached them as they spoke. "Pardon my interruption. If you wish to travel, I volunteer as your transportation. It was never my intention to linger here at the castle. I possess a powerful lust to see the world."

Jandra's cheeks tingled at the word "lust." But with Hex flying her, the journey to find Zeeky and the real Bitterwood might only take a few days. Perhaps by then she could trust herself to work with Pet without risking becoming another of his conquests.

"Hex," she said, "It would be an honor. Do you need anything before we go?"

"I arrived with only the scales on my back and so I shall depart. There is nothing I need that the forests and the streams cannot provide."

"Wonderful. I travel light as well," she said, fingering the pouch of silver dust that hung on her belt. If she needed a change of clothes, she would simply weave them from materials at hand. In fact, her skirt seemed a little impractical for dragon-riding. She ran her fingers along the velvety cloth, willing it to transform. The fabric responded almost instantly, reweaving itself into a pair of riding pants.

"Wow," said Pet. "I didn't know you could do that. Change your clothes just by thinking."

"I've been able to transmute matter for a while," she said. "I've just gotten better at it."

"Do you, uh, take off your clothes the same way? Just think about it and, whoosh, they fall off? Because that's just... I mean—" Pet's voice trailed off dreamily.

"Take care, Pet," she said as Hex crouched, giving her access to his broad back.

She glanced toward Pet as she straddled Hex's neck, grasping his mane of long feather-scales. She was out of range of Pet's aroma once Hex rose to his normal height. Pet didn't look as delicious as he had a second before. He looked a little pathetic, actually, small from where she sat on the back of a dragon. Which only made it all the more urgent to her that she not be near him should her senses run wild again.

"Let's go, Hex," she said.

Hex ran forward, spreading his wings. With a flap they were airborne and Jandra clenched her knees, holding on for her life.

JANDRA HAD NEVER ridden a sun-dragon before. When she was younger, she'd often flown with Vendevorex, riding in a harness strapped to his chest, looking out over the world upside-down. But once she'd gone through the growth spurt of puberty, she'd become too heavy for him to carry easily, and slowly she'd come to accept that she'd spend her adulthood earthbound.

Hex carried her across the night sky as if she was weightless. Sun-dragons' enormous wings had always reminded her of sails. Sun-dragons moved through the air the way ships sailed across the water, slowly, taking turns in great arcs. Sky-dragons moved more like fish, darting and flashing in any direction with the speed of thought.

As Jandra watched the moonlit landscape unfolding beneath her, she suddenly found a deep appreciation of the sun-dragon's command over the air. The relative slowness of their flight felt graceful, as if they were drifting down a river of wind, with Hex's wings carefully dipping and tilting in the current. From time to time he would beat his broad wings. His powerful muscles rippled beneath Jandra's legs as they climbed into the sky. She felt as if they must be miles above the earth. Yet, even as she thought this, her brain began to buzz as her helm gathered various bits of data—the angle of the crescent moon above in comparison to the size and shape of Hex's shadow below—and a string of numbers flashed through her mind to inform her they were roughly three hundred yards above the countryside.

The terrain below was gentle hills. It was late fall and most of the trees had shed their leaves. Cottages and barns dotted the hills; rail fences divided the land into large parcels, marking the boundaries of farms. It seemed odd that the Earth should look so peaceful, with Albekizan's castle so near. Most humans had returned home after the battle of the Free City. It mattered little to them who sat upon the throne. They would continue their daily lives of raising families, planting, harvesting, and trading goods.

Vendevorex had told her long ago that humans benefited from the rule of sun-dragons. War had become a thing that dragons waged against other dragons. The armies that dragon kings amassed weren't aimed primarily at the oppression of humans, but at protecting themselves from the threats posed by other dragons. It was true that, under the law, humans owned nothing. They were legally little more than parasites upon the king's property. All the products of their labors could be taken from them on a whim. But, in practice, most humans were allowed to live their lives unmolested. The human arts of farming and tending livestock had never been activities dragons embraced. Humans produced food, the dragons took their portion, and beyond this most people spent their lives catching only the occasional glimpse of dragons. In return, humans lived in a state of relative peace. They weren't allowed to amass armies. The ruling sun-dragons would quickly quash any human militia before it could become a threat. While humans did skirmish with neighboring villages from time to time, most humans spent their lives never having to pick up a weapon to use against a fellow man. For centuries, there had been no human-against-human battle that involved more than a few dozen men. This time in history, Vendevorex had told her, was known as the Pax Draco—the Peace of Dragons.

Was Shandrazel risking this peace with his talk of freedom? Having grown up among dragons, Jandra had spent most of her childhood assuming that the existing world order was essentially fair. Perhaps the world would be better if the dragons continued to rule.

As she thought this, they passed over a high hill and on the far side found what looked to be a city of tents. Smoke from a hundred smoldering campfires scented the air. In addition to the hundreds of small and tattered tents, there were thousands of humans who were slumbering on the bare ground, with not even a blanket to cover them.

"Who are these people?" Hex asked.

Jandra wasn't sure. "I suppose they're refugees," she answered. "People from the Free City who don't know how to find their way home."

"This is why Shandrazel's vision of a new world order is doomed," Hex sighed.

"Why?"

"Humans will care nothing for Shandrazel's proposed reforms after what my father has done," said Hex. "They may even take up arms to avenge my father's misdeeds. And what then? Shandrazel will use the armies he now commands to force the humans to respect his new laws. He'll become as much a tyrant as my father was no matter how good his intentions."

"You're something of a pessimist, I take it."

"On the contrary," he said. "I believe there is every chance a new and better world is only a few years away. Perhaps Shandrazel will lose control of his armies. The various domains that make up the kingdom will revert to local control. No longer ruled by a higher authority, the inhabitants of the land may learn to work together for the good of all. Simple self interest will lead dragons and humans to peace, once the claw of tyranny is lifted."

Jandra now found Hex's world view overly optimistic. Then she remembered the sound of the executioner's axe falling and taking the lives of her friends. She remembered the cries from the courtyard as Albekizan had all the humans in the palace slaughtered. Maybe Hex was right—perhaps all authority in this world did derive from violence.

She grew quiet, lost in thought, as the refugee camp vanished in the distance behind them. Hex said, "Perhaps I should have asked this an hour ago, but where are we going?"

"Oh," said Jandra. "Excellent question. I wish I knew. You were heading west, and I know that's right, at least. Zeeky said her village was called Big Lick. Supposedly, it's in the mountains near Chakthalla's castle."

Hex stiffened at the word "mountains." Jandra had always been mystified that dragons were afraid of the western mountains. Vendevorex had told her that dragons lived in lands beyond, but for some reason dragons avoided journeying to those distant lands.

"I don't think it's far into the mountains," she said, hoping to reassure him.

"It won't matter if it is," Hex said, sounding defiant. "I've never placed much weight in the legends of the cursed mountains, though others do. Dacorn, the most rational dragon I've ever known, told me that it was certain death for a dragon to risk traveling over them. I've faced things in life worse than death; a cursed mountain isn't all that worrisome."

"There's still the matter of finding it. I know we follow the river, but as it heads west more and more tributaries join it and I'm not sure which one Vendevorex followed when he took me there. Perhaps we should turn back. There are atlases at the palace."

As she said this, she saw in her mind's eye the giant pedestal that sat in the main library, and the atlas upon it, containing all the maps of the kingdom. She could still feel the weight of the parchment in her hand as she looked through the tome—a book scaled for sun-dragons had pages nearly as tall as she was.

As she thought about the atlas, it loomed in the air before her, luminous yet convincingly solid. She reached out to the floating book and opened its cover. Her head tingled as the helmet reached into a thousand folds of her brain simultaneously, reconstructing the book from memories.

Stunned by the detail of the maps before her, she realized, with a sudden thrill, that every book she'd ever studied lurked in the hidden corners of her mind. Would the reconfiguration of her brain that Vendevorex had told her about produce total recall? Would every page of every book she'd glimpsed be available with just a thought?

No wonder Vendevorex had always seemed like such a know-it-all.

CHAPTER SIX

JUDGMENT BY SWINE

BANT BITTERWOOD THOUGHT the valley below looked like a giant's patchwork quilt, as squares of tan fields jutted up against blocks of gray trees. In the distance were mountains, the peaks barely visible through blue haze. Zeeky didn't seem interested in the scenery. Zeeky, a nine-year-old girl with golden hair and dirty cheeks, only had eyes for animals. It was she who guided their mount, Killer, a barrel-chested ox-dog that carried two humans and a pig on his back as if they weighed no more than kittens. Zeeky was currently occupied teaching the pig to talk.

"Zeeky," she said.

Poocher, the pig, squealed, "Eee-ee."

Bitterwood hoped the pig would provide Zeeky better conversation than he could. Though he tried to hide it from Zeeky, he was currently wracked with fever. The wounds he'd suffered when the dragon king Albekizan had buried his dagger-length teeth into him had festered. Yellow-brown pus glued his shirt to his torso and soaked through his makeshift bandages.

Bitterwood sucked in a sharp, pained breath as Killer slipped on a slick rock along the stream bed they followed. The ox-dog was as steady a mount as could be hoped for, and Zeeky's praise brought out an exceptional gentleness in him. Still, the terrain was rugged, and the broken things inside Bitterwood cut ever deeper.

Bitterwood found the sharp focus of the pain a welcome distraction. It brought him momentary relief from the torment of his memories. He never intended to survive his final battle with Albekizan. He'd nearly died beneath that river, drawn toward a light where he found his beloved wife, Recanna, dead to him for twenty years.

She'd told him to turn back.

She'd told him he wasn't ready.

For twenty years, Bitterwood had slain dragons, never wavering in his conviction that his cause had been just. Had he been turned away from death to continue that fight? Or had heaven shunned him because the struggle had warped him beyond redemption? Had twenty years with nothing but murder in his heart changed him into a worse monster than the creatures he battled?

"You can end this," Recanna had said.

Bitterwood picked at those words like a scab. End what? End his struggle against the dragons? Or did she mean he wasn't finished with the war, that he still had the power to end it by continuing to fight? Had she been telling him his life's work had been worthwhile? Or had it all been a mission of vanity?

Perhaps it had only been the dream of a drowning man. Could he tell the difference between dreams and reality any longer, after the life he'd led?

"Zeeky," said Zeeky.

"Eee-ee," said Poocher.

The ox-dog paused to drink from a pool of clear water at the stream's edge. Crayfish darted about the rocky pool, above a carpet of corn-yellow leaves. Bant grew more alert as he saw the crayfish. Despite his fever, he felt his appetite stirring.

"Any objection to me eating those?" Bant asked, pointing toward the darting figures.

Zeeky stared intently at the pool as she pondered the question.

"They aren't saying anything," she said, her face relaxing. "I guess it's okay."

Zeeky wouldn't let him eat anything she could talk to. Fortunately, not all animals met this criterion. She didn't seem to have any special rapport with bugs or fish, but late at night he'd caught her gossiping with owls, and she could be downright chatty with Killer and Poocher. Poocher was a few months old, no longer at an age where he could be called a piglet, not yet a full-fledged hog. He was at an awkward stage in a pig's life, too long and hairy to be cute, yet still too skinny to make a man think longingly of bacon. Poocher had a mostly white hide marked with patches of glossy black, and his dark eyes would sometimes fix on Bitterwood with a contemptuous gaze that caused Bitterwood to look away.

Bitterwood knelt next to the pool. Even in his weakened state, the swiftly darting crayfish didn't stand a chance. Long ago, his hands had been bitten off by a dragon, and an angel—or perhaps a devil—had given him new ones. She'd also altered his eyes and arms, leaving him fast enough to empty a quiver in under a minute, with every arrow finding its target. The crayfish may as well have been frozen in place as his agile fingers dashed about the pool, quickly gathering a score of the fat mud-bugs.

"We should stop here for the night," Bitterwood said, looking up at the darkening sky. "I'll start a fire."

"I want to keep moving," Zeeky said. "I think we're close. The air has a familiar smell to it. We're almost home."

Killer looked up from drinking and let out a quick snort.

"Oh, all right, I know you're tired, stop complaining," said Zeeky. "That's two votes to one. What about you, Poocher?"

Poocher lowered his head in a human-like nod and gave a squeal that made Zeeky frown.

"I know you're hungry," she said. "You're always hungry. Oh, all right. We'll make camp here. Go ahead and start the fire, Mister *Bitterwood*."

She said Bitterwood in a mocking tone. Zeeky knew Bitterwood only by legend, a near mythic dragon-slayer, a hero of humanity. Bant looked nothing like anyone's hero. His hair was thinning; he was missing quite a few teeth, and, though he was strong and wiry, he wasn't as tall as a hero should be. His clothes were little more than rags, and twenty years of survival beneath an open sky had left him with a face of wrinkled leather.

It wasn't important to him who she thought he was. Though they journeyed together, in truth each traveled alone. They were refugees, survivors of Albekizan's death camp. Except for the mundane details of travel, they had little to discuss. Zeeky was usually too busy talking to animals to allow bad memories to sweep over her. Bitterwood was nothing but his bad memories. Strip away the ghosts that haunted him, and his skin would collapse like an emptied sack.

Poocher bounded off into the woods to search for mushrooms and edible roots for dinner. Bitterwood pulled a wad of charred cotton wrapped in waxed parchment from his pocket. He set to work striking his fire flints together to make sparks. A moment later a tendril of acrid smoke rose from the cotton. He knew the smell well. It was the exact smell of the blackened remains of one of Adam's diapers. It was an odor that had haunted him for twenty years. He lifted the black cotton to his lips and gently blew, giving birth to a delicate flame. He lowered it to the bed of twigs he'd prepared.

Zeeky had the pig and the dog for companionship and protection. The small useful role Bitterwood served in her world was maker-of-fire. It was enough. It was the one thing he could do that made him feel as if his continued existence served some purpose.

As the flames grew, he arranged the crayfish on a stone facing the fire. Some were still alive, struggling to crawl away. He pressed down on their backs, breaking them, until they could do nothing but lie there and cook.

"How close are we?" Zeeky asked.

"You said it smelled like home," he said. "Your nose is pretty smart. After we follow this stream across the valley, we'll be at what's left of Chakthalla's castle. The town of Winding Rock was near it. You say your village was close?"

"Big Lick," said Zeeky. She sighed. "I miss everyone. Even Papa."

"Still think he'll try to eat the pig?" Bitterwood asked.

"He's learned his lesson," Zeeky said, in a firm, matter-of-fact way that spooked Bitterwood. For a little girl far from home and family, she sometimes sounded as if she were in control of the world.

The crayfish were turning red. Bitterwood snatched one up, snapped it in two, and chewed on the steaming meat in the tail. He sucked down the yellowish gunk inside the head. It tasted good, fatty and bitter. It felt like medicine sliding down his throat. A bucketful of these and a week in bed might cure his fever.

Zeeky wrinkled her nose. "It looks like a bug."

Killer gave a huff and Bitterwood looked up to see the giant dog staring at him. The dog seemed to like him, even if the pig didn't.

"Oh, you think everything smells good," Zeeky said.

Bitterwood tossed Killer the remains of the head and watched him greedily gobble it down, the shell crunching between his teeth. The grateful look in his eyes led Bitterwood to throw him a second crayfish, a whole one this time.

The darkening forest murmured as a breeze rustled through it. He thought for a moment he heard a woman whispering. From the corner of his eye he saw Recanna standing by the water's edge, waving. He turned and saw it was only a low branch of a tree, draped with pale leaves, shuddering in the chill air.

Bitterwood shuddered as well, and drew the tatters of the blanket he wore as a cloak tightly around him.

WINDING ROCK HAD been looted. Only a month ago, the little mountain town had been clean and full of life. Now, the place looked haunted. The doors stood open to the elements. The panes of glass that had filled the windows were gone. Not smashed, Bitterwood noted, but carefully removed. Gazing into a nearby house, Bitterwood couldn't see a scrap of furniture. The type of stuff that had been looted told a story. Dragons wouldn't bother stealing window glass or chairs. This was done by humans—quite possibly Zeeky's people, from Big Lick.

This was the sort of thing that had driven Bitterwood to hold humanity in nearly the same contempt as dragons. The people of Winding Rock had been rounded up in the middle of the night and forcibly marched to the Free City. The dragons had acted swiftly, gathering only those they found in a single night. Certainly these mountains were full of people the dragons had missed. Bitterwood had spotted other villages in the valley that were unmolested by the king's attempted genocide. The neighbors of the town of Winding Rock could have banded together and attempted to rescue their captive brethren. Instead, they'd stayed hidden until the dragons were gone, then stolen everything that wasn't nailed down. Passing a house from which the slate roof tiles were missing, Bitterwood realized that actually being nailed down hadn't provided any protection from theft either.

"This place is spooky," Zeeky said.

"It's just empty," said Bitterwood. A spark of anger ignited as he realized that this village was the vision Albekizan—the dragon king—had possessed for all of humanity. The spark of anger was instantly quenched by a wave of guilt. Albekizan's genocide order had come in response to Bitterwood's actions. He had triggered this violence by killing Bodiel, the king's most-loved son. His hands weren't clean in the death of this place.

They passed through the town, finding a wellworn trail that followed a creek higher into the mountains. The path was nothing but rocks and roots. Killer was a powerful mount, but even he slowed on the steep incline. The creek splashed beside the path in a series of waterfalls.

"We're close!" Zeeky said, fidgeting in her seat.

"Hallelujah," Bitterwood said. He felt somewhat better today, after the meal of crayfish and a solid night of sleep. Last night he'd slept free of dreams. He'd simply succumbed to exhaustion and illness and slumbered from dusk to dawn. His fever had broken. He was still tender, but he felt some of his old strength returning.

Poocher sniffed the air, then grunted.

"Smoke?" said Zeeky.

Bitterwood took a sniff. The pig was right. There was a slight hint of smoke in the air, burning wood, with an undertone of sulfur.

"They burn coal in these parts?" asked Bitterwood.

"Yes," Zeeky said. "The menfolk dig it up and trade it down in Winding Rock."

Poocher grunted again.

"You're right," said Zeeky. "It does stink."

They continued up the mountain path. The rocks were rising at steeper angles now, the forest growing denser and darker. The cliffs high above were riddled with shadowy caves.

They'd come several miles from Winding Rock when Bitterwood heard a scream. Somewhere in the distance ahead, a woman—or perhaps a child—cried out in pain.

"Stop here," said Bitterwood.

"No!" Zeeky said. "We're almost there! It's just around the bend!"

"Let me go ahead to check things out."

"Run, Killer!" Zeeky yelled.

Killer lunged forward. Bitterwood grabbed fistfuls of bristly dog hair to keep from toppling as Killer swerved around a steep curve on the trail.

Zeeky let out a gasp.

Ahead, the village of Big Lick was nothing but a mound of smoking ruins. Killer stopped in response to Zeeky's gasp, suddenly as paralyzed with shock as she was.

Bitterwood vaulted from the ox-dog and said, "Wait here," before moving further up the path. The village had been burned several hours ago, judging from the remains. What had once been homes were now just heaps of charcoal, sending up a fog of smoke. The coal dust that had clung to the village gave the charred remains a sickly egg-fart stench.

Bitterwood searched the ground for tracks as he walked closer to the village. If an army of dragons had done this, they'd not traveled up this path. Of course, it could be sun-dragons or sky-dragons behind it. They could have flown in. However, for some reason he'd never understood, the winged dragons normally didn't journey into these mountains.

He crept forward carefully, crouched low, his eyes seeking out natural areas of cover he could dive for in case of aerial attack. Unarmed, he searched the ground for a good heavy rock. Fortunately, Big Lick had no shortage of stones. As he picked up a smooth, fist-sized rock, he noticed a scrape in the ground beside it. A claw mark... a dragon? It was too small for a sun-dragon, and whatever had left the mark had been heavier than a sky-dragon. Quickly, his eyes picked out a dozen other marks, then a hundred more, in all directions, with human footprints mixed among them. Curiously, he spotted no blood. Sniffing the air, he found no trace of the sweet hammy smell of burnt human flesh. The dragons—if that's what had attacked—must have taken the villagers as captives.

It was growing dark and cold as he stepped into a square of ash and blackened logs that had once been a cabin. A small tower of stone jutted up from the center, the remains of a fireplace. The smoke danced like ghosts as the wind pushed tiny ash-devils across the stone hearth. He spotted a fallen fireplace poker, a length of black iron with a forked end and a coil of wire for a handle. It was hot enough to blister a normal man when he lifted it, but his hands were tough as leather gloves. The poker had a pleasant heft. He'd killed dragons with lesser weapons than this.

The hair on the back of his neck rose. Something was running in the woods on the other side of the chimney, coming fast. It sounded like human footsteps. Bitterwood pressed himself against the chimney. Seconds later a boy rushed past, breathing hard, tears leaving trails down his soot-darkened cheeks. The boy was older than Zeeky, rail thin, with bright blond hair of a nearly identical hue. The boy caught sight of Bitterwood from the corner of his eye. As he turned his head he tripped, skidding amid the ash, sending up a shower of dull red sparks as he fell. Bitterwood gripped the poker tightly with his left hand, and readied the fist-sized stone in his right hand to throw.

As the boy struggled to stand, Bitterwood saw blood on his burlap shirt. The boy looked back over his shoulder, past Bitterwood and the chimney toward the woods beyond, his eyes wide with terror.

From the crunching of leaves, it sounded as if a small army was approaching.

Every muscle in Bitterwood's body coiled, ready to spring. The pain in his chest vanished as a reptilian odor was carried toward him—a dragon! But what kind?

A copper-hued, horse-sized head of a dragon darted past the edge of the chimney, low to the ground. The creature's long neck was quickly followed by a pair of shoulders supporting thick, strong legs that ended in three-clawed talons. This was the creature that had made the tracks. Another yard of the beast passed and another set of shoulders and a second set of legs appeared. The boy had gotten to his feet again, and was darting away like a rabbit. The dragon steered toward him, as a third set of legs scrambled past the chimney. Bitterwood had never seen anything like this creature.

Time slowed, as it always did in the heat of battle. Though the creature charged as quickly as a galloping horse, it moved at a crawl in Bant's eyes. He could see every individual scale of the creature as it passed. He watched its muscles as they moved in precise choreography beneath a gleaming metallic hide. A fourth set of limbs came around the edge of the chimney, then a fifth, but the fifth set wasn't part of the creature's body. They were human feet, resting in stirrups.

The human in the saddle was revealed as the creature advanced. He was a short man, with skin pale as milk, dressed in a shimmering white tunic. A large silver visor hid his eyes. He somehow guided his reptilian mount without the benefit of reins, leaving his hands free to aim a large crossbow at the boy. He too caught sight of Bitterwood and cocked his head, his lips parting as if he were about to speak.

Bitterwood wasn't interested in what he might say. The springs in his legs uncoiled. He swung the iron poker in an upward arc, catching the rider underneath his chin. The rider was lifted from his saddle by the blow.

As the white-clad man fell through the air, the serpent's back curved, instantly aware of the rider's missing weight. Bitterwood spun as the beast's head whipped around, its jaws opening to reveal a pale pink mouth-roof. Twin rows of teeth hurtled toward him, the jaws spread wide enough to swallow his head.

Bitterwood raised the stone he carried, a good, hard chunk of stream-polished granite. As the dragon's mouth reached him and the jaws began to snap, he placed the stone precisely at the back of the creature's jaw. When the beast chomped down, its spiky rear teeth snapped. Bitterwood ducked to allow the dragon's momentum carry it over him. The dragon let out a grunt as it hit the chimney with a wet smack. Its body twitched and coiled as Bitterwood jumped free.

Long years of fighting dragons had left Bitterwood with a reliable internal map of where a dragon's claws, teeth, and tail would be in close combat. Alas, he still hadn't figured out how many limbs this weird long-wyrm had. As he jumped away something sharp snared his ankle. His leap to freedom aborted in a painful crash. A second set of claws tore into his calves, then a third, and a fourth. Bitterwood twisted around to see the long-wyrm shake its bloodied head, then turn its dark eyes to face him.

Bitterwood kicked, loosening two of the claws. The beast jerked, dragging Bitterwood closer as claw after claw sank into his legs. By now the entire creature could be seen. It was fully fifty feet long from snout to tail, with fourteen pairs of claws. The long-wyrm's mouth dripped blood, and the lower jaw was set at a funny angle, perhaps broken.

Behind the dragon, the rider rose to his knees, looking dazed. His visor had been knocked off, revealing large, pink eyes amid the ghostly flesh of his face. He raised a hand as if to shield his eyes from the light, despite the deepening shadows. The man looked around, and reached for his visor. Before he could grab it, a black and white form flashed into view and snatched it up in its jaws, then dashed away. *Poocher?*

The long-wyrm suddenly stopped pulling Bitterwood closer. Its eyes were set on something behind the fallen hunter. The creature braced itself. The ash all around Bitterwood swirled in a rush of wind. A large shadow flew over his head. Killer, the ox-dog, let out a thunderous bark in mid air, then sank his massive jaws into the lizard's copper throat. The long-wyrm released Bitterwood, coiling up to rake and tear at the giant dog. Killer whipped the wyrm's head back and forth, its broken jaw flopping. The beast let out a series of hissing yelps as Killer pinned it to the ground and clamped his jaws even tighter.

Even though the serpent was losing, it continued tearing out bloody chunks of fur as it curled around the dog in a whirlwind of claws. Bitterwood scrambled back to his feet, taking the poker in both hands, and lunged for the long-wyrm, ignoring the slashing pain from his damaged legs. He planted the forked edge of the iron poker in the center of the beast's left eye and threw his full weight onto the handle. The thin layer of bone behind the eye snapped as he drove the rod into the creature's brain. The dragon fell limp, its claws stilled at last.

"Jeremiah!" Zeeky shouted.

Bitterwood looked down the path, to see the boy running toward Zeeky.

"Ezekia!" the boy shouted. Zeeky jumped into his arms as they reached each other. The boy's legs collapsed at the weight, and they both wound up on the ground.

Bitterwood yanked the poker from the dead reptile's eye. The white-skinned rider was now on his feet, his back toward Bitterwood. The rider, hearing Bitterwood's approach, turned. He'd recovered his crossbow. He raised the weapon and pulled the trigger.

Bitterwood's eyes were still swift enough to trace the razor-honed tip as it sliced through the air toward him. His arms felt like lead weights as he tried to lift the poker to knock the bolt from its path.

To the amazement of both the rider and himself, the poker reached the same point in space as the bolt less than a yard from Bitterwood's chest. The bolt deflected upward, leaving a trail of sparks, as it whizzed past Bitterwood's left ear.

The rider looked stunned. Bitterwood had witnessed the same look countless time in the eyes of dragons. It was a look that gave him a certain amount of pleasure, but experience had taught him it was not a pleasure that should be prolonged. He willed his torn legs to leap the few yards that separated him from the man, swinging the iron rod in a vicious arc. He slammed it against the side of the man's neck with such force the poker bent. The man fell to his back, twitching, his eyes rolling up in their sockets.

Bitterwood sucked down air in great gasps, his legs trembling. The world slowed back to normal speed. He studied the fallen rider. Though blood was seeping from his ears, the man still breathed. Perhaps he would live. Perhaps he would have answers as to what had happened here.

On the other hand, the man had been riding a dragon, or something very much like a dragon.

Bitterwood thought of women and children being dragged from their homes by reptilian claws, imagined the destruction of Big Lick with great clarity. He could hear the screams of the villagers, just as for twenty years he'd heard the screams of his own family.

There was only one way to silence those voices.

Glancing over his shoulder he saw Killer limping back to Zeeky and the boy, who were sitting on the ground, talking. No one was looking toward him.

Bitterwood fell to his knees. His arms were losing strength; his legs were bleeding in copious streams. He wanted to fall over, to collapse forever into sleep.

There could be no rest while the voices howled.

Bitterwood raised the poker above his head and swung it, planting the full weight into the man's face. A bubble of blood rose from the man's lips.

Bitterwood felt too weak to move as he stared at the damaged face. A lightness took hold of him, like the fevers that had given his world such a dreamlike quality. The unconscious man's features suddenly struck him as familiar—eyes, ears, nose, mouth—a universal visage, belonging to almost any man. Bitterwood could even see himself in the shared structures, and as the world slowly began to tilt he could no longer tell if it was the rider who lay upon the ground, or himself.

Bitterwood raised the poker and swung at the face that might be his own, then swung again, and again, until what he was hitting no longer looked like a face.

The screams now silent, Bitterwood toppled into the ash.

He closed his eyes, then opened them to discover Poocher by his head. The pig was wearing the rider's visor, standing on two legs.

"Evil man," Poocher said, in a smooth and high-cultured tone. He pointed a cleft hoof at Bitterwood in a gesture of condemnation. "All your works amount to dust. All that remains of you will scatter with the winds."

Bitterwood found himself concurring with the judgment of the pig. He welcomed this fate. It seemed a very light thing, to be carried off by air, unremembered, unmourned.

"Take care of Zeeky," he whispered before the world spun in a whirl of white embers, then turned black.

CHAPTER SEVEN

MAGICAL GIFTS

A MISTY RAIN veiled the mountains, hiding
Zeeky's ruined village. Zeeky gazed out from
the shelter of one of the caves overlooking Big
Lick. It had taken hours for her and Jeremiah to
drag Bitterwood to the shelter. Killer was too
wounded to carry anyone, though he could limp
along. Poocher sat beside her, watching her intently
as she used Bitterwood's kit to start a fire. The logs
they'd dragged up to the cave were damp. The
flames from the kindling licked the bark, causing
the logs to sizzle and put out fumes that were more
steam than smoke.

She checked Bitterwood's bandages one last time.
Jeremiah had found scraps of unburned blankets in
the rubble and they'd used these to bind his
wounds, but she was frightened by how much
blood he'd lost. He was burning hot, and his
breathing was shallow and raspy. She wished she
knew something more to do.

Finally, with the fire putting out at least a little heat and everyone in safe from the drizzle, she asked, "What happened, Jeremiah?"

"For a couple of years, the menfolk have been whispering about the new kind of demon they were seeing in the mines," said Jeremiah. "Big copper-colored serpents with a hundred legs. But the demons were afraid of light; the men kept mining, they just needed more lanterns than before."

"I know that. I heard Papa talking to Uncle Silas about the demons," said Zeeky. "But why'd they attack?"

"I don't know," said Jeremiah. "They just showed up in the middle of the night and dragged everyone out of bed. I tried to fight but the demons were too strong. The demon just got hold of me. There were men with them who tied me up. They carried everyone up to Dead Skunk Hole. I was slung over the back of one of the demons, but there was some slack in the ropes holding me. I wiggled loose and ran like a jackrabbit. Didn't look back to see if I was followed. I hunkered down in some bushes for better than a day. Then I took off running for Big Lick to see if anyone was left. I guess one of the demons also came back to look. I thought sure I was a goner when I heard it coming up behind me."

"You think Mama and Papa are still alive?"

"I reckon," said Jeremiah. "I didn't see nobody get killed. Wonder what them demons want us for?"

"I'll just have to go up to Dead Skunk Hole and find out," Zeeky said.

"Zeeky, you saw that demon. It ripped up your friend and hurt this big dog something fierce. You'll get eaten alive."

"No I won't," said Zeeky. "The serpents aren't demons. They're animals. I could make out some of what it was saying while it was fighting. I bet I could talk to one. Animals won't eat me if I tell 'em not to."

"Yeah," said Jeremiah. "You did talk that ol' bear out of eatin' Granny."

"Told him he'd only get indigestion," said Zeeky.

"But these long-wyrms ain't natural," said Jeremiah.

"It ain't natural that I can talk to animals," said Zeeky. "I'm not scared of things just 'cause they ain't natural. I'll just go into the mine and look around some. I'll take Poocher. You stay here with Mr. Bitterwood and Killer. Keep the fire going. Fetch them some water from the creek when they wake up."

"All right," said Jeremiah. "I know I ain't going to talk you out of it. Just promise you'll be careful."

Zeeky nodded but didn't actually say the words, so it didn't count.

IT WAS DAYLIGHT when Zeeky lit out for Dead Skunk Hole. She soon arrived at the sturdy wooden ramp that led up to the entrance. Fog hid everything more than thirty feet away. She held the rail for balance on the slippery wood, as Poocher crept along beside her, looking wary.

"Guess this is it," she said to Poocher as they reached the entrance of the mine. The gaping hole in the mountainside looked like a giant mouth looming in the mist. It had a faint wet skunk atmosphere drifting out of it. She gave Poocher a scratch under his bristly chin as she knelt to gaze into his dark eyes. "Not too late to turn back if you want. I'll understand."

Poocher snorted and twitched his snout, indicating he wouldn't abandon her.

She stepped into the mine and looked around. The entrance was huge, big enough for an entire army of dragons to take shelter. All around were carts and picks and lanterns, equipment the miners used in their daily chores. The mines had been worked for centuries. Her Papa used to say that the mountain was almost hollow now. Yet, each time a vein of coal would play out, a new vein would be discovered, a little deeper down, a little further in. The men complained it took a full day to walk to the current vein they worked. The miners labored in five-day shifts. Zeeky couldn't imagine spending so long away from the sun. No wonder all the men always looked so tired and haunted.

Zeeky lit the oil lamp closest at hand. It wasn't as heavy as it looked. Long, jagged shadows stretched out against walls blackened by centuries of lantern smoke. She stepped further into the mine, away from the pale, fog-filtered daylight. Poocher stayed close by her heel. She walked several hundred yards down the main shaft when she reached her first obstacle. The shaft split into five different tunnels. A wooden elevator, designed to be powered by a team of mules, sat in a shaft that hinted at even more tunnels beneath. She wished the mules weren't gone. She could have asked for help.

"Any ideas, Poocher?"

Poocher roamed over the floor, sniffing. He spent several minutes at the entrance of each tunnel before letting out a grunt.

"Good job," she said.

Poocher snorted a thank you and trotted ahead. She followed, her eyes straining at the shadows. The white patches of Poocher's hide grew increasingly gray. Was Poocher getting dirtier, or was the lantern getting dimmer? She tried to adjust the wick. The light brightened briefly, but as she fiddled with the lantern she could hear a sloshing of what could only be a few teaspoons of oil. She suddenly realized why the lantern had felt so light. It was her first time using a lantern. She'd watched her father use them, and was pretty sure she knew how to refill it. Her father said there were oil barrels all through the mine. Had she passed one yet? Had there been one back near the elevator?

She turned around.

The lantern flickered, the glass darkening with sooty smoke. She started to run.

Everything went black.

BROWN GUNK COVERED the marble floor of the grand hall of Chakthalla's castle. Here and there in the muck, bright shards of the broken stained-glass windows that had once lined the hall glinted in the firelight. This room was vivid in Jandra's nightmares—it was the room where her throat had been slit. Some of the nastiness on the floor might be her own decayed blood, mixed with rain and rotting leaves that had blown into the abandoned room. Here, she'd watched the sun-dragon Zanzeroth gut Vendevorex and leave him for dead. This was the room where she'd learned the truth behind the biggest secret of her life—that it had been Vendevorex who'd killed her parents, for no other reason than to prove himself to Albekizan.

Despite her terrible memories of the place, she'd known the castle held rooms large enough to shelter Hex. They'd been only a few miles away when the weather became too dangerous to continue their journey by air. Once the fogs rolled in, flight was a foolish risk.

Hex was curled up near the fireplace at the rear of the room, slumbering. His belly gurgled as it digested the young buck he'd swooped down upon and killed earlier. He'd eaten most of the buck raw, hooves and all, but had saved Jandra some meat from a haunch. She'd roasted it over the fire and had her fill. Jandra would have joined Hex in sleep, but, oddly, despite her full belly and the fact she'd barely slept in days, she wasn't even mildly tired. Vendevorex had seldom slept. He'd needed no more than a few hours each week to remain alert. Was this another side effect of the helmet?

Jandra passed the time by reweaving and altering her clothes, doodling with the physical qualities of the fibers. She'd altered the color of the fabric, changing it from black to a red shade resembling Hex's hide. She'd adjusted the fit of her loose mourning clothes until they clung to her like a second skin, though not too immodestly. From just beneath her chin down to her toes, there was no hint of exposed flesh save for her fingers and palms—even the backs of her hands were hidden by a red, feathery, scale-patterned lace she'd created. Her breasts were modestly concealed by a leather vest she'd crafted by replicating the molecules of leather in her shoes. She was sufficiently occupied with her newfound talent as a mental seamstress that the ghosts of the room didn't haunt her.

Unfortunately, the same wasn't true of Hex. His sleep grew fitful. His jaws clenched with rapid snaps, as if he was biting at some unseen foe in his dreams. His claws flexed and twitched. Suddenly, he jerked his head up, his eyes open wide, as he shouted, "No!"

Jandra reached out and placed a hand upon his hind-talon.

"It's okay, Hex. Just a bad dream."

Hex stared at her, confusion in his eyes. He shuddered, and released a long breath. "I was dreaming of the contest of succession," he said.

"Oh," said Jandra. The contest of succession had pitted two of Albekizan's sons against one another in a ritual hunt of human slaves. The victor had had a chance to challenge Albekizan in combat for the throne. The loser had been castrated, and sent into a life of servitude to the biologians. Jandra could see how such an event could lead to unpleasant dreams, even thirty years later.

Hex rose to his hind-talons, stretching his wings, shaking off the effects of sleep.

"Everyone expected me to win," said Hex. "But the slave I hunted drowned while swimming the river. It took three days for his body to be discovered. The human my brother hunted broke his leg falling from a tree within sight of the palace. His howls of anguish made him easy to find. Dacorn tried to console me with talk of destiny. He said that fate required someone else to wear the crown."

"Perhaps there's truth to it," said Jandra. "No one expected Shandrazel to become king. And now, he may be the king that brings an end to kings."

"Destiny played no part in this," Hex said. Now that his limbs were awake once more, he crouched down near the fire, his legs beneath him, his wings folded against his body. In this posture, with his long serpentine neck, he resembled a giant, scaly, blood-red swan. "Life is essentially random. Shandrazel is king by chance alone. Bitterwood killed Bodiel, then my father. No guiding power put him on the throne."

"These things aren't random," said Jandra. "Bitterwood wanted revenge against your father because your father took his family. Things happen for reasons. Our lives are entangled with the lives of those around us."

"Just because our lives are tied together doesn't make us puppets. We're free to cut our strings."

Jandra thought this was a nice image. She said, "There's a poet inside you."

"Nonsense," said Hex. "Poets seldom have any meat on them. I'd have to be starving to eat one."

Jandra smiled. "I don't think I've ever heard a sun-dragon make a joke before. Most always seem so serious."

"Why do you assume I'm not serious?" Hex said. Then, he winked at her. "I decided long ago that life's absurd. If you don't develop a sense of humor, it will drive you mad. Especially in this part of the world."

"What's special about this part of the world?"

"Why, the noise, of course."

"Noise?" said Jandra.

"The song of the mountains," said Hex. "Though we are some miles distant, I can already hear whispers of the infernal melody. They may have caused my unpleasant dreams."

"I don't hear a thing," said Jandra.

"Humans have always been deaf to the noise. It's a low-pitched dirge that drives some dragons to insanity. Fortunately, it's still faint. If the windows of this room were intact, I doubt I would hear it at all."

"Hmm," Jandra said. "I want to try something. Can I touch your ear?"

"If you wish," said Hex, snaking his head closer to her. The ears of sun-dragons were saucer-sized disks just behind the jaws. The sheer size of the ear meant they could hear certain sounds that eluded humans. She gently traced the edges of the smooth disk. With the increased sensitivity of her fingertips, she could feel a faint vibration. Hex wasn't imagining things. The noise was real, and coming from the direction of the fog-draped mountains. What caused it?

"I might be able to help you," she said. "Vendevorex taught me that sounds travel through air like waves across water. You can neutralize sounds with a counterwave, just as you can disrupt ripples from a rock thrown into a pond by throwing in a second rock."

She dipped her fingers into the pouch that hung from her belt, grabbing a fist full of the silver dust. These tiny machines were the key to her control over matter. Right now, however, she needed a bigger machine. The silver in her hand changed from dust to long metallic threads. The shimmering strings coiled into the shape of a concave disk the size of her palm. It pulsed slowly, like a heartbeat. The remaining threads braided through the air, forming a long silver chain that draped down to the floor. A moment later she was done. The firelight danced upon a silver amulet. The necklace that held it was no thicker than a human hair.

"Put this on," she said. "Let's see if it works."

"What is it?" Hex asked, extending his foretalon.

"It's an amulet that emits a frequency that neutralizes the sound you're hearing. Most of the things I make with the dust only exist a second or two, and draw power from ambient heat. This should be a stable construct, but it will need to be warmed by your body to keep working."

Hex slipped the chain on. The amulet rested against his breastbone, just beneath his throat. He cocked his head, tilting his ear toward the broken windows above.

"I don't hear the mountains anymore," he said. "Let's hope your magic dust doesn't run out."

"It won't," said Jandra. "It's self-replicating and self-assembling. I drop raw materials in the pouch from time to time—iron nails, sand, the occasional bit of gold. I charge them with sunlight, and the machines draw everything else they need to function out of the air. With a little care, it will last forever."

"With so much power, why are you a servant of Shandrazel?" Hex asked.

"I didn't think I was," said Jandra.

"Since Vendevorex served my father, I assumed you would serve my brother," Hex said.

"When I was younger, I dreamed I would grow up and be Bodiel's personal wizard. He was so clever and elegant; I would gladly have devoted my life to him. I like Shandrazel. I think he means to make life better for humans. Still, it's difficult to overlook the fact that most dragons accepted Albekizan's dreams of genocide. It would be difficult to swear my loyalty to a dragon, even one as visionary as Shandrazel."

"So you'll serve humans instead? Perhaps this young Bitterwood should he become the human king?"

"I most especially won't be serving young Bitterwood," Jandra said. "I don't know what I'm going to do with my life. I haven't had much time to consider the matter. It wasn't so long ago that Vendevorex made all my decisions for me. I studied what he told me to study, and we traveled where he decided to travel. It's still sinking in that I'm the only one in charge of my life now."

"We sun-dragons believe that no son is truly grown until his father is dead. I, too, lived my life by my father's choices rather that my own."

"Then you know how I feel. What are you going to do with your life?" she asked.

Hex fixed his eyes on the fireplace that warmed them. He studied the dancing flame with a long and thoughtful gaze before answering. "Somehow, I would like to change the world."

Jandra thought this sounded like a noble, if broad, goal.

"Hopefully for the better," Hex continued, "but I'll take what I can get."

ZEEKY PLACED ONE hand on Poocher's shoulder, holding her other hand in front of her as they crept toward the entrance, guided by Poocher's infallible sense of smell. Even blind, he knew where they had walked. When they got back to the entrance, she would grab every lantern she could carry, and this time she'd make sure they were full. She'd even let Poocher carry one.

The mine was full of odd noises. Water trickling down some unseen stream. A distant moaning, like wind passing through a tunnel. The echoes of Poocher's hooves as he shuffled along. Her own stomach grumbling.

Then, ahead of her, the sound of something she couldn't identify, a scraping, scratching, clicking noise. She stopped. It sounded like claws upon the stone, drawing closer. Poocher tensed, suddenly frightened.

"Is someone there?" she asked.

The scraping noise stopped. Now she could hear the deep, slow breathing of the beast ahead of her.

"H-hello?" she asked.

"Hello," said a voice. It sounded like a man, but not someone from her village. The accent was one she'd never heard before.

"Who are you?" she asked.

"My name is Adam," the man answered. "You must be Zeeky."

"How do you know my name?"

"The goddess planted you," Adam answered. "I've come to harvest you."

Zeeky was confused by the man's response, but her focus shifted to the beast that accompanied the man. It was drawing closer. Its hot breath washed over her like humid wind, carrying the odor of dead things. Then, the wind shifted direction as the creature took a long sniff. The beast was only inches from her. Something damp gently flickered across her cheeks. She scrunched up her face, recognizing the wet thing as the creature's tongue exploring her features, tasting her. She reached out and stroked the beast's nose. It was hard and smooth and cool, covered with individual scales the size of her palm—it felt like the same sort of dragon that Bitterwood had slain. The beast flicked its forked tongue across her fingers. She could tell the creature meant her no harm—it was merely curious. From the location of the man's voice, she assumed he was riding it, which meant it was tame.

"Pleased to meet you," she said, addressing the dragon. "I'm glad you found me. Can you see in the dark?"

"The long-wyrms can see shades of heat with an organ in their snout," Adam said. "It helps them maneuver in absolute darkness."

"How can you see?" Zeeky asked Adam.

"Let me show you." There was a crunch of coal dust as he hopped from his saddle. He walked toward her, drawing very close. He smelled a lot better than the long-wyrm. He put something cold and metallic in her hand. It was a circle of metal, with a gap at one end. It felt like the visor poocher had taken from the rider Bitterwood had killed. She still had the object in her bag.

"Put that on," he said.

She slipped the visor over her eyes. Suddenly, she could see clearly. Adam crouched before her. Unlike the first rider, Adam was handsome, with a mane of chestnut hair and boyish features. He stood up, smiling. "Better than stumbling around in the dark, isn't it?"

"We were doing okay," Zeeky said. "Poocher wasn't lost."

"Oh?" Adam asked, sounding skeptical. "I didn't know pigs could see in pitch black."

"He can see with his nose almost better than with his eyes," Zeeky said, kneeling next to Poocher. Poocher turned his snout toward her as she opened the bag over her shoulder and pulled out the visor. He quietly advanced into her hands as she slipped the visor onto him. Poocher's head was bigger than hers. In a few months, he'd be too big for the visor. As it was, he gave an approving grunt.

"Yes," she said. "It is better isn't it?"

"So it's true," said Adam. "You understand the pig?"

"Of course," said Zeeky. "Mama says I was born able to talk to animals. I could talk with Mulie, our old hound-dog, before I could talk to Mama."

Zeeky took a closer look at the long-wyrm. She gave it a scratch near the back of its jaw. It tilted its head to accept her touch. Its claws flexed in the packed coal dust.

"Yes, I know you like that," she said.

"You can understand Trisky too?"

"That's his name? Trisky?"

"Her name. Her full name is Triskaidekaphobia."

"That's a funny name."

"It means 'fear of the number thirteen.' It's appropriate because she was the thirteenth and final egg to hatch, and, unlike her siblings, she only had thirteen pairs of legs instead of fourteen. She was born when I was only seven; it was lonely for me growing up underground because I had no parents, and I felt sorry that Trisky had no parents. I asked the goddess if I could care for her and she said I could. I fed her cave crickets when she was little—she was no bigger than a garden snake. Now, she's the strongest and fastest of the long-wyrms."

"Granny told me there was no goddess," said Zeeky. "She said that the goddess was really the devil, and the only things that lived underground were demons. But I knew that wasn't true, because I've talked to bats, and they aren't demons."

"Do you know why you can talk to animals, Zeeky?" Adam asked.

"Nope," she said. "I just can."

"I know why," said Adam. "The goddess is always trying new things in the world. She gave the long-wyrms life out of clay."

"I thought you said they came out of eggs?"

"But she sculpted the eggs out of clay. They weren't laid by a mother. And, sadly, Trisky and her siblings never laid any eggs themselves. When they die, they'll all be gone. The goddess said it's just part of life; most kinds of animals that have ever lived died out long before you and I were born."

"That's sad," said Zeeky.

"The goddess says it isn't sad. She says the world must constantly change; nothing lives forever, save for her. And, for all the things that die, she makes new things. Some thrive, some don't."

"If Trisky and her kind are so rare, why do you ride them? Why do you attack people? It will only make them get hurt."

"Trisky likes to be ridden. She enjoys having a purpose in life, as long as that purpose is to serve the goddess."

Trisky let out a bubbling gurgle that showed that she agreed with Adam's words.

"See?" said Adam.

"You can understand her?" Zeeky asked.

"Yes, but I need the visor. It contains all the knowledge of the subtle sounds and gestures that allow me to talk with her. Though, 'talking' isn't exactly the right word."

"No," said Zeeky. "It's like talking, but it's more than talking. Animals speak with their whole bodies. They even speak with smells."

"Right," said Adam. "I need the visor in order to talk to long-wyrms, and that's the only animal I talk to. But you can talk to most vertebrates, and I know why."

"Why?"

"You were born with a catalogue of animal signals already memorized. You instinctively know the right tones and postures to convey your thoughts to animals, and you can read all the signals they give off and understand their intentions. The goddess made you this way. She reached into your mother's womb and shaped your brain so that you would be gifted with a thousand times more knowledge than my visor holds."

"Oh," said Zeeky. This news worried her. Sometimes, the other kids in Big Lick would whisper behind her back that she was a witch child. Had the devil touched her while she was still in her mother's belly? She shook her head. She wasn't a witch child. She was a good girl. Maybe the goddess wasn't the devil. But then—

"What happened to my village, Adam?" Zeeky asked. "Did you help destroy it?"

"We didn't destroy it," said Adam. He smiled, but Zeeky could tell this wasn't a real smile. "We simply returned it to nature. In a year or two, no one will know it was ever there."

"That was my home!" Zeeky said, in her sternest voice, placing her hands upon her hips. Poocher drew close to her, his head tilted toward Adam, his head lowered, as if prepared to attack with tusks he hadn't yet grown. "Where is everybody? What did you do with Mama and Papa? Tell me!"

Adam shook his head. "I can't tell you. However, I'm supposed to bring you to Gabriel. You can ask him."

"Why can't you tell me?"

"I'm sorry. I don't have permission. And, truly, I don't know what the goddess plans for them. She's been preparing the people of Big Lick for many generations, I'm told. She's given all its people magical gifts. Gabriel said that the goddess planted her seeds in Big Lick, and decided now was the right time to harvest them. Be assured that if the goddess wants your family brought to her, it must be for some greater purpose."

Zeeky frowned. Judging from his body language, Adam was telling the truth. He didn't know what was in store for her family. She didn't see any choice but to go with him to Gabriel, whoever he was.

"Looks like I'll get to ride you, Trisky," she said, stroking the beast's copper-scaled neck.

Trisky gurgled her approval.

CHAPTER EIGHT

BURKE'S TAVERN

Every town needs an old man whose only purpose is to sit near the main road and talk to strangers as they pass. Dealon served that role at Burke's Tavern, a small village on the Forge Road, ninety miles from Albekizan's palace and equally as far from Dragon Forge. Dealon had filled the role of unofficial greeter for over forty years, since his wife had died in labor. He'd been too lonely simply sitting alone in the ramshackle cabin he'd built for her. The place looked abandoned after all these years, with weeds all about and moss growing on the wooden shingles. Dealon only returned to the cabin late in the evening to sleep, sharing his bed with a one-eyed cat named Gamble. The rest of his time was spent on the porch at the local tavern, or had been since the tavern was built.

The curious thing about the village of Burke's Tavern was that it had possessed the name for centuries, yet, in Dealon's youth, there was no tavern, nor any memory of anyone named Burke. In the first decade after his wife's death, Dealon had spent his days leaning against a fence near the Forge Road. The traffic of the road often resembled a parade. Great-lizards as green as unripe apples ridden by darker-hued earth-dragons would traverse the dusty, packed earth, guarding caravans of wagons towed by monstrous ox-dogs.

Yet, it had not been dragons that had proved to be the village's most important visitor. Roughly twenty years ago, Dealon had been looking toward Dragon Forge, watching the sun set. Under this crimson sky, a lone man had walked toward the village. As he grew closer, Dealon discovered the man wasn't truly alone; an infant was cradled in his arms.

The man was a curious sight. His skin was darker than anyone Dealon had met before, a deep, ruddy hue, like a sunburn beneath a suntan. His long, jet-black hair was pulled into a braid, secured by bands of leather. His buckskin clothes were worn and dirty, but the blanket he carried the infant in was white as a daisy petal. He wore two disks of curved glass over his eyes, held in place by a golden frame that sat upon his hooked nose. Dealon had heard of spectacles, but he'd never seen a pair before. The spectacles were such an oddity, Dealon almost didn't notice the man's second prominent feature—three parallel scars, running from beneath his right eye down to his chin, barely missing the edge of his lips. The spacing of the scars hinted they'd been inflicted by an earth-dragon.

The man was aware of Dealon watching him, and as he drew close, he said, "Greetings. I've walked many miles today. Could you direct me to the nearest tavern?"

"Ah," Dealon had said. "You've been confused by the name."

"The name?"

"Burke's Tavern. Our town. There's been no tavern here in my lifetime."

"I see," said the man, thoughtfully gazing around the motley collection of shacks that composed the village. "The name is sort of wasted, isn't it?"

Dealon nodded. "I suppose. What's your name, stranger?"

The traveler had smiled, his eyes twinkling behind his spectacles, as he said, "Call me Burke."

In the years since Burke had built his tavern, the town had thrived. Burke was famed not only for his hospitality, but also for his cleverness. He was an inventor, and people would travel far to witness such marvels as the guitar under glass that played without the touch of fingers, and the tall clock from which a copper frog would hop and croak the time. This fall, Burke had installed the chess-monkey on the porch, which had grown to be the bane of Dealon's existence.

Though a chill breeze had driven everyone else inside, Dealon remained on the porch, seated before an upturned rain barrel with a chessboard atop it. Across from Dealon sat the chess-monkey—a three-foot tall tin ape with long nimble fingers and glass eyes that fixed on Dealon with infuriating confidence. Dealon studied the game before him as if he were locked in a contest with a player of the highest caliber. With a cautious hand, he twisted his white bishop from its square and picked it up. The bottom of the bishop wasn't flat; it held a slender rod covered with small pegs—a key. Dealon placed this key into a corresponding slot three diagonals up and to the left. He twisted it into position to complete his move. Now the monkey either had to take the bishop with his queen and lose the queen to Dealon's rook, or move the queen and expose the monkey's rook to capture.

Within the barrel, clockwork whirred and clicked. The monkey tilted his head toward the board and reached out to grasp his knight. With a heart-breaking *click*, the rook protecting Dealon's bishop rose in its slot. The monkey retrieved the lifted piece with his left hand and moved his knight into the now open slot. A chime inside the box struck three times. The flat metallic disk of the monkey's jaw lowered, forming a wide grin.

"Sonova..." Dealon grumbled. He was in check. He could move his king out of it, but only in such a way that his rook no longer protected his bishop. The monkey's queen would take his bishop, and he'd be in check again.

Dealon stood up, stretching his back, taking a minute to think. He'd been insensitive to the cold while he'd been concentrating; now he felt it in his bones. He should go inside, sit next to the fire, and warm himself with a cider. However, when he walked inside, Thorny would ask him how he'd fared against Burke's monkey. Since the installation of the device, Dealon had played one hundred and seventeen games. Five of these had been stalemates. The others he'd lost. He knew the exact total not because he kept track, but because Thorny kept track, and reminded him every time he entered the tavern.

Of course, he hadn't lost yet. True, things looked bleak, but it was vaguely possible he could win. The problem was, the damn monkey didn't get tired. Its butt didn't get sore sitting on a wooden chair. Cold winds didn't make its back ache. All it had to do was grin and let its clockwork brain think about chess.

Dealon looked back at the board. He glanced toward the door of the tavern, and could hear the conversation drifting from within. The scent of warm cider flavored the air. Of course, he could just go home. It would be dark soon. He looked down the Forge Road, toward the east.

A mob of humans was approaching, led by a naked man. Dealon stepped from the porch for a better look, thinking his eyes might be playing tricks. They weren't. Hundreds of men, perhaps thousands, were marching down the Forge Road, most carrying makeshift weapons: pitchforks and scythes and clubs.

The late afternoon sun gave Dealon a good look at the man out in front of the group. Their leader stood tall and muscular, his whole body covered in dark wiry hair. His face was all but hidden beneath an untamed mane of brown hair that hung past his shoulders in a tangled veil. His thick, curly beard reached the center of his chest. He wore no clothes, not even shoes.

In contrast to the makeshift weapons his men carried, the leader held finely crafted scimitars in each hand. Dealon spun around and darted up the porch steps. He burst into the tavern and shouted, "Burke!"

"What's wrong?" Thorny asked from his seat at the table by the fireplace. His grizzled old face broke into a cruel grin revealing his three remaining teeth as he asked, "Monkey beat you again?"

"There's an army," Dealon said as the door closed behind him, guided by the invisible hand of a counterweight that Burke had installed. "They're heading here!"

At this pronouncement, the scattered conversations in the room fell silent. There were only ten people in the tavern's great room, eight of them farmers like Thorny, plus Anza, Burke's daughter, who worked as the tavern's barmaid. Behind the bar stood Burke himself, wiping a glazed ceramic mug, his spectacles reflecting the orange flames dancing in the fireplace.

"Earth-dragons?" Burke asked, sounding uninterested.

"Humans!" said Dealon.

Burke's lips pursed ever so slightly downward. "How many?"

"Hundreds!"

"I see," said Burke. He took off his spectacles and cleaned them with the same cloth he'd used on the mug. "It's a good thing we just stocked up on cider. Anza, would you go down to the cellar and count the stock for me?"

Anza nodded, looking serious, as if Burke's words meant something that only she understood. Anza had grown into a fine woman, several inches taller than her father, with the same perfectly straight black hair and tan skin. In all her life, no one had ever heard her speak. Though she understood everything that was said to her, she communicated only with her gestures and expressions. Among the gestures she was famed for was her rather swift response toward any man who laid a hand on her. She could break a man's fingers faster than he could finish saying, "Aren't you a pretty thing?"

As Anza vanished into the kitchen, Burke asked, "How far off? How long before they get here?"

In response, the door to the tavern was kicked from its hinges. It crashed to the floor, knocking over a table, which sent chairs toppling in a domino effect. The thick floorboards of the great room trembled as the mob trampled in, led by the naked swordsman. Dealon ran to the bar, scrambling over it as fast as he could manage, getting on the side with Burke. Others sought refuge beneath tables, or in the corners of the room. Burke alone seemed unfazed by the invasion as he picked up another mug and began to wipe it.

More of the army crowded inside—Dealon guessed at least a hundred men. A dozen of the largest hung close to the muscular leader as he approached the bar. Like their leader, they were armed with actual swords. Unlike him, they wore clothes. Some even had bits of ill-fitting armor: breastplates and bucklers and skirts of chainmail that had obviously been crafted for use by earth-dragons.

The naked man raised his hand and the men who followed him stopped where they stood, utterly silent. He stared across the room at Burke. Burke patiently waited for the man to speak first.

The naked man shook the room with a deep and thunderous voice: "The southern rebellion. The town of Conyers. Among the heroes of that battle was a man known as Kanati the Machinist. He was of the ancient race of the Cherokee, and legendary for his inventiveness. You are this man."

Burke shrugged, then shook his head. "Seems you know a little history. You must know Albekizan crushed that rebellion. The sun-dragons held a public feast to devour the captives. Whoever this Kanati was, he's dead now. Everyone who lived in Conyers is dead."

"Not everyone," said the naked man. "I was born there. I was eight when the king's army came against the city. Despite my youth, I would gladly have stayed and fought. My father, however, gathered my family and fled in the darkness. We weren't the only refugees. Don't tell me that everyone died."

"Maybe there were some survivors," said Burke. "Your family was one of the fortunate."

"No," the man said, shaking his wild locks. "My mother and father survived Conyers only to be slain five years later by Albekizan and his accursed wizard. Little about my history can be called fortunate save for discovering you, Kanati."

"Kanati, I assure you, has long since been digested. Sorry to make your trip here a pointless one. Why don't I give your men a round of cider for your troubles, then you head off to wherever it is you're going?"

"My men may not partake of alcohol."

"I see. Well then, Ragnar, I'm not sure there's much more I can do for you."

"Ah!" the naked man said, his eyes brightening. "You know my name! Can it be you remember me from long ago?"

"Were you this hairy when you were eight?" asked Burke. "I know your name because I've been hearing rumors about a prophet named Ragnar who's vowed not to cut his hair or wear clothes until the last dragon has been slain. You seem to fit that description."

Ragnar drew back his shoulders. "I am that prophet. I have been the tongue by which the Lord speaks of the final days of the dragons. Now, I am the sword that will cut them from this earth!"

"Everyone needs something to do with their time," Burke said with a gentle smile. "I confess, I'm not sure I grasp the strategic value of fighting a dragon buck naked."

"The prophet Samuel wandered the desert clad only by prayers," said Ragnar.

"Interesting," said Burke, nodding slowly, as if appreciating the logic behind Ragnar's words. "Did this Samuel fellow also swear off soap? Because, I gotta tell you, Ragnar, you're making my eyes water."

Ragnar slammed the hilt of his scimitar onto the bar, causing the mugs that sat upon it to jump. Spittle flew from his lips as he shouted, "Do not mock me! I am the Lord's chosen! With a word, my army will destroy this town. Stone will be knocked from stone. Your barns will be burnt and your livestock slaughtered. Your women will weep as we behead the men of this village one by one for treason!"

Dealon cringed a little lower behind the bar in the face of Ragnar's rage. Burke was no longer smiling.

"You make a compelling argument," Burke said, in a cool tone. "Still, I can be a little thick. Why, exactly, are we accused of treason?"

"Albekizan, king of the dragons, is dead, as I prophesied. The dragons are in disarray. All men must now stand together to strike the accused serpents. Those who refuse are traitors. I march from village to village, bringing all men the divine message: *Join or die!*"

Burke smirked. "At least we get a choice."

"No, Kanati," said Ragnar. "Your only choice is to join. The Lord has told me the legendary machinist will fight by my side."

Burke reached up and scratched the pale scars above his lip as he thought. He said, "Why would you even want Kanati? The machinist didn't do much good the last time he stood up to dragons. He spent months preparing Conyers for battle. The dragons overran the town in hours. All this Kanati fellow managed to do was spread false hope and get a lot of people killed."

"You lacked divine guidance," said Ragnar. "The holy scriptures state that the great dragon will hold dominion over the Earth for a millennium before perishing in a final battle. The thousand years have passed. I now wage the last war. You will build me the weapons I need to fight it. Should you refuse, my men will find your daughter—Anza, I believe she's called. Terrible things will be done to her before your eyes."

Burke lowered his hands to the bar. His voice was cold as the breeze outside as he said, "Leave here, Ragnar. You no longer amuse me."

"I'm not here to amuse you," said Ragnar.

"I'll give you until the count of ten," said Burke. His hand fell below the bar. Dealon noticed a long iron rod that Burke pulled back. From beneath the floor came the clatter of cogs and clockwork, like the sounds the chess-monkey made, but on a grand scale. "After that, I'm going to start killing your men."

"Do it," said Ragnar. "Kill them."

Burke frowned, his eyes darting about the room as if he were counting the number of forces arrayed against him. Most of the time, Dealon thought of Burke as the same youthful man who'd wandered into town those long years ago. Now, Burke looked as if he'd aged twenty years since Dealon had last seen him. Light gray hairs streaked his braid and deep wrinkles lined his eyes. The expression upon Burke's face as he surveyed the mob wasn't so much a look of anger as one of weariness.

"This one," said Ragnar, grabbing the guard to his left. "His name's Ugnan. Start with him."

"Sir," Ugnan said, looking startled. He was a big, lumpy man, with thick arms and a thicker belly. His pumpkin-shaped head sat upon his shoulders without the intervention of a neck. Plates of rusted armor hung over his dirty brown shirt and trousers.

"Your faith will protect you," said Ragnar.

Ugnan didn't look confident in this, but he stood still, obedient to the holy man.

"If your power is as great as you wish me to believe, prove it now," Ragnar said to Burke.

"Don't make me do this," said Burke.

"Think of Anza," said Ragnar.

Burke grimaced, his eyes locked onto those of the prophet. Suddenly, he barked out, "A-seven!"

A powerful spring in the cellar uncoiled with a twang. The bar stool next to Ugnan splintered as a long, sharp iron rod sprang six feet into the air. Ugnan looked over at the rod, only inches away, his eyes wide. "It missed," he whispered. "It's true... my faith saved me."

Burke sighed. "Sorry Ugnan. It's not divine will, just bad memory. It's been, what, twelve years since I built the grid?"

Ugnan looked confused.

Burke looked down at his feet, cupped his hands to make a fleshy megaphone, and shouted, "A-six!"

Dealon turn away as a pained shriek tore from Ugnan's lips. His twitching body lifted into the air and his sword hit the floor with a clatter. Blood splattered the ceiling. Ugnan's eyes remained open as he lifelessly slid down the spike.

"Alas," said Ragnar. "Ugnan's faith was weak. But my faith is strengthened. Perhaps Kanati the machinist is long dead. The Lord has delivered us a man who matches his talents. Join me, Burke. Together, we cannot fail."

"What I did to Ugnan I can do to every man in this room," said Burke. "Even you."

"You didn't kill me, though you could have. You know that should I die, the men outside this tavern will run wild."

"True," said Burke with a sigh. "The only thing worse than an army led by a fanatic is an army led by no one at all."

Burke stared into the eyes of the naked prophet. His hand rested on a second lever beneath the bar. Dealon wondered what intricate machinery that lever would set in motion. Yet the look on Burke's face was one familiar to him. It was the same expression Dealon often saw reflected in the glass eyes of the chess-monkey, the look his own face wore when he was in check and any move he made was going to cost him dearly.

Burke's fingers slipped from the handle.

"No one else," he said. "I'll join you if no one else from the town is taken."

Now it was Ragnar's turn to stare as he silently contemplated his opponent's offer. He studied the twisted form of Ugnan, standing like a fleshy scarecrow, supported by the steel rod. Ugnan's blood pooled around the prophet's bare feet. With a look of satisfaction in his eyes, Ragnar turned to Burke. "Agreed."

Burke relaxed. He crossed his arms and said, "You've picked up a fair little army with this 'join or die' tactic. Do you have any other plans up your sleeve? If you had sleeves, that is?"

The prophet smiled, his yellow teeth gleaming amid the dark tangle of his beard. "It's not by chance we travel the Forge Road."

Burke nodded, as if Ragnar had just explained everything.

CHAPTER NINE

fEVER DREAMS

BITTERWOOD DREAMED OF fire. He fled down corridors of flame-wreathed stone in Chakthalla's castle, holding his breath to avoid the deadly smoke. He emerged into a courtyard to find his home village, Christdale, ablaze. All the wooden buildings glowed apple-red, yet were still intact; the black cinder bodies of women and children stood in doorways, beckoning to him. He stumbled through the inferno of the village, his lungs aching, blisters rising on face, to arrive at the church he'd built board by board with his own hands. The structure collapsed in a spray of bright sparks. As the burning walls fell away, stands of living trees were revealed. It was the temple that had stood in this village long ago, the temple of the goddess.

He peered through the smoke into the heart of the temple, toward the statue of the goddess. In Bitterwood's youth, the goddess had been a wooden carving, immobile, but in this dream she was walking toward him, a voluptuous female form with skin of rich mahogany. Where her hair should have been there were gouts of flame, slithering together like glowing snakes, flicking their tongues in evil hisses.

The fire spread across her polished skin as she drew closer. The goddess stumbled, her glowing arms stretched toward Bitterwood, as if begging him to catch her. He tried to run, but couldn't move as the goddess fell against him and his own skin caught fire. In his panic, he jerked his eyes open.

He was lying under a stone outcropping. A small, pathetic campfire sputtered at his side. White smoke drifted from the coals and wrapped around his head like a cloud. With every breath the acrid stench filled his lungs. He was under a heavy wool blanket that smelled like manure. He was awash with sweat. The breath that passed between his shivering lips was hot and dry as a summer wind. He tried to wipe the sweat from his eyes. The hand he lifted was barely recognizable as his own; it was a yellowish gray lump streaked with purple. Bitterwood tried to wiggle the swollen fingers and they didn't move. He dropped the limb to his chest.

Glancing around the shelter, he couldn't see Zeeky or Poocher, but the boy he'd saved was near, leaning up against Killer's massive body. Both were sleeping. Killer's legs were covered with brown bandages. Bitterwood tried to speak, but wound up coughing. The intended effect was the same. Killer and the boy opened their eyes.

Bitterwood licked his dry lips and whispered, "W-where's Z-Zeeky?"

The boy shrugged. "Gone," he said.

"G-gone where?"

"Dead Skunk Hole," the boy said.

Bitterwood nodded, as if the boy's words made sense. Then he closed his eyes and slipped back into dream.

THE FIRST DRAGON Bitterwood had ever killed had been a sky-dragon. The beast had been flying overhead, little higher than the tree tops. Bitterwood had been practicing with a bow since the fall of Christdale, never wanting to again be unprepared to defend himself. Bitterwood hadn't needed to defend himself from this dragon. The sky-dragon never even glanced down as it passed. Bitterwood had been, quite literally, beneath its notice. Bitterwood could have ignored it and continued his training. Instead, he'd made a lucky guess as to how far ahead of the beast he needed to aim and loosed the shot. The beast had yelped a single word— "*What?*"—when the arrow caught in its breast, then spiraled through the air as its damaged chest muscles tried to maintain its flight. It crashed at neck-snapping speed.

Bitterwood had stood over the dead dragon a long time, trying to feel something. Guilt, perhaps, for killing a creature that had nothing to do with the deaths of his family. Or, satisfaction, at least some small flicker, that his shot had found its target and the population of dragons was now reduced by one.

He'd felt nothing. Intellectually, he was aware he'd just killed a fellow intelligent being, capable of thought and speech. Until this moment, the only large thing he'd ever killed had been a deer when he'd hunted with his brother Jomath. He'd felt some small twinge of remorse looking down at the deer, though that emotion had changed to satisfaction when he'd later dined upon a steak cut from his kill.

Remembering that meal, he'd cut the dragon's thigh free from the body and left the rest to be picked over by buzzards. That evening, he'd roasted the thigh over a fire. He could still smell the aroma of dragon fat as it dripped from the leg and sizzled on the coals below. He remembered the way the tough, chewy meat played upon his tongue, the gushes of smoky grease. He could still be warmed by the glow that filled him after that meal as he stretched out under the stars, his belly full.

To this day, there was no sound more satisfying to his ears than a startled dragon yelping, "*What?*"

Deep inside his dream, Bitterwood was aware of his nostrils twitching. He was keenly tuned to the smell of dragons, the way their hides stank of fish, the way their breath smelled of dead things. His nose served as an extra eye, alerting him when dragons waited in the dark, unseen. His lids cracked open the barest sliver.

A dark red shape loomed at the mouth of the cave. Then it was blotted out by a second shape, scaly like a dragon, but shaped like a woman. The woman's face drew closer. Did he know her?

"Recanna?" he mumbled before his eyes closed again.

"He's burning up," the woman said, pulling the blanket and taking away a fair number of scabs with it. The smell of rotting meat wafted through the air. The woman audibly gagged. "By the bones," she said softly, strange words from a human's lips. It was normally an expression of dragons.

"That's a lot of pus," said a deep voice. Bitterwood recognized the timbre of the sound, the bass formed by a belly wide enough to digest a man. *A sun-dragon.* Was he still dreaming?

He opened his eyes once more. A sun-dragon peered into the small cave, his eyes glowing green in the firelight. Bitterwood was certain that he was looking at a ghost: Albekizan, coming to claim his revenge. Yet, despite the similarity, this dragon was younger than the king. Bodiel? No, Albekizan's youngest son was dead too. Who was this?

This dragon didn't seem to be watching him. His eyes were focused above Bitterwood. Bitterwood tilted his head to find the woman he'd glimpsed kneeling over him. He flinched as her fingers probed his wounds. Yellow fluid oozed beneath her fingertips as she applied pressure. She closed her eyes. Bant struggled to recall where he'd seen her before. Her helmet was familiar... it looked like the one the wizard-dragon Vendevorex had worn.

"J-Jandra?" he asked. It had to be her. She looked different since their time together in the Free City. Older, somehow, though only weeks had passed.

"I'm here," she said. "What the hell did this to you, Bant?"

"Dragon," he mumbled. "N-never seen one like it."

"I can't believe you're still alive." Her voice sounded distant and distracted. Her eyes were closed, flickering back and forth under the lids. "I've never seen so much infection."

"I-I've felt w-worse," he said.

"You'd lose your left leg if I weren't here," Jandra said. "Still might. This is going to take some work."

She said something else a moment later, but her voice seemed far away, lost beneath some hiss, like the fall of a hard rain. Was it raining? He couldn't see anything beyond the veil of black mist that slid across his vision, blotting out Jandra, the dragon, and the fire beside him.

at the end of his arm were wriggling fingers again. It wasn't just his hands that felt restored. He tossed aside the blanket, which was now clean. Beneath, he was naked. All the wounds inflicted by the long-wyrm were healed. His body was covered by a hundred smooth crisscrossing scars, but he felt fine. All traces of the fever and weakness were gone.

"I'm sorry about the scars," Jandra said. "Once I got rid of the infection and repaired the deep structure damage, I simply accelerated your body's own healing systems."

Jandra wasn't looking directly at him as she spoke, averting her eyes from his nudity. Bitterwood grabbed the blanket and pulled it back over his lap to hide himself.

"You must command the same magic Vendevorex used," Bitterwood said. "He healed himself after being gutted. He should have died."

"He did die, later, in the Free City. I'm not sure how much you know about what's happened since I left you."

"Not much," Bitterwood said. "I've been traveling with Zeeky... *Zeeky*! Where is she?"

"Missing," said Jandra. "Her brother said she went into the mines."

"That fool girl," he grumbled. "She'll get herself eaten. Why didn't you go after her?"

"I've been saving your life," she said, looking hurt by his scolding tone.

Bitterwood looked around for his clothes. If Zeeky had gone into the mines, he'd have to follow her. "Where did you put my—?"

"Here," Jandra said, lifting a folded bundle of leather and linen. "I took these off because I didn't want to get the fibers entangled in your wounds. I repaired them as best I could. Nothing fancy. There wasn't much to work with."

She tossed the bundle to Bitterwood. He caught the familiar fabric, recognizing at once the linen shirt and buckskin pants he'd worn for so many years. He couldn't recall the last time they'd been so completely free of blood stains. The tattered blanket he'd worn on his journey had been fashioned into an actual cloak, complete with a drawstring hood.

"I didn't know you were a seamstress as well as a witch," he said. He took a sidelong glance at her. "You've changed your hair again." Her long brown locks hung freely past her shoulders from beneath the silver skullcap. In the Free City, her hair had been black, and barely shoulder length. Her clothes also caught his attention, as it looked like dragon hide. The material clung to her body in a way that seemed part of her. Elaborate flourishes of feathery lace around the cuff and collar seemed more appropriate for a palace than for a cave in the wilderness. "Your clothes look like something that peacock you consorted with might have worn. What was his name? Pet?"

Jandra frowned. "Pet wasn't my consort. I don't appreciate being judged simply because I want to wear something nicer than rags."

As she spoke, Bitterwood sniffed the air. "It's not my imagination. There was a sun-dragon here."

"Hexilizan," said Jandra. "He likes to be called Hex."

"Ah. The disgraced first-born."

"You've heard of him? I lived in the castle all my life and didn't know who he was." She turned her back to him. "Put your clothes on so we can go see the others."

"I know Albekizan's family well," said Bitterwood, unfolding the bundle. "He had six sons and four daughters. Only two of the sons survive—Hexilizan and Shandrazel. Lancerimel followed the Dragon Road beyond the Cursed Mountains and never returned. The other three I killed… though only Bodiel's body was discovered."

"Don't brag about that to Hex," she said. "In fact, before we go further, I want to lay down some rules. Back at Chakthalla's, you gave me your word not to kill Vendevorex, and you kept it. Now, I want your word that you won't kill Hex. He's my friend, and I won't have him become another notch on your bow."

"I don't carve notches in my bow," said Bitterwood, struggling to pull his pants over his thighs. The buckskin had tightened. "It would weaken the wood."

"You know what I mean. At Chakthalla's castle, you didn't take sides. If it had scales, you put an arrow into it. But all dragons aren't alike. Hex has done nothing to hurt you."

"You know nothing of the real world, girl," Bitterwood answered, finally getting the pants up to his waist. Despite the snugness of the buckskin, Bitterwood could tell he'd lost weight during his time of fever. The skin of his belly lay tight against the muscles beneath, all hint of fat eaten away in an effort to keep him alive. "As Albekizan's son, Hex trained in the art of hunting humans. Your so-called friend has feasted on the meat of slaves he's brought down. No dragon is innocent."

"Sun-dragons' reputation for eating humans is vastly exaggerated," Jandra said. "Most of them eat the same stuff people do—fish, beef, bread— just a whole lot more of it."

"Foods produced by human labors, which the dragons steal. You don't know that because you've led a sheltered life, protected by a dragon who treated you as affectionately as some men treat their dogs."

"I'm not naïve," said Jandra. "I've killed dragons. I've killed humans. Nothing about my life is sheltered anymore."

Bitterwood silently pulled his shirt on, considering her words as he laced the front closed. Jandra was forever corrupted by having been raised by a dragon. However, he knew he wouldn't be alive without her. She would also be helpful in finding Zeeky. Despite being a witch, she seemed to have a kind heart. Finally, he sighed. "What is it that you want of me?"

"Don't kill Hex. Or Shandrazel, should you meet him. We're at the dawn of an age when dragons and humans can finally live in peace. I don't want you destroying that with your blind hatred."

"My hatred is far from blind, girl," Bitterwood said. "It's clear-eyed hatred, seeing the world that is, not the world you wish it to be. Still, I will honor your request... for now."

Jandra looked relieved. She moved toward the edge of the cave and leapt onto a rock below. "Come on," she said, motioning for him to follow.

They were several hundred feet above the ruins of Big Lick. The mountain here was a series of rocky shelves and overhangs, some quite deep. Jandra navigated the narrow path that led between the ledges with the sureness of a mountain goat. Bitterwood sensed that the change in her since last they'd met was more than just a change of wardrobe. He strained to keep up with her. She definitely hadn't been this strong or fast when they'd first met. Then, she'd been little more than a child in a young woman's body. She'd been brave, yes, but also irrational and overly emotional. She seemed more in control now. When she'd told him not to kill Hex, she hadn't been pleading or bargaining. She'd simply been telling him the rules he would live by in her presence.

He wondered if she'd laid down the same sort of rules with Hex.

THEY WALKED UP a wooden ramp toward the great gaping mouth of the mountain. Judging from the picks and shovels laying around, this was the entrance to a mine. Inside the shelter of the mine a fire burned, and beside this fire sat Killer and the boy. Killer looked healthier, though the ox-dog's hide was now as scarred as his own.

"Did you heal the dog before you healed me?" he asked.

"His wounds were mostly superficial," Jandra said. "After he was better, I had Hex bring him and the boy here. The first cave was too small for Hex, and I wanted us to have a little privacy after you woke."

It was getting dark outside, and the roof of the cave was so black with the soot of centuries it looked like a formless void.

"Where's Hex?" Jandra asked.

"I don't know," the boy said. "He smelled something strange. Said he'd be right back. He only left a minute ago."

"Where's Zeeky?" Bitterwood asked.

"We found her footprints," the boy said, pointing toward the rear of the shaft. "She's looking for our folks."

"You're related to her?" As he asked this, Bitter-wood saw that the family resemblance was undeniable. The same cornsilk-blond hair, the same pale-blue eyes. The boy's face was a bit more angular, however, his nose sharper, his chin more prominent. Bitterwood guessed the boy to be about twelve. He had the same wiry limbs that Zeeky possessed, a body shaped by poverty and the physical demands of climbing over this harsh landscape.

"Ezekia's my sister," he said. "I'm Jeremiah."

"You're older than your sister," said Bitterwood. "Why did you let her go?"

"Ain't nobody can stop Zeeky when she sets her mind to do something."

Bitterwood nodded. He knew this from experience. "Jeremiah and Ezekia... these are names from the Bible."

"Yes sir," the boy said. "My great grandfather was converted by a prophet named Hezekiah. He came to these mountains as a missionary."

"I see," said Bitterwood. "People in this area are usually devotees of the goddess Ashera. I saw her temple in the town of Winding Rock."

"If you know the Bible enough to know our names, are you a follower of the Lord, mister?"

Bitterwood felt anger stir inside him at the question. He knew the boy meant no harm in asking; no doubt he was merely looking for common ground with a stranger. The boy couldn't know that the only thing Bitterwood hated more than dragons were the words of the so-called prophet Hezekiah.

Apparently, the boy sensed Bitterwood's anger, because he turned his face toward the floor and grew quiet, as if he was afraid.

"I didn't know you were such an expert in religion," Jandra said to Bitterwood. "Of course, almost anyone would know more about religion than I do. Vendevorex didn't teach me anything about spirituality."

"If you stay in these mountains long," the boy said, "you'll learn more than you want to know about spirits. These mountains are full of devils."

"Some people think these mountains are the home of the goddess," said Bitterwood, not so much to argue with the boy as to explain things to Jandra. "Jeremiah's people think the place is full of devils, but in the village where I was born it would have been unthinkable to mine these mountains—this was sacred ground. The goddess both lived in the earth, and was of the earth. Digging a hole this deep into her would have been like digging into her heart."

"Hmm," said Jandra. "When I get back to the library I'll have to read up on theology."

"Don't you carry the books inside your head?" asked a deep, strong voice from the growing darkness outside the cave. Bitterwood spun around, his body instinctively steeling itself for combat.

Jandra looked toward the shadows outside, and said, "I can only recall books I've actually seen. This wasn't something I studied."

The shadows at the mouth of the cave took on shape and substance as the ruby hide of a sun-dragon slinked forward. Bitterwood surveyed the room for a weapon. He'd never killed a sun-dragon barehanded. The pickaxes that lay at the entrance could do the deed.

However, the way this dragon moved gave Bitterwood a reason to relax. This dragon was no threat; he was limping, and there was a hint of freshly spilled reptilian blood in the air. Indeed, more than a hint—Hex must be bleeding freely to unleash such an odor.

As Hex moved nearer the light of the campfire, it became apparent that he wasn't limping. He was dragging something he grasped with his fore-talons, something quite heavy. From the corner of his eye, Bant saw Jandra toss a handful of silver dust into the air. Suddenly, the room was as brightly lit as if the noon sun was overhead.

The burden that Hex dragged behind him was copper colored and its body seemed to stretch on forever out of the mouth of the cave. It was studded with muscular legs ending in fearsome claws.

"I heard what you were saying about the goddess," said Hex, as if the fact he was dragging a slain beast into their presence was hardly worth mentioning. "We dragons don't believe in gods exactly, though we do believe in a life flame that endures beyond death, and we believe in spirits. These mountains are said to be haunted; perhaps the strange noise that permeates these rocks causes both men and dragons to seek supernatural explanations."

"What noise?" Bitterwood asked.

"What in the world is that?" Jandra said, walking over to the beast, ignoring Bitterwood. "I've never seen anything like it."

"I'm not sure what it is. I smelled something odd in the wind earlier. I found this thing emerging from one of the nearby caves. It attacked when it saw me; I killed it in self-defense."

"Those are demons," Jeremiah said. "They live in the underworld."

"This isn't a demon," said Hex. "It's an animal, and it was being ridden by a man. Unfortunately, he escaped as I was fighting the beast."

Bitterwood nodded. "There was a man on a beast I slew as well. He didn't escape. I'd never seen anything like it either. But I've heard about a lot of legendary beasts over the years, and once was told of a race of long-wyrms that lived in the mountains. This must be one of those."

Jandra ran her hands along the long-wyrm's hide as Killer, the ox-dog, drew up beside her and started to sniff. "A creature like this shouldn't exist," she said. "I've been studying biology since I was old enough to hold a book. All vertebrates are limited to four limbs. It's biological law."

"The beast must not have read the same books," said Hex. "If it can read at all. Despite its draconian head, I didn't get the feeling it was intelligent. It didn't speak during the battle, although its rider let out a string of scatological commentaries as he departed."

"Jeremiah, what else do you know about these creatures?" Jandra asked.

"Not a lot, ma'am," the boy answered. "Occasionally the menfolk of my village spot the demons when they're in the mine. The demons shy away from light. But they weren't scared of fire when they attacked Big Lick."

"Why did they attack?" Hex asked. "What provoked them?"

"I don't know," said Jeremiah. "They just came in during the night and started dragging people from their beds. I don't think they killed anyone, their riders just tied us up like hogs and carted us back to the mountain. I'm lucky to have got away. Luckier still to find Zeeky."

"And now Zeeky's gone into the underworld to find your parents," said Bitterwood. "Can you lead us through the mines?"

"I... I'm afraid to, mister," the boy said. "They say these things don't just eat you... they also eat your soul."

"If you live a life of cowardice, your soul has already been chewed up," Bitterwood scolded.

The boy hung his head in shame.

Hex said, "Zeeky's footprints are easy enough to spot in the coal dust. I can smell where her pig walked. We won't need the boy to guide us."

"You're crazy to go into the mountain," Jeremiah said, directing his words at Bitterwood. "That one demon right near killed you. There were at least a dozen that came to Big Lick."

Bitterwood smiled grimly. "I've faced stiffer odds. I only fared badly because I was already injured. If Jandra can make me a bow and some arrows using her—" he stopped suddenly. Killer had lifted his head with a jerk, and turned to face the back of the cave. He let out a low growl toward the darkness.

"What is it, boy?" Jeremiah asked.

"I hear something," Jandra said, looking in the same direction. "Something's moving back there."

Hex dropped to all fours and strained his neck forward, sniffing the air. "Another long-wyrm," he said. "More than one, in fact."

Bitterwood's eyes searched the darkness. The back of the cave was a tangle of rock and shadows, and the light Jandra had created only made it more difficult for him to see what was approaching. Then, at the edge of his vision, a patch of shadow moved closer, until its eyes caught the light and flashed golden.

"Jeremiah," Bitterwood said, as a second pair of eyes joined the first. "Now would be a good time to run."

Jeremiah darted toward the entrance of the cave and, having barely traveled twenty feet, skidded to a halt. Bitterwood glanced back. Three more long-wyrms and their riders were at the entrance of the cave. This brought the total number they faced to five, plus the riders.

The middle long-wyrm at the front of the mine had two riders. "That's him," the hindmost rider said, pointing toward Hex. "He killed my mount."

The long-wyrms crept closer, eyeing the sun-dragon. Their riders carried loaded crossbows. All possessed the same pale skin of the earlier rider, and all wore the same shimmering white tunics and strange visors. Though Bitterwood couldn't see their eyes, it was apparent from the tilt of their heads that the riders were focused on Hex.

Jandra said firmly, "Don't come any closer. I'm sorry we killed your mount. There's no need for further violence."

"The hell there isn't," growled the rider whose mount had been slain. "The goddess was furious when Fondmar and his wyrm were killed. I'll not face her without bringing the head of the dragon who killed my mount."

"Why did you attack the town of Big Lick?" Jandra asked. "What have you done with its people?"

Bitterwood noticed that as she spoke, Jandra had dipped her hand into the pouch on her belt and was now allowing the fine silver dust to trickle through her fingers and vanish into the air. The atmosphere around Bitterwood began to faintly hum. What was she doing? There was already enough light to see by. Too much light for his taste. He fought better in the shadows.

Of course, in a second, it would no longer matter. In unison, all the wyrm-riders lifted their crossbows. Everyone aimed their weapons at Hex.

Bitterwood tensed, waiting for the triggers to be pulled, so he could spring into action before they reloaded. In his head, he was already mapping out the path he would follow, which wyrm he would attack first. He could have one long-wyrm dead in twenty seconds; a second would fall half a minute later. Beyond that, the situation had too many variables to plan. Hopefully, his attack would be enough of a distraction for Jandra to turn invisible and get Jeremiah to safety. He wished he had a second to share his plan. He would have to trust her instincts.

The time for planning abruptly ended as the vengeful rider shouted, "Fire!" The crossbow strings sang out with a single deadly note.

CHAPTER TEN

THE BATTLE OF DEAD SKUNK HOLE

BITTERWOOD CHARGED AS the bolts whistled through the air. A flash of light caught his eyes. The bolts flared, lit by an internal fire. Three feet from Hex's hide the missiles vanished in puffs of smoke.

"Yes!" shouted Jandra, sounding pleased. "Finally!"

Hex looked puzzled by the dusty cloud wafting around him. Then he grimaced, as if in pain, before unleashing a sneeze that echoed through the cave like thunder.

With all eyes on Hex, Bitterwood grabbed a shovel that leaned against a mine cart as he closed in on the nearest long-wyrm. He jumped atop a crate and threw himself at the beast. The long-wyrm whipped toward him, drawn by the sudden movement. Bitterwood planted a hand on the dragon's snout and somersaulted over its toothy maw. He landed on the beast's back, two yards from the rider, who dropped his crossbow and hastily drew his sword.

As the weapon cleared its scabbard, Bitterwood swung. The wooden handle cracked as the iron blade of the shovel connected with the man's head. The rider tumbled from his saddle, his sword flying from his fingers. Bitterwood dropped the shovel and snatched the sword as he leapt from the beast. He landed on the stone floor, crouching, his cloak concealing the blade. The shadows on the floor revealed the long-wyrm snaking back toward him. Bitterwood spun around, burying the blade in the underside of the beast's jaw. Hot spittle flecked his cheeks as the long-wyrm's mouth slammed shut. The upper six inches of the sword jutted from the creature's snout like a bloody horn.

Bitterwood braced himself. He'd missed the long-wyrm's brain. The beast recoiled in pain. Bitterwood held onto the blade with both hands as he was jerked from his feet. With a slurp the blade pulled free, and Bitterwood dropped back to the stone. The creature shook its head back and forth in agony. Bitterwood aimed carefully and thrust upward, his feet braced for maximum leverage. The tip of the sword found the spot he wanted, nearer the back of the jaw. This time, the blade broke into the beast's skull with a gratifying crunch. A spasm ran the length of the long-wyrm, all its claws clenching in sequence. Bitterwood pulled the blade loose as the beast slackened. He jumped free of the collapsing serpent, his eyes searching for the next target.

None of the long-wyrms even looked his way. Two of the remaining beasts were fighting Hex, one was locked in combat with Killer, and the last creature and its rider were engulfed in flames. Jandra was focused on their writhing bodies; her hands grabbed at the air. It looked as if she was gathering the smoke that rose from her victims into a tight ball.

Satisfied that Jandra was in no immediate danger, Bitterwood sprinted across the room toward the long-wyrm that fought Killer. In a replay of the earlier battle, the ox-dog had buried his teeth into the creature's throat. Unlike the earlier battle, Killer's new wounds were more than just scratches. The wyrm had coiled around it and was digging deep gouges in the giant dog's underbelly. A pool of gore grew beneath them as the creature's copper claws pulled out bluish-red loops of intestine. Killer's jaws went slack. A noise, part howl and part sigh, came from somewhere deep inside him. The rider, still in his saddle, leaned forward with his silver blade and buried the tip of the weapon between the dog's eyes.

Bitterwood had seen a lot of creatures die, but seldom had he ever felt such loss. Killer had been a good dog. Bitterwood snarled as he flew at the rider. The rider looked up, struggling to pull his sword free from the dying canine. Bitterwood leapt and swung his blade, chopping into the man's sword arm near the elbow. The rider pulled back, a gasp of agony escaping his lips. The rider's pale face turned even whiter as he saw his arm dangling by a thread of flesh. Bitterwood spun to face the jaws of the long-wyrm as the rider slipped from his saddle. Unfortunately, the rider wasn't dead. With his good hand, he reached out as he fell and grabbed Bitterwood's cloak, jerking him backward.

Bitterwood fought for balance as his feet slipped on the slick gore beneath him. An instant later he was flat on his back. He clenched his jaws as the first of the long-wyrm's talons dug into his right shin. With reflexes trained by years of constant battle, Bitterwood swung his blade without thinking, severing the talon at the wrist. He kicked, scooting backward, as the long-wyrm pulled back. He tried to rise, but everywhere his feet and hands fell he found the hot, stinking slime of Killer's entrails. He could get no traction. The long-wyrm recovered and rose, swaying, then flashed toward him, a bolt of serpentine lightning.

Before it reached him, a second long-wyrm came flying through the air, catching Bitterwood's attacker in mid-strike, knocking it backward.

Bitterwood rolled to his side, trying to figure out what had just happened. He saw one of the long-wyrms now lying dead and broken at the sun-dragon's feet. Two riders lay still and bloody nearby. Hex was down on all fours, the tail of the remaining long-wyrm clamped in his mouth. He spun in circles, whipping his foe through the air in dizzying arcs. This was what had saved Bitterwood—Hex's foe had collided with his. The rider of the spinning long-wyrm was still in his saddle, his feet tangled in the stirrups. His visor was gone, and he had a look of sheer terror in his eyes.

Rising to his feet, sword in hand, Bitterwood searched for the long-wyrm that had killed Killer. It was undulating toward the back of the shaft, vanishing once more into darkness. Bitterwood considered giving chase, but decided against it. The bleeding long-wyrm would leave an easy trail. Bitterwood was greatly interested in where it would lead.

With a sickening crunch, the long-wyrm in Hex's jaws smacked into the wall of the mine, its body nearly flattening with the impact. Hex let the now-dead beast drop, pinning its still-living rider beneath it.

Hex looked dizzy, swaying drunkenly in the aftermath of battle. He was covered with countless cuts, though none looked serious.

Bitterwood examined the body of the rider who'd grabbed him by the belt. The man had finally died from blood loss. He looked around the room. Jeremiah was nowhere to be seen.

"Where's the boy?" he asked.

"I don't know," Jandra said, looking down at something small in her hands. "I got a little over-confident after my success at dismantling the bolts and fried this one with Vengeance of the Ancestors. I forgot that I might kill the rest of you with the poison smoke. I had to gather up all the particulate matter and compress it so it wouldn't be harmful." She held up a black ball the size of a walnut. A skin of silver flowed over it like paint as she turned it in her fingers. "I'll be more careful next time."

Hex said, "I saw Jeremiah flee from the mine. I admire his finely honed instincts for avoiding danger."

"He's only a child," said Jandra. "He's probably safer wherever he ran to than wherever we're going."

Bitterwood knelt next to Killer, placing his hands on the dog's bloodied body. The bristly fur was warm to his touch. He remembered Killer's gentleness as a mount, the look of genuine gratitude the dog conveyed whenever Bitterwood had thrown it some scrap of food. Bitterwood's leg throbbed from where the long-wyrm had dug into it, but the pain felt so distant compared to the cold fingers of grief that clamped around his heart.

"Jandra," he said softly. "Can you help him? He's... he's a good dog."

Jandra walked over and placed a hand on Bitterwood's shoulder. "I'm sorry. Most of what I do is augment a body's own healing mechanisms. I can't bring the dead back to life."

Bitterwood shuddered, feeling the icy hands inside him closing tighter. He closed his eyes, locating the core of hatred that forever burned in him, and instantly his grief washed away in a flood of outrage. These long-wyrm riders had much to pay for.

He stood and limped toward the only rider left alive, the one trapped beneath the long-wyrm. The man's face was twisted in agony as he clawed at the floor, trying to pull himself free. His pale features were now smudged with black coal dust.

Bitterwood stamped down with his full weight, using his uninjured leg to snap the man's fingers beneath his boot. The man released an anguished cry.

"I'm going to kill you," Bitterwood said, pressing down harder and giving the fingers under his heel a twist.

"Wait!" Jandra shouted, rushing up behind him. "We need him alive! We need to ask him questions."

"I'll never talk!" the rider vowed between clenched teeth. "I'd die before betraying the goddess!"

"Then die!" said Bitterwood, raising his sword.

"Stop," said Jandra, taking Bitterwood's arm and pulling him back. "He can tell us what happened to Zeeky!"

"He won't talk. He's a disciple of the goddess Ashera. I know better than anyone the blindness of faith. Let me end his pathetic life!"

"The goddess shall avenge me!" the man said, struggling to sit up. His legs were free of the long-wyrm now but they were twisted in a way that told Bitterwood he would never walk again.

"Your goddess has no power," Bitterwood said. "I've seen her temples gutted, her idols desecrated.

She cannot stop these things, just as she cannot save you!"

"Blasphemer!" The rider spat the word out as if it tasted vile. "I've seen the goddess with my own eyes! If you were to gaze upon her glory, you would tear out your own tongue in penance for your foul lies!"

Hex's long face drew closer to the rider. His jaws still dripped blood. "I, for one, would like to meet this goddess. Can you take us to her?"

The man grimaced as he tried to move his broken legs. He sighed, sagging back against the long-wyrm's corpse. "It would serve you right if I were to lead you to her, dragon. She would melt the flesh from your bones with but a glance."

Jandra knelt before the rider. "I'm willing to take that chance. I have the power to heal your legs. Would you lead us to your goddess if I do?"

The man looked at her skeptically.

Jandra reached out and placed her hands on the man's foot. His boot had been lost beneath the long-wyrm, leaving his bloodied and twisted flesh exposed.

She closed her eyes as a look of concentration fell over her features.

"Compound fractures in both legs," she said. "Extensive internal bleeding. You'll die if you don't accept my help."

In answer, the man's one good hand darted out and grabbed Jandra by her hair. Her helmet flew from her head as he yanked her to his chest, pinning her with his other arm. His free hand flashed to his belt and an instant later a dagger rested against her throat.

"Stay back!" he snarled. "I'll kill her if you move so much as an inch!"

"This really isn't a smart move on your part," Jandra grumbled.

"I've summoned other riders," the man said, eyeing Bitterwood, then the dragon. "You should flee if you value your life. I'll release the girl when they arrive."

Bitterwood raised his sword and took a step closer. "The girl is a witch. It was only a matter of time before I killed her myself."

"I swear I'll do it," the rider screamed, jerking Jandra's hair back and denting her throat with the tip of the blade.

Before Bitterwood could react, Jandra grabbed the man's wrist. Though the man's arms were twice as thick as her own, she pushed the dagger away from her throat as the man struggled to regain control.

Suddenly Hex darted in, his jaws wide. He clamped down with twin rows of knife-length teeth over the man's head. The rider screamed briefly before Hex silenced him forever with a sharp twist that tore the man's neck from his torso. Hex rose, his jaws spraying blood as he crunched the man's skull into ever-smaller fragments.

Jandra turned pale as she watched Hex swallow. She scrambled away from the corpse who still had an arm around her and grabbed her helmet.

"He tasted better than his mount, at least," said Hex, wiping blood from his jaws onto his wing. "Why didn't you simply melt his dagger, Jandra?"

Jandra didn't look back at Hex as she pulled on her helmet.

"I need my helmet to…" her voice trailed off, as if she thought better of completing her sentence. "It's not important."

Her eyes caught Bitterwood's. Bitterwood could tell that this was the first time she'd ever seen a dragon devour a man. Perhaps now she could understand his hatred of the beasts. She turned away, looking ill.

Hex remained oblivious to the unspoken communication between the humans. His eyes were fixed on the back of the shaft.

"There's one more," he said.

Bitterwood looked into the gloom. A single long-wyrm slithered forward. At first, he thought it might be the one he wounded, but he soon saw that this one was unscathed, as was the rider upon its saddle. The rider's outfit was slightly modified from that of his brethren, with a large red star above his left breast. Like the others, he wore a silver visor. Unlike the others, whose hair had been cropped short, this new rider's locks hung to his shoulders. His skin was the same pale tint, but his hair was a dark chestnut, a shade that reminded Bitterwood of his now dead wife, Recanna. He carried a crossbow, but it wasn't loaded. Bitterwood had learned to read bodies well over the years; whoever this was, he wasn't planning to attack.

"What a waste," the new rider said, looking over the corpses of his brethren. "This combat wasn't authorized. They betrayed the goddess by coming here on a mission of petty revenge. They've paid the ultimate price for their folly."

"You'll not try to avenge them, then?" asked Hex.

"No," the rider said. "Through our visors, we may send messages to one another. They signaled that they were entering combat; I ordered them to stand down and they disobeyed my orders. I watched the battle as if through their eyes. They struck first. You fought in self-defense. There is nothing to avenge."

"Perhaps *you* have nothing to avenge," said Bitterwood. "But there's a town below that was destroyed by your riders. Why?"

"The goddess decreed it was a time of harvest," the rider said in a matter-of-fact tone as his long-wyrm carried him to within a few yards. To be coming into the presence of a sun-dragon, the rider and his long-wyrm looked strangely unworried. "The goddess planted them. She may reap them."

"Planted them?" Jandra said. "They weren't stalks of corn."

"Are they still alive?" Hex asked.

"The fate of the villagers should not concern you," the rider said.

"The fate of one villager is of great concern to me," said Bitterwood. "Her name is Zeeky."

The wyrm-rider smiled. "The girl with the pig. Quite resourceful, that one. The goddess has taken special notice of her."

"We want to meet this goddess," said Hex.

"Her temple is a long journey from here," said the rider. "You must travel underground for several days. It isn't a journey to be taken lightly; men have gone mad contemplating the weight of the earth above them."

"Perhaps men do go mad," said Hex. "I believe I'm made of sterner stuff."

"I'm not afraid," said Jandra. "Take us."

Bitterwood didn't answer. It didn't seem, from his posture, that the rider was planning to lead them into a trap. Still, if the temple was many days away, had Zeeky arrived there yet? He wasn't certain how many days he'd lost to the fever.

"Before we go, introductions are in order," Hex said, apparently impatient with Bitterwood's silence. "I am Hexilizan; my friends call me Hex.

The woman is named Jandra. I fear I haven't been introduced to the gentleman yet."

Bitterwood thought carefully of what to say. Jandra apparently had kept his true identity secret. A wise move, perhaps, but now that he had a sword in his hand he didn't care what Hex knew about him.

"My name is Bant Bitterwood," he said. He saw the muscles beneath Hex's hide go instantly tense. More curiously, the rider also stiffened in his saddle. The man's mouth opened, but he seemed unable to speak.

Shaking off his shocked expression, the rider dismounted. He took off his visor and stepped toward Bitterwood. The look on his face was an expression half of disbelief, half of reverence.

"Do you..." he asked, his voice soft. "Can you truly be Bant Bitterwood?"

"Is my name known so well in the underworld?" Bitterwood asked.

The rider drew closer. Despite the pallor of the man's skin, Bitterwood noted the rider's features in many ways echoed his own, from the sharp angle of the nose to the firm line of the brow. Yet while Bitterwood's face was leathery and wrinkled, the rider's visage had a baby-skin smoothness that no doubt came from avoiding the sun. The man was taller than Bitterwood, better muscled and much younger, at most a few years older than Jandra.

"I worried you were dead," the rider said.

"I've done little to discourage that belief," Bitterwood said.

"Your legend has preceded you," the rider said. "As I grew up, I took pride in your exploits whenever Gabriel reported back news from the world of men. I feel as if I've known you my whole life, though I have no true memories of you."

"No memor... Who are you?" Bitterwood asked, his voice trailing to near silence as he realized why this man might resemble him.

The rider nodded, as if recognizing that Bitterwood had figured out the puzzle. "Yes," he said. "I'm Adam Bitterwood."

CHAPTER ELEVEN

UNHEALTHY PHILOSOPHIES

THE BRILLIANT MORNING sun was a welcome change from the gloom and rain Graxen had flown through the last few days. The palace of Shandrazel stood in the distance, a small mountain of granite. The frost that covered this ancestral seat of power sparkled like jewels. Since Shandrazel had taken the throne, Graxen had spent little time at the palace. He'd traveled to the far reaches of the kingdom to summon guests to Shandrazel's conference. Today, sun-dragons would arrive, lords of the various territories that swore alliance to the king. Humans would attend as well, represented by the mayors of the larger towns, like Richmond, Hampton, Chickenburg, and Bilge. The earth-dragons would be underrepresented. Save for Dragon Forge, they claimed no territory as their own. They lived primarily in the service of sun-dragons, and depended upon these superior beasts for leadership. Male sky-dragons from all nine of the Colleges would be in attendance, but the female sky-dragons would only have one voice—the representative from the Nest. Graxen wondered how Shandrazel could hope to bring equality to races of such uneven power and resources; he couldn't even bring equal numbers of representatives to the discussions.

Still, there was an atmosphere of optimism about the palace. The red and gold flags that served as the banner of Albekizan fluttered everywhere. Earthdragon guards in crimson uniforms stood at each door, and above the towers of the palace the brilliant blue figures of the aerial guard could be seen. The aerial guard were those rare male sky-dragons who had chosen lives of combat over scholarship. Graxen himself had wished to join the guard when he was younger. He'd trained his body to endure the hardship of combat, and his childhood as an outcast had toughened him for a life of constant vigilance. Yet, his letters of application to the commander of the guard had never been returned. No matter. As messenger of the king, his life at last had purpose.

The one dark spot on the landscape of this historic day was a literal one—the Burning Grounds, the blackened funeral field still smoking with the pyres of the previous night. Many noble dragons who had valiantly given all in the battle of the Free City still awaited the ceremonial cremations. All winged dragons were due this honor; it would be a long time before any hint of grass returned to that charred field.

Beyond the Burning Grounds, almost hidden by the long shadow of the palace, stood the Free City itself, the cause of much of the recent trouble. This city had been built as a trap for humankind. Albekizan had promised a life of luxury and ease to its chosen residents, a reward, it was said, for their faithful service. In truth, the city had been designed by Albekizan's demented brother, Blasphet, to serve as an abattoir. Albekizan had authorized the genocide in order to produce a definitive end to the legendary dragon-hunter Bitterwood. Of course, in the end, Albekizan had underestimated the humans; on the day the residents were to be massacred, a rebellion had spread. What was to be a day of human slaughter turned into a day of human victory.

The Free City was empty now. Graxen wondered what would become of it. It seemed pointless to tear down the structure after so much wealth and effort had been expended to construct it. The Free City could house thousands of people. Perhaps humans would one day settle there peacefully, if they could overlook its sinister origins.

Graxen's reverie ended as he passed over the palace walls. He tilted his body toward a balcony, angling his wings to slow his descent. He gracefully lit on the balcony then walked into the marble-tiled hall beyond. The murmur of voices told him many of Shandrazel's guests had already arrived.

This was the Peace Hall. Albekizan had always referred to it as the war room, but Shandrazel had renamed the chamber as a sign of his intentions. Yet, despite the room's new name, its history still hung on the walls. Tapestries depicted a dozen scenes of Albekizan's conquests. Even the floor of the room was inlaid with a map fifty feet long showing the entirety of Albekizan's kingdom, laid out in precious metals and polished stones of exotic colors.

Groups had gathered in the four corners of the chamber. Four enormous sun-dragons leaned in closely with one another in conference in the corner

nearest the balcony. Graxen knew them all as dragons he'd personally summoned. In the opposite
corner, a crowd of humans stood. Graxen recognized a few: the mayor of Richmond was
noteworthy for being unusually squat and round,
and the mayor of Bilge he remembered due to the
fact he only had one arm. Few of the other humans
looked familiar. Graxen prided himself on his eye
for details and his excellent memory, but he still had
difficulty telling one human from another. It wasn't
that they all looked alike, rather, there was too
much variance. It was impossible to catalogue all
the countless configurations of the human form.
Adult sky-dragons varied little in color and size;
adult humans came in hundreds of shades of tan,
and could vary in height by several feet and weight
by hundreds of pounds. Their faces were an equally exasperating mish-mash—some hairy, some
hairless, some with hair on their scalp and none on
their cheeks and jaw, some with the pattern
reversed. And that hair could come in an array of
colors: white, black, gray, orange, brown, and gold,
each in dozens of shades and mixtures.

With a fellow dragon, there were only a few simple identifying cues: the bumps of the snout; the
curve of the jaw; subtle variations in the shape of
the eyes; the way that no two sky-dragons' scale
patterns were ever exactly alike. A sky-dragon face
instantly triggered recognition as the mind filtered
through the logical system of organizing who was
who by these differences. With humans, most iden-
tities were drowned out by the cacophony of
possible features.

As he mused on identity, Graxen cast a glance
toward a third cluster of gathered guests—sky-
dragons like himself, all male—the biologians, the

scholar-priests that guided the intellectual life of the kingdom. A few cast glances toward him with suspicious eyes. Graxen felt a sense of shame. Did the dismissive attitude he felt toward humans mirror the feelings the biologians had about him? Too different to ever be worth the effort of knowing? No biologian ever studied his face for his identifying features. He was forever marked as "other." Something deep in the brains of sky-dragons would never accept him as a fellow member of the species.

In the final corner of the room sat Shandrazel, resting upon a throne pedestal topped with a large golden pillow. The young king looked quite noble: his red scales freshly groomed, golden rings decorating the edges of his wings. Before him stood Androkom, the High Biologian. Androkom wasn't much older than Graxen. It was odd to see a dragon of his youth wearing the green sashes that denoted such important rank. Androkom's most notable feature, however, was his lack of a tail; he'd lost most of the appendage after an encounter with Blasphet. Normally, sky-dragons placed great emphasis on physical perfection; the worst punishment any sky-dragon could face was to become a tatterwing. Graxen wondered if having an amputee dragon holding such high rank might lead to greater acceptance of deformities among sky-dragons.

Graxen approached as Shandrazel and Androkom quietly conferred. The king glanced up as he neared.

"Welcome, Graxen," Shandrazel said. "Thank you for your work in summoning everyone. The day is still young, but already many of the guests have arrived. However, I won't need your services today. You've worked hard these past weeks. You should take today to rest. Tomorrow as well."

"History will unfold here today," Graxen said. "I can think of no other place I'd rather be."

"Understood," said Androkom, sounding impatient. "However, you can't stay here. The talks must remain closed. Everyone who isn't a representative of their race must leave the chamber."

Graxen looked toward Shandrazel. The sun-dragon looked apologetic as he said, "He's right, I'm afraid. You can remain while the guests arrive, but I must request that you leave when the discussions begin."

Graxen nodded. He could see the logic of having the talks be private, but there was still something condescending about Androkom's emphasis on the words "representative of their race." Graxen looked around the room. If he couldn't remain, he still might play one small role in helping the talks succeed. The historic tapestries on the wall may have been effectively invisible to Shandrazel; no doubt he'd seen them his whole life, and paid little attention to their contents.

"Before I leave, may I assist in removing the tapestries?" he offered.

"Why?" asked Shandrazel.

Graxen motioned with his gaze to a tapestry behind Shandrazel's left shoulder. It showed a young Albekizan with a human body crushed in his jaws and a severed human head hanging in his left fore-talon. The glorified dragon stood upon a mountain of dead men.

"It hardly seems fair to the humans to negotiate a new government under such a reminder of the power of dragons," Graxen said.

"I understand your concerns," Shandrazel said, contemplating the image. "However, I value truth above all other virtues. My father was known for his blind spots. He acted as if Hex had never been born. He claimed that the map inlaid on the floor showed the entirety of the world when it actually only shows the narrow sliver he conquered. My father erased history as it suited his needs; I prefer to let the evidence of the past stand. Perhaps these glorifications of violence will inspire us to greater fairness."

Graxen thought this highly unlikely. He said, "But what if the humans—"

"The tapestries will stay, Graxen," Shandrazel said. "There's no point in arguing with me. You know that during my time at the College of Spires, I never lost a debate."

Graxen himself had witnessed many of these debates. Did Shandrazel truly believe he'd always won due to his superior intellect? Was he blind to the fact that he owed his victories to being Albekizan's son more than to any special gift for logic?

"Of course, Sire," said Graxen.

He glanced once more at the growing crowd of humans, wondering what their thoughts on the matter were. He took note of a tall young man with long blond hair dressed in silk finery—he'd seen this human before, often in the company of Shandrazel. It was the one Albekizan had labeled as Bitterwood. Perhaps Shandrazel was right about Albekizan's blindness to truth. The man was obviously too young to be the source of the original Bitterwood legend.

The young Bitterwood was leaning in close to talk to a shorter man. The second man was bald save for a few whispery gray hairs, and sported a long braided mustache. In contrast to the robust form of Bitterwood, the man was stooped and thin, supporting himself with the help of a gnarled stave.

Watching the two whisper to each other, Graxen was struck by a possibility. What if the older man were the original Bitterwood?

"I'M GLAD TO see you again," Pet said, keeping his voice low as he leaned in to confer with Kamon. Kamon was a prophet from the town of Winding Rock. His people had been among the first brought to the Free City. Kamon was well known throughout the kingdom; for decades he had preached a philosophy of subservience to dragons, telling men they must not take up arms until the arrival of a nameless "savior." Kamonism was a popular philosophy. It promised better days coming, without requiring any immediate action on the parts of his followers.

Kamon nodded. "It was my duty to answer this call. For over half a century I've preached of the time when men would be free. I'm glad I lived long enough to see this day."

"You certainly had a loyal following in the Free City," said Pet. "Speaking of loyal followings, any idea where Ragnar is?"

Ragnar and his men had been the most ferocious fighters in the battle of the Free City. Pet owed his survival to Kamon and Ragnar. Both were genuine leaders, while Pet knew, deep down, he was a fraud. People believed him to be a fearsome dragon-slayer. In truth, even during the heavy fighting of the Free City, he'd never so much as scratched a dragon.

Kamon lowered his eyes at the mention of Ragnar. His lips trembled as if he was about to speak, but after several long seconds the old prophet merely shook his head.

"You don't know?" Pet asked.

"The most accurate answer is, yes, I don't know," Kamon said.

"What's a less accurate answer?"

"All I've heard are rumors. It may amount to nothing."

"I've always listened to rumors," said Pet. "What's going on?"

Kamon's voice fell to a whisper that Pet strained to hear. Kamon's breath smelled like sour milk as Pet leaned closer. "After the fall of the Free City, many of the captives returned to their homes. But I've heard that some of the men have formed a small army led by Ragnar."

"Small army? How small?"

"A few hundred. Perhaps a thousand at most."

Pet silently contemplated the news. Maybe this wasn't so bad. One right that was going to be discussed was the right for humans to assemble militias to defend themselves. Just because Ragnar had an army didn't mean he planned to go out and kill a bunch of dragons.

"According to rumor," Kamon said, so close now his mustache touched Pet's cheek, "Ragnar plans to capture the Dragon Forge and kill all the dragons within it."

"I see," Pet said neutrally. He kept his face impassive as various scenarios boiled in his mind. Ragnar would launch a war and lose, showing humans to be both hostile and weak. Or, Ragnar would win, showing humans to be hostile and dangerous. Neither was a good position for negotiating peace. Pet thought of informing Shandrazel of the rumor and possibly halting Ragnar's army before it did real harm. Yet, on a gut level, this felt wrong. He'd be dead if not for Ragnar. He couldn't just betray him. Where was Jandra when he needed her? She was the one with the brains. Not to mention an actual sense of right and wrong. Pet's moral compass normally steered him toward the path of least resistance. He wasn't entirely without his limits; having been the victim of torture, he'd had no trouble standing up to Androkom when he'd suggested torturing the captured assassin. Right now, however, he didn't know what to do, so he decided to do nothing.

Before he could confer further with Kamon, the doors of the Peace Hall swung open and six earth-dragons marched in, clanking and clunking as they advanced toward Shandrazel. Most earth-dragon soldiers wore light armor, but these were arrayed head to tail in elaborate steel exoskeletons, the individual pieces polished to a mirror finish that reflected the room's vivid colors. The earth-dragons snapped to a halt before Shandrazel. They saluted crisply and, in unison, removed their helmets.

Pet couldn't help but stare at the one in the center. The dragon's face was horribly disfigured, with a crack in his beak large enough that Pet could see his tongue even with his mouth closed. All that remained of the eye above this gash was a horrible tumor of scars.

"My lord Shandrazel," the earth-dragon said, his voice deep and authoritative, with a slightly wet whistling noise from his injured beak. "I am Charkon, commander of the Dragon Forge, a loyal servant of your father for sixty years. I've received your summons and am here to serve you."

"Thank you, esteemed guest," Shandrazel said. "Though, it is not your service I seek today, but your wisdom and counsel."

"Sire," Charkon said, "my wisdom comes from my service. For an earth-dragon, there is no greater purpose than to devote his life to the will of his superiors."

"I do not like the word 'superiors,'" said Shandrazel. "It implies that your race is an inferior one; these talks are to promote the equality of all races."

"Yes, sire. So I've heard. Let me be blunt: We earth-dragons aren't the equals of sun-dragons. You winged dragons see the world from up high. You're dreamers and planners and leaders because of your elevated view. We earth-dragons are simple creatures. We think of little in life beyond what we will eat next. We seldom ponder the world outside our immediate grasp. Our greatest joy comes from hitting things. We make fine soldiers and blacksmiths; we have no gift for politics."

"The eloquence of your words argues differently, noble Charkon," said Shandrazel.

Charkon started to answer, but his voice was drowned out by a flapping of wings. Pet looked toward the balcony to find a small army of sky-dragons alighting on the marble rail. Pet instantly recognized them as valkyries. He'd never actually been in the presence of these fabled female warriors, but as a performer he knew the ballads that sung their praises, and the valkyries had been popular subjects of the painting and sculptures at Chakthalla's castle.

The valkyries quickly fell into formation behind the tallest of the sky-dragons. Their armor and spears glinted in the warm morning light. The tallest valkyrie was unarmed and unarmored, but something about her eyes told Pet she was the most dangerous of the group. Her claws seemed especially sharp as they clacked upon the marble on her march across the room.

"Sire," she said, in a short, clipped syllable. Unlike the deferential Charkon, this valkyrie showed no hint of submissiveness or even respect as she stared into Shandrazel's face. "I am Zorasta, commander of the valkyrie legion, the matriarch's appointed representative for these so-called 'talks.'"

"So-called?" asked Shandrazel, sounding somewhat taken aback by Zorasta's forcefulness. "I assure you these talks are genuine. I hope that all of us working together will be able to form a more perfect union."

"Sire, you're still quite young," Zorasta said in a condescending tone. "You've led a sheltered life. The biologians who educated you have failed you, filling your mind with unhealthy philosophies. I've been sent to bring you back to the sane and rational path."

Shandrazel wrinkled his brow, looking quite bewildered by the aggressive manner of a creature half his size.

Kamon cast a sidelong glance at Pet and whispered, "This is their diplomat?"

"At least the talks aren't going to be boring," said Pet.

Pet looked at Androkom, trying to judge his reaction, since he was one of the biologians most responsible for Shandrazel's "unhealthy philosophies." The new High Biologian didn't look all that worried. Indeed, while dragons could neither smile nor frown, there was a tilt to Androkom's head and a gleam in his eye that told Pet he was amused by Zorasta's attitude.

But the thing that really caught Pet's eye was the sky-dragon standing behind Androkom—Graxen the Gray. Graxen's eyes were positively starry as he cast his gaze at Zorasta. No, not Zorasta. Graxen was focused on a different valkyrie, the one standing behind the right shoulder of the diplomat. At first, Pet couldn't spot anything particularly unusual about this sky-dragon, who stood stone-still, a living prop to symbolize Zorasta's authority. However, Pet had finely tuned instincts for spotting sexual attraction. There was a flicker in the valkyrie's eye, a slight change in her breathing, that told Pet that she was fully aware of Graxen's presence. Did the two know each other? Or was this some kind of love at first sight thing? Pet was an expert in human romance and knew more than he wanted to about sun-dragon affairs, but he had no clue what would stoke the flames of passion for sky-dragons.

He felt himself relax a bit at the sight of this unspoken emotion between the two dragons. He stopped worrying about Ragnar and felt a flicker of hope. Dragons weren't so unlike people. They had the same basic needs—food, clothing, shelter—and an all-consuming desire to mate. As long as he could help ensure a world where those basic needs were met, perhaps it was possible for all the species to live in harmony.

"...which brings me to my next demand," Zorasta said. She'd been talking this whole time, Pet realized, he just hadn't been paying attention while he was focused on reading Graxen's body language. He suddenly wished he'd been listening, though, as Zorasta swung toward him and extended her wing in an accusatory fashion.

"Bitterwood cannot be a representative of the humans. No dragon can know peace until this man has been brought to justice for his crimes. If these 'talks' are to take place at all, he must be arrested and taken to the executioner's block without delay!"

BLASPHET, THE MURDER God, rested upon a giant cushion stitched together from the hides of sky-dragons. The Sisters of the Serpent demonstrated remarkable aptitude for tanning and taxidermy. The only downside was that Blasphet's temple reeked of the tanning solutions. Huge vats of brine and urine and various tree saps gave off fumes that permeated the air.

Perhaps another god might have taken offense that his temple had such a foul atmosphere, but Blasphet was too impressed by the ingenuity of his worshipers to judge them harshly. From the air, Blasphet's temple was indistinguishable from the thousands of abandoned and derelict buildings scattered through the kingdom. It had been a warehouse in centuries past. Now it was almost completely buried beneath a tangle of vines and brush; there were low, gnarled dogwoods growing upon the roof. Yet, somehow, the warehouse had survived the assault of centuries of vegetation and remained mostly intact. The vast, open space within proved comfortable for a creature of his stature. The Sisters of the Serpent had painted the walls of the place black. The floor was carpeted with the hides of various beasts; even the skins of sun-dragons. His followers had been busy. Colobi, the human leader of this sect, said they had worked on the temple for some years, long before he'd been released from his first imprisonment to design the Free City. He was touched that they had shown such faith in his eventual return.

The temple was lit by the light of a thousand candles; the scent of burning tallow mixed with the tanning fumes. In this candlelight, a score of his followers were guiding a flat-bedded wagon drawn by an ox-dog. Upon the wagon lay the immobile form of a sun-dragon. Blasphet knew him: Arvelizan, a distant cousin, and the sun-dragon charged with the administration of the territory of Riverbreak, a rather poor and unimportant domain on the edge of the Ghostlands. Arvelizan had been captured within sight of Shandrazel's palace. He now lay paralyzed by Blasphet's poisons, though Blasphet could see the slight rise and fall of his belly that signaled he was still alive.

Colobi, the serpent of the first order, approached him. She was dressed in robes created from the soft leather of a sun-dragon's wings, stained black. Her face was in shadows below a broad hood, revealing only her blood-red lips and pale chin in the candlelight.

"We have captured a live sun-dragon as you commanded, O Murder God," Colobi said, kneeling before him. "Two sisters were killed in combat with his guards; no one who traveled with him escaped. His absence at the talks will be a mystery."

"Well done," Blasphet said. "Have the sisters administer the antidote. I wish to speak to Arvelizan."

"At once, my lord."

Arvelizan was now only a few yards away. Blasphet watched as Colobi issued her orders and one of the sisters injected the antidote into Arvelizan's long, scaly neck using the fine tip of a hollow dagger. Moments later, the sun-dragon's eyes opened. His deep green irises were still dilated, leaving his eyes mostly black.

"W-where…" he whispered, still too weak to lift his head.

"Hello Arv," Blasphet said. "Remember me?"

Arvelizan's gaze drifted toward the voice. Suddenly, he jerked his head up, the motion halted by the sturdy hemp ropes that bound him to the wagon's bed.

"Blasphet!" he cried.

"Here in the temple, I prefer to be addressed as the Murder God," said Blasphet. "Lord is acceptable as well. My true name is sacred, you see."

Arvelizan responded by increasing his struggles. His tail came free and whipped around blindly, catching one of the sisters off guard and knocking her from her feet. Other sisters leapt back and drew daggers as the ropes groaned and the wood creaked.

"You'll only injure yourself if you keep struggling," said Blasphet.

Arvelizan showed no fear of self-injury. He kicked and strained and wriggled, working slack into the ropes. Suddenly his left wing extended, now free of its bonds. Three more sisters were thrown to the ground by his struggles.

"Colobi," said Blasphet. "Feed him this paste." He held out a gallon-sized iron pot. Colobi grabbed it and removed the lid. In contrast to the background stench of the room, a pleasing aroma of orange-scented honey rose from the oily yellow paste within.

Colobi grabbed the iron pot and fearlessly jumped onto the bed beside the thrashing dragon. He turned his jaws to snap at her; she crouched down inches from his teeth. She calmly slipped on a waterproof leather glove that covered her slender arm up the elbow. Arvelizan snapped his jaws again, straining harder to reach her as she dug her hand deep into the pot. The paste within was the consistency of dung; she lifted a large fistful. Arvelizan opened his jaws to attempt to bite her a third time and she flung the golden gunk toward the back of his throat. Arvelizan coughed, spraying Colobi's black robes with flecks of yellow. She readied a second handful, then a third, tossing it with expert aim into the creature's gullet as he strained to reach her with his teeth. Soon the sun-dragon's entire tongue was coated in the stuff, and his saliva dripped like mustard-colored paint. His struggles slowly calmed. Colobi reached out and placed her hand upon his snout, then nudged his lower jaw open as he stared at her vacantly. She rubbed the last few scoops of paste directly onto his tongue.

"There," said Blasphet. "Isn't that better?"

Arvelizan turned toward Blasphet once more. "Yes," he whispered.

"Yes what?"

"Yes, Murder God," said Arvelizan.

"Untie him," Blasphet said.

Colobi looked calm as she stood and removed her paste-covered glove. She tossed it aside as the other sisters ran forward and cut away Arvelizan's ropes.

"Rise," Blasphet said.

Arvelizan stood, looking more alert than Blasphet had suspected. Save for the yellow spittle dripping from his jaws, he showed no obvious signs of having ingested the powerful drug.

"Now bow before me," said Blasphet.

Arvelizan dropped to all fours, lowering his chin to touch the floor. He spread his wings like giant red carpets to his side as he pressed himself into a pose of unquestioning submission.

"Truly, your works are mighty, O Murder God," said Colobi, staring at the now obedient dragon.

"I won't deny it," said Blasphet. "However, I'm not certain how long our friend here will be useful to us. The paste has dissociative properties; Arvelizan is obedient because his own sense of identity has been suppressed. Alas, the paste rots the brain. He's functional now, but he'll grow increasingly drowsy and clumsy in the coming days. Hopefully, a few days will be all we need. Take him outside and fit him with the harness. Make sure all the sisters on the sky team get a chance to practice riding. I'll guide the kitchen in preparing more paste. I want you to select the stealthiest crew you can assemble. Soon, I'm sending you back into the belly of the beast."

CHAPTER TWELVE

TRACES OF KINDNESS

THE VALKYRIES LOWERED their spears and advanced toward Pet. He'd long suspected he'd meet his end facing a mob of vengeful females, but somehow he hadn't seen it playing out like this.

"Halt!" Shandrazel shouted, his voice booming through the Peace Hall. "Stand down, valkyries!"

The valkyries stopped in their tracks, looking back toward Zorasta. The valkyrie diplomat turned toward the king.

"Bitterwood's sins demand justice," Zorasta said firmly. "He killed your father and your brother. Why would you taint these talks with the presence of a confessed murderer?"

"This man did not kill my father," said Shandrazel. "His whereabouts are well known at the time my father died."

"What of your brother, Bodiel? This man confessed to the crime."

Which was true. Pet had confessed; he'd even bragged about it. He just hadn't actually done it. He'd confessed because the king's army had been slaughtering the people of his home village one by one until they produced Bitterwood. He'd confessed and stopped the slaughter, partly driven by some faint flicker of courage within him, partly driven, he would admit, by a desire to finally impress Jandra. If she hadn't been chiding him for his cowardice all day, he doubted he would have made the decision he did. Acting and deception were Pet's innate talents; it hadn't been that hard to play the role of hero. Still, perhaps now was a good time to come clean? Perhaps he'd calm things by claiming his confession had been a lie. Or would that only make matters worse?

Before he could answer, Shandrazel rose from his golden cushion. He strode toward the center of the room, taking a stand in the middle of the world map. He was silent, as if gathering his thoughts as he looked down at the inlaid gemstones beneath his talons. Everyone grew quiet as they awaited his words.

Shandrazel lifted his head. "My honored guests," he began, in a thoughtful voice. "I've summoned you to this Peace Hall for a noble cause. Four intelligent species share this world." He motioned toward the map beneath him with a sweep of his wings. "This is our common wealth. We hunt in the same forests, we drink from the same rivers. I was born to a family that viewed this land as our domain, and ours alone. Everything on this map was the property of my father; by law, it now belongs to me. The labors of humans, earth-dragons, and even sky-dragons are never truly their own. If a human planted a crop, my father could claim the harvest. If an earth-dragon smelted gold, my father could claim that treasure. Any book a biologian wrote was instantly considered the property of the king's library. This is the history we share."

Pet looked around the room. Everyone stood in rapt attention at Shandrazel's words. Even Zorasta seemed to be attentive.

"As of this day, the book of the old world is closed," said Shandrazel. "We in this room must turn to a new page, and write the history of a reborn world. Let them remember me as the king who brought an end to kings. After these talks, dragons and men will no longer live in a kingdom; we shall all dwell together in a Commonwealth."

Pet noticed that, as Shandrazel spoke, Graxen the Gray gave a nod toward the valkyrie with the teardrop scale on her cheek. The valkyrie gave a subtle nod back.

"We have a golden future ahead of us," Shandrazel continued. "Each of us can leave the Peace Hall knowing we've made the world a more just place. To do this, we must free ourselves from old hatreds and grievances. I know that every race in this room has suffered in some way; I don't wish to diminish the injustice that has occurred in the past. As of this moment, however, we must turn our eyes away from our yesterdays and face our tomorrows. To make a world that is truly free, we must release ourselves from the chains of memory.

"Will you do this? Will you join me in drafting the future? Can I count on your hard work and dedication to ensure the birth of this Commonwealth?"

Shandrazel's stirring words echoed through the hall. He'd delivered the speech with a voice that rang with confidence and leadership. Pet applauded enthusiastically, his long-practiced response to any speech a sun-dragon gave. The humans around him clapped in a more sullen fashion.

Charkon and his guards slapped their gauntleted claws against their breastplates, then unleashed a single cheering syllable: "WHOOT!" which sounded to Pet like a noise of support.

Even the biologians broke out in scattered applause.

Only the valkyries remained stock-still. Zorasta glowered at Shandrazel with eyes that could have shattered stone.

PET LEFT THE Peace Hall twelve hours later. He was giving serious consideration to finding a fast horse and being far away come dawn. Shandrazel had neutralized the demand for his execution with his speech, but that was about the only positive thing accomplished with the day. Once all the representatives had arrived, the room had quickly fallen into bickering over such trivial details as which part of the room each delegation was to stand in. It wasn't an auspicious start.

While Pet had been the immediate beneficiary of Shandrazel's insistence that the talks wouldn't dwell on the past, Pet found himself disturbed by the logic. Centuries of oppression of humans were to be dismissed as no worse than the murder of a few dragons. As attractive as it was to focus on a better future, Pet couldn't forget the things he'd witnessed in the Free City. But, was it necessary to forget? Or only to forgive? Was one the equal of the other?

Pet climbed the stairs to the roof. He walked to the edge and looked out over the Free City, ghostly in the light of a crescent moon. The frigid night air made his lungs ache; it was crisp and clean, yet somehow it couldn't quite remove the scent of blood and piss and muck that washed through his mind whenever he looked at the wooden palisades surrounding the Free City.

Pet froze as he heard a loud, long sigh behind him. Turning, he saw Graxen the Gray perched on a wall on the opposite side of the roof. The sky-dragon seemed oblivious to Pet as he stared across the open courtyard toward one of the many towers that studded the palace skyline. Graxen almost looked like a statue, immobile against the backdrop of stars. Pet followed his gaze and saw a valkyrie standing at attention on a distant balcony. Suddenly, the Free City no longer loomed in his mind; Pet was ever the romantic. He couldn't turn his attention away from a case of unrequited love.

Pet cleared his throat, startling Graxen from his reverie. Graxen flinched, as if he'd been caught doing something embarrassing.

"So," Pet said, hopping onto the wall next to Graxen. From here it was a long, steep plunge into the courtyard. Luckily, Pet was immune to vertigo. "What's her name?"

"W-whose name?" Graxen asked.

"The valkyrie. You know her?"

Graxen sighed. "Nadala. In truth, I know little more than her name."

"I thought that sky-dragons of different sexes didn't mingle. How'd you meet her?"

"She tried to stop me from entering the Nest," said Graxen. "I met her at the point of her spear."

"Aren't they irresistible when they play hard to get?" Pet said with a knowing chuckle.

"I don't know what you mean," said Graxen.

"Human women don't like to appear too easy. I assume the same is true with your females. They like to make you work to prove your interest."

"I fear you know nothing of sky-dragon propagation," Graxen said. "My interest has nothing to do with mating. Desire may rule the reproductive choices of humans, but sky-dragons value their species too much to leave breeding to individual whims. Our biological destinies are determined by the matriarch and her advisors. We mate only with whom we are told to mate."

"Where's the fun in that?" Pet asked.

"What does *fun* have to do with *mating*?"

Pet felt a gulf arise between Graxen and himself that he wasn't sure could ever be crossed. Yet, there was no mistaking the look in Graxen's eyes. This dragon was lovesick, even if he didn't know it.

Pet studied the valkyrie across the way. He could see nothing remarkable about her except, perhaps, that she was standing at such diligent attention.

"She shows a remarkable commitment to duty," Pet said.

"Yes," Graxen said. "She's guarding Zorasta."

"She's probably on duty for hours. She might appreciate some company."

"I don't wish to disturb her," Graxen said.

"You won't disturb her. I saw the way she looked at you. She's as fascinated by you as you are by her."

Graxen wrinkled his nose as if the concept disgusted him. "Valkyries are too disciplined to ever be 'fascinated,' especially by one such as myself. You know nothing of our ways."

"I saw the two of you nod to one another earlier."

"It was only a respectful greeting."

"If you fly over there, does your conversation carry any danger of turning into a session of passionate mating?"

"What? No!" Graxen looked genuinely mortified by the suggestion.

"That takes all the pressure off, then. You can hop over knowing all you're going for is a polite chat. There's no risk of anything messy. What's the harm?"

Graxen didn't answer. Pet could practically hear the wheels turning in the dragon's mind as he allowed himself to be convinced. Pet gave him one last nudge.

"At the very least, since she's stuck standing out here in the cold, you could ask if she'd like a cup of hot cider to fight the chill. You can bring her some from the kitchen if she says yes. It's not flirting. It's just being kind to a fellow dragon. It's showing respect and appreciation for her hard work."

Graxen's eyes softened. "It *is* cold tonight. It would be simple kindness to offer."

"Go," Pet said, giving Graxen a gentle push on the back. The sky-dragon tilted forward, looking for half a second like he would plummet into the courtyard, until he spread his gray wings and shot toward the distant balcony as if pulled by some powerful, unseen spring.

Pet decided at that moment he wouldn't flee the castle. For one thing, he was curious as to how this meeting would work out for Graxen. Secondly, he hoped that, sooner rather than later, Jandra would return. He didn't want to miss the chance to see her again. He grinned as he dreamily watched the distant dragons talking. He drifted into a fantasy that began with the offer of a cup of warm cider on a cool evening, then moved to a vision of Jandra's gown and his pants tangled together at the foot of a bed. Some small, quiet voice inside him warned that he might be skipping some steps in this scenario, but he'd honed to a wonderful degree the ability to ignore such small, quiet voices. He closed his eyes and let his body grow warm in the embrace of Jandra's invisible arms.

NADALA REMAINED RIGIDLY at attention as Graxen landed on a rainspout above her. Only the slightest tilt of her head revealed her awareness of his arrival.

"It's, uh, chilly tonight," he said. His tongue felt stiff in his mouth as he spoke. His voice seemed to belong to someone else.

She whispered her answer, so softly he had to strain to hear it. "It's not so cold. I've stood watches in snow. Tonight is almost balmy."

"Oh," said Graxen. "Then, can I get you some warm cider?" He cringed as the words came out of him. She'd just said she wasn't cold!

"We're not allowed to drink on duty," she whispered. She kept her eyes focused on the horizon, as if watching for the approach of invading armies.

"It's... it's quite a difficult job, I imagine, being a valkyrie. I-I want you to know I... uh... appreciate your hard work." He grimaced at the prattle falling off his tongue. Why had he listened to the human?

"Thank you," Nadala whispered.

Graxen found himself with nothing further to say. He'd thought he'd be flying off for cider about now. His heart pounded out the long seconds as neither of them spoke.

Nadala cast a brief glance upward, as if to assure herself he was still there. Her body quickly resumed the stance of an alert sentry as she whispered, "It's kind of you to offer. Under different circumstances, I would take the cup."

"You're going to be here at the palace for a few days, at least," said Graxen. "Perhaps we could meet—"

"I don't think that's wise, Graxen the Gray."

"Oh," he said.

"I wish the world were more fair," she sighed.

"I know," he said.

"Zorasta won't allow this conference to succeed," Nadala said, sounding bitter. "The matriarch has commanded that we cannot risk the existing world order. I wish she were open to the possibility that the world could be improved."

Graxen felt his heart flutter as the implications of her words took hold.

"Then, you aren't happy with the world as it is? You dream of changing the old ways?"

"A valkyrie is devoid of dreams," Nadala said, her voice firm and, somehow, not her own. It was as if she were speaking the words from rote. "A valkyrie has no will of her own, no desire, save to serve the matriarch. We live and die for the greater good."

Graxen dropped from the rainspout down to the balcony rail, twirling to face her, landing as silently as a leaf. With his voice at its softest, he said, "We both know that isn't true. You treated me kindly when your sisters turned me away. You're an individual as well as a valkyrie."

"In the heat of battle, there can be no individuality," Nadala said. She no longer sounded as if she were repeating slogans. She believed these words. "A valkyrie must be a part of a greater unit. In unity, we will never know defeat."

"But life isn't always a battle," said Graxen. "Shandrazel wants to bring an era of peace to the world."

"There will never be lasting peace," said Nadala. "Especially not in this time of upheaval, following the death of a king. I know with the certainty that night follows day, I'll be called to battle soon. My subservience to the unit must be complete."

Nadala sounded resigned as she spoke. Her eyes looked past Graxen, into the distance, as if seeing that future battle.

Graxen nodded, accepting the wisdom of her words.

"You're right," he said. "Mine was a foolish dream."

Her eyes suddenly met his. She whispered, "Tell me of your dreams, Graxen the Gray."

"I'd only lower myself in your eyes to speak of such fantasies," he said.

"No," she said. "I'm fascinated by dreams. I envy your freedom to dream them."

Graxen wanted to leap from the balcony and flee rather than confess his thoughts. Yet, for so long, he'd wanted to talk to someone about his most cherished hopes. He'd never been asked before; he couldn't run away now. "Before I visited the matriarch I dreamed... I dreamed I would be allowed to mate. It's utterly foolish. I know that centuries of careful planning aren't going to be set aside to accommodate the hopes of an aberration. Yet... still I dreamed, and still I hope."

"I admire that you can hold on to your dreams," she said. "It's been many years since true hope burned in my heart."

"But, certainly you'll be allowed to mate," he said. "You must be highly respected, to be chosen

ure of four limbs, a torso with a
a spine, and a skull. The bones of
·s were similar in size to a human's
erent proportions. The thighs were
length, bending forward from the
hins bent backward at the knees.
shins were long. Sky dragon shins
the bones that formed the human
ackward bending knee. The bones
were stretched into a long lower
dragon. Where humans had short
ame bones in sky-dragons splayed

·al, the sisters had tried to make a
me work by chopping off the shins
rder and teaching her to walk on
led sky-dragon legs. The experi-
: well, and the sister had died of
t suspected that if he had a human
th, he could devise a device that
: shins. He could lengthen the feet
by the use of screws and clamps.
s became pregnant, he would give
thought.
he sisters were demonstrating a
ragon turned into a puppet. The
that held the preserved corpse
he candlelit room. A team of sis-
tugged and tweaked the beast's
he fine details proved effective—
yes blinked in a realistic fashion
were manipulated with enough
puppet could pick up a quill.
larger movements that seemed
beast's stride was off. Even the
ead bobbed upon its neck felt

as a guard for Zorasta. I know from experience you're a formidable warrior."

Nadala lowered her eyes as he spoke, as if embarrassed to discuss the matter. Despite her discomfort, she said, "I find the possibility that I'll be selected as breed stock as dreadful as I do hopeful. I won't be allowed to choose my mate; he'll be assigned to me. The matriarch selects biologians who excel in intellectual arts, yet frequently these biologians lack even the most basic sense of decency. They spend their lives being lauded for their greatness, and they approach the mating as just another award they've earned."

"I've heard the boasts of the chosen ones," Graxen admitted. "They do seem to relish in describing how they, um, dominated the female. I think they overcompensate. Many biologians fear the power of valkyries; they become overly aggressive when confronted with a creature they secretly believe to be their superior."

"We don't wish to be your superiors," said Nadala. "Only your equals."

"Those are the sorts of words that Shandrazel is hoping to hear. It's a shame you aren't the ambassador."

"And it's a shame that the matriarch is blind to your virtues. It was kind of you to come speak to me tonight, Graxen. I fear for the future of our race, should the last traces of kindness be bred out of it."

There was a noise in the chamber beyond the balcony, a soft mumble, like someone speaking in their sleep.

Nadala whispered softer than ever. "If Zorasta wakes, it will be difficult to explain why I haven't gutted you."

"Understood," said Graxen. "It's been worth the risk of gutting to speak to you. I feel… I feel less alone after hearing your thoughts. I wish we could continue our conversation."

Nadala shook her head. "You mustn't take further risks. Leave, knowing that you're less alone in the world, yet also knowing we cannot speak again."

Graxen swallowed hard. Could this really be the end? Ten minutes of conversation was so inadequate for the lifetime of words he'd stored up inside him. He could hear in her voice that she was also full of such words. She was simply too disciplined to risk speaking them. She had so much more to lose than he did. He should go and be satisfied. Still, some desperate part of him wanted more.

"I could write you," he said.

She cocked her head at the suggestion, intrigued.

There was a further mumble in the chamber beyond.

"I know where you could leave the letters," she said, her voice rushed. "On my patrol, midway between the nest and Dragon Forge, there's a crumbling tower, long abandoned. It's easy to find if you follow the river. Atop its walls stands a single gargoyle; there's a hollow in its mouth big enough to hold a scroll. You could leave letters for me there, if you wish. Perhaps I'll answer them."

"I'd like that," said Graxen.

In the room beyond, there was a sudden snort, the sound of a dragon jerking awake.

"Fly!" Nadala whispered, raising her fore-talon and stroking Graxen's cheek. He tilted his cheek against her touch, feeling the smoothness of her scales, and the fine, firm strength of her talons.

Graxen tilted backward, then kicked into space, corkscrewing until he caught the air. He flew out

beneath t
his heart.

La-la-la
Na-da-l

He shud
as "*Yo ho*
get that ac

AFTER TH
Blasphet fe
tion. This
himself ove
his spirit and
His successes
analytical, wond
because he'd lo
he should have
of research a
wondering w
the poison
paste plea
a gallon
thetic sen

A lack
rent dem
Sisters
themselv
the art.
stuffed

Anato
assembl
glance,
backwa
duplica
level o
were b

same basic struc
rib cage and hip
a sky-dragon's le
bones, but of dif
nearly the same
hips. Then, the
However, huma
were short, and
ankle became a
of a human foo
leg for the sky-
roes, the
out as talons.

Before his arr
ky-dragon cost
one of their
ilts that resem
ment hadn't go
infection. Blasph
baby to work w
would confine th
as the child grew
If any of the siste
the matter furthe

This evening,
mummified sky-
black silk thread
were invisible in
ters in the rafter
limbs. Curiously,
the sky-dragon's
and its fore-talon
dexterity that the
Alas, it was the
exaggerated. The
way the corpse's

false. Blasphet doubted the illusion would fool a real sky-dragon. Their eyes were the sharpest of the dragon species. You could never make a puppet string so fine it wouldn't stand out like thick rope to them, even in candlelight.

"I've seen enough," Blasphet said, shaking his head. "Leave me to my thoughts."

The sisters looked disappointed as they carried the puppet away. Only Colobi remained in the room. Rather than retreating, she walked toward him and knelt, placing her head against his left foretalon.

"They meant well, my Lord," she said softly.

"I know," Blasphet said.

He gently stroked her cheek. Colobi was proving to be his favorite of the hundred clever girls willing to die for him. His responsibility for their lives was sobering. He'd wasted five of them in the castle due to a momentary whim. Eventually he'd send the rest to their deaths as well. But for what cause? Revenge against Shandrazel seemed petty now that he was free. The unfinished genocide of the human race still sat in his belly like an undigested meal. Would his plan have worked if Albekizan hadn't ruined things?

He was certain he could have succeeded. But did he want to? Humans were among the creatures he hated least. Time and again they'd proven useful. Humans treated him with deference and respect. Humans had proven to be clever and quick-witted. An army of a hundred, guided by a mind as powerful as his own, could do astonishing things. Genocide was still a challenge that seemed worthy of his unique talents. But perhaps he had chosen the wrong species as his target?

A sliding door rumbled open on the far side. A cross-current swept across the cavernous room; the winter air was a welcome relief from the fumes of the tannery. The night outside was blustery. The wind whistled through a thousand tiny gaps in the building's decaying walls.

Three sisters came through the door, leading a bound and blindfolded sky-dragon. Blasphet recognized the frail creature immediately. The sisters tugged at the ropes that held the dragon, guiding him to stand before the Murder God.

Colobi rose and angrily demanded, "Why do you interrupt our Lord's solitude?"

The leader of the trio gave Colobi a hateful stare. Blasphet had noticed that the other sisters were becoming aware of her status as his favorite.

The woman said, "We captured this unworthy one on the road leading to the College of Spires. He claims to be the former High Biologian, Metron. He says he has served the Murder God loyally in the past."

"Remove his blindfold," said Blasphet. "Cut his bonds. He speaks the truth."

The three produced knives hidden in folds in their garments and thrust them expertly at the old, trembling dragon, slicing away his ropes in violent strokes, yet never so much as scratching him.

Freed, Metron shook his limbs. His wings had been slashed to ribbons, the fate of all criminal sky-dragons. He lifted his ragged limbs to remove his blindfold. He squinted as if the candlelight caused him pain. His nose wrinkled as tears welled up in his eyes.

"What is that stench?" he gasped.

"Oh, did you notice the tannery?" said Blasphet with a chuckle. "You grow used to it."

Metron looked around, visibly disoriented by the black walls and the candlelight. He stared down at the hide he stood upon, a fellow sky-dragon, and trembled.

"Where are we?" Metron asked.

"My temple," said Blasphet. "Modest, perhaps, but roomier than the dungeons."

Metron shook his head. "So you've found more humans to believe your lies of godhoo—"

Before Metron could complete the thought, Colobi sprang forward and delivered a powerful kick to his gut, her black leather robes spreading wide like the tail feathers of an enormous raven. The old dragon folded over, collapsing, struggling to breathe.

"Give me a knife that I may cut out his blasphemous tongue!" Colobi snarled. Her hood had slipped backward in the attack, revealing a face twisted into naked rage.

"Not just yet," Blasphet said. "I'm curious as to what he was doing traveling toward the College of Spires."

"I-I've been banished for assisting you," Metron said, his voice faint as he rocked in pain from Colobi's blow. "I'm no longer High Biologian. Other biologians will kill me if they discover me."

"I know," Blasphet said. "Which makes your destination baffling. Half the biologians in the kingdom dwell at the College of Spires. It's not a healthy place for you to be."

"I'm old," Metron said, still lying limp at Blasphet's feet. "This may be the last winter I see on this earth. I've little time left to tell certain truths to… interested parties."

"To your bastard son, you mean," Blasphet said.

"H-how did you—?"

"I'm a god," said Blasphet. "I know things. The whole time that you assisted me in the palace I knew of your little secret. I have a network of spies that provide useful fodder for blackmail. You always gave in so easily it was never required. You proved exquisitely corruptible."

Blasphet motioned to the trio who had brought Metron before him. "Help him rise. Give him shelter and food. We must help this poor lost soul find his son."

"Why, Lord?" Colobi asked, sounding hurt. "Why do you spare this blasphemer?"

"Even a Murder God may know his moments of mercy," said Blasphet. "This pathetic creature has done me no harm. He was useful to me once; you must know I can be kind to those who are kind to me."

Colobi's face softened. Her cheeks blushed pink in response to his words.

"Metron," said Blasphet. "Your journey to the College of Spires would have been in vain. The dragon you seek resides there no longer; he now serves Shandrazel in the palace."

"Truly?" said Metron as he stood, assisted by the women. He winced as he rose; the tatters of his wings were covered with scabs. A dragon's wings were sensitive; Blasphet suspected Metron was in constant agony.

"I know you can enter the palace anytime you wish," said Blasphet. "You may know more of its secret passages than even I. Indeed, your son owes his existence to your knowledge of secret passages, does he not?"

Metron lowered his gaze. "I don't wish to discuss the matter."

"I do," said Blasphet. "And we both know you'll eventually do whatever I wish. So, have a seat, Metron. You look weary. The sisters will bring you food and drink and a blanket to help fight the chill. Then, you can tell me your story. I've heard the rumors. But only you can tell me the true origins of Graxen the Gray."

CHAPTER THIRTEEN

UNSEEN MOUTHS WHISPER

BURKE THE MACHINIST stood on a hill overlooking Dragon Forge. The continuous pollution of the foundries had rendered much of the surrounding countryside barren; the red clay soil lay naked, cut through with gullies. Here and there a few particularly tough and ancient trees rose above the landscape, gnarled and defiant. In the low areas sat the camps of the gleaners, shanty towns built around small mountains of scrap metal and refuse. Burke studied the workings of the town at the heart of this desolation, using one of his inventions, the spy-owl. The spy-owl was a copper version of the night bird with large glass eyes, standing almost three feet tall. The big round lenses on its face directed light into a series of carefully crafted mirrors. Burke rested the heavy device upon a tripod. Looking into twin lenses at the back of the spy-owl allowed him to see the goings-on in the town below as clearly as if he were standing in the center square. He studied the doorway of the central foundry, counting the earth-dragons who came and went. Knowing how many dragons it took to keep the foundry in operation was crucial information.

He hadn't created the spy-owl to prepare for war. He'd built it to discover the truth behind the stories of life on the moon. The stories were true; the moon was teeming with cities and lakes and forests beneath the glint of crystal domes miles across. Yet, learning the truth had left him wishing he'd never built the spy-owl. What did the knowledge gain him? The discovery of a world he could never reach filled him with a hunger that could never be slaked.

He looked up from the owl, stretching his back. His daughter, Anza, climbed the hill toward him. Dressed in buckskin dyed black, her dark hair in a tight braid, Anza looked quite formidable. She was a walking armory, with a longsword slung over her shoulder, a dagger strapped to her shin, an array of throwing knives on small scabbards lining each bicep, and two steel tomahawks at her belt. Of course, even without all this weaponry, Anza was a woman who'd earned the fearful respect of men back at the tavern. She could silence anyone with a glance.

Burke didn't know why Anza had never spoken; she wasn't deaf. She had a keen mind. She could work calculations in her head that took him two sheets of paper to solve. She read voraciously, yet she'd never taken up a pen to write. She spoke to him with a few dozen hand signals that she'd devised while still in diapers. Everything else she had to say she conveyed with her eyes.

She nodded toward the spy-owl as she reached him. He stepped back to let her look inside. She turned the owl, then motioned for Burke to examine her new target. He did so, and found his vision focused on the city gates. He quickly saw what she had noticed without the aid of the spy-owl. The gates were sunk into the dirt. Or rather, over the centuries, the grime and dust of the city had built up and covered the lower parts of the gates. Burke guessed the bottom two feet of the doors were buried.

"I'm not surprised those gates haven't closed in centuries. Walls around towns lost some of their defensive value once the winged dragons took over the world," Burke said. He moved the spy-owl around, studying further details of the walls. "This place was built by humans before the ninth plague, when the biggest threat was still other people. That plague gave the dragons their opening; they flourished as mankind withered. Human numbers have built back up, but we've never truly thrived again. As you can imagine, this doesn't sit well with folks like Ragnar, who believe they were given dominion of this world by God."

Anza gave him a curious look.

"Don't worry that you don't know. I deliberately haven't told you much about God, the Great Spirit, or whatever. I felt there were other educational priorities for you than the study of invisible men who live in the sky."

She frowned slightly. She glanced toward the horizon, to the exact spot where the moon would be rising in a few hours.

"No, it's nothing like that," said Burke. "The men on the moon are real. Even if they weren't, people aren't going out and launching wars to please them. No one has ever been killed because of the moon men."

Anza pursed her lips. She made a stabbing motion, like she was driving an invisible dagger into someone's belly, then tilted her head, inviting further explanation.

"No," said Burke. "I'm not saying it's wrong to kill, if you've got a good reason: self-defense, financial gain, political advantage, or even just to stay in practice. Killing for a rational purpose is fine. Killing because you think it will make an invisible man in the sky treat you kindly when you're dead is deranged."

Anza nodded, finally clear on his point. Then she looked down the hills and gave a disgusted wrinkle of her nose. Her eyes said, "Look who's coming." Her nose said, "Ragnar."

"Speaking of deranged," Burke mumbled.

A chill wind rushed over the hill as Ragnar, prophet of the Lord, walked toward them. A whistling moan rose from the rust heaps in the valley below. Burke shivered within the folds of his heavy woolen duster. Ragnar, clothed only by his sunburned, leathery skin and a mane of wild hair, looked blissfully insensate to the cold. Bliss was perhaps exactly the right word, thought Burke. Ragnar's eyes were permanently narrowed in an angry expression, yet Burke was slowly starting to see the man underneath this mask of rage. The true dominant quality of the prophet wasn't his anger but his serenity, a calm, faithful confidence that came from his absolute certainty that every breath he breathed had been waved across his lips by the fingers of God. It wasn't that Ragnar wasn't angry, boiling with vengeance and wrath—he was simply at peace with this rage.

"What have you learned with your magic bird?" Ragnar asked as he drew near.

Anza moved to Burke's left side then retreated several yards, so that she was no longer directly downwind from the prophet.

"The first thing I've learned is that earth-dragons are uniformly near-sighted," said Burke. "If they see anything more than shadows and shapes past fifty yards, I've found no evidence of it."

"How can you tell?" Ragnar asked.

"For one thing, I've been up here two hours without anyone but the human gleaners glancing my way."

"My spies are moving among the gleaners," said Ragnar. "I want to learn how loyal they are to the dragons."

"I don't think loyalty is a virtue gleaners hold in high regard," said Burke. "They make their living destroying relics that could teach us much about the days when humans ruled the world. I personally don't trust them."

"Do you fear they will betray our presence?" Ragnar asked.

"Maybe," said Burke. "We *are* going to mess with their livelihood. Fortunately, gleaners aren't noted for their bravery. I can't imagine they'll take up arms against us. Once we control the forge, they won't care who they're selling their junk to. Not that we'll be needing to buy much from them. We can pour for weeks just by melting down all the armor and weapons cluttering up the place."

"My men need those weapons," said Ragnar.

"The armor doesn't fit right, and swords and axes are poor weapons to fight the winged dragons. If you want to win, let me outfit your army properly. We need bows more than swords."

"Many of my men already have bows," said Ragnar.

"At Conyers, longbows weren't enough," said Burke. "The sun-dragons can fly above their range. From that height, anything a dragon drops turns into a weapon. At Conyers, they'd fly overhead and drop bucket-loads of steel darts, only a few inches long, weighing barely an ounce. You couldn't really see the darts as they fell, only a dark shadow released by the dragon's claws as they zoomed over you. One minute, the walls are full of archers, vainly firing arrows at dragons out of reach. The next minute, half your archers are dead, ripped to shreds by the dart swarm."

"Now you admit to being at Conyers," said Ragnar.

Burke placed a hand on Anza's shoulder. "Go back to camp," he said.

Anza gave him a worried glance. She detected something in his tone, perhaps.

"I'll be fine," he said.

Anza walked away, slowly at first, then breaking into a sprint. He was envious of her energy, the way her body seemed so light. She bounded down the hill with the grace and speed of a doe.

"You shouldn't have brought your daughter," Ragnar said. "War is no place for a woman."

"Anza is better trained than any of those farmers you've pressed into service. With a hundred like her, I could take this fortress and hold it against every dragon in the world."

"You wouldn't succeed unless it was the will of the Lord," said Ragnar. "He cannot look kindly upon the fact you allow your daughter to dress in such tight clothing. Did the ancient race of the Cherokee always permit its women to dress like whores?"

Burke flicked his wrist, triggering the spring-loaded knife he had in his sleeve. In a flash, he buried the razor tip in the prophet's beard, stopping the second he felt the blade graze flesh.

"You call yourself a prophet," said Burke, his voice trembling. "Can you see what I'm going to do if you insult my daughter again?"

Ragnar's lips curved into a smile. His eyes kept the look of frustrating serenity that tempted Burke to give his blade one last push.

"You've brought bad times upon us, prophet," Burke said, trying not to shout. "You're about to unleash a war. A lot of people are going to die. Cities will be burned. No crops are going to be planted in the spring and by next winter men everywhere will starve. We might see the dawn of the tenth plague, thanks to you. This is a tremendous burden of misery I could spare the world right now by slitting your damned throat."

Ragnar's expression changed from serenity to outright glee. "War!" he said. "Plague! Famine! Death! These things you fear are the Four Horsemen of the Apocalypse. Kill me if you wish; you cannot halt their ride!"

The blade Burke held was among the finest he'd ever machined. It was sharp enough to shave with. The prophet's leathery hide wouldn't even slow it. Burke saw madness in Ragnar's eyes, horrible visions dancing in their black centers. Looking into this darkness, Burke remembered the battle of Conyers with perfect clarity. The deadly rain of darts had been nothing compared to what had happened next. The sun-dragons had dropped onto the fleeing and broken survivors and tore them, simply tore them, ripping flesh from bones with as little effort as a man might use to tear the husk from an ear of corn. Did he want to witness that nightmare again?

No.

And Ragnar was his best hope of never seeing it replayed.

His hand trembled as he pulled the knife away.

"I don't like you," said Burke. "I don't believe in your God. I don't believe in your prophecies. But you have an army. In a few days, you'll have a foundry. I need both of these things if I'm ever going to show the dragons why humans once ruled this world. Twenty years of nightmares have given me a very strong incentive to plan the right way to fight an army of dragons. I know the weapons we'll need; I know the training we'll require; I know the tactics and strategies we'll follow. I can win this war, but only if you obey me."

"I'm the chosen of the Lord," said Ragnar. "I obey his orders alone."

"Damnit, no!" Burke shouted, throwing up his arms. "That's exactly what I'm talking about. You aren't going to win by obeying the voices of your invisible friend. If you want even a slender hope of surviving this, I have to be the only voice you listen to. Your mob can take Dragon Forge through sheer brute force, but can they hold it? The sun-dragons will come and take it back from you. I have a plan to defeat them. It's going to require turning a hundred of your farmers into foundry workers in the span of a few hours. It's going to mean that I'm the one mind that will guide their hands in building weapons that you can't even imagine. If we're fast enough and lucky enough, the dragons that fly over us will be slaughtered. Their blood will rain from the sky. Our biggest logistical problem will be clearing the carcasses from the streets before they rot."

Ragnar looked toward Burke's spy-owl. He walked over, lowered his head, and looked into the lenses. He moved the owl on the tripod with surprising confidence and dexterity. For several long minutes, he silently studied the city.

At last, he pulled away. His face was blank; for the first time, there was no hint of anger, no trace of insane joy. For the first time since Burke had met him, Ragnar appeared lost in thought.

"It wasn't the Lord that guided me to you, Kanati," Ragnar said. His voice had lost its normal prophetic vibrancy. With the madness gone from his eyes, Burke realized how much younger Ragnar was than himself. There was something boyish and innocent about him. "When I was a child, my father told me you were the smartest man he'd ever known. He said if the others had listened to you instead of Bitterwood, they might have won."

"We'll never know," said Burke. "We made the choices we made. Bitterwood's plan wasn't a horrible one. We just didn't know what we were up against. No one at Conyers had ever faced an army of sun-dragons. The normal way of the world is for men to waste their energies fighting men, and dragons to focus their aggression on other dragons. We didn't have the experience we needed to plan for victory. Now, some of us have it. Bitterwood, I hear, has been fighting a one-man guerrilla campaign ever since. It's not a bad strategy if all you want to do is make dragons suffer. But you need a smarter plan if you want humans to once again rule at least a patch of this world."

"An unseen mouth whispers that you have that smarter plan, Machinist," said Ragnar, with a sly grin. Some of the heaven-sent madness again flavored his speech. "A rain of blood. Carcasses filling the street. You have the soul of a prophet."

"I have the mind of a man who's seen too much," said Burke, shaking his head. "I wish you'd died in the Free City, Ragnar. But, since you didn't, I'll make the best of a world with you in it. I pride myself on understanding reality. You're my reality now."

"I shall spread the word," said Ragnar. "My army will obey you as they would me."

"Good. Before we take the city, I need twenty men, your brightest. I've been canvassing your mob and have a few candidates in mind. I've got plans sketched out, diagrams. I need to teach them the what, why, and how of the items we'll be manufacturing. They'll be the foremen who lead the rest of the workers when we take the town. With the right advance work, we can pour metal within hours of taking the foundry."

"How long will you need?" asked Ragnar.

"Several days. At least a week," said Burke. "There's a lot to cover."

"That's too long to tarry," said Ragnar as he once more looked into the spy-owl. "The earth-dragons may be dim-witted and half-blind, but it's only a matter of time before they realize there's an army encamped mere miles from their fortress."

"Haste will lead to failure," said Burke. "Still, you're right. Every hour we wait is a gamble. The gleaners could betray us; a sky-dragon could fly over. Hopefully from the air your rag-tag army looks like gleaners, but that's probably wishful thinking. Let me get started; I'll teach the men as quickly as possible. Anza can help. I can get the training down to five days. Maybe four. There are tests I've written up. Until I have twenty men who can pass those tests, taking the town will do us more harm than good if the sun-dragons retaliate before we're prepared to fight. The moment we're ready, I'll let you know.

"So be it," said Ragnar. "It's been nearly sixteen years since my parents were killed and I took up preaching the gospel of war. The victory of the Free City has left me hungry to spill more dragon blood; yet, if I must, I can wait a few more days for this feast of vengeance."

Ragnar smiled with the serene rage that Burke found so disquieting. Burke shivered, pulling his collar higher to fight the chill and rising wind.

WHEN ZEEKY WOKE she sensed something was different. The odor and sounds surrounding her had changed. Trisky was gone, as was Adam. The only one with her was Poocher. She reached for the visor, sitting up in the pitch black. She'd been too drowsy to keep her eyes open when Adam had taken her back to his camp. How long had she been asleep?

She froze as she slipped on the visor and the darkness became light. She wasn't alone after all! Leaning against the mine wall across from her stood a tall, broad-shouldered woman in a long black coat. No, not a woman—a man with long white hair and a beautiful, feminine face. He watched Zeeky with an unblinking gaze, smiling as he realized she saw him.

"Sleep well?" he asked with a gentle voice.

"Who are you? Where's Adam?" she asked. Poocher stirred at the sound of her voice.

"Adam was called away. Some trouble with the other members of his squad. He summoned me to take you. I wanted to let you sleep. You've had a tiring journey."

"Are you Gabriel?" Zeeky asked. "Adam said he was taking me to see someone named Gabriel."

"An excellent deduction," said Gabriel.

"You look like the angel in the bible at the church. At least the bible that used to be there. I guess it's burned up now."

"Do you believe in angels?" Gabriel asked.

"Sure," said Zeeky. "Are you one? Is that why you're not breathing?"

Gabriel raised an eyebrow. "Adam told me your perceptions were strong. I didn't fool you at all, did I?"

"If you're an angel, why don't you have wings?"

"Who says I don't?" Gabriel asked. He took off his coat, revealing a bare chest. He was well muscled, yet slender; he looked more like an animated statue than a living thing. He shrugged his shoulders and a pair of golden wings began to sprout, covered in golden feathers. The wings unfolded in an intricate dance, soon reaching several yards in length. He shook his open wings and the metallic feathers sang with the delicate ringing of a thousand tiny chimes.

Poocher sat up. He'd nudged the visor onto his eyes himself and now sat beside Zeeky, staring at the winged man. Poocher grunted.

"I know," said Zeeky. "But maybe angels are supposed to smell that way. It's like summer rain."

"You're a curiously fearless girl, Zeeky," said Gabriel, kneeling down before her. "Adam said you weren't afraid of Trisky. You aren't afraid of the dark. You obviously aren't afraid of me."

"I get scared sometimes," she said. "I got scared in the Free City, when the dragons started killing everyone. I got scared when I saw Big Lick all burned up. Do you know why it got burned? Do you know what happened to my parents?"

"Yes," said Gabriel. "The goddess decided that few people would notice their disappearance at this particular moment. The other villages they traded with would assume they'd been killed by Albekizan's soldiers in his purge of the human race. She needed people to help her learn things. She designed the people of your village to help her study."

"Study what?"

"Ah," said Gabriel, with a grin. "That is a difficult question to answer. The goddess knows almost everything. The few things she doesn't understand aren't going to be easily explained to mortals, not even to a girl as clever as you."

"Adam said the goddess touched me in my mother's belly and changed me. Did she do this to learn something?"

"Of course," said Gabriel. "Everything the goddess does she does in the name of knowledge. The alterations to your mind help bridge the perceptual gap between humans and animals. You see the world with the same sensory openness of a beast, yet still possess the cognitive gifts of a human. You're the harbinger of what the goddess envisions for all future humans."

"What's a harbinger?"

"A forerunner," said Gabriel. "You're the first of your kind. But, you're displaying such promise, I'm certain you won't be the last. We're happy you came back, Zeeky. The goddess was disappointed you weren't with your family."

"If this goddess has my family, will you take me to her?"

"Of course," said Gabriel, offering his hand.

Zeeky placed her fingers into his outstretched palm. Gabriel helped her rise. She could hear things inside him as he moved, soft clicks and purrs that sounded nothing like a normal human body.

"How far away are they?"

"A long way by foot," said Gabriel. "But I know a short cut."

He reached his arms out in a dramatic gesture; his slender fingers grabbed the air. He began to pull, as if at some unseen rope. A rainbow formed where his fingers moved. Poocher squealed and backed away as the arc of colorful light grew, stretching from floor to ceiling.

Zeeky backed away as well. There were terrible sounds coming from the rainbow, distant sobs and moans, the sound of men and women in horrible torment.

Gabriel looked puzzled by her reaction.

"For one so fearless, I didn't expect you to be bothered by a little light," he said.

"Can't you hear it?" she asked.

"Hear what?"

"Those voices," she said, as she backed up all the way against the wall. The cool wet rock dampened her shirt. "All those people. Listen to them. They're hungry and lost and afraid."

"Interesting," Gabriel said, looking at the rainbow arc. "I don't hear anything. No one ever hears anything. There are no sounds in underspace."

"They're not just in the rainbow," Zeeky said, covering her ears. "They're all around us. They're in the air, and in the rocks. It's like the voices of ghosts!"

Poocher paced back and forth, emitting a series of short, soft, panicky squeaks, as if he wanted to erupt into a full blown squeal but was afraid to make the noise.

"If you can hear them, can they hear you?" asked Gabriel. "Can you talk to them?"

Zeeky felt her rising fear suddenly plateau as the question lodged in her mind. She could talk to animals. Could she talk to ghosts as well? Her curiosity overwhelmed her terror.

"Hello?" she cried out. "Hello? Can you hear me?"

At first, the change in the moaning was very subtle. It was difficult to tell if there had been any reaction at all. Yet, perhaps a few of the voices had fallen silent. Some of the ghosts had stopped to listen to her.

"Hello!" she called out again, aiming her voice toward the rainbow. "Is anyone there?"

Now more of the voices grew quiet. One by one, the sobs fell away. The agonized moaning trailed off, to better pay attention.

"My name is Zeeky," she said. "Who are you?"

At first, she could barely hear anything. Then, the whispers rose, repeating her name: "Zeeky... Zeeky... Ezekia..."

The hairs on the back of her neck rose as she realized the ghosts knew her true name.

"Zeeky?" a woman asked. She knew this voice.

"Mama?"

"It's cold here," the woman answered.

"Where are you?" Zeeky asked.

"Where are you?" the woman answered, her voice fading.

"Mama?" Zeeky repeated. "Mama?"

There was the faintest whisper in response, a word just beneath the edge of comprehension, and then the voices were gone.

"I don't hear them anymore," she said. Poocher seemed calmer as well. Had he heard the voices, or just been responding to her fear?

"Extraordinary," said Gabriel. "Opening the underspace gateway creates millions of fine-scale wormholes. Can it be you heard voices from underspace through these tiny rips? The goddess will definitely want to study this further. We must see her at once."

"You keep saying underspace," Zeeky said, crossing her arms, looking stern. "You know I don't know what it means. Are you trying to make me feel stupid?"

"I'm sorry," said Gabriel, with a sincere tone that convinced Zeeky he meant the words. "Underspace, is, well, it's like a world under the world."

"Like this mine?"

"Not quite," said Gabriel. "Perhaps I should say it's a world beside this world. But really, it's more like... hmm. I don't think I can explain it well without using higher math. I'll let the goddess try. She's very good at making things easy to understand."

"All I want to know about underspace is, is my mother there? Is that why I could hear her?"

"Possibly," said Gabriel. "Let's go to see the goddess. She can explain everything."

Zeeky looked down at Poocher, who looked up at her. He shrugged, as if to say, "Too late to turn back now."

Zeeky nodded, and walked toward the rainbow.

CHAPTER FOURTEEN

ENCOUNTERS IN THE NIGHT

S HANDRAZEL HAD COMMANDED Graxen to leave the palace on the second day of the talks and go someplace where he could simply enjoy his day. Graxen would have preferred to stay near the palace in hopes of seeing Nadala again, but an order was an order. Graxen had no true friends to spend time with, so he flew downriver to the brackish swamplands, mentally replaying every word of his conversation with Nadala as he flew. Near the coast, the river swelled so wide it was nearly a bay. Countless fishing villages stood on stilts. Humans by the thousand plied the waters here. Using wide flat boats they harvested shrimp and crabs, oysters and eels, and fish from inch-long anchovies to sharks that rivaled sun-dragons in size. Graxen had grown up in the eternal poverty of a student, but as Shandrazel's messenger his purse was suddenly full. On his trip to Hampton to summon the mayor, he'd glimpsed an item worn by the mayor's wife that seemed as if it would make an appropriate gift for Nadala. Of course, at the time, he didn't have any clue he would ever see Nadala again. Now, he returned to the fishing town, landing on one of the countless docks that edged the harbor, hoping he could find her a gift.

The second he landed on the salted wood, vendors from a dozen nearby shacks began to shout. His first instinct was to ignore them, but to his left a wizened old woman in a yellow scarf thrust her arm into an oak barrel and pulled out a still-living catfish. Graxen's eyes immediately locked onto the fat, blue-gray morsel, nearly two feet in length. The woman held it high with her knotty fingers jammed into the fish's wide mouth. She smiled knowingly as she met Graxen's hungry gaze.

There was no meal more beloved of sky-dragons than raw fish. While the necessities of commerce and transportation meant that most seafood was dried, smoked, or pickled, when the opportunity arose nothing compared to biting into a freshly caught fish, drinking down its living fluids as it struggled against your tongue.

Almost before he knew it, his purse was two coins lighter and his belly was many pounds fuller. His tongue repeatedly flickered across the gaps between his teeth, searching for any remaining essence of the meat that lingered there.

Feeling fat and happy, Graxen moved along the docks, browsing the various wares. He lingered at shops where the local women sold their specialty, tiny flat beads carefully carved from opalescent mother of pearl and shaped into a variety of bracelets, necklaces, belts, and capes.

At last, Graxen found the item he sought. It was a belt made of the pearly shells, with each bead carved into the shape of a curved sword. The hips of a sky-dragon were similar in size to the hips of a human female. He tried it on himself and found it fit snugly, given that his belly was swollen with fish. He knew Nadala wouldn't be allowed to wear it openly; indeed, she might find the gift trivial and pointless.

Still, Graxen couldn't resist. The belt was a lovely thing made from blades; Nadala was a lovely thing who used blades. He could write her a letter explaining the symbolism. Or, would that be insulting her intelligence? Every time he thought about the contents of the letters he wanted to write her, his mind quickly locked as doubts and possibilities slid against one another and ground to a halt.

The hours he'd spent in Hampton resisting the pitches of hawkers left him weary by mid-afternoon. The flight back to the palace felt especially long. He wondered if Nadala would be standing guard. It was nearly nightfall when he caught sight of the palace. The first things that captured his attention were several earth-dragon guards rushing back and forth in the courtyard. The fringes on the back of his neck rose as he sensed something terrible had happened in his absence.

Graxen swooped into the Peace Hall and found a chaotic scene. Humans were shouting at humans in one corner of the room, biologians were bickering in an opposite corner, and the valkyries were nowhere to be seen. Charkon and the other earth-dragons were filing from the room. Charkon glanced back with a look of disgust in his one good eye as Graxen's claws touched down on the marble. For an instant, Graxen wondered if his arrival had somehow offended the elderly earth-dragon; it took a few seconds to realize the disgust wasn't directed at him, but toward the bickering humans.

Shandrazel looked glum as he sat perched on the golden cushion at the head of the room. All the optimism and energy that normally animated him had vanished. Behind him, a tapestry depicted the face of his father, Albekizan, glowering down at the room. The emerald-green threading of the eyes shimmered against the blood-red scales, making the eyes look almost alive.

"Sire," Graxen said, approaching Shandrazel. "What has transpired? Did Blasphet attack again?"

"No," Shandrazel said. "A gang of assassins would be relatively easy to deal with. Zorasta and her contingent flew away, saying the talks are over. The humans won't agree on anything, and now even Charkon has left angry. Why is this proving so difficult?"

"What was the point of contention? What caused the crisis?"

"I'll tell you what caused the crisis," the young Bitterwood called out, having noticed Graxen's arrival. The tall blond man looked quite agitated, completely unlike the wise and fatherly friend who had counseled him on how to approach Nadala.

Bitterwood walked before Shandrazel, addressing his words to both Graxen and the king. "Zorasta condones human slavery. She wasn't here to discuss freedom. She wants to keep all men in chains!"

Shandrazel sighed. "That really wasn't the issue being discussed. Zorasta merely proposed that bows be outlawed. It is the weapon of choice for a human to use against a dragon. Her proposal shouldn't have produced such a violent reaction from you humans, if you'd only stopped to consider the point. My brother was killed with a bow, as was my father. It strikes me as a reasonable item to be discussed."

"Are dragons being asked to give up their teeth and claws? Are they being asked to stop flying above us with spears? A bow is the only weapon that gives a human a chance of defense!" The young Bitterwood was shouting in a most disrespectful tone, Graxen thought. Perhaps the matriarch was correct in saying humans couldn't control their emotions.

"There will be nothing to defend against," said Shandrazel, sounding weary, as if he'd repeated the words many times before Graxen's arrival. "Dragons will no longer hunt humans under the new laws. What need do you have for arms that have no use other than killing dragons?"

"Most bows have never been raised against dragons," Bitterwood said. "We use them for hunting, or to—"

"Hunting?" Shandrazel scoffed, incredulous. "Humans plant crops. You fish. You herd cattle and sheep. Hunting plays no real role in your diet."

"You called this meeting to grant humans rights. On the second day you're already talking about taking a right away."

Graxen leaned forward and interrupted the argument. He didn't care whether humans had bows or not. He did care that Nadala might no longer be in the palace.

"Sire, did you say the valkyries flew away? Did they return to the Nest?"

"I assume that is their destination," said Shandrazel.

"With your permission, sire, I'll give chase to their party. Perhaps I can persuade them to return."

"Zorasta doesn't want to return," Bitterwood said. "She arrived wanting to thwart these talks. We should just move ahead without her."

Shandrazel thought the matter over. Graxen waited impatiently, feeling the miles between Nadala and himself growing by the second.

"I doubt you can change her mind, but if you choose to try, I wish you good fortune," Shandrazel said. "Go."

Graxen dashed toward the balcony, the weight of the bead-belt heavy in the satchel slung over his shoulder. If he didn't catch Nadala before she made it to the Nest, he might never see her again. Though he was already tired from his trip to the coast, he threw himself into the air beyond the balcony and beat his wings with all his strength, flying as fast as he had ever flown before.

GRAXEN NEVER CAUGHT sight of Nadala and her party as he chased after them. He'd hoped that a group of armored sky-dragons might stop frequently to rest. Despite sky-dragons' prowess in the air, flying could be an exhausting endeavor. While a dragon with Graxen's youth and stamina might cover a hundred miles without stopping for rest or water, the average sky-dragon seldom put their endurance to the test. Flying to the point of exhaustion was dangerous—a muscle cramp striking a human runner might cause a stumble; a similar seizure in a dragon even a few dozen feet above the earth could prove fatal. Combined with the facts that male sky-dragons often led sedentary lives of study, and female sky-dragons seldom strayed out of sight of the Nest, this meant that most sky-dragons broke long journeys into smaller flights of ten or twenty miles at most.

Unfortunately, while the need to rest apparently wasn't slowing the valkyries, Graxen himself was trembling with weariness. When he'd returned to the palace, he'd already flown over three hundred miles that day. Adding another hundred fifty to it meant that as he neared Dragon Forge he was pushing a limit he'd never fully tested. At what point would his wings simply fail?

His heart wanted nothing more than to see Nadala again, but his mind was wracked with doubt. He was too late. If they'd already made it to the island, there would be fresh guards preventing his entrance. His earlier stunt of invading the island was one he doubted he could duplicate. He'd caught the guards unaware, and surprised them with his speed. Now that they knew how fast and agile he was, they would take no chances, and simply overwhelm him with numbers.

His lungs burned. His shoulders felt as if the muscles were riddled with fish hooks, tearing deeper with each flap of his wings. The day was now long gone, and he found it difficult to judge his distance above the earth in the dark. Several times he'd been forced to pull upward as he discovered himself only a few feet above the treetops.

Ahead, he could see the glow of the foundries, still some miles distant. The air carried the faint trace of burning coal, which mingled with the more woodsy smoke of the hundreds of campfires dotting the landscape beneath him. Graxen grew curious. He knew that human gleaners lived near Dragon Forge, but were they truly so numerous? The campfires below spread across the hilly landscape for the better part of a mile. Was this some human festival he was unaware of?

Curiosity combined with his exhaustion finally drove Graxen to find a place to land. His keen eyes located the main road beneath him. His wings wobbled as he attempted to hold them steady. The ground came up faster than he'd anticipated and his hind-talons buckled as they slammed against the hard-packed earth. He tumbled tail over snout, skidding to a halt on ground worn bare by generations of travelers. He landed on his back, his wings spread limply to his sides.

Dragons didn't normally lie upon their backs, but Graxen found the position unexpectedly comfortable. He stared up into the stars, which twinkled softly behind the haze of smoke. Rocks polished by countless footsteps pressed into his shoulders and hips, but this discomfort was outweighed by the relief of absolute surrender to gravity after a long day in the air. He felt as if it would be a welcome sensation simply to sink deeper into the earth.

He closed his eyes, feeling lost and alone. What was he doing out here in the darkness, pushing himself beyond all safety and sanity on such a hopeless mission?

"Nadala," he whispered. "Where are you?"

He listened to the night, as if expecting a reply.

There was a crunching sound from the nearby brush. Someone was moving. Several someones. Humans? They sounded like human males as they spoke in soft hisses. Graxen could only catch every other word: *Dead? Fell. Spy? Kill?*

Realizing there was the very real possibility that he was the subject of their conversation, Graxen opened his eyes. Why would gleaners be worried about anyone spying on them? Was there some especially valuable chunk of rust left unclaimed this close to Dragon Forge?

Graxen rolled over, his body stiff and protesting. He tried to rise, and found sudden motivation as the nearby whispers turned to shouts.

"Get him!" a man commanded. Footsteps slapped against the ground all around him. In the darkness, Graxen counted two-three-four-five shadows rushing toward him.

Graxen instinctively whipped his tail toward the men. The gambit worked, tripping the man who led the charging quintet. The second human stumbled over the first, dropping a jagged sword as he fell. The third man leapt over his brothers, looking quite athletic and heroic as he sailed through the air, brandishing a pitchfork overhead, preparing to drive the sharp prongs into Graxen's brain.

Graxen jumped forward, leaning toward the man, allowing the pitchfork to pass over his head. The prongs scraped along the scales of his back as he sank his teeth into the man's stomach. The man gave a gurgling howl as Graxen pushed him aside in time to see his fourth assailant swinging a club in a swift arc toward his snout. Graxen jerked backward, the wind from the blow filling his nostrils. He jumped up and flapped his wings, kicking out with his hind-claws, tearing a long and messy strip of flesh from the clubber's rib cage.

The fifth man never reached him, wheeling in the space of a single step to dart back toward the woods shouting, "Spy! A blue one! We need bows!"

The two humans he had tripped were almost back on their feet, though one was still unarmed. Graxen skipped backward, getting clear, before tilting his head up and jumping toward the stars. He wanted to be well out of range before the archers were ready. The adrenaline that surged through him from the brief stint of combat proved a perfect remedy for his exhaustion.

A blue one? thought Graxen, climbing higher. In the dark, all sky-dragons must look alike. He took a deep breath, the oxygen clearing his mind and renewing his spirit. He decided on a new destination. He would no longer try to reach the Nest. But he would find the abandoned tower and rest for the night. When morning came, he would write Nadala her letter.

THE NIGHT TURNED crisp and cold by the time he located the tower. The structure wasn't terribly imposing: four vine-draped walls of ancient red brick, perhaps forty feet high. Back at the palace there were single rooms in which this "tower" could have fit. The walls looked as if a hard wind could topple them. Graxen picked the most solid-looking point on the walls and glided to a landing. His muscles had stopped burning—they'd stopped feeling anything at all. He was numb with weariness.

The tower was built on a square floor plan, about half as wide as it was tall. The roof of the structure had long since caved in. Peering down, he could see in the tangled darkness faint hints of what had once been stairs and wooden floors long succumbed to rot. Dim light seeped through windows lined with jagged shards of glass. Graxen guessed the tower was the handiwork of humans, but what purpose the building had served he couldn't deduce. The landscape surrounding the structure was nothing but wilderness. It was as if the building had wandered off from a more developed setting and gone feral.

As Nadala had described, at the southwestern corner of the building a single stone gargoyle was perched, staring down at the weeds below. Its jaws were opened to reveal lichen-covered fangs, with just enough of a gap between them to allow a folded note to be tucked into the mouth where it would be protected from the elements.

The gargoyle looked like a large cat with a mane, with wings sprouting from its back in a way that made no sense to Graxen. Did this sculpture depict an actual animal? Sky-dragons usually engaged in representational art, depicting creatures and events found in reality. It seemed unsettling to think that someone had deliberately carved an animal that so obviously had no place in the physical world. What kind of mind would be moved to construct such an impractical hybrid?

However, the longer he studied the sculpture, the more he felt a sense that it wasn't so alien after all. This thing should not have existed; it was the product of unknown creators that had long since abandoned it to a world that cared nothing of its existence. Graxen placed a fore-talon on the creature's stony mane, suddenly feeling a sense of kinship.

He reached into his satchel and produced a small bound book. Like most biologians, he never traveled without a notebook. He opened it, seeking a sheet of fresh parchment. He produced a jar of ink and a quill made from one of his own feather scales and used the gargoyle's back to form an impromptu desk.

He uncapped the ink, releasing the pleasing aroma of walnut and vinegar. He dipped the quill into the jar, and then placed the tip against the parchment.

He stood there without moving a muscle, the seconds passing into minutes, the minutes building into what must surely have been an hour, unable to scribble the first letter. His mind became a maze that not even the simplest thought could navigate.

Dearest Nadala? Dear? Was "dear" a presumptuous greeting for a soldier who was still in so many ways a stranger? Perhaps just start with her name. Nadala? Was Nadala spelled n-a-d-a-l-a? It sounded like it should be spelled that way. But Graxen sounded like it should be spelled g-r-a-k-s-i-n, and it wasn't.

Part of him wanted to toss aside all caution and fear. Beloved Nadala? No, that bordered on insanity. Love was an emotion of sun-dragons and humans; as a verb it was normally employed by sky-dragons only when discussing books. What was he doing here? This was an exercise in futility. A sane dragon would go to sleep and reconsider this whole matter in the morning. Of course a sane dragon wouldn't have flown so far in the darkness, beyond all exhaustion and hope. He'd already established his lack of sanity. My darling Nadala? Perhaps he should let her see the madness that consumed him. If she became frightened, so be it. Better she should know the truth.

He noticed, as the night grew ever colder, that he was shivering.

He remembered the first words he'd said to her.

He wrote, in shaky, uneven letters, "It's chilly tonight."

A moment later, he ripped the page from the book and crumpled it, before tossing it away. He watched the white ball of paper fall. In the first second of its flight, he realized how much the wad of paper served as an adequate representation of himself—a thing filled with meaningless words, falling through the air toward the litter of the forest floor. If words were written and never read did the words ever exist?

The paper fell in a slight arc away from the wall for a few more seconds. Inches from the ground, a large dark shape swooped in and snatched the paper from its fall. The leaves on the forest floor swirled as the winged creature pulled up from its dive. Graxen's heart skipped as the dark shape took on recognizable form, a beat of long blue wings pushing it higher, up above the roof of the building. The stars were suddenly blotted by the distinctive profile of a sky-dragon passing overhead.

The dragon swerved and spun, dropping down to a landing crouch on the opposite corner of the building. Even in the darkness, he recognized her scale patterns, her sleek and symmetrical muscula-ture. She had shed all her armor and carried only a small leather pouch hanging from a cord around her neck.

"Nadala?" he asked, feeling as if he might have slipped into a dream.

Nadala didn't answer. She unfolded the crumpled ball of paper and studied it. Her brow wrinkled.

"It's chilly tonight?" she said. "Perhaps, in your future letters, you can write of more significant top-ics than the weather?"

"I... in all fairness, I had discarded that," he said. "I've yet to write your true letter."

"You've flown all this way without bothering to write the letter first?" she asked.

"I didn't know you would be here," he said.

"I didn't know you would be here," she said, "but I wrote you a proper letter before I arrived." She patted the leather pouch with her fore-talon.

"I was hoping to catch your party before you made it to the Nest," he explained. "I gave chase, wanting to convince Zorasta to return."

"She'll go back eventually," said Nadala. "Our leaving will throw the talks into chaos. Shandrazel will expend much of his diplomatic capital convincing Zorasta to take part. Then, just as he gives up and proceeds without her, Zorasta will return to the talks and once more obstruct the process. She can delay progress for months, even years with this tactic."

"Why?" Graxen asked. "Why obstruct Shandrazel's reforms?"

"The matriarchy has an interest in maintaining the status quo. Zorasta will not permit radical changes to the world order."

"How strange," said Graxen. "All my life, I've craved change. I honestly don't care what the consequences will be if Shandrazel succeeds in creating a new form of government. I simply welcome a tomorrow that I know will be different than today. I welcome a world where nothing can be truly thought of as permanent."

Nadala flapped her wings and hopped to the same wall Graxen stood on, though still keeping her distance. "Would you truly embrace that?" she asked. "A world where nothing is permanent?"

"Some things must be permanent, I suppose," he said. "The sun will continue to rise and fall for all eternity; the moon will forever wax and wane among the stars. Ten thousand years from now, the ocean waves will still beat against the sand, and crickets will still chirp through summer nights. But I won't be here to see these things, and all the books of the biologians will have long since crumbled to dust. We already live in a world in which we're not permanent; to believe otherwise seems to require the willing embrace of an obvious untruth."

"Ah," said Nadala. "You have a flair for poetry after all. These are the sorts of words you should put in your letters."

"Wouldn't reflections on our impermanence be a depressing topic for a love letter?" asked Graxen.

"Oh," she said, with a coy tilt of her head. "Are they love letters now?"

Graxen was too tired to be flustered. The word had slipped out; there was no point in pretending otherwise.

"From the moment I saw you, it's been love," he said, looking at her directly.

"You're lying," she said, hopping closer. "The first moment you saw me you wondered if I was going to kill you."

"True," he said, still meeting her gaze. His exhaustion and her presence had left him feeling slightly drunk. Words that he couldn't have imagined uttering earlier now spilled out of him. "But I felt love from the moment you chased after me to return my satchel. Your kindness was more than I expected or deserved. The grace of your act made the world a more hopeful place."

"It's a lucky thing I missed when I tried to skewer you, then."

"If you had killed me, you would only have been doing your duty."

"If my sisters discovered me here with you, they would kill us both. Would you still be so forgiving in the name of duty?"

"I know you're taking a risk in coming here," he said. "Yet, you did come. Why?"

"Because I too crave change," she said, looking down into the tangled darkness in the tower's interior. "What you said about impermanence, about how we won't be here in ten thousand years... these words resonate with me. What does a valkyrie's pledge to duty matter when the years will eventually wash away even her memory? The only slim thread of immortality in this world is to produce offspring, and hope that they will produce offspring. Perhaps some small echo of the self will endure through the ages."

"I'll never produce offspring," said Graxen. "Perhaps this is why I've come to my views on impermanence."

Nadala flapped her wings once more, hopping directly beside him. She was close enough that he could smell her, a soapy scent, sandalwood and rosewater. She'd apparently had the opportunity to bathe after her return to the Nest. Graxen suddenly felt unclean, his hide sticky and musky.

She leaned her head close to his, her nostrils wide as she breathed in his scent.

"I like the way you smell," she said, closing her eyes, her voice sounding dreamy. "There's something primitive about it. Bestial. Beneath the veneer of culture, we are, in truth, only animals."

"There's nothing bestial about the way you smell," Graxen said, his mouth hovering over her scales. "It's the scent of a civilized being, a smell like architecture and music."

"Oh, that must definitely go in your letter."

She opened her eyes and their gazes locked. Their nostrils were so close together they were breathing each other's breath. They stood facing for a long silent moment, he inhaling as she exhaled, she reciprocating an instant later. The air passing between them was hot and humid. They were sharing the very essence of life itself.

She leaned her snout against his and pushed. Their cheeks rubbed against each other with a slow, firm pressure. Her smooth scales were the perfect surface for his own scales to rub against, the most satisfying thing that had ever touched his hide. She continued to slide along him, her cheek slipping along his neck, until their shoulders met and each had their head nestled against the other's spine. Her aroma left him dizzy; the warmth of her skin and the firm yet yielding texture of her muscles beneath caused a thousand tiny storms to erupt within him. He felt full of lightning—energized, but also on the verge of being torn apart.

At the thought of being torn apart, he pictured Nadala's fate if they were discovered by other valkyries.

"We can't do this," he whispered. "I don't care if your sisters rip me to shreds; if they harmed even a scale on you I couldn't live with myself."

"We can't do this," she whispered back. "But not because I fear death. I don't. I've always been willing to die for a cause. Now I'm willing to die for you."

"Oh," he said, feeling the storms within him raging even stronger. "Then I guess we *can* do this."

"No," she said, pulling back, stepping away from him. The sudden absence of her warmth left him shivering. "We can't do this because I don't know how."

Graxen was confused. "You don't know how to love?"

"No," she said. "I mean, yes, I believe I know how to love. Perhaps. I don't know what love is; it's more the domain of poets than warriors. I only know that I want you more than I've ever wanted anything."

Graxen was now even more confused. "Then, what, exactly, is it that you don't know how to do?"

Nadala looked away demurely. She said, in a low voice. "I mean, I haven't had training. In reproduction."

"Oh," he said.

"Those initiated in the process are under strict vows of secrecy," she explained. "But perhaps the biologians...?"

"No," Graxen sighed. "I've heard... whispers. But I've never received an education in these matters either."

"Then we're shackled by our ignorance," she said, sounding bitter. "That veneer of culture I mentioned has separated us from our animal natures."

Graxen nodded. "Perhaps we could simply proceed and let our instincts guide us?"

Nadala shook her head. "It may be just stories meant to frighten us, but I've been told that mating without the proper training can lead to injury. I want you, Graxen. I just don't know what to do with you."

"I, um, am very good at research," Graxen said, thinking of the Grand Library back at the palace. Certainly some biologian had recorded the technical details of reproduction among those countless tomes. "I'll return once I learn the details."

"How long will this take?" she said.

"A few days, perhaps?" he said. "That should be time enough..."

"I don't know if I can wait that long," she said. "I feel as if I'm going to be torn apart by the desires within me."

"I understand better than you think," he said, though the storms within him were fading now that he had put his mind to the thought of research. "I promise to read as quickly as I can."

She wrapped her wings around him, still facing him. It wasn't a correct fitting somehow; their bodies felt pleasant pressed against one another, but somehow mismatched. Whatever the actual reproductive act entailed, Graxen suspected they wouldn't be facing one another.

Wordlessly, she pulled away. Her eyes glistened as she studied him for a long moment, then leapt, straight up, climbing toward the sky.

He thought of the beaded belt in his satchel; the gift could wait for another time. A moment later, a small leather pouch fell from the stars. He caught it in his fore-talon. The satchel smelled like she smelled. He opened it to find a neatly folded square of translucent paper, the black outlines of letters visible through the surface. He didn't open it. He felt so full of Nadala's presence that he wasn't yet prepared to replace the words she'd spoken with the words she'd written. The melody of her voice was still fresh; he would hold onto it as long as he could.

Soon, her dark form vanished into the night. He watched the stars for a long time before spreading his wings and drifting off into the sky, light as hope.

CHAPTER FIFTEEN

BROKEN SKY

JANDRA KEPT A soft, even glow around them as they traveled. They rode in silence through long and twisting tunnels of black rock. Bitterwood sat astride the long-wyrm behind Adam, while Jandra rode Hex. The journey had taken place so far in an uncomfortable silence. Bitterwood and Adam had barely spoken. Jandra was herself an orphan; if she ever met a surviving family member, she couldn't imagine remaining silent. Vendevorex had informed her that her parents had died in a fire while she was an infant, conveniently leaving out for fifteen years the detail that he had been the one who ignited the blaze. Beyond this, she knew nothing of her family. She didn't even know if Jandra was a name she'd been given by her parents or a name Vendevorex had chosen for her. He had told her that the name meant "God is gracious" in some old human tongue, which hinted that he hadn't chosen it. Vendevorex didn't believe in gods. Indeed, he was openly scornful of religions and the supernatural in general.

"The world thinks we are supernatural beings wielding powers drawn from some invisible world," Vendevorex had said when he had first given her the tiara ten years ago and began training her in his art. "In truth, there is nothing supernatural about our abilities. The invisible world we manipulate is the very foundation of what is natural. It is a world of magnetism and light. All matter is an assemblage of infinitesimal building blocks. In time, I'll teach you to manipulate these blocks with the assistance of equally small machines." As he'd spoken these words she'd placed the tiara on her head and her world had changed. She became aware of a fine silver haze that coated every inch of her skin—the residue of Vendevorex's powers. Vendevorex had opened her hand and allowed a trickle of shimmering powder to drift from his foretalon into her palm.

He'd told her, "I will show you wonder in a handful of dust."

She pulled herself from her reverie as the tunnel they traveled through joined with a larger shaft. The shaft was almost perfectly rectangular. She could see from the gouges in the rock that this tunnel had been carved by some machine wielding massive steel teeth. She could still see traces of the iron scraped into the rock, now turned to rust by the ages.

Adam broke the silence. "I've been told this was all carved by men, long ago," he said. "The world wasn't always ruled by dragons."

"The very rocks that surround us disprove you, Adam," Hex said. "The libraries of the biologians are filled with fossils of the giant reptiles that eventually became the dragon races. We inherited the world from these ancestors. The evidence is clear that humans are merely apes who've gained the ability to speak only recently, from a geological perspective. I say that with no malice; it's simply a truth written into stones. A few radical biologists argue that the ruins of the world show evidence of a once dominant human culture. But if your kind was ever more technologically evolved, it must surely have been under the guidance of dragons. If humans were as advanced as some argue, how did they possibly lose control?"

Adam shrugged. "The goddess judged the time of human dominance to be at an end."

"The goddess?" the elder Bitterwood scoffed, his voice low and firm. "We worshipped Ashera in the village of my birth. I was later shown that she was nothing but a block of polished wood. The carving was destroyed and the world carried on. The seasons still changed, the rains still fell, the sun continued to rise. Everything we were taught about her power was demonstrated to be a lie."

Adam didn't look angry at his father's words. He answered in a patient voice, "You saw only an idol of the goddess. The true goddess is the living embodiment of the earth. She's the model for all the statues that have been carved of her, but that is all they are—statues."

Jandra found herself intrigued. Her upbringing had left her certain, despite Adam's eye-witness testimony, that they weren't truly being led to a goddess. Jandra couldn't help but wonder: were they being led to a woman who wielded power similar to her own? Invisibility, command of elements, a healing touch—it wouldn't be too difficult to convince some people that these were the powers of a god.

Vendevorex said he'd stolen the helmet. What if he'd stolen it from her parents? Could it be that this so-called goddess might be related to her? Jandra tried to suppress the thought, knowing it was absurd. And yet... she hadn't simply sprung from dust. She had parents. She had to be related to someone in this world. If she were to ever meet a brother or sister, would she recognize them?

Would she be any less tongue-tied than Bitterwood and Adam?

They walked on in silence once more. Hex slowed his pace slightly. Jandra, astride his shoulders, wondered why he was creating the additional distance between them and the Bitterwoods. Hex twisted his serpentine neck back toward her and said, softly, "I notice you've had little to say to me since I killed that long-wyrm rider."

She was surprised he'd interpreted her silence so effectively. Vendevorex had never known what to make of her quiet moments; Bitterwood and Pet hadn't displayed much skill at it either.

"I don't think it was the killing that bothered me," she whispered back. "It was the way you swallowed him, and then announced that he tasted good. I know that Albekizan used to hunt humans for sport. Did you?"

"Of course," said Hex. "It was part of my upbringing."

"Did you always eat the men you killed?"

"It would have been wasteful not to," he said.

"When I first met you, you denounced the oppression of the weak by the strong. How can you justify eating humans if you truly believe the things you say?"

"I haven't hunted men for sport in thirty years," said Hex. "I didn't hunt that long-wyrm rider; he attacked you, and I acted in your defense. I wasn't making a political statement by eating him. I had meat in my mouth; I swallowed. Pure instinct. I'm sorry that this disturbed you. I'll be more careful in the future."

Jandra again found herself surprised by his words. Dragging an apology out of any other male she'd ever known had been almost impossible.

"I'm not angry with you," she said, realizing that, in truth, she wasn't. "I suppose I've just been having an identity crisis. I grew up among dragons. I've come to think of dragons as my family. It's always a shock when I'm confronted with the reality that I'm human, and that dragons aren't my family, but are, quite possibly, my mortal enemies."

"I'm not your enemy," he said.

"I know," she sighed.

"As long as we're on the subject of enemies, however," Hex said, "is your friend the true Bitterwood? Is he the man that killed my brother and father?"

"Yes," she said.

"Why didn't you tell me?"

"I worried you'd kill him when we met him."

"Would he not deserve it?"

"No," said Jandra. "You yourself said your father deserved his fate. Bitterwood has given me his vow he won't harm you. I don't want you seeking revenge against him."

"Unlike my father, I haven't a vengeful bone in my body," said Hex. "Endless cycles of revenge poison all our cultures, both dragon and human. I do, however, have a strong sense of self-preservation. If your friend so much as looks at me with evil intentions, I won't suffer the least remorse when I bite his head off. However, I will promise not to swallow."

Hex's words sounded loud to her in the relative quiet of the mine shaft. By now, Trisky was several hundred feet ahead of them. Could the Bitterwoods hear their conversation?

BITTERWOOD, ASTRIDE THE long-wyrm behind his long-dead son, listened closely to the whispered voices behind him. Were the sun-dragon's words a ruse? Perhaps Hex was attempting to lull him into lowering his defenses. He sensed that this dragon was craftier than others he'd tangled with over the years.

Bitterwood welcomed this threat so near his back. He'd grown used to the life of the hunt. He'd become accustomed to the daily risk; the knowledge that the next dragon he faced might be the one to spot him at the last second and lunge, faster than he could react. What did it mean that he only felt alive when he faced such danger? When he'd killed Bodiel, he could have put an arrow into his brain on the first shot. Instead, he'd targeted his arrows into non-lethal spots, crippling the giant dragon, leaving him struggling in the mud, slowly bleeding to death. He'd taken his time, savoring Bodiel's anguish. Was he courting death by indulging in such sadism? Was he, in truth, as much a monster as his prey?

The close presence of a potentially hostile dragon gave Bitterwood a welcome distraction from the obvious question of why his son was alive, in service of the goddess, and dwelling beneath the earth.

Adam, perhaps growing tired of waiting for questions that never came, began to answer them.

"I was too young to remember, of course, but I'm told I was discovered by Hezekiah. He found me in the well in Christdale and gave me to the angel Gabriel, who brought me here to the goddess."

Bitterwood's guts twisted at the mention of Hezekiah. "Hezekiah disdained the goddess. And Gabriel isn't associated with the goddess myth at all. You've gotten your religions confused. Gabriel is the Biblical angel who informs Zechariah that his son will be John the Baptist."

"The Bible is a false document. Hezekiah is a false prophet. The goddess created him to play the role of deceiver; she said Eden wouldn't be paradise without a serpent."

Bitterwood saw no point in arguing his son's fractured theology. Adam's tone was that of a true believer. Had Adam inherited this gullibility from him? He'd been deceived by Hezekiah. Adam was correct, at least, in calling Hezekiah a false prophet.

Adam continued, "The goddess told me you were still alive. She said that the fabled Bitterwood that dragons feared so greatly was, in truth, my father. I asked permission to find you. She said I wasn't ready. Now I see that she planned to guide you here all along."

"No one guided me here," said Bitterwood. "No supernatural force, at least."

Adam turned around to face his father. "You've been somewhat argumentative since we met. Have I in some way offended you?"

Bitterwood swallowed. It was impossible to look at his son without seeing the echoes of Recanna. He glanced away as he said, "You've committed no offense. All the sin is mine. I'm sorry."

"There's no sin," said Adam. "You've nothing to apologize for. You didn't know I survived."

"No. I didn't search the village. Hezekiah told me if I didn't repent he would kill me. I fled from Christdale in grief and fear. The only emotion that gave me strength was my hatred. A more loving or courageous man would have stayed to search the ruins and bury the dead. I would have found you had I been a better man."

"You couldn't know," said Adam. "And if Hezekiah told you he would kill you, he would have. While he wore the clothes of a human, he was, in truth, an angel like Gabriel. No human could have stood against him."

"Hezekiah was no angel," said Bitterwood. "It took me years to learn the truth, but he was nothing but a machine. I don't understand his workings, but he was no angel."

"Wasn't he?" asked Adam. "Perhaps angels are machines built by a mind beyond the understanding of men?"

Bitterwood could see no way to argue this point. He was distracted, anyway, by a change in the atmosphere. The rotten-egg stench of the mine was slowly giving way to fresher air. He could smell the faint hint of flowers carried by an underlying brine-tainted breeze.

In addition to the change of scent, the tunnel ahead no longer stretched into dark infinity. A bright square showed the tunnel was leading toward a daylit sky. Twenty minutes later, they came to a ledge awash in warm sunlight.

Hex drew up on the ledge next to Trisky. A valley stretched before them, long and green, untouched by the early winter they had left behind on the surface. A placid lake, its waters deep and blue, filled much of the valley. The odor told Bitterwood the waters were saltwater, not fresh. In its center sat an island speckled with flowers of every color. Thick forests covered the island, the tree branches sagging with fruit. In the center rose the marble pillars of a temple. Bitterwood recognized the structure instantly; it resembled the temple that had stood in his home village, only on a much larger, grander scale.

JANDRA STUDIED THE valley, feeling dizzy as her enhanced senses struggled to catalogue the scents, colors, and sounds before her. The songs of countless exotic birds filled her mind with images—parrot, canary, gull—though the birds were only specks of color in the distance. The walls of the valley were sheer rock covered with vines, stretching so high that it seemed as if the sky was merely a painting resting upon them.

"Daylight!" said Hex, sounding joyous. "I thought we'd never leave that accursed tunnel!" Jandra dug her fingers into his neck fringe as he suddenly bounded toward the edge of the cliff.

"Wait!" shouted Adam. "It's dangerous to fly here!"

"It's dangerous to fly anywhere," Hex answered, as he leapt into space and soared toward the blue above. "Every dragon lives with the knowledge that his next flight could be the one where gravity wins!"

Hex said the words with such defiant joy that Jandra felt joyous herself. Hex seemed utterly fearless as he climbed upward. Jandra clenched her legs tighter around his neck as he spiraled toward the upper reaches of the stone walls and the open sky beyond. The hairs on her neck rose as her eyes began to pick apart the sky racing toward them. Suddenly she realized that the expanse above was mere illusion.

"Watch out!" she shouted, thrusting her right hand forward, willing the blue sky to vanish. As she willed it, the sky obeyed, parting in a wave, revealing the valley to be capped by the same stone as the tunnel, a solid ceiling now mere yards away. Hex twisted in the air, nearly dislodging Jandra. She fought to maintain her hold, grateful for her improved strength and reflexes. Hex had pulled his head back in time to avoid a collision, but there was a terrible jolt as his tail smacked into the stone. He fell toward the water, seemingly in complete surrender to gravity.

Then, Hex's wings caught the air and their descent quickly halted. Hex soared over the lake in a long circle, turning back toward the cliff they'd leapt from. The bright sunlit room was growing dim. The sky continued to ripple like water into which a heavy object had been dropped, the waves growing in violence. In places the sky was ripping, with large fragments of blue sloughing away in sheets. A snow of silver dust filled the air as the sky crumbled, revealing that they were still completely encased beneath rock. A moment later, only a few shards of blue sky still stubbornly persisted, carrying on as if unaware that the illusion was now pointless.

Jandra let some of the silver dust settle on her outstretched hand. They were part of a Light-Emitting Nanite System—a LENS—something she herself knew how to use to create images from light. But, the sky had covered miles... Who could possibly have the concentration to maintain such an illusion?

Hex alighted next to the long-wyrm. It coiled backward, skittish at his approach.

"Steady," said Adam, stroking Trisky's neck.

"What witchcraft is this?" Bitterwood said as he stared wide-eyed at the shattered sky.

"This is no witchcraft," Adam said. "The goddess transformed this cavern into the paradise you see. Have no fear. The sky will repair itself."

Jandra had a hundred questions about the goddess. Before she could ask even one, however, there was an angry shout from the island, loud enough to be heard even though it was miles away.

"My sky! Who broke my sky?"

A woman emerged onto the stone steps of the temple. Jandra again found her eyes confused by the strange perspectives of the cavern. Either the island and the temple were much smaller than she'd judged, or the woman was at least twelve feet tall. The trees around the marble columns must have been half the height Jandra had assumed. The woman looked toward the cliff where Jandra stood. She walked toward them, growing with each step. After two steps, the trees were no higher than her waist. After four steps, they were at her knees. Then, she had left the trees entirely and walked across the lake, her body now hundreds of feet high, her eyes at the level of the cliff where they stood. The lake water dented beneath the woman's footsteps, yet the waters held her.

"The goddess, I presume," said Hex, his body tensing as if preparing to fight.

Jandra suspected Hex had good reason to anticipate combat. The goddess didn't look happy. Her face was mostly human, but her eyes glowed like twin bonfires. Her skin was the color of new spring grass, with her lips a darker, mossy shade. Her hair was a tangle of kudzu, the locks draping down her shoulders to cover the nipples of her otherwise bare breasts. Whether the draping was due to modesty or chance was debatable, however, for there was no such cover for the lower parts of her body. Her pubic mound was a tangle of thick, dark ivy. Her broad feminine hips rested upon shapely legs, long and artful.

In comparison to Jandra's more girlish proportions, the goddess was of a more womanly shape, heavy-breasted and lushly curved. She walked with a hip-swaying gait that Jandra found slightly obscene. As the goddess drew near, the heat radiating from the fury of her eyes caused Hex to step backward. Jandra raised an arm to protect her face. Beside them, Trisky lowered herself to her belly and Adam dove to the ground, pressing his face to the stone in either fear or reverence. Bitterwood had drawn his sword and was crouched low beside the great-wyrm.

"A sun-dragon?" the goddess said, sounding both puzzled and pleasantly surprised. Her voice was powerful yet not overwhelming and, save for its volume, not that different from the voice of a woman of normal size. The flames in the green woman's eyes faded, revealing orbs of a more human structure, albeit still over a yard across. The irises were made of brilliant turquoise. Within the dark circles at the core, stars twinkled in the void.

"I haven't seen one of your kind in my little kingdom in centuries," the goddess said, focusing on Hex and ignoring Jandra. "I've taken precautions to keep you away, in fact. How curious that you overcame your fears to come here."

Hex stepped forward, drawing up into the normal two-legged stance of the sun-dragons. Jandra leapt from his back, not wanting to weigh him down if he was about to do something risky. Hex inhaled, puffing out his chest in a manner that reminded her of Albekizan, and announced, "My name is Hexilizan. I have no fears to overcome; I'm of royal blood. Courage is my birthright."

"Aren't you the bold one?" asked the goddess. "Boldness can be dangerous here, dragon. You've discovered that things aren't always as they seem. I'm curious... How did you break my sky? Mere collision shouldn't have caused such chaos."

"I don't know," said Hex. "I was flying when it parted of its own will."

Jandra stepped around him, facing the goddess, raising her hand in a shy wave.

"Actually," she said, "it was my will. I, um, sensed what it was made of at the last second. I didn't mean to cause so much damage. I just lost control."

The goddess narrowed her eyes. It was difficult to tell due to the scale of her gaze, but it seemed to Jandra that she was focusing on her helmet.

"That is an interesting toy, little one," the goddess said.

"Perhaps we should sit down and talk about toys," said Jandra.

"That could be amusing," said the goddess, the corners of her mouth pulling into what Jandra assumed was a smile. It was difficult to read facial expressions when that face was too wide to take in all at once. "Very well. Meet me at my temple."

After she spoke, her body broke apart, becoming a swarm of insects. Everyone coughed and covered their mouths as whirlwinds of iridescent green bottle-flies spun through the air for several minutes before dispersing.

Afterwards, Adam stood and guided Trisky as she rose. Everyone stared at him, as if expecting him to explain everything with one sentence.

"I told you," he said, with a knowing smile. "The goddess."

CHAPTER SIXTEEN

MERCIFUL

P ET SAT UP, mildly disoriented. He blinked his eyes, feeling as if he'd moved back in time a year to his old life of comfort and privilege. He was in room with a vaulted ceiling and a stained-glass window similar to the ones that had adorned Chakthalla's castle. He was sleeping on a large red silk cushion, the sort of cushions Chakthalla used to sleep upon with him curled up beside her. As he rubbed the sleep from his eyes he remembered he was in Shandrazel's palace. As leader of the human diplomats, he had been granted these plush accommodations.

It was just after dawn judging from the soft light coloring the high windows. He was freezing, naked upon the cushions without an inch of blanket. The thick wool covers were all pulled off to the side of the cushion and wrapped around the slender figure of a sleeping woman. Pet stared at her for a long moment. Who was she? How had she gotten here?

She had her back to him. Her long brown hair was tousled from the night's activities. Pet started to wake her, but his fingers stopped inches from her shoulders. He decided to let her sleep. He couldn't recall her name, but the memory of meeting her was beginning to resolve from his mental fog. After the fiasco of the previous day's talks, when the valkyries had stormed out, Pet had decided it was time to get out of the palace and run far, far away. He'd only made it as far as Richmond when he'd decided to fortify his resolve with an ale or two at the local tavern. A trio of musicians had been performing and the girl beside him had been their flute player. He recalled how she reminded him of Jandra in the color of her hair and the shape of her jaw. Yet, while Jandra was never impressed by anything Pet did or said, this girl had been quite enamored by Pet's claims that he was an advisor to Shandrazel. He vaguely remembered inviting her back to his room, deciding he could put off fleeing the talks at least one more day. His memory grew cloudier after that. In truth, he hadn't drunk enough to affect his memory, though it was possible she had—she'd accepted his generosity in buying rounds readily enough.

Pet suspected the real reason he couldn't remember the further details of their encounter was that he'd simply found it boring. His true pleasure in seduction came in the early stages, when women were attracted by his smile, his wit, and his fine breeding. The sun-dragons who found it fashionable to keep humans as pets engaged in selective breeding to exaggerate certain desired traits. Pet's lineage was that of a purebred, and he enjoyed being admired for his physical perfection.

Pet rose and went to the mirror. His body was a work of art; he knew that women enjoyed feasting upon him with their eyes, and more. It was the rare woman who could resist reaching out to touch his flowing golden locks, or feel his broad and well-formed shoulders. He was proud of his appearance, and took care with his diet and exercise to hone its finest details. His face possessed the same perfection. He paid attention to the smallest items that could detract from his appearance. He tried to maintain even numbers of eye lashes, for instance, and was ferocious in seeking and snipping any split ends in his hair. He possessed an array of fine brushes he used to clean and polish his teeth after every meal; he even washed his tongue three times daily to ensure the freshness of his breath.

Yet, staring into the reflection of his brilliant blue eyes, Pet wondered if all his outer perfection had left him tarnished on the inside. He'd witnessed purebred dogs. The prettier the breed, the crazier they tended to be. Had breeding him for physical perfection left him with a damaged personality? He frequently seduced women he didn't truly desire. He only wanted Jandra, he suspected, because she didn't want him. Was this perverse? To impress her, he'd repeatedly risked his life. This couldn't be healthy. And as irrational as his behavior was around Jandra, his actions around dragons were becoming outright insane. Why had he yelled at Shandrazel over the whole bow thing? What did he care if men had bows? Perhaps his long years of subservience to sun-dragons had left him with a pent-up need to yell at one?

Or perhaps he could only summon passion when he was pretending to be someone else. He embraced the role of Bitterwood because the man was a hero.

Pet was only, well, a pet. He was the exact philosophical opposite of a hero. If he were honest with the other humans at the talks, he would tell them what he truly believed: humans would have better lives if they just worked harder to make dragons happy. Treat a dragon with flattery and obedience, as he had Chakthalla, and you would be rewarded with a life of ease.

Would he dare march into the Peace Hall and speak the truth to his fellow men?

He sighed, shaking his head. If the truth ever came out of him, they'd lynch him. Better to be praised for a lie than hanged for the truth.

Feeling he'd had his fill of introspection for the day, he dressed himself quietly and crept from the room, careful not to wake his guest.

As PET ENTERED the Peace Hall for the third day of talks he noticed that the room seemed empty. None of the dozen sun-dragon representatives had arrived yet. Shandrazel, Charkon, and Androkom were huddled together in conference. A few of Pet's fellow humans were gathered across the room, murmuring among themselves, looking worried. Only a handful of the biologian representatives were present, and there was no sign that the valkyries had returned.

Pet bypassed the humans and walked straight to Shandrazel. The giant dragon looked agitated. Before Pet reached the throne pedestal, a trio of earth-dragon guards stepped into his path, blocking him. They barked out, "Halt!"

Pet stopped, confused. "Are you new or something? I'm supposed to be here."

"No humans are to approach the king!" one of the guards snarled, lowering his spear until the point was aimed at Pet's neck. "Any closer and we'll run you through!"

Fortunately, the commotion caught Shandrazel's attention. "Lower your weapons!" he commanded. "I gave no such order!"

"I did," Androkom said. The High Biologian was less than half Shandrazel's size, but somehow this morning he looked more composed and in charge than the young king. "I felt it would be a logical precaution."

"A precaution against what?" Pet asked as the guards lowered their spears.

"It may be nothing," said Shandrazel. "But, during the night—"

"During the night all of the sun-dragon representatives vanished," Androkom said.

"What do you mean, vanished?" said Pet. The word "vanished" had taken on subtle shades of meaning ever since he met Jandra. Just because something couldn't be seen didn't mean it wasn't there anymore.

"No messages were left," said Shandrazel. "And there were no signs of struggle. I've sent out members of the aerial guard to try to—"

"We believe it was the work of Blasphet," said Androkom, sounding impatient. "And there *are* signs of struggle; there are seven dead earth-dragon guards."

"I meant we've found no signs that any of the sun-dragons were harmed," Shandrazel said.

"The guards died from puncture wounds crusted with black poison," said Androkom.

"The sisters attacked again?" Pet asked. "Why didn't anyone hear them? They were so vocal last time."

"No one heard anything," said Shandrazel. "We still have more questions than answers."

"It doesn't make sense," said Pet. "I mean, yes, they could sneak in during the night and kill some guards. But how could they kill a dozen sun-dragons without making a sound? What could they have done with the bodies? I don't see how the Sisters of the Serpent could be responsible for this. Maybe the sun-dragons learned that Blasphet had assassins in the palace once more and fled?"

Charkon, the boss of Dragon Forge, who had been listening patiently, cleared his throat.

"Sire," the elderly dragon said. "Blasphet remains on the loose and you are unable to protect even your own castle. I regretfully must withdraw from these talks. My duty to my brethren at the forge must be my first concern. When you've established security in your kingdom, I'll come back."

"Charkon, you're the wisest of earth-dragons," said Shandrazel. "If Blasphet is planning some master scheme, I would find your presence at my side most helpful. Since Kanst died, my armies have been without a field commander. I'd like to offer you this position."

"Sire?" Charkon said, his one eye opening wide. "No earth-dragon has ever held such rank. It is the birthright of sun-dragons to fill such roles."

"Those are the old ways, Charkon. From this day forward, positions will be filled not by birthright, but by merit. No one can surpass you in experience and judgment, noble Charkon. You've fought in countless battles, and proven yourself a worthy leader as boss of the forge. I can think of no better candidate."

Charkon raised a thick paw to scratch at a patch of flaky flesh just behind the scar-tumor where his eye had once been. He looked lost in thought.

"It will be my honor," said Charkon. "I'll start by increasing security here in the palace. You've allowed the gates to be too open. Humans are coming to and fro with impunity."

"Humans who were invited to these talks," said Pet, bothered by Charkon's tone. "However Blasphet's assassins are getting in, I don't think they're walking through the front door. Beefing up security at the gates is pointless."

"You would say that... human." Charkon stepped close to Pet, his eye narrowed into a thin slit. "I'm not making accusations. But the ease with which the sisters pass suggests that they must have inside help."

"And you're saying that I—"

"I'm saying that your loyalties lie with humans, and the Sisters of the Serpent are human."

"Charkon," said Shandrazel. "Your theories have been noted. Your desire to improve security is reasonable. Do what you must; however, the free movement of the human diplomats must be allowed. I trust you'll find an appropriate solution."

Charkon punched his gauntleted fist to his steel breast plate with a loud clang. "At once, sire," he said before marching from the room. The contingent of armored dragons who traveled with him followed. Once in the hall, Charkon began to bark out commands.

Shandrazel sighed wearily. He was still a young dragon, no older than Pet, but recent events were taking their toll. The skin around his eyes was puffy, as if he hadn't been sleeping well. He slouched on his golden cushion, and the feather-scales of his wings weren't groomed as well as they should be. He sounded on the verge of despair as he said, "My father kept Blasphet imprisoned for over a decade. Why am I so powerless to halt his schemes?"

Pet searched for the words to console the sun-dragon. "It was your father who set Blasphet loose, and then gave him an army of construction workers to build the Free City. Blasphet could have constructed a score of secret entrances with the resources at his command."

"Perhaps," said Shandrazel. "Yet I could have ended his threat. I could have ordered his execution."

"Why didn't you?" Pet asked.

"I don't believe that death should be used as punishment," said Shandrazel. "I know of innocent dragons accused of false crimes and slain by my father for political gain. I wanted to break with the past, and put an end to executions."

"That's a noble goal," said Pet. "But perhaps, for Blasphet, you can make an exception."

"Perhaps not just for Blasphet," said Shandrazel. "The events of the past few days have opened my eyes. I believed that concepts such as equality and freedom would appeal to the reason of any thinking creature. I held, in my heart, that these truths were self-evident. Obviously, I was deluded. The world has been controlled by force for too long. Rule by brute strength didn't start with my father, and cannot end with him, I fear."

"What are you saying?"

"It's time for me to stop wishing that peace and justice will spontaneously arise. If I'm to be the king who brings an end to kings, it seems I must first embrace the role of king." Shandrazel looked toward the tapestry that depicted Albekizan crushing the human rebellion at Conyers. "I must establish safety and security by capturing Blasphet. I must win back the respect of my fellow sun-dragons by showing that I'm still in control of the greatest army this world has known. And, if I wish to have valkyries present to discuss the future of this Commonwealth, it seems I must drag them here in chains."

"Don't overreact," said Pet. "You've suffered set-backs, yes, but—"

Before Pet could finish his sentence, an earth-dragon guard approached. He was holding a wooden bucket, the interior nearly glowing with the remnants of a lemon-yellow paste.

"Sire, we've found several of these buckets. I thought you'd want to see one."

Androkom took the bucket, examining the contents. He lowered his snout inside and sniffed. "Honey and citrus oils," he said. "And... an undertone of jimsonweed."

"Jimsonweed?" Pet asked.

"There's a whole chapter devoted to it in Dacorn's treatise on botany," Androkom explained. "When ripe, it produces a spiky seedpod filled with pink berries. The juice has hallucinogenic properties. There's only a two or three day window of ripeness when it is effective as a drug, however. If ingested at the wrong stage, it's poisonous."

The earth-dragon guard had something further to say. "Sire, I've also been told that one of the guards on the roof saw two sun-dragons flying away in the night. They didn't appear injured. The only thing that struck the guard as odd was that it looked like they were being ridden."

"Ridden?" asked Androkom.

"By humans," the guard said. "Females, he thinks."

"The Sisters of the Serpent, no doubt," said Androkom.

"What evil is Blasphet planning now?" Shandrazel said, rising from his cushion and stalking to a long sheet of parchment hung on the wall. The parchment bore a map of existing political boundaries in the kingdom. Various cities and landmarks were sketched upon the sheet with dark charcoal. Shandrazel tore the map down and rolled it up roughly. He turned to Androkom and said, "Follow me."

"Where are you going?" Pet asked.

"This is none of your concern," Shandrazel snapped. His eyes were narrowed in anger as he moved toward the hallway. Androkom gave a nod toward the earth-dragon guards. As Pet attempted to follow, the guards rushed forward, blocking his path.

Pet backed away, wondering what to do next. He cast a glance to the other humans in the room. Kamon, the elderly prophet from the mountains, approached. "What's happening?" he asked in a hushed tone.

"I don't know," Pet said. "Apparently Blasphet has done something to the sun-dragon representatives, and now Shandrazel is mad at us."

Kamon took Pet by the arm and led him further from the earth-dragon guards. "Do you think he's heard of Ragnar's exploits?"

"He hasn't said anythi—*exploits*? What have you heard?"

"Ragnar's men have been recruiting soldiers from throughout the kingdom," said Kamon. "So far, they haven't killed any dragons. This may be why Shandrazel remains ignorant. The movements of humans throughout the kingdom are of little interest if no dragons are being harmed."

Pet ran his hands through his hair. With Shandrazel looking for a way to prove he was still in charge, the worst thing possible would be for Ragnar to actually start killing dragons. Pet had caught a subtle look of hunger when Shandrazel had looked at the tapestry of Albekizan tearing apart humans. "What's Ragnar hoping to accomplish? Shandrazel isn't Albekizan. He wants peace; if we humans would work with him and try to keep him happy, he'll grant us our freedom."

"It doesn't matter what Shandrazel wants," said Kamon. "You've heard the hatred of his fellow dragons. He's alone in his desire to grant us rights."

"At least we have a dragon on our side right now," said Pet. "Shandrazel was just talking about how he may need to use his army to gain respect. If Ragnar provokes a war, Shandrazel's going to crush him."

Kamon leaned closer, his voice dropping to a conspiratorial whisper. "What if the dragons were deprived of Shandrazel's leadership?"

"How? What are you getting at?"

Kamon reached out a boney hand and took Pet by the arm. He pulled Pet further across the room from the guards, guiding him until they were behind a marble pillar, out of sight of the earth-dragons. Standing beneath a tapestry that displayed Albekizan in flight, his forty-foot wingspan depicted lifesize, Kamon whispered, "Shandrazel trusts you. Daily you stand close enough to end his life with a single thrust of a poisoned dagger."

Pet peeked back around the pillar, expecting the earth-dragon guards to be running toward him. They stared in his direction, but gave no sign of having overheard Kamon. Pet found himself feeling dirty for even having heard the idea.

"That's the dumbest thing I've ever heard," Pet said. "We finally have a dragon king who wants to treat mankind fairly and you're proposing we poison him? I know he sounded angry when he left the room a few minutes ago, but this is only a minor setback. I just need to talk to Shandrazel in private. Get his mind back to where it naturally wants to be. I've had a lot of experience dealing with moody dragons. Chakthalla could get into funks over the smallest things, and I could always cheer her up."

Kamon's face fell. He looked as if he'd just heard the worst news in the world.

"What?" said Pet.

"It's true," said Kamon. "There have been... whispers. Some have said that you aren't the dragon-slayer Bitterwood. That you're an imposter, who lived a life of comfort as the pet of Chakthalla."

"Oh," said Pet. "That. Didn't you know that I just acted as her pet so that I could pass unnoticed among the dragons?"

"If you've killed so many dragons, why did a look of fear pass through your eyes when I mentioned killing Shandrazel? The men of the Free City believed you were Bitterwood because of Albekizan's public accusation. Has it all been a lie?"

"I'm not going to waste my breath arguing with you," said Pet. "You stood before the crowd and proclaimed me the savior of humanity. You said God had revealed the truth to you. Are you going back to your followers now and tell them God screwed up?"

Kamon looked as if he'd swallowed a bug.

Before they could resume their argument, a faint sound caught Pet's attention. Though muffled by stone, Pet recognized the cry of a woman in tremendous pain. He remembered the musician he'd left in his chamber. This wasn't a good morning for an unidentified young woman to be discovered in the palace. His guts knotted as he thought of the consequences of his pointless passions. If the girl was harmed, he'd never forgive himself.

Pet moved toward the exit. The earth-dragons lowered their spears to block him. Pet kept advancing, coming right up to the tips of their weapons. He couldn't hear the girl now. Had they stopped hurting her? Or had something worse happened?

"Move back, human," one of the guards said.

"Has no one told you who I am?" Pet said, lowering his voice to a chill growl. "Have you never heard of Bitterwood? The Death of All Dragons, the Ghost Who Kills?"

"Bitterwood isn't real," the first guard scoffed.

"I heard his legend years ago," the second guard said. "You'd have been in diapers."

"I'm older than I look," said Pet. "Also, faster."

Before the guards could react, Pet dove for the hall beyond them, slipping beneath their outthrust spears. Earth-dragons had many virtues as soldiers—strength, toughness, loyalty—but rapid reflexes weren't among these attributes. Pet was halfway down the hall before the guards made it out the door. He turned the corner as a second wail of pain came from below. It wasn't coming from the direction of his bedchamber. Had they taken her to the dungeons?

The stairs down had two parallel tracks, a broad set of steep steps for sun-dragons, and a smaller, more shortly-spaced set of stairs for earth-dragons. Pet leapt his way down the sun-dragon stairs. His long years as a companion of a sun-dragon had left him well-practiced in traversing the landscape of giants.

Soon he found the torch-lined tunnel leading to the dungeon. A crew of earth-dragons stood guard, their heads turned to listen to the cries of anguish that came from an iron door standing open at the end of a short hall. Dim lantern light spilled from the chamber, and the jagged shadow of a winged dragon danced into the hall. Pet raced past the guards before they could blink. Their reptilian brains barely realized he'd passed them before Pet reached the lantern-lit chamber.

Pet froze, at first unable to untangle the scene before him, the mix of shapes, light and dark. The sounds of the woman screaming echoed so loudly within the windowless chamber he couldn't tell where her voice was coming from. His nose was the first sensory organ to ground him in the reality before him. Deeply wired channels in his brain recognized the smell of urine and vomit, and the stale, acrid stench of a human body unwashed for days. Slowly, his eyes made sense of the nightmare before him. The giant moving lump in the center of the chamber was Shandrazel. Half his body was in shadow, half lit by a single bright lantern. His emerald eyes glowed in the gloom like a cat's. Androkom stood opposite Shandrazel, his blue, shadowy shape ghostly in reflected light. The High Biologian's eyes were fixed on a limp thing in Shandrazel's foreclaws, something pale white and shaped vaguely like a human woman. The serpentine tattoo on her scalp identified her as the assassin Hex had captured. Her limbs were twisted in ways a human body shouldn't bend. Both her ankles were broken, and her fingers were knotted in unnatural configurations. Nonsense grunts spilled from her blue lips and tears wetted her cheeks. Her eyes were filled with terror as Shandrazel shook her.

On the floor beneath her was the map Shandrazel had ripped from the wall.

"Show me where his temple is," Shandrazel shouted, his deep draconian voice nearly deafening Pet. "Show me or I'll break you further! Show me!"

"Put her down!" Pet shouted, clenching his fists. "Have you lost you mind? Let her go!"

Shandrazel's tail swept through the air, catching Pet in the chest. It knocked him from his feet as easily as Pet could have kicked aside a yapping lap dog. Pet smacked into the stone wall. His knees buckled and he slid down to rest on the slimy floor.

Shandrazel's face was suddenly inches from his own. Shandrazel was normally such a gentle soul, Pet forgot just how big and powerful the full-grown bull sundragon truly was. His teeth were longer than Pet's fingers. Pet had time to get a good, careful look at those teeth as Shandrazel growled at him.

Finally, Pet's breath returned in a painful rush. "What's happened to you?" he asked, his voice on the verge of tears. "You're one of the good guys. You don't torture women."

Shandrazel snorted. "You self-righteous fool. I'm doing what I should have done the moment we captured this woman. She knows where Blasphet is. Blasphet is only a danger because humans treat him like a god. Why haven't your kind stepped up to the responsibility of stopping him?"

Pet swallowed, fighting back his fear. He'd barely heard Shandrazel's words as his attention remained focused on the white teeth flashing only inches from his face. Was Shandrazel somehow blaming humans for Blasphet?

"Blasphet was trying to wipe out humanity in the Free City!" Pet protested. "It's insane to think I'm helping him."

"We hadn't accused you of helping him," said Androkom. "Though, if you were, it would explain many things. Isn't it odd that the Sisters of the Serpent knew to find Shandrazel in the bath while you were there?"

"What?" Pet felt as if he'd gone crazy. "The sisters were attacking at random! And they attacked me! Shandrazel, don't let the actions of a few misguided girls turn you into a monster like your father."

Shandrazel swooped Pet up in his fore-talons, his claws biting into Pet's biceps. He lifted Pet with no more effort than a man would expend picking up a kitten. He shouted, "*I am nothing like my father!*"

Pain blanked Pet's mind and fear locked every muscle. He wanted to beg for mercy but couldn't find the words and couldn't have spoken them if he had.

Behind Shandrazel, Androkom craned his neck down to the face of the captured sister, who lay crumpled on the map where Shandrazel had discarded her.

"I fear his distraction has cost us," Androkom said. "This woman has stopped breathing."

Despite being trapped in Shandrazel's grasp, Pet felt himself stirred to rage at Androkom's words. Suddenly, his mind unlocked, and words gushed out of him. "Are you happy?" he shouted at the sundragon. "You've killed a helpless girl! Do you feel strong now? Do you feel like you're the king your father wanted you to be?"

"Silence! My father will be remembered as a tyrant! I will be remembered as the king who brought an end to kings!"

Shandrazel punctuated this sentence by spinning Pet around and slamming him face-first into the bedrock of the dungeon.

Shandrazel growled again, his anger building, "History will proclaim me Shandrazel the Just!"

Again the bull-dragon slammed Pet into the stone. Pet heard snapping noises echoing through his skull. With an odd sense of detachment, he realized that his front teeth were loose against his tongue. He pushed them out of his mouth and felt them slide down his chin amid the drool and blood.

Shandrazel dropped him. Pet rolled to his back, staring dumbly at the towering reptile above him. His limp right arm fell against the broken fingers of the dead woman. He coughed as the blood in his mouth hit the back of his throat. Shandrazel gazed down at him with a look that was half rage, half fear.

"Shandrazel... the wise," the sun-dragon said, his voice growing calmer. He swallowed hard as he stared at Pet. Pet could see himself reflected in the sun-dragon's eyes. His once sharp and shapely nose was now flattened against his face. He was bleeding freely from a gash over his right eyebrow. Slowly, his vision faded. Shandrazel's voice sounded dreamy as he said, "Most of all, I shall be remembered as Shandrazel... the merciful."

Pet closed his eyes. He was vaguely aware of the sounds of chainmail jangling; the guards from the hall had finally arrived.

Androkom's calm, authoritative voice said, "Cart the corpse away. This cell has a new occupant."

Distantly, an earth-dragon voice barked out a reply, but Pet could no longer understand the words. His ears filled with a sound like rumbling surf. He felt as if those waves were lifting him, leaving him adrift, tugging him ever further away from the shore of awareness. He floated into darkness, utterly alone.

CHAPTER SEVENTEEN

ATTRACTIVE
SOULLESS
MONSTERS

THE SCHOLAR'S GATE was a thick oak door hung on iron hinges. The door was tall enough that a sun-dragon could enter, and so heavy that Graxen feared he wouldn't have the strength to open it. Beyond the Scholar's Gate was the Grand Library, the domain of the High Biologian, a research collection surpassing the contents of all other libraries in the kingdom. Only the High Biologian and a few chosen attendants could freely enter the Grand Library. A student needed the High Biologian's consent to pass through the gate, and this consent was rarely granted.

Fortunately, Graxen wasn't a student anymore. He was Shandrazel's messenger, and as such had permission to travel anywhere in the kingdom. What's more, by tradition, copies of the keys to all libraries were given to the king, and as messenger Graxen had access to them. The ceremonial key was a work of art, a rod of iron over a foot long with a head shaped like a dragon's skull, the teeth plated with silver. Silver letters were scrolled along the black shaft, spelling out a quote from the *Ballad of Belpantheron*. The string of syllables was interpreted by some scholars as reading, *"My lord is wise according to the wisdom of an angel, to know all things that are in the earth."* The words were meant to remind kings that the battle between dragons and angels wasn't won by brute force. Dragons had once fought only with tooth and claw, while angels fought with swords and spears. Victory came, according to the poem, when dragons stole the knowledge of angels, and learned to forge metals and create their own weapons and armor.

Graxen wasn't certain the key would actually work, or if it was merely for decoration. To his relief, the key slipped into the lock easily. The lock clicked open. The massive door then swung away from Graxen with only the slightest push, its balance a testament to the engineering prowess of the biologians.

As he stepped within, Graxen froze at the magnificent vision before him. The Grand Library was nearly a hundred yards across, a vast open tower filled with all the knowledge of the dragon races. The roof high overhead was a giant dome intricately crafted of steel and glass, allowing the pink rays of sunset to spill into the chamber. Iron staircases twisted in elaborate intertwining helixes giving access to rings of walkways lined with tall bookcases. Looking up at the tomes that lined the room, it seemed impossible that the world was old enough that so much could have been written down. All the books he had dusted in the College of Spires might possibly have filled this central chamber, but dozens of hallways opened from each floor leading to more book-filled rooms. Graxen felt a sense of vertigo as he tried to take in the sheer scope of the information before him. Certainly, the knowledge he desired would be somewhere in this library.

Besides the books, the library featured an impressive collection of fossils and sculptures that showed the ancestry of the dragons. An enormous skeleton of a tyrannosaurus rex dominated the center of the room, its huge jaws dwarfing even those of sundragons. High above, sculpted recreations of pteranodons hung from chains, seemingly frozen in mid-flight among the stacks. He'd long heard the argument that the winged dragons were descendents of pteranodons, but it was a claim he found dubious. While the torsos and wing limbs held an undeniable similarity, he found their stubby hindlegs almost comic, and had always felt the primitive beasts must have been horribly clumsy in the air with no tail to serve as a rudder. Of course, bats flew gracefully without significant tails, so he knew intellectually it wasn't a barrier to flight. Still, when he was in the air, his tail was as important to the fine-tuning of his maneuvers as his wings. On a gut level, it didn't make sense that these ancient reptiles led in a direct path to him.

Graxen moved across the smooth floor, passing through the shadows cast by the replica reptiles above him. As much as the sheer scope of the library stirred his hopes, it also filled him with a sense of despair. No two libraries were ever organized the same. Centuries ago, clans of biologists had engaged in armed conflict to impose a standard system for categorizing information. The War of Words had ended with hundreds dead and left libraries throughout the kingdom vandalized, with countless books stolen and restolen by marauding colleges. In the aftermath, all hope of a standardized system was lost. Each library was organized via secret and unshared systems that helped protect the knowledge within them from predation, theft, or destruction by competing scholars. Unfortunately, it meant that Graxen would now need to find one of the few dozen biologians who directly served Androkom to act as his guide, or he would have to figure out the organizing principle of the library on his own, wasting hours, perhaps even days, in his search.

Still, he wasn't quite willing to walk up to a stranger and announce, "I seek a manual that will instruct me in the art of procreation." There was the chance that, if Androkom learned of his presence, so would Shandrazel. While Graxen was deeply in Shandrazel's debt, he couldn't afford the distraction of checking in with his employer and risking a new assignment. So, trusting to luck, he ventured down a nearby hall. He chose his path because it was the most poorly lit of all the halls leading from the main room, and he guessed that forbidden knowledge would be entrusted to the parts of the library most enshrouded by shadows.

Using this guiding logic, when the hall he traveled forked, he chose the darker of the two paths, and then repeated this again at his next choice. Now, however, the futility of this search method became clear. Randomly lifting a book off the shelf, he found the lighting too poor to discern the title. Perhaps he would need to find a guide after all. The biologians who knew these stacks could no doubt maneuver through them in total darkness. It was said that the former high bioligian, Metron, was able to navigate through the maze of books with his eyes closed and unerringly lay his claws upon any tome he desired.

"Ah, Metron," Graxen sighed. "I wish you were here now."

"Truly?"

Graxen spun around, searching for the source of the voice. It seemed to have come from a narrow gap between two shelves. It was difficult to tell, though, if there was a chamber beyond, or if the shadow merely gave the illusion of such. He crept forward.

"Who's there?" he said, keeping his voice low.

"Metron. The one you seek," the voice said. Graxen found that the gap between the shelves was filled with a tall stack of books. The chamber stank of dust and aged paper.

"You don't fool me, stranger," Graxen said, listening for any further noise. There was a scrape on stone. Behind the shelf? Or on the same row he was on, in the darkness at the end? The long tall rows of books baffled sound, and confused his senses. "Metron was banished. Who are you truly?"

"I *am* Metron," the voice said. "And, I am banished, a tatterwing cast out into the wilds."

"These aren't the wilds," said Graxen.

"True," the voice said. "Fate has led me back to my long-time home. No one knows the hidden chambers of this library better than myself. I could elude detection for the remainder of my days. Yet, this is not why I've returned. I've come seeking an individual dragon."

"Who?" asked Graxen. Then the answer seemed obvious. "Androkom?"

"No. Androkom and I didn't part on good terms. The dragon I seek, as difficult as this may be to believe, is you, Graxen the Gray. I've returned to the palace to speak with you, since I've learned you now reside here in service to Shandrazel. I entered through a passage that only I know of. I didn't expect to find you in the library, however."

"This does give me reason to be skeptical of your claims," Graxen said, straining his neck to try to see over the top of the stack of books. Only dim shadows lay beyond.

"Some biologians argue that there are no coincidences. They see in chance encounters the guiding claws of an architect of fate. Some days, I wonder if my life is not a testament to this fundamental truth."

"Why would you seek me out?" Graxen asked, still not convinced that the voice belonged to Metron, but willing to accept it until more information emerged. "I know of your betrayal of Shandrazel and your alliance with Blasphet. You'll find no favor from me."

"What leads you into this dark corridor, my son?" asked Metron. "Is there something you seek? Why not ask one of the attendant biologians?"

"What I'm looking for is none of your business," said Graxen.

"Everything in this library is my business," said Metron. "I've had over half a century to organize this collection. It will take Androkom decades to unravel my system. If there is anything you wish to find, there's no one better equipped to lead you to it than myself."

Graxen looked down the long hall of books, back toward the distant light of the main hall. How many books were here? Ten million? More? He could spend years looking at them one by one.

Haste was of the essence. Shandrazel was no doubt wondering why he hadn't reported back from his pursuit of the valkyries. He also knew he should inform the king of the unprovoked attack by the gleaners he'd encountered near Dragon Forge. Yet, he could do neither of these things until he found the information he needed for Nadala.

"You've taken a long time to consider your answer, my son," said Metron.

"Don't call me your son," said Graxen. "I know you mean it in a metaphorical sense, due to your greater age, but I find the word distasteful."

"That's most unfortunate," said Metron. "Because I don't intend the word in a metaphorical sense. I've come here, Graxen, to confess my greatest secret to the one most harmed by it. I've carried this terrible burden for many years. I've watched you grow, witnessed the cruelties you've endured, and I stood in silent cowardice. I've betrayed you, Graxen, by never admitting to the world that I am your father."

"What is the purpose of these lies?" Graxen said, his voice loud enough that, should any attendants be near, they would almost certainly hear him. "Metron was famed for his celibacy."

"You speak of my public refusal of the invitation to the Nest. I did feel that way, in my early years as High Biologian. However, the matriarch and I were the two highest authorities among the sky-dragons. We often had contact on a purely professional basis. There are ceremonies at the Nest that the High Biologian attends. The matriarch and I would sometimes retreat to private chambers to discuss the burdens of our shared duties. Neither of us was young. Both of us were past the sanctioned age of breeding; even if we weren't, breeding between us was contraindicated by our genetic threads. Yet, despite this knowledge—or perhaps, perversely, because of it—we soon found our attraction overwhelming, and succumbed to mutual passions. We carried out our secret trysts for years—until the matriarch reported she was pregnant. There are poisons that can terminate a pregnancy, but they can be fatal for an older female. When you were born, it was her intention to have you killed. I pleaded with her to spare your life. As you were my only offspring, I couldn't bear the thought of your death. My rank prevented me from claiming you as my own, but through the years I've watched your progress with great interest."

Graxen wanted to dismiss these words as lies, but found he couldn't. The greatest mystery of his life was why the matriarch had allowed his survival beyond infancy. Of all the sky-dragons, only the High Biologian would have had sufficient sway to ensure his survival. Instinctively, he knew Metron was telling the truth. Still, not everything made sense.

"Why did my survival matter? I was a freak, fated to never breed. If the sole value of a child lies in passing along the parent's genetic material, I was of no value to you."

"This is not an easy thing to explain, Graxen." Metron sighed. There was a soft scraping sound on the row behind the niche. Was he moving something? "If my sole desire in this life had been to pass along my genes, I had that opportunity many times over. The threadlines dictated a half-dozen valkyries I could have productively mated with. I refused; my brother Pachythan was selected in my place."

"Why did you refuse?"

"Intellectual arrogance, I suppose. I've witnessed the mating behavior of lower animals. The hard-wired desire to rut seems to be the driving force of life; only in the sky-dragon has the intellect advanced sufficiently for reason to take command of those baser instincts. At least, so I thought. In reality, the first moment I felt the matriarch's cheek against my own, all reason left me, and I surrendered to the same animal lust that drives all other creatures."

"Truly?"

"Truly. I remember the first time I met the matriarch. I cherished her strength and her humor. I recall the gemlike quality of her eyes, and the way that sunlight danced upon her lustrous scales. Every time I met her, my infatuation deepened. I grew fond of her scent; days spent without hearing the music of her voice were as cold and barren as the depths of winter. When at last I confessed my desires, and found she felt the same, it was the first moment of my life when I was wholly alive. Don't you see, Graxen? I didn't mate due to some intellectual scheme to produce the perfect scion. I wanted you to live because you were a testament to the feelings I had for the matriarch. I wanted you to live because you were product of my love."

"Love?" said Graxen. "All my life I've been taught that love is a folly of the lesser races, an unworthy emotion for a sky-dragon."

"I know. I preached this doctrine. I've written books defending it. I've been a hypocrite of the highest order. Falling in love with the matriarch changed everything I knew about the world. Publicly, due to the gravity of my office, I couldn't speak out against the chosen method of propagating our species. But, privately, I fear for the long-term prospects of our race. What does it matter if we become as numerous as ants and as powerful as gods, if we breed away all compassion and love from our species?" As Metron spoke, his voice seemed in motion, beginning in the book-filled niche and ending in the hall behind Graxen. Graxen turned to find the elderly sky-dragon, his wings torn to strips. His wounded limbs weren't fully healed; he smelled of rot and corruption.

Metron continued: "I fell victim to Blasphet because he flattered my intellect and I ignored my heart, which knew what he wanted was wrong. I believe the underlying amorality of sky-dragons led us to stand silent as Albekizan attempted genocide against the humans. We hold the intellect as the highest virtue while denouncing the value of emotion. We mock as philosophical illusions such concepts as good and evil. We're following a genetic road to becoming a race of brilliant, attractive, soulless monsters."

"Your words are hollow to me," said Graxen. "Where was your defense of love when you held power? You once had the authority to change the world. Now that you've lost your rank, you confess to your regret?"

"Yes," said Metron, lowering his head, looking woeful. "Yes, when I held power, I sought to protect the status quo. I may be the greatest hypocrite in all of history, yet it may not be too late for me to make amends."

"How?"

"While I've lost my rank and power, the matriarch remains in her position. I must speak to her. I must appeal to the last embers of her affection and ask her to end the centuries-old traditions that separate the sexes. I believe it's time to allow love to again play a role in the pairings of sky-dragons. It may be that she'll have me slain the moment she sees me. But what if she's as riddled with regrets as I am? The seeds of my words may fall on fertile soil. It's a slim chance, but I feel I must try."

Graxen contemplated the words. The matriarch had shown such hostility toward him. Did that hostility mask a regretful heart? Would she listen to Metron?

"Why do you need me?" he asked.

"As a tatterwing, I cannot simply fly to the Nest. I can't make this journey alone, Graxen."

"I've met the matriarch," said Graxen. "I don't think my presence will help your case."

"But—"

"But I didn't say I wouldn't help. I can't condemn you for falling in love. I, too, have recently tasted this emotion. I've met a female who I want to be with and, against all odds, she wishes to be with me. It's why I was searching through this library."

"You... were going to meet her here?" Metron sounded confused.

Graxen felt embarrassed, but he'd already said enough that he could see no harm in confessing all. "No. I need information. Neither Nadala nor I have been trained in the, um... skills... of biological pairing."

"Oh?" said Metron, still sounding bewildered. "Oh! You mean you don't know how to copulate."

"I chose not to use such crude terminology."

"Crude terminology is one of the more enjoyable spin-offs of the process. However, it's understandable that you don't know what to do. Mating comes quite naturally to lower animals, but for thinking creatures the act can appear slightly absurd and impractical. I assure you, however, with a little practice everything makes sense. It's mainly a matter of changing the way you look at your body's plumbing. You see, the organs of reproduction and the organs of waste lie very—"

"Stop," said Graxen, raising his fore-talon. "I'm uncomfortable discussing this matter with you. Isn't there a book I could read? Some manual of instruction?"

"Oh," said Metron. "Why, most assuredly. There's a book for everything, you know. In fact, you're in luck. Albekizan's father was a collector of such manuscripts. The subjects are all sun-dragons, of course, but the biological differences between our species are mostly a matter of scale. The *Prime Codex of Pleasure* is an excellent reference work, due to the illustrations. Two of the five known copies reside in this library. I drew quite extensively from its pages during my encounters with—"

"Enough!" said Graxen. Despite his intense interest in the subject, he was disturbed by the thought of learning details of the encounters between his parents. "Show me the book. Then I'll take you with me to meet Nadala. I suspect she'll be interested in your mission. Perhaps she'll know of a way for you to see the matriarch."

PET GINGERLY TOUCHED his face. His left eyebrow was a hard, swollen knot. He wasn't certain he could open the eye beneath it—in the pitch-black cell, there was no difference with his eyes opened or closed. He was missing three teeth, two on the top and one on the bottom. His hair was tangled and glued to his face by dried blood. His nose was too painful for him to explore its new contours. He couldn't breathe through it, which was just as well. He could taste hints of the odors that haunted the cell. He'd barely been awake earlier when the guards fastened the manacles onto his arms and legs. An earth-dragon had sullenly washed the floors by pouring stagnant water from a wooden bucket onto the area where the girl's corpse had been. The traces of urine and vomit that crossed his tongue were dreadful; he was glad his broken nose spared him the full impact of the stench.

He drifted in and out of wakefulness. He wasn't certain how much time had passed; though it felt as if he'd been here an eternity, he suspected he hadn't even endured a day, since the guards hadn't yet fed him.

In the tomblike silence, Pet's attention was drawn to a scratching, clicking noise nearby. A rat? No, the scraping was more metallic, like long needles tapping against iron. A moment later, a loud *clank* echoed through the chamber, the distinctive sound of a padlock opening. The hinges of the iron door groaned as they inched open. Dim light seeped through the ever-widening gap.

Two women squeezed into the doorway, their faces barely visible in the light of a small vial that glowed with a yellow-white phosphorescence like an oversized firefly. The women had shaved heads tattooed with serpentine designs; their bodies were hidden beneath heavy black cloaks. They moved barefoot across the floor toward Pet.

A yard away, they drew to a sudden stop.

"That's not Deanna," one said.

"Help me," Pet whispered, his voice sounding like someone else's as it passed through his damaged mouth.

"Kill him," the sister who carried the light said, drawing her dagger.

"Wait," the sister on the right said. "I've seen him before. He's the one they chained before the crowd in the Free City. His face is messed up now, but I remember his hair."

"That's me," Pet said, summoning the strength to sit up. "I was the one Albekizan tortured. You were in the Free City?"

"Yes," the girl said, bending down to take a closer look at his face. "Is it true? You're the great dragon-slayer?"

Pet turned his head, ashamed that these girls were staring at his damaged face. He felt like a monster. "I'm not a great anything anymore," he whispered.

"We should free him," the woman said, kneeling and grabbing his chains.

"Are you crazy?" the other one hissed. "This isn't the mission."

"Missions change," the woman answered as she started working her lockpicks within the manacle that bound Pet. With a *snick*, the band loosened. He rubbed his free arm. It felt cold as ice.

"Were you here to save the other girl?" said Pet.

"We heard that Deanna was captured," the girl said as she worked on the lock binding his ankle. "Blasphet wanted us to make certain she was finally able to complete her suicide mission."

"Shandrazel completed it for you," Pet said. "He killed her trying to make her reveal Blasphet's location."

"Did she?"

"No."

The girl holding the light-vial grumbled. "We were going to kill one of our own, but we're rescuing some stranger now? This is going to be difficult to explain."

The first girl finished working on the manacle. She stood up as it clattered to the floor. "My name is Shanna," she said. "My companion is Lin. She wasn't at the Free City or she wouldn't question why I'm doing this."

Pet tried to stand, but his feet were numb, and he wound up flat on his back. He sighed, and said, "I *was* there, and I'*m* not sure why you're doing this."

"All survivors of the Free City will forever be connected by our shared hatred," said Shanna. "If you go from this dungeon and kill even one more dragon, you will be fulfilling your life's most sacred purpose."

Pet started to point out that Sisters of the Serpent worshipped the very dragon who'd designed the Free City, but decided that this was a bad time and place to launch an argument.

Pet again tried to stand. By bracing himself against the slimy wall, he was able to once more find his footing. His head felt heavier than it should be, swollen and throbbing. He was a foot taller than either woman. Shanna looked up at him with a curious emotion in her eyes. Admiration? Pet was used to seeing attraction in the eyes of young women, but admiration was something new. Lin didn't seem so impressed. She scowled at him with an expression that told him he would need to watch his back.

"If Deanna is dead, we're finished here," said Shanna. "We'll take you back to the leader. He can no doubt find a good use for the hero of the Free City."

Pet found the idea of being to put to good use by Blasphet a rather ominous one.

Lin, the scowling girl, said, "He can't be Bitterwood. He's too young."

"Anyone can be Bitterwood," said Shanna. "He's not so much a man as a spirit. Anyone can open their hearts to him and become the Death of All Dragons, the Ghost Who Kills."

"Are you Bitterwood?" Lin asked Pet.

Pet tried to smile, to make some charming quip, but couldn't. His torn lips reminded him of what he'd lost. His whole life, he'd been little more than a doll, a living plaything valued for his pretty face. And now, he was broken. He wanted to lie, and tell these women what they wanted to hear, but couldn't summon up his old talents.

So, in the dim, chill dungeon, with the stench of death still tainting the damp air, the truth spilled out of him: "My name is Petar Gondwell," he said. "I'm the man everyone rallied around at the Free City, though I've never killed a dragon. But, as you say, I'm young... and I'm eager to learn."

CHAPTER EIGHTEEN

BIG PROBLEM

JANDRA AND HEX waited on the shore of the island while Bitterwood and Adam rode Trisky down the steep, rocky path from the high ledge of the lake. As Jandra looked around the cavern, she easily picked out what was real and what was illusion now that she knew to look for it. The restored sky was fake, but the sands they stood upon were real enough, despite their exotic appearance. The sands were made of fine black gravel mixed with sparkling flecks of gold. Jandra surmised the gold was iron sulfide. The waters of the lake should have been highly acidic given the volume of sulfur leaching into them, but the sulfur had been bound with iron to create enough fool's gold to build an island out of, apparently. The effect of the gold as it glittered under the waterline was quite stirring. A person less knowledgeable in chemistry would no doubt think the goddess lived in unimaginable wealth.

The waters of the saline lake were full of strange fish?s. Albino, eyeless minnows no longer than her pinky swam in the shallow waters near the shore, but further out dark gray-green creatures as long as sharks knifed through the water. Yet they weren't sharks, despite their prominent fins. The creatures surfaced from time to time to breathe through a long mouth full of teeth. They were covered with scales that seemed more reptilian than fishlike. Some sort of water-dragon? Jandra had never heard of such a thing, but she'd never heard of the long-wyrms either, and by now Trisky was striding confidently across the surface of the water toward her. She could see the water beneath the long-wyrm solidifying into a thick sheet of ice as the beast loped forward. It was the same sort of phase transition she was able to invoke in water. Was the long-wyrm responsible, or was the goddess doing it remotely?

As Adam guided Trisky to the shore, Jandra noticed the look on Bitterwood's face—it was a mix somewhere between awe and terror. She imagined the effect that this strange place must have on a mind less trained than hers. It angered her to think that this so-called goddess was only a human like herself, taking advantage of the ignorance of others to make her seem more powerful than she truly was. Not that the goddess wasn't powerful, of course. Jandra knew she was up against someone with more experience in using the technology. Also, the goddess definitely had more imagination than she or Vendevorex had ever applied to their abilities. Turning invisible, starting fires, changing water to ice or steam—these seemed like parlor tricks compared to building an island paradise deep in the bowels of the earth.

"I would speak with you in my temple," an ethereal voice said, coming from all directions at once. The bright golden flakes in the sands shifted and congealed, forming a path of gleaming bricks that led into the interior of the isle, vanishing amid the broad-leafed vegetation. Jandra took the lead in stepping onto the path with Hex following close behind. Jandra didn't feel afraid. Ever since donning the helmet, she'd noticed that her actions were more confidant and decisive. Was the helmet suppressing her fears? Or had her adventures in the previous months simply toughened her so that nothing bothered her now? She only used to feel this confident whenever she'd been around Vendevorex. It had made her feel safe to know that he was watching out for her. Perhaps her growing friendship with Hex was providing a similar boost to her confidence. It wasn't so hard to walk down strange paths in unfamiliar jungles knowing there was a sun-dragon watching your back.

The air was humid and warm as they moved past the thick foliage walls along the pathway. Butter-yellow birds flitted among the leaves, eating a collection of exotic beetles with carapaces gleaming like jewels. Snakes as green as algae draped over branches like vines. Flowers in countless hues perfumed the air.

They soon arrived at the temple, a thicket of tall trees surrounding a platform of aged marble. Jandra walked up the steps to a gap in the trees. In the large chamber beyond, a tall mahogany statue stood. It was a carving of the same woman they'd seen before. The figure was disturbingly immodest by Jandra's standards, with no attempts at concealing the nipples or genitalia. The face of the figure had full lips and a seductive stare. She'd heard rumors that followers of the goddess celebrated the solstices with ritualistic orgies. The statue looked as if it would approve of such unbridled passion. Jandra was surprised Pet had never tried to become a high priest in such a religion.

Adam stopped when Trisky reached the steps of the temple.

"I can go no further," he said. "I haven't had the proper cleansing."

"The goddess invited us," said Hex.

"Her invitation wasn't directed at me," said Adam.

Bitterwood dismounted and followed Jandra up the marble steps, his eyes wide with a look she could only interpret as reverence. Bitterwood crept toward the mahogany idol. He stared at it in silence.

"Have I been wrong all these years?" he asked softly. "Did Hezekiah's lies turn me from the truth?"

At his words, the statue came to life. The goddess tilted her head and looked down at Bitterwood. A smile crossed her lips. The expression of sexuality changed into the gaze of a mother looking at her child.

"A faith untested is no faith at all, Bant Bitterwood," the goddess said. Her voice was soothing and gentle. "You've faced many trials since you left my fold, dragon-slayer. What have you learned? Tell me of your wisdom."

"I-I've been a fool," said Bitterwood, dropping to his knees, staring up at the living statue. "There's nothing wise about me."

"Knowing this is a step toward wisdom," the goddess said.

Bitterwood lowered his head and stared at the goddess's feet as she stepped down from the pedestal and placed a hand on his shoulder.

"Forgive me," he said, his voice on the verge of tears.

It was more than Jandra could take. She could see what was happening quite plainly with her finely tuned senses. The statue was crawling with the same tiny machines that gave life to Jandra's own illusions. It sickened her to see Bitterwood so callously toyed with. It was obvious from his voice he was in tremendous emotional pain.

"This has gone far enough," Jandra said, lifting her hands toward the statue. She reached out with mental fingers and grabbed at the machines that animated it, attempting to wrest control. The statue jerked in response, its arms falling limp, its head flopping back and forth, as if someone had taken it by the shoulders and given it a good shake. Jandra felt needles of pain prickling against the interior of her skull as something fought her control. She'd never experienced this feedback before; always in the past, her mind had been the only mind in command of the invisible engines. Now, a second force resisted her.

The eight-foot-tall mahogany statue marched toward Jandra in slow, forceful steps, as if walking against a powerful wind. The fingers of the statue's right hand extruded into long wooden spikes. Jandra's muscles strained as she fought to keep the statue from moving nearer. She knew if she relaxed her concentration for even a second, the statue would spring forward and bury the spikes in her heart. Bitterwood still sat on his knees, dumbfounded, watching in useless bewilderment.

"A-a little help here, Hex?" she said, as the statue drew ever closer.

"Of course," Hex said, as his long scaly neck shot over her shoulder like a jet of red flame. The sundragon's teeth crunched into the statue's head, splintering it. The statue stabbed upward with her spikes but Hex easily caught the attack with his fore-talon. With a *crack*, he ripped the wooden arm free of the torso and tossed it across the room. He whirled, catching what was left of the statue with his tail and batting it. It crashed against the living trees that formed the walls of the temple, then clattered to the floor, lifeless.

"Okay, bitch, it's on," a disembodied voice growled. The air in front of Jandra was suddenly full of rainbows, and the largest of these rainbows ripped between the yellow and the green revealing a black void beyond. A woman's arm shot out from the darkness and grabbed Jandra by the wrist.

"Nobody fucks me like this," a voice on the other end of the darkness shouted. The slender arm yanked Jandra from her feet with superhuman strength. The walls of the temple vanished as Jandra fell into the rainbow. Beyond the colors, everything turned dark. Somewhere in the distance behind her, seemingly miles away, she heard Hex bellow her name. Then the rainbow closed, and she could hear and see and feel nothing at all.

BITTERWOOD ROSE FROM his kneeling position as Hex stood gaping at the empty space where Jandra had stood. Biiterwood charged across the room and grabbed the broken wooden torso of the goddess. He gripped the statue's shoulders with both hands and cried, "What did you do to her? Bring her back!"

His voice trailed off as he realized that the thing in his hands was only a heavy lump of polished wood, utterly lifeless. Had he once more slipped into the dreamland between life and death? Was he sleeping, to have imagined this statue had been alive only seconds before?

"Jandra!" Hex bellowed, the force of his lungs causing the leaves of the surrounding vegetation to tremble. "Where are you?"

"This was real?" Bitterwood asked Hex.

"I saw it," Hex said.

Bitterwood raced toward the steps of the temple. Adam was still outside, sitting astride Trisky. "What happened to Jandra?" Bitterwood shouted. "Where did she go?"

Trisky skittered backward at the sound of Bitterwood's voice. Adam looked taken aback. "What do you mean? I know less of what's happened than you."

"Your goddess attacked Jandra," Hex said, his head jutting out parallel to Bitterwood's shoulder. "She was simply standing there when the statue attacked without provocation."

"The goddess knows our hearts," said Adam. "Perhaps Jandra was corrupted beyond redemption."

"Jandra was a good-hearted girl," Bitterwood said, stepping toward Adam, clenching his fists. "She cannot possibly be as corrupted by this world as I've been. Make your goddess bring her back."

"Father, choose your words carefully," Adam said. "The notion that the goddess can be made to do anything other than her own divine will is blasphemous."

"I've committed sins much worse than blasphemy," said Bitterwood.

"The goddess is the embodiment of wisdom," Adam said. "If she acted in a hostile fashion, you must have faith that your companion was deserving of this judgment."

Bitterwood wanted to leap over the head of the long-wyrm and tear Adam from his saddle. Perhaps if he beat him to a pulp, Adam would agree to pray for Jandra's return. Bitterwood was chilled to discover his violent rage rising against his own blood. The memory of his brother Jomath dying at the foot of a temple much like this one rose in his mind. His hatred had ended his brother's life. Would the darkness within him demand a similar fate for his own son?

Bitterwood let out a long, slow breath. It wasn't his son who needed to be beaten until he prayed. He slowly sank to his knees. He bowed his head, aware of Hex only inches away, fully cognizant of his vulnerability if the great beast chose this moment to take his revenge. In an act of surrender, he closed his eyes and whispered, softly, "Goddess, please. Show mercy upon Jandra, just as she showed me mercy. Return her to us."

Above him came the sound of giant wings flapping. It wasn't Hex—even with his eyes closed, Bitterwood could sense the sun-dragon looming over him.

Bitterwood opened his eyes and looked up.

A bare-chested angel in black pants dropped from the sky toward him, his descent slowed by gentle flaps of gleaming golden wings. The angel carried something in his arms: a human form, judging from the legs jutting out—a girl? Jandra? No, the legs were too small and spindly.

As the angel landed on the steps of the temple, Bitterwood at last caught a flash of blonde hair as the girl lifted her head from the angel's breast.

"Zeeky!" Bitterwood cried, his heart swelling to discover she was alive. He experienced a strange and unfamiliar sensation. Could this be joy he felt, after so many years of knowing nothing but hatred and regret?

"Mr. Bitterwood!" Zeeky shouted as she dropped from the angel's arms and ran toward him. "You're okay!"

Bitterwood caught the girl as she sprang up to hug him. Her arms around his neck stirred memories of his own daughters, now dead. Yet somehow the memories were altered by the presence of Zeeky, becoming bittersweet rather than simply bitter.

"Where's your pig?" Bitterwood whispered.

"Poocher's okay," Zeeky said. "We gave him a bath."

Hex cleared his throat. "I don't believe we've been introduced."

Bitterwood lowered Zeeky to the ground.

"This is Zeeky," he said. "She's my... friend." The word felt foreign to his tongue. It had been many years since he'd used it. "Zeeky, the dragon is Hex. The man on the long-wyrm is—"

"Adam!" Zeeky said, waving. "You made it back!" She ran down the steps and hugged the snout of the long-wyrm. "Good to see you, Trisky!"

Bitterwood looked up from Zeeky to once more study the angel. The creature had long white hair and stood as tall as the statue that had just attacked Jandra. The angel's wings folded in an elaborate origami, the feathers tinkling musically as they furled up behind his broad shoulders until they vanished. The angel took the long piece of black cloth draped over his shoulders and shook it, revealing it to be a coat. He pulled the coat on and from somewhere within its folds a hat appeared in the angel's hands. It was broad-brimmed and black—exactly like the hat Hezekiah used to wear. Indeed, Hezekiah and the angel were almost identical in stature and garb, with only hair coloring and tones of skin to differentiate them. Bitterwood tensed. The only thing he despised more than dragons was the prophet Hezekiah. Of what relation was this angel to him?

The angel smiled once he was done adjusting his garments.

"As long as introductions are being made," he said, "call me Gabriel."

AFTER A BRIEF second of nothingness, Jandra was pulled into blinding light. She couldn't see a thing as two strong hands grabbed her shoulders and slammed her up against a wall. Her helmet striking the surface caused her head to ring like a bell.

"I run the show down here," a throaty female voice hissed, inches from her face. "If you were told I'd let some Atlantean skank waltz in here and piss all over my territory, you've been sadly misinformed. Who sent you? Cass? It was Cass, wasn't it?"

"I don't know who Cass is," Jandra protested, her eyes struggling to adjust to the light. The woman before her was little more than a dark outline, taller than Jandra by several inches, and judging from her grip, much stronger.

The woman slapped her hard. Jandra sucked her breath as the pain followed an instant later.

"Don't lie to me! My sister has ruined one plan after another and I'm sick of it. I'm going to use you to send a message. There won't be enough of your DNA left for her to clone your turds when I'm done with you!"

Jandra rubbed her cheek and cringed as she said, "I probably can't stop you from killing me but would you please stop cursing while you do so?"

The woman chuckled and released her shoulders. "Really? That's your big problem with me? My potty mouth?"

"No," said Jandra, straightening up. "My big problem is you pretending to be a goddess and letting my friend humiliate himself. Bitterwood may not be a saint, but I don't want to see him grovel in front of anyone."

As she blinked her eyes, Jandra slowly began to see the woman more clearly. She was tall, with broad shoulders and sharply chiseled facial features. With her big hips and ample breasts, she was obviously the model for the goddess statue. Thankfully, she was clothed, wearing a loose white cotton blouse tucked into tightly fitting blue pants. She was barefoot and her toenails were painted green, matching her hair, which had a dark, grassy hue. The woman was staring at her intently. Her eyes softened from anger into thoughtfulness. She chuckled again, and backed away.

The green-haired woman moved to a metal table that sat in the middle of the cluttered space. The room they were in was long and relatively narrow, filled with tables and shelves. There were no visible doors or windows. The most eye-catching items in the room were the multitudes of frames lining the walls, filled with strange paintings that seemed made of light and motion, showing creatures and landscapes of countless variety.

The surface of the metal table was covered with hundreds of sketches, most in gray pencil, a few inked and colored with washes of faint pigments. The woman picked up a white cylinder of paper and put it between her lips. She raised a finger, its nail also painted green, but chipped from heavy usage. She touched the finger to the paper cylinder and a small puff of smoke rose from the point of contact. The woman took a long, slow drag, bringing the embers at the end of the cylinder to a bright cherry red. She then opened her mouth and released a long stream of smoke. The acrid fumes stung Jandra's eyes.

"You know why I keep the human race around?" the goddess asked.

"I didn't know you'd been the one to make that decision," said Jandra.

"Tobacco," the goddess said. "I can build an exact replica of this cigarette molecule by molecule using nanites. Under a microscope, no one could tell the difference. But the taste just isn't right unless the tobacco has come through the whole process; the growing, the drying, the rolling. So, I decided to let humanity live, as long as they kept planting my favorite drug."

"I see," said Jandra. She had known that the goddess would be fake. She hadn't considered the possibility she might be insane. Jandra backed away from the smoke, trying to get a feel for her surroundings. Instinctively, she felt they were still underground. Her eyes were drawn from one flickering image in the frames to another. Was that Shandrazel? In another frame, she saw sky-dragons conversing in a room filled with tapestries. Something was odd about them... were they female? The valkyries? Jandra had never seen them before. Finally, Jandra felt her heart leap as she spotted the island temple in one of the frames. Hex and Bitterwood were on the steps, looking as if they were shouting at Adam. Even if she didn't know where she was, it was comforting to know they were still okay.

"You seem easily distracted," said the goddess.

Jandra brought her attention back to the woman.

"What are all these pictures?" she asked.

"I like to keep watch over my various projects," the goddess said.

"Your projects?"

"Little social experiments I've nudged along over the centuries. Living for a thousand years means you have time to follow a lot of different plotlines. I like to tune in from time to time. They're like my soaps, you know?"

Jandra didn't know. She couldn't see any correlation between the images and something you would use to bathe yourself.

"Judging from that glassy stare, you're not getting my jokes," the goddess said, crossing her arms. "Which clinches it that you're not Atlantean. Know what first tipped me off?"

"No," said Jandra.

"Your accent. Dragons speak a variant of English, but they do it without the benefit of lips, so the sounds are all shifted. They fake sounds like 'b' and 'p' by pressing their tongues against the roofs of their mouths in a slightly different location than 'd' or 'n'. You do the same thing despite having perfectly serviceable lips. I could hear it when you said, 'big problem.' It sounds like 'dig drodlen,' sort of. Which gives me a good clue who you must be. You're that dragon's daughter. Jandra, I think it is? And your father—for lack of a better term—was Vendevorex?"

"Did you know him?"

"Maybe," said the goddess. "It's not important. What is important is that I'm not going to tear you apart atom by atom and scatter your component parts out in a long smear through underspace. You didn't know what you were doing. Punishing you would be like slapping a retard for breathing through her mouth. It's not something a socially conscious ex-hippy such as myself is comfortable with."

"Are you an Atlantean?" Jandra asked.

"Lord no." The goddess rolled her eyes as if it was an absurd suggestion. "I'm the exact opposite of an Atlantean. An anti-Atlantean, if you will. I crippled the damn city when it first came to Earth. If the Atlanteans ever figured out how badly I screwed them I'll be the one who ends up as a skid mark in underspace. I'll be... You don't have a clue what I'm talking about, do you?"

"I confess, I'm having a difficult time following what you're saying. Your accent is odd to me. And you really expect me to believe you're a thousand years old? And you kept the human race alive to grow tobacco?"

"1174, with a birthday just around the corner. The candles on the cake will be seen from Mars. Just kidding. About the cake. God, you have the glassiest expression when I'm talking over your head. You should work on that. Make your default listening face kind of a grin. Seriously, you've got good teeth for a girl living in an era without dentistry. Show them off."

The goddess walked closer to her again. Jandra started to back away, but found herself paralyzed. She couldn't move a muscle as the green-haired woman came to within a few inches of her.

"Know what I'm doing?" the goddess asked.

Jandra couldn't speak.

"Oh, sorry, let me give you back your jaw."

Jandra's mouth returned to her control. "Why can't I move?" she asked.

"You haven't put any locks on your genie, sweety," the woman said, reaching out and rapping Jandra's helmet with her knuckles. "You really don't know how to use this thing at all, do you?"

"I've survived this far," Jandra said, straining to even wiggle her fingers. The same tingling sensation inside her skull she'd felt fighting the statue returned, only now a hundred times as intense.

"For starters, wearing it as a helmet isn't terribly flattering. You have nice hair. Don't hide half of it." The goddess ran her fingers through Jandra's locks. Jandra's head felt suddenly lighter. The helmet seemed to be melting off her scalp and dribbling down her spine.

"Reconfiguring it to run along your spinal column will make you modestly faster and stronger," the goddess said. "The real benefit is appearance, though. You have a lovely face; this will let people see more of it. I like the natural, no make-up look. Fresh and healthy, almost virginal. Still, you could benefit from a little tarting up. Lower the neckline on that fancy blouse of yours. Show some cleavage and you could make men stupid."

At the mention of the word cleavage, Jandra couldn't help but think of Pet.

"The men in my life are stupid enough, thank you," she said.

"Heh," the goddess chuckled. Suddenly Jandra felt free to move again. "Yeah, a thousand years of evolution has really improved the brains of dragons, but I can't tell a damn bit of difference in men. Of course, humans haven't benefited from my benevolent intervention like the dragons have."

"Now you're claiming to have created dragons?" said Jandra, feeling her hair. Her helmet was gone; only a few thin fingers of metal ran along her scalp beneath her hair line. The rest of the metal had turned flexible and clung to the back of her neck, trailing down to the tip of her spine beneath her clothing. She again felt her senses altering ever so slightly. What had the goddess done to her?

"I didn't create the dragons. I just tweak them from time to time. When Atlantis triggered the great collapse, there were only a few dozen dragons around. My friends and I helped them survive those rough early years. Then the sky-dragons diverged from the sun-dragons and started that brilliant eugenics program. Following the ninth plague of the humans, the dragon population really exploded. After that, the earth-dragons showed up and... You following this, honey? Am I talking too fast? Maybe you should start taking notes?"

The goddess shuffled through the papers on her desk. Jandra spotted a sketch of a long-wyrm with a cryptic note penciled in the margin—*mutagenic expression of multiple limbs*. The goddess found a sheet of blank paper and held it out to Jandra, along with a pencil.

Jandra shook her head. She'd had her fill of note-taking under her tutelage of Vendevorex. "I didn't know there was going to be a quiz," she said.

Over the goddess's shoulder, Jandra noticed that Bitterwood and Hex had been joined by a tall man in dark clothing, and a smaller, blonde figure. Zeeky?

"So," said the goddess, "I want you to understand something. Your genie? Since it's unlocked, I could wiggle my fingers and it would crumble into dust. I'll completely destroy your mojo if you mess with my toys again. We clear on that?"

"I understand you. I think," said Jandra. Was genie another name for the helmet? She could only guess what a mojo might be. Despite the unfamiliar words, she was certain she understood the main point. Now, she had her own terms to deliver. "I don't care what you tell Adam or anyone else about your powers. If you want to pretend to be a god, fine. However, I don't want you to make any further claims of godhood to Hex, Bitterwood, or Zeeky. They're my friends, and under my protection."

The goddess took one last drag of her cigarette, her eyes fixed on Jandra in a cool calculating stare. She stubbed the remnant of the cylinder out in a ceramic plate that sat on the edge of the table. Her expression remained inscrutable for a moment, then, suddenly, she smiled.

"You've got balls. I like that. I have a feeling we can be friends." The goddess leaned forward and held out her hand. "Put her there, Jandra Dragons-daughter."

Jandra was unfamiliar with the gesture, but instinctively extended her own open hand. The goddess grasped it, palm against palm, and gave her arm a vigorous shake.

"I can use a girl like you on my team," the goddess said. "Welcome aboard."

"Oh," said Jandra, who had been unaware she was being recruited to a team.

"It's Jazz, by the way," said the goddess.

"What's jazz? By what way?"

"My name," the goddess said. "My real name is Jasmine Robertson, but all my buddies call me Jazz. At least they do before I get tired and kill them."

Jandra let go of Jazz's hand, not sure what to say.

"You gotta work on that glassy-eyed thing," Jazz said. "Seriously, even if you don't get the jokes, a grin's going to make you look a lot smarter."

Jandra started to tell Jazz that she was growing tired of her insults. Then, she decided to play along, and grinned.

"If I'm on your team," said Jandra, "I'd like some further answers. You said you knew Vendevorex? Did you give him his helmet?"

"No," said Jazz. "If I had, I'd certainly have taught him to lock it."

"But, you watch the palace, right?" Her eyes were on the picture showing Shandrazel consulting with Androkom. "And you've been doing it for a long time? You saw me living there?"

"Sure," said Jazz.

"Did you see me when I was just a baby? Do you know who my parents were?"

"Not really. I watched Vendevorex kill them, but never cared to learn their names. I was more interested in how a dragon had come to possess such a fancy toy. Man, he was so clumsy with it back then. I thought for sure he'd kill himself."

"Oh," said Jandra. "Then, you don't know anything about my family?"

"I see where you're going with this. Sure, I know a little something. Not everyone died that night. You have an older brother who escaped."

"Really? What's his name? Is he still alive?"

"How the hell would I know? I don't follow the lives of every last living being. I just follow the major players. Sorry, kid. All I can tell you is he's at least twelve years older than you, and he looked a lot like you with the hair and eyes."

Jandra tried to imagine what her older brother must look like. The task was nearly impossible; there were simply too many men in the world with brown hair and brown eyes.

So, she had a second question. "What did you do to Zeeky's family?"

Jazz met her gaze with a cryptic smile. The air took on an odd energy. Jandra looked around to find another of the rainbows she'd traveled through floating behind her.

Before she knew what was happening, Jazz gave her a rough shove with both hands against the small of her back. Jandra stumbled toward the rainbow, and again the world went black.

CHAPTER NINETEEN

PRODIGAL SON

IT WAS MID-DAY when Shanna and Lin drew their horses to a halt in front of a small farmhouse. Pet slid down from the horse he shared with Shanna while Lin went into the farmhouse to secure fresh mounts. This was their second change of horses in twelve hours. Pet didn't know how far they were planning to travel; the girls proved frustratingly tight-lipped as to their destination or the reason for the frantic pace they kept.

As the horses they'd ridden for the last six hours wandered over to a nearby trough, Pet joined them, dropping down to his hands and knees to take a long drink of the icy water. Its chill freshness helped him overlook the horse drool streaming into the trough. The light was such that his face was dimly reflected in the water; he was grateful the image wasn't sharper. He could see that both his eyes were ringed with black circles from his broken nose. The knot on his brow looked as if someone had shoved a hen's egg under his skin. His lower lip was split and purple, pulling his mouth into a permanent pout. Fortunately, his right nostril had opened up a few hours earlier. While he'd been breathing through his mouth, the air had made his missing teeth ache. With his mouth closed, the pain was tolerable if he didn't smile or frown or move or think.

Soon, they were astride fresh horses.

"Tell the others you lost sight of me during our escape," Shanna said to Lin. "It may be some time before I can return to the temple. Inform Colobi that the pigeon made it safely to the roost."

Lin nodded and spun her horse to ride off on a dirt path that intersected the road they had traveled. Shanna spurred her horse into a rapid trot heading in a direction Pet was pretty sure was west. Geography hadn't been a subject he'd had any use for. He dimly recalled learning that the sun sat in the west, but never before in his life had that knowledge been of any importance. In truth, he cared little what his destination might be. All that was important now was that he was putting miles between himself and Shandrazel.

Pet wrapped his arms tightly around Shanna as she pressed her horse into a faster pace. He leaned his right cheek on her shoulders; it was the least damaged surface on his face. Her dragon-wing cloak was soft, the dark leather warm. He closed his eyes, grateful for at least this small comfort.

IT WAS THE following morning, and their fourth horse, when they arrived at the edges of a human encampment. The countryside was full of rolling hills and forests; it seemed that with each hill they'd pass over, he would spot more and more tents. Were these refugees from the Free City? Certainly these couldn't all be worshippers of Blasphet. Pet had no flare for math, but it seemed like the humans here must number in the thousands.

If Blasphet did have an army of thousands, so be it. Pet had never been passionate about anything in his life. His philosophy had been simple—if you desired a life of comfort, follow the path of greatest comfort. Yet, during his journey, he'd spent a great deal of time thinking that comfort might not be the most worthy goal. The true Bitterwood, who he'd met once before, had dedicated his life to revenge. At the time, Pet had thought the old man was insane. Now, with his swollen, scabbed-over face sagging from his skull, Pet was starting to appreciate the value of vengeance.

If Blasphet placed a poison dagger in his hand and ordered him back to the castle, Pet suspected he would accept the mission. All his life, he'd allowed sun-dragons to shape him into the man they wanted him to be. Intentionally or not, Shandrazel had shaped him into a man with murder in his heart.

Shanna guided their horse toward the largest of the tents. Pet recognized it instantly and shuddered—it was the tent that had once belonged to Kanst, Albekizan's cousin and general of the king's army. It was a tent he'd slept in many nights after he'd been taken prisoner.

"What's going on?" he asked as Shanna halted before the tent flaps. "This is Kanst's tent."

"Not since Vendevorex killed Kanst," said Shanna, dismounting. "After the Free City fell, our leader appropriated supply wagons used by Albekizan's armies. They were already packed up neatly outside the gates of the Free City. The Lord himself placed these supplies into our hands."

Pet again glanced around at the city of tents. "I'm surprised that so many humans associate themselves with Blasphet after what he intended to do in the Free City."

"Our association with Blasphet is a matter of strategic importance," said Shanna. "It's all part of our leader's master plan."

Pet felt confused. Shanna was talking about the leader as if he were someone different than Blasphet. "I thought Blasphet was your leader."

"So does Blasphet," said Shanna. "But the truth isn't so simple."

"Then Blasphet isn't who we've ridden out here to see? Just who is this leader of yours?"

As he spoke, the flaps of the tent pushed outward. A pleasant smell was released by the movement, an aroma like corncakes frying in bacon grease. Suddenly, a tall, naked, wild-haired man stepped from the tent. Pet recognized him instantly.

"Ragnar!" he said. "What are you doing here?"

"The Lord's work," said Ragnar, eying Pet skeptically. "Do I know you?"

"Yes," said Pet. "I was at the Free City, on the platform. Albekizan accused me of being Bitterwood. You helped free me."

Ragnar studied Pet's face. Slowly, recognition dawned in his eyes. "It looks as if you've fallen on hard times. I take it this is your reward for negotiating with the great serpent?"

Pet swung his legs over the saddle and dropped to the ground. His inner thighs felt blistered and raw as he walked toward the naked prophet. If he never sat on a horse again, it would be fine by him.

"Negotiations can only get you so far," said Pet. He drew up next to the hairy prophet and met his gaze, unflinching. At this distance, the smell of cornbread was no longer the dominant odor in the area. Ragnar hadn't bathed since the Free City, apparently.

Yet it was Ragnar who wrinkled his nose as Pet leaned near him, as if Pet smelled rank. No doubt he did. Between the dried blood, the foulness he'd laid in back in the dungeon, and more than a day of constant horseback riding, he was in no position to judge anyone for their odor.

"If you're building an army to fight Shandrazel," Pet said, "consider me your newest recruit."

"Kamon reported the talks devolved into chaos from the first hour," said Ragnar. "I'm not surprised by your change of heart."

"Kamon?" said Pet. "He's here?"

"No," said Ragnar. "He remains at the palace. He serves as my eyes and ears there, just as Shanna, Lin, and others serve me within the temple of the Murder God."

"Then the Sisters of the Serpent aren't really devotees of Blasphet? You're the guiding force behind them?"

"No," said Shanna. "The core of the Sisterhood is composed of actual devotees of the Murder God. Colobi, the serpent of the first order, truly believes the dragon to be a supernatural being."

Ragnar said, "Even before the Free City, however, I'd planted my followers within the ranks of the cult. I'd long planned to free Blasphet."

"What? Why?"

"Blasphet is far more dangerous to dragons than to men. I'd hoped he would rid us of Albekizan if we freed him. Now, it looks as if he will still be of use."

Shanna added, "The Sisters draw their members from among the poorest, most wretched women in the kingdom. Women who have lost all hope. I was recruited from a camp of refugees from the Free City. But my true loyalty will always lie with Ragnar."

"This sounds like a very dangerous game," said Pet. "Blasphet sends his followers on suicide missions. Even if he likes you, associating with him is a good way to die."

"My followers' faith is their shield," said Ragnar. "There is no true danger in this world. Life only begins after you're free of your mortal body."

Pet nodded, though he had no clue what Ragnar was talking about.

"Kamon said you intended to attack Dragon Forge?"

"Soon. We're waiting for the right moment to attack."

"I have some potentially useful information," said Pet. "The boss of Dragon Forge, Charkon, was just appointed general. He seemed worried about the danger to Dragon Forge with Blasphet on the loose. It wouldn't surprise me if he sends reinforcements to the Forge any day now. For all I know, they've already left."

"This is useful to know," said Ragnar. "However, we cannot attack the Forge prematurely." Ragnar lifted the flap of his tent. The smell of breakfast wafted through the air. For the first time since his beating, Pet felt the stirring of appetite.

"Come in," Ragnar said, motioning for Pet and Shanna to follow. "Your arrival is well timed. We've cooked a breakfast fit to welcome a prodigal son."

THE FLIGHT BACK to the abandoned tower was a slow and difficult one. Metron obviously could no longer fly alone. Graxen found the option of walking back unacceptable. So, they'd developed a system where Metron would cling to Graxen's back in flight. Few dragons would have been strong enough to carry the weight, or graceful enough to remain balanced with a fidgeting burden pressed against their back. Yet, in many ways, it was as if Graxen had been training his whole life for this flight. The endurance he'd developed serving Shandrazel now gave him the stamina to carry Metron for many miles before requiring rest.

They could have flown even faster if not for the *Prime Codex of Pleasure*. The leather-bound tome was indeed an illustrated manual of acts of erotic love between sun-dragons. It had been drawn on the scale of sun-dragons as well; the pages were a yard high. The book weighed almost as much as Metron did; Graxen carried it strapped to his chest to balance the weight on his back.

During their rests, Graxen would find a spot of privacy to peruse the tome, his mood alternating between boredom, fascination, and a mild sense of terror. Some of the activity depicted looked as if it must certainly be painful. On an intellectual level, so many of the poses struck him as awkward and uncomfortable. Yet on a gut level, the process simply looked right. He almost felt as if he could have figured it out on his own if he'd been less timid.

Their travel was also slowed by Graxen's choice of flight path. The road leading to Dragon Forge would almost certainly have produced witnesses. Graxen was too easily identified and Metron was too well known to take the chance that they might be sighted. So, they took a path over less-traveled terrain, with Graxen trusting his long study of maps and his innate sense of direction to lead him to his destination.

His faith in his navigational abilities were rewarded when, at last, the vine-covered tower once more loomed from the leafless forest. Graxen swooped down to a landing on the tower wall, near the gargoyle.

Metron dropped from his back.

"Why did you land on such a narrow wall?" Metron grumbled. "The structure looks unsafe."

Graxen sighed. Much of his life, he'd entertained fantasies of what he and his father would discuss should they ever meet. Most of their actual conversations on this journey consisted of Metron complaining of his weariness or discomfort. Graxen had expected that meeting his father would be a joyous event. In reality, his feelings were far more complex. He felt a sense of satisfaction knowing the truth; discovering he was the son of the high biologen was almost like discovering he was a long lost prince. Yet he also felt anger and resentment, thinking of how different his life could have been if Metron had showed more courage. Graxen assumed that Metron's complaints were a manifestation of the guilt that tore at the elderly dragon. During his quiet moments, Metron had the look of a dragon being savaged from the inside by his demons. Rather than being overwhelmed by larger emotions like love or anger, Graxen mainly felt pity for his father, and more than a little annoyance.

"Why couldn't we land on the ground?" Metron asked, staring down at the leaves below.

"You're free to wait on the ground if you wish," said Graxen. "I choose to wait here for Nadala."

"Ah, yes, your lover," said Metron. "Are you certain we can trust her?"

"What do you mean?"

"I mean that love can blind a male to the faults of a female. How much do you truly know about her?"

"I confess, we've had precious little time for conversation. But the words we've shared resonate. She wrote a letter that revealed her most private thoughts, and the things she said could have come from my own quill. I trust her with my life."

"I believe you," said Metron. "But, the very act of falling in love with you requires her to be a law-breaker."

"Who are you to judge anyone for breaking laws?"

"I'm not judging her. I'm merely expressing my concern."

"The passion I feel transcends laws. I can't claim our shared passion is rational. All I know is that when I see her, I feel as if the world is a much more wonderful place than I have ever realized. When we're apart, my thoughts can focus on nothing but her."

Metron looked wistful. "Yes," he said. "Yes, that is how I felt about Sarelia. In truth, that flame still burns within me."

"Sarelia?"

"The matriarch's true name. It's seldom used since the matriarch doesn't enjoy the luxury of indi-viduality. As the guiding force of the sky-dragons, it's imperative that all the individuals who have ever served as matriarch seem to be of one mind and one will. It enhances their authority."

"You and she both possessed great authority," said Graxen. "With a joint decree, you could have made your love lawful. You had the power to change the world. Why didn't you?"

Metron looked forlorn as the evening sun hov-ered over the hills behind him. He was a small, elderly dragon, shivering in the chill air. His voice trembled as he answered. "You make it seem sim-ple. Can't you see we were chained by the very authority we wielded? Perhaps we simply lacked the courage to overthrow the traditions that gave us our power. Now, I've discovered a certain bravery that comes with knowing my remaining days are few. I've lost everything that was ever important to me. I've nothing to lose in speaking to Sarelia. It may be that future generations have much to gain. I want to try one last attempt at making the world a better place."

Graxen nodded. He could think of a dozen arguments, a hundred questions, and a thousand frustrations he wanted to shout at this creature that stood before him. In the end, he knew words simply wouldn't matter. The past was past. Metron now represented a slender hope for a better future.

"The wind on this wall is worse than it would be below," Metron said. "It cuts into me like a knife."

Graxen turned his back to his father.

"Climb on," he said. "I'll take you down."

Once Metron had found a comfortable spot to rest below, sheltered from the wind, Graxen flew back up to the top of the wall. He didn't know when Nadala might show up, and he wanted to be in plain sight when she arrived. He perched next to the gargoyle and unstrapped the enormous book from his chest. He placed it on the gargoyle's back and opened its pages. During his many years as a student, Graxen had been repeatedly drilled in the art of debate; he suspected this training could prove useful. He thought it likely Nadala would react with disbelief when he explained what was involved in the mating process. He would need to carefully present each step as a logical extension of the step that preceded it.

He lost track of the time as he studied the manual. The sun was nearly gone when he turned the page to find himself confronted with a detailed drawing of a male sun-dragon's reproductive organ.

The organ was depicted approximately life-sized, stretching diagonally across two pages, and was painted in vivid red and pink watercolors that seemed to glow in the dimming light.

A shadow fell across the book.

"What are you reading?" a female voice asked, full of curiosity.

Graxen spun around. "Nadala!" he yelped. "I didn't hear you approaching!"

"I can land as silently as a dandelion wisp when I wish," she said. "Is that a book behind you?"

Graxen held his wings in such a way that he blocked her sight of the illustration. He didn't know what her reaction might be to the lurid material.

"It's a work of anatomy," he explained. "Of sun-dragons."

"Can I see it?" she asked.

"I worry it might offend you," he said. "It's a matter of chance that..."

"Stand aside," she said, in a soldierly tone, snaking her long neck over his shoulder to get a glance at the concealed material.

She suddenly grew very quiet.

"Goodness," she said, a moment later.

"Please note this is not the organ of a sky-dragon," he said. "I don't want you to experience alarm. Or disappointment."

She took a step back and held out her fore-talons. Instinctively, he placed his own talons in hers. She squeezed them with a gentle pressure as they stared into each other's eyes.

"I find it charming that you're embarrassed," she said.

"I hope you continue to find it charming," said Graxen. "I fear I may embarrass myself repeatedly in the coming days."

"The coming days, the coming weeks, the coming years," said Nadala, squeezing his talons tighter. "I've made my choice, Graxen. I'm leaving the Nest. You and I will carve out a new life together somewhere, even if we have to cross the haunted mountains."

"I'm happy to hear this," said Graxen. "I'm even happier to tell you it may not come to that. There is a chance, however slender, that our love could be sanctioned by the matriarch."

Nadala shook her head. "You're deluded to entertain such fantasies. I know you're her son, but the matriarch will never allow us to be together. And what if she did let us breed? It's not a brief tryst ending in pregnancy that I desire. I want you as my life-mate. Why should only sun-dragons know the pleasure of a life-long love?"

"It's as if you're speaking the words that dwell in my heart," said Graxen. "The matriarch won't listen to me. But there is one she may listen to. Indeed, someone she did listen to, once, or else I wouldn't exist."

"What are you talking about?"

"My father," said Graxen.

"Metron?" she asked.

Graxen felt as if he might topple from the wall. "You... you know that? How can you know that?"

"Everyone at the Nest knows it," said Nadala. "It's whispered in the dead of night, the tale of how even the matriarch once knew love. It's a story that brings shame to some and hope to others."

Graxen trembled. Nadala stroked his fore-talons.

"What's wrong?" she asked.

"This has been the central mystery of my life," said Graxen. "I would have paid any price to know who my father was. And now I learn that everyone at the Nest knew the truth? It's difficult to accept that the secret I most longed to discover was common knowledge to fully half our species."

"I didn't know you didn't know," said Nadala, sounding apologetic. "When I told you that Sparrow was sired by Metron's brother, I thought you understood that her aggression toward you was a matter of familial pride. She sees herself as the true inheritor of Metron's bloodline. I promise I never meant to deceive you."

Graxen tried to control his emotions. There was nothing rational about the feelings swirling in his mind. Why should he be angry at Nadala? Why should he suddenly feel such a sense of loss? How would his life be different if she had blurted out the truth when they first met?

"I'm confused," Nadala said, looking concerned. "You obviously know that Metron is your father; I take it you only learned recently. Who told you?"

"I told him," a voice shouted from below.

"A spy!" Nadala shouted, releasing Graxen's claws. She leapt from the ledge, diving into shadows toward the voice.

"Wait!" Graxen shouted, but it was too late. There was a terrible grunt below as Nadala found her target. Graxen leapt down to join Nadala, and found she had pinned Metron roughly to the ground. The old dragon had a look of terror in his eyes.

"It's a tatterwing!" she growled.

"Nadala," said Graxen. "That's Metron."

Nadala's eyes widened in sudden understanding. She released her grip on the elderly biologian.

"My apologies," she said.

"You have nothing to apologize for," said Metron, struggling to stand and failing. "I am nothing but a tatterwing now. I deserve whatever contempt is heaped upon me."

Graxen moved to Metron's side and helped him rise. A moment later, the ancient biologian found his balance on unsteady legs.

"Why is he here?" Nadala asked Graxen. Was there a hint of fear in her voice?

"I want to see the matriarch once more," said Metron. "Graxen has told me about your situation. You two are not the first sky-dragons to find your desires in conflict with the carefully crafted eugenics of our race. There was once a logic to our strict planning. A thousand years ago, the dragon races were birthed from a stock of fewer than thirty individuals. Inbreeding could have doomed our species. Instead, careful planning guided our kind through the dangerous maze of a confined genespace. However, a thousand years have passed. Mutations have arisen, and there's been enough variation that one race became two—for, you see, sun-dragons and sky-dragons have both grown from this small group of common ancestors. Our race has flourished due to its intelligent design; but, in the long term, nature provides a more powerful shaping force through natural selection."

"I thought we were the product of natural selection," said Graxen. "You yourself taught that we're descended from the ancient reptiles called dinosaurs."

"All lies," said Metron. "We were created in a laboratory by humans. The first dragons were designed to be hunted by men for entertainment. A thousand years of history have brought the cycle of predator and prey full circle. I shed no tears during the sun-dragon's ritualistic hunt of humans."

"Humans... created us?" said Nadala. "How?"

"It's difficult to believe, I know," said Metron. "Still, you would have to be blind not to recognize that mankind was once the dominant species on this world. A thousand years ago, they had access to technologies we can only imagine. The brutes who now toil in the fields once strode this world like gods."

"This is difficult to accept," said Nadala.

"Early biologians worked hard to obscure the facts surrounding dragon origins. I don't expect two minutes of truth to overturn a millennium of lies. However, it's not important. The important thing now is that I see the matriarch. I alone may convince her that our race no longer requires her guidance to thrive."

Graxen took Nadala's fore-talon once more and looked into her eyes. "I believe him," he said. "He wants to change the world. And it's a world I would like to live in. However, the choice is yours. If you want to run, escape together beyond the mountains, we shall. If you want to stay and try to help Metron see the matriarch, I will be by your side as well."

"She'll kill him," said Nadala. "This is foolish."

"More than foolish," said Metron. "It's very close to insanity."

"We cannot fly to the island," Nadala said.

"No," said Metron. "But, there's a tunnel leading into the heart of the Nest. I traveled through it often, but time has washed its exact location from my memory. If I were inside it, I could find my way to the matriarch. You wouldn't even need to accompany me."

"If you go alone, you won't survive," said Nadala. "I'm a valkyrie. I won't shy away from a just course of action simply because it's dangerous. I know of the tunnel."

She turned to Graxen. "Whatever this insanity is that drives you, I'm infected as well. Perhaps a single night of courage can change the future. Yet we must not lie to ourselves: taking Metron into the Nest will likely lead to our deaths."

Graxen nodded. He squeezed her fore-talon tightly. "With you at my side, I don't fear death."

Nadala rubbed her cheek against his, holding it there for a long moment. He savored this touch, this tenderness. When she pulled away her eyes were soft, glistening, yet shining with determination.

"I do fear death," she whispered. "But I cherish you more than life. You're a cause worth dying for. I'll take you through the tunnel."

CHAPTER TWENTY

ONE DAY LOVE

"I WELCOME YOU to the abode of the goddess," said Gabriel. The timbre and cadence of his voice had a songlike quality. "You came here searching for Zeeky. As you see, she is unharmed."

"And what of Jandra?" Hex asked as he lowered his long jaws to within inches of Gabriel's hat brim. As the sun-dragon spoke, Gabriel's silvery locks fluttered.

Bitterwood watched the angel carefully. Gabriel showed no sign of being intimidated by Hex. Indeed, against the backdrop of the white jungle flowers blooming in the trees behind him, Gabriel's androgynous face looked positively serene.

Gabriel answered calmly, "Jandra was invited to commune more closely with the goddess. I assure you, she hasn't been harmed. She will return to you soon."

"It didn't look like an invitation to me," Hex said. "It looked like an attack; an obscenity was used. I want Jandra returned now, unharmed, or..."

"Or?" said Gabriel, his pearly teeth gleaming as he smiled. "Choose your words carefully, dragon."

Bitterwood moved down the steps, clearing a path for Hex to take action. He glanced toward Zeeky, still standing near Trisky. If combat broke out, he could quickly reach her and move her to safety. The jungle behind her was thick with ancient trees. Perhaps he could find a safe place for her amid the branches.

He assumed that if Hex attacked Gabriel, Adam and Trisky would fight on the angel's side. Bitterwood felt no loyalty toward Hex, but he also knew that Gabriel was lying. Jandra hadn't been invited anywhere; she'd been taken away by force. If a fight broke out, was he prepared to take Hex's side? Even if it meant standing against his own son?

From Hex's tone, a fight seemed increasingly likely: "Don't threaten me, angel. You would do well to remember the *Ballad of Belpantheron*. Dragons long ago evicted angels from the domain of the earth. History is on my side should we come to blows. Tell your goddess to return Jandra. Now."

Gabriel's beatific face hardened. Bitterwood stepped closer to Zeeky. Adam's hand rested on his crossbow, his eyes fixed on the sun-dragon. Trisky paid no attention to the fight, munching contentedly on the handful of grass that Zeeky held out to the copper-colored long-wyrm.

Suddenly, a disembodied voice once more rang through the air.

"There's no need for this argument," the goddess said. Her voice was an ethereal thing. The syllables sounded almost as if formed by chance from the noise of leaves rustling in the breeze, the buzzing of bees, and the soft cries of distant birds. Yet as she continued, the words became more human, and gained more directionality. Bitterwood looked toward the entrance to the temple as the voice said, "You are all my guests. Jandra is unharmed."

The goddess emerged onto the temple stairs. She had reverted to a mostly human appearance, clad in a long flowing gown of spun emerald. Her skin looked liked flawless marble and her hair curled down her back in stony locks. She was ten feet tall, towering above even her angel, Gabriel.

There was a movement further in the temple, half-concealed behind the goddess's statuesque frame. Jandra stepped from behind the goddess. Her helmet gleamed with the blue of the artificial sky overhead. She raised her hand in a wave, looking mildly embarrassed at the commotion she had caused.

Bitterwood called out, "Jandra! Are you safe?"

"I'm fine," Jandra said. "The goddess and I have just been engaged in girl talk."

Bitterwood felt hairs rise on the back of his neck. Something about Jandra's voice was off. And, as she stepped onto the stairs beside Gabriel, she had no visible reaction, as if the angel's presence wasn't worth her notice.

He looked toward Hex, whose nose twitched as he sniffed Jandra. Hex shifted his head, glancing back toward Bitterwood. The second their eyes met, the unspoken truth passed between them.

Whoever this woman was, she wasn't Jandra.

JANDRA EMERGED FROM nothingness under a starry sky. The ground beneath her yielded like fine, loosely packed snow, with a slight crunching sound as it compressed beneath her feet. The landscape was a bleak, uniform gray, a fine gravel dustscape that spread in every direction for as far as she could see.

The setting was curiously odorless and eerily quiet. Jazz stood with her back to Jandra twenty feet away, her eyes turned toward the sky. Jandra stepped toward her, and was startled to find herself flying. No, not flying... but a single step had somehow transformed into a long, slow jump. She gently floated back down to the gray dust beside Jazz. She turned her face to the sky, her body posture mimicking the older woman's. She was bewildered by what she found in the sky. The moon? Only now ten times larger, and covered with wispy white clouds and enormous blue-gray oceans.

"Where are my friends?" said Jandra. "Where are we?"

"Your friends are still at the temple. I've sent ambassadors to entertain them. We're on the moon. We're in a prep zone that has atmosphere but hasn't been terrascaped yet. That big ball above us? It's our home. It's the planet where you've lived your whole life. Pretty cool, huh?"

Jandra felt queasy and lightheaded. Not just lightheaded, light-bodied. The contents of her stomach seemed to be lifting toward her throat as easily as her feet had lifted from the surface.

Jazz said, "You may ask yourself, well, how did I get here?"

"We're on the moon?"

"I thought it would be nice to give you a little perspective. I like you, Jandra Dragonsdaughter. You came a long way and put yourself in a lot of danger to help a friend. You've got good instincts. We're going to get along fine."

"I've heard legends of men who live on the moon," Jandra said.

"Yeah. They're all jerks. We won't be meeting them."

"Then why are we here?"

"Look," said Jazz, waving toward the glowing blue-white orb above them. "Have you ever seen anything so beautiful in all your life? That's an entire biosphere you're looking at. It's not just a big ball of wet rock. It's the largest living thing you're ever going to lay eyes upon. You have to understand something important: if it weren't for me, that wonderful living planet above us would be dead. The world owes me big, but I'm not expecting any thanks. I did it out of love."

Jandra stared at the earth, trying to make sense of what she was seeing. Icecaps and oceans and land masses green and gray and tan. It seemed unimaginably small and impossibly big at the same time.

"I was born into a world that was dying," said Jazz. "The world had already toppled over the brink of environmental catastrophe before I was out of diapers. The atmosphere and oceans were poisoned in order to satisfy the consumption of the wealthy. The richer nations could afford the illusion of environmental health by shipping their most polluting industries to remote corners of the globe. Except, there were no remote corners of the globe—pollute the air in Timbuktu, and eventually the poison spreads everywhere."

"I've heard that mankind once ruled the world, then fell," said Jandra. "Did the environmental catastrophe cause this?"

"Curiously, no," said Jazz. "The more poisoned the world became, the wealthier people grew. It was a perverse cycle. When people are rich enough, they can afford to live disconnected from nature. What does it matter if the atmosphere is fouled when you live cradle to grave in sealed vehicles and buildings where the air is finely controlled? Sure, there were millions of people who cared and tried to save things. But there were billions more who carried on their happy lives as planetary parasites, shopping and gorging with endless appetites, forever plugged into an endless stream of distracting entertainments that allowed them to ignore the greater truth around them."

"So what—"

"Double, triple, quadruple whammies," Jazz said, anticipating her question. "Atomic warfare in Asia was followed quickly by big bioterrorism attacks in the world's largest cities. Seventy percent mortality in London and New York, almost ninety percent in Hong Kong. The biggest earthquake ever seen flattened California and set the world ringing like a bell. Tidal waves, volcanoes, earthquakes; it was a lousy year. Economies collapsed faster than consumers could shop them back to health. Mega-amolds evolved and ate half the south. Then, right in the middle of this mess, Atlantis showed up."

"You keep talking about Atlantis like I should know what it is," said Jandra.

"Well, you should, girl. You're using Atlantean tech."

"Vendevorex mentioned it but didn't go into detail. Who are the Atlanteans?"

"The Atlanteans are us," said Jazz. "Just people. But Atlantis isn't us at all. Right around the time that the world was falling apart, the Navy built a fancy piece of equipment called a warp door. It functioned using the concept of spooky action at a distance—entangled particles are able to communicate information instantaneously no matter what their distance, as if they are connected via some higher space. The Air Force built a very fancy and very expensive portal that connected a room in

Dover, Delaware to a room in Houston, Texas. The two sides of the warp door were separated by over a thousand miles on the map, yet occupied the very same space due to the higher dimensional nature of entangled particles."

"I don't understand a thing you're saying to me," said Jandra.

"Don't worry about it. The important thing is, use of the warp door created ripples through under-space, and an alien intelligence came to Earth to check us out because of this."

Jazz pointed to a gleaming silver snowflake in the center of an ocean. Jandra's enhanced vision could see that the snowflake was actually an island, covered with gleaming spires miles high.

"That's Atlantis. I don't know who designed it, but it arrived as a tiny seed of intelligence and grew into a city searching for inhabitants to care for. It's nearly godlike in power, and almost limitlessly altruistic. It was going to share its advanced technology freely with mankind—until I crippled it."

"Why would you cripple something you say was altruistic?"

"Because mankind had done so much damage with its primitive tools, I could only imagine the horrors unleashed if every man had the power of a god. Fortunately Atlantis was, at its heart, a machine intelligence. I was the FBI's most wanted cyberterrorist. So, when I met Atlantis, I hacked it. I wasn't able to destroy it, but I was able to give its omnipotence some boundaries. Its altruism ends at its shores now. The people of Atlantis live in bliss, but Atlantis withholds its blessings from the remainder of the world. The Atlanteans are mostly blind to the rest of the planet. The passage of a thousand years has proven I made the right call. As the rest of mankind has fallen back into barbarism, the Earth has slowly begun to heal."

"I have so many questions I don't know where to start," said Jandra. "I feel like I only understand every other word you're saying."

"Yeah," said Jazz. "I suppose I could patiently explain the entire history of mankind to you over a long course of lectures. Or, I could do this."

Jazz reached out and touched a finger to Jandra's forehead. Images splashed through her mind, like the pages of a million picture books being flipped at blinding speed. A city of gleaming spires; a small reddish dragon attacking a marble angel; a black doorway that opened into emptiness; an apple; a starry sky; a silver key. She dropped to her knees, dizzy, stirring up a cloud of fine gray dust. She saw a dead man walking even though he was plainly disemboweled. She saw emaciated monkeys dropping down from rainbows. She brought her hands to her scalp. Her temples throbbed. It felt as if her brain were swelling against the confines of her skull.

"What are you doing to me?" she gasped, as tears blurred her vision.

"I commanded the nanites to physically rearrange your synapses to give you some of my memories. You won't be able to understand them instantly, but as we talk you'll discover you have the context to understand me. You're going to have the mother of all headaches for a while, but in the long run you'll be much more pleasant company."

"I don't remember agreeing to be around for the long run," said Jandra, certain she was going to vomit. When had she last eaten? All she could think of was that unidentified jerky that Adam had offered her. Salty and tough, the way it kept growing in her mouth as she chewed. Her body spasmed, yet, somehow, she held it all in. Trembling, she said. "I-I just want to find Zeeky and her family and take them home."

"Right," said Jazz. "That won't be happening."

"W-why?" said Jandra. The pain in her grew worse. Her head was being stabbed at its core by a million sharp knives. Her intestines knotted. She fell as her strength fled. It seemed to take forever to fall to the gray dust. "W-what d-did you do to them?"

"You won't understand yet," said Jazz.

"That h-hasn't s-stopped you so far," Jandra said, her fingers digging into the moon soil. She clenched her jaws and closed her eyes, trying to calm the storm within her. She wanted Jazz to keep talking. Her voice was a welcome distraction from the cacophony within her own skull.

"True," said Jazz. "Those rainbows that got us here pass through underspace. When I go through them, there's nothing in between. I step in one side, I step out the other. But a thousand years ago, I met a man who got lost between the rainbows. His name was Alex Pure. He was the first human ever to use the door, and he survived in underspace for years. He told me that being inside was akin to being omniscient. He said you see anything you want from inside: the future as well as the past. It's possible he was delusional, but I'd like to find out. I'm already immortal; omniscience would be a nice bullet point on my godhood résumé."

"What does Z-zeeky's family have to d-do with this?" Jandra said. She felt on the verge of insanity as a thousand years of unearned memories found purchase in her mind. Only the conversation was holding her in the here and now.

"When any normal person passes through under-space, they don't experience it. Artificial beings like

Gabriel don't record anything. But if you send a monkey in, it doesn't always come out. Alex Pure had fried his brain with thirty years of substance abuse; something about his damaged cerebral cortex allowed him to perceive the imperceptible and get lost in a place that isn't a place. I've been carefully tweaking Zeeky's family for generations, breeding a new kind of human with a functional form of autism that bridges the higher human thought world and the more primitive monkey mind at its core."

"Y-you've purposefully damaged the m-minds of an entire village?" Jandra asked, as sweat dropping from her face darkened the soil beneath her. "What gave you that right?"

"Rights are a philosophical myth," said Jazz. "I do it because I can."

Jandra wanted to summon the Vengeance of the Ancestors to consume Jazz in flame, but her aching brain couldn't remember how. She wasn't even certain she knew how to stand up again. Her own thoughts seemed to be in the wrong place inside her head, roughly shoved aside by Jazz's memory bomb. How long would it be before she recovered?

"Are... are you going to throw Zeeky into the rainbow?" she asked.

"No. The little girl passed through underspace without getting lost. But her mother and a few others didn't. They're still inside and I don't know how to guide them out. Zeeky, however, somehow can hear them inside. She's my key to retrieving them. Once they return, I'll take their brains apart and discover the secret to getting inside."

Jandra struggled to control her limbs once more. In the fractional gravity she rose, lifting her chin, summoning the most defiant gaze she could manage.

"I w-won't let you hurt Zeeky," she said.

Jazz tilted her head back and laughed. "Nice," she said. "I like this side of you. The resistance. I haven't had a lot of challenges lately. It's been, what, three hundred years since I tracked down the last person who knew how to make gunpowder? Things have been a little dull since. I mean, I keep busy, but I need someone like you from time to time to keep me feeling human."

As Jazz spoke, Jandra mentally reached out to touch the nanite swarm surrounding the thousand-year-old woman. Slowly, the invisible dust settled on Jazz's skin, too faint to arouse her attention. Then, Jandra willed the machines to ignite and engulf Jazz in flame.

Nothing happened.

"Good try," said Jazz, walking over. She lifted her hand to brush the hair from Jandra's face. Jandra wanted to slap her fingers away, but found she once more had no control over her arms.

"That look in your eyes right now," Jazz said, looking deep into Jandra's eyes. Jazz's own eyes were shockingly human; dark blue verging on gray, the faint traces of crow's feet at the corners. There was nothing within her gaze to suggest her age or power. "I love it. Everyone else I've talked to in recent centuries just looks at me with awe, or terror. You've got higher emotions in your eyes. Sure, there's anger and fear. But I see curiosity as well. You want to know what I can teach you. I think you want to be my friend; you just don't know it yet."

Jandra's skin crawled as Jazz ran her fingers along the line of her jaw. She felt sickened by the fragrance Jazz wore: faintly floral, yet corrupted by the scent of tobacco.

"We're going to be best friends, Jandra Dragonsdaughter. You're so pretty, you're like a little doll. I'll dress you like I want to; we'll play games together. You'll always lose, of course. And you know what?"

Jandra couldn't answer. Even her tongue was no longer her own.

"One day," whispered Jazz, bringing her lips to Jandra's ear, her hot, dry breath stinking of ash. "One day love will be the only thing I see in your eyes."

BITTERWOOD HAD MET the gaze of many dragons over the years. In his hatred of the beasts, he'd come to know them intimately. He could read the finest subtleties of thoughts that crossed the visage of a dragon as it lay dying: the futile hopes, the unrequited angers, the remorse over promises unkept, even the last faint flicker of peace as a beloved memory swept across a fading mind.

At this moment, however, looking into Hex's eyes, he experienced something he'd never felt before: camaraderie. Suddenly, in this strange and terrible paradise, the two blood enemies became the only ally the other could truly trust.

Hex gave a slight nod of his head. Bitterwood nodded back, his hand falling to the sword he'd taken from the long-wyrm rider, still tucked in his belt.

Hex lunged, his reptilian muscles uncoiling with the speed of a rattlesnake striking. With his powerful jaws he clamped down on the marble torso of the goddess, biting her hard enough to send cracks spiderwebbing through her body. He whipped the living statue around, slamming her head straight into the center of Gabriel's chest. The angel was knocked from his feet by the blow, landing on his back on the grass at the bottom of the steps.

Bitterwood leapt, raising the sword overhead with both hands, then driving it down with his full weight into the angel's belly. To his relief, the sword penetrated the angel's flesh. Bitterwood's momentum drove the sword deep. The blade sank into the earth beneath the angel. Bitterwood sprang away before the angel could recover sufficiently to grab him.

Gabriel didn't look so much hurt by the attack as embarrassed to have been pinned like a bug. He grasped the hilt and started to withdraw the blade, when suddenly Hex struck again with the living marble, driving the ten foot statue down onto Gabriel's head like a hammer. The goddess shattered from the blow. Gabriel was suddenly obscured by dust.

Bitterwood spun around as the false Jandra leapt toward him. He caught her in mid-air with an uppercut to her jaw that left his whole arm numb. Jandra was knocked back but seemed unfazed by the blow. Where he'd punched her, the flesh of her chin peeled away, revealing a steel jawbone beneath.

So. This, too, was a machine, just as Hezekiah had been.

He danced backward as she charged him, swinging her feminine fists in rapid punches that would have killed him if they'd connected. Suddenly, she fell, tripped by something long and serpentine—Hex's tail! The false Jandra looked up as a shadow passed over her. Hex's open jaws shot toward her. Bitterwood cringed as the sun-dragon's jaws snapped and Jandra's body was suddenly headless. Sparks flew from the neck as Hex spat out the feminine head, the hair now wet with saliva and blood. Bitterwood could see that several of Hex's dagger-like teeth had snapped from their sockets. Bitterwood was familiar with the ache of freshly missing teeth, but he had no time to express sympathy for the dragon.

Suddenly, the jungle itself came to life. The tree branches jerked toward Hex, throwing out long lassos of vines. Hex snarled and kicked, leaping from the ground, his powerful wings beating. Bitterwood was nearly knocked over by the force of the wind.

Hex's attempt at flight proved futile. The vines continued to shoot from the trees, wrapping him in a net of green, dragging him down beneath their weight. Bitterwood turned to run, aiming his flight toward Zeeky. Adam and Trisky still stood frozen, no doubt in shock at seeing the goddess shattered to dust. Zeeky was only inches from Trisky's jaws; if Adam recovered, he could make things unpleasant.

Bitterwood reached out to scoop up Zeeky, wrapping his arm around her chest as he ran past. Yet, Zeeky was not to be scooped. She stood her ground and seemed to weigh a thousand pounds. Bitterwood was thrown from his feet as his dash came to an abrupt halt. He skidded on the grass, trying to make sense of what had just happened. He rolled to his back as Zeeky came flying down from above, her small foot landing on his midsection with breathtaking force. He doubled over, unable to breathe, feeling as if her blow had pressed his bellybutton against his spine.

His vision blurred as he fought to remain conscious.

"What is it with you people?" Zeeky growled. "Do you go into other people's homes and break all their pretty things? I should kill you right now, asshole!"

"Goddess, please," Adam said, leaping from Trisky, throwing himself prostrate before Zeeky. "Spare him. He knows not what he's done."

Zeeky frowned. She stared at Bitterwood with murder in her eyes. Then, just as quickly, she relaxed, and grinned.

"Oh, why not?" she said. "You're spared, Papa Bitterwood. But, I'm warning you." Zeeky bent down and waved a finger in his face. "Damage one more of my toys, and I'll break your arms and legs and dump you in the middle of the Nest wearing only a Bitterwood nametag. My valkyrie buddies would love using you for target practice. Understand?"

Bitterwood did understand. Zeeky was a machine like Jandra, also animated by the mind of the goddess. He should have known Zeeky wouldn't be here without Poocher.

"If you've hurt Zeeky, I'll kill you," Bitterwood whispered.

"Yeah, yeah," said the false Zeeky, shifting her foot to stand on Bitterwood's throat, pinning him, cutting off his breath until the world faded away.

CHAPTER TWENTY-ONE

THE LAST EASY KILLS OF THE NIGHT

PET HAD BEEN allowed to sleep in Ragnar's tent to recover from his grueling ride. He woke as night was falling. Distant shouts had pulled him from sleep, but when he sat up everything was silent. Perhaps he'd dreamed the voices. He hadn't slept well. His bed was a mat of woven reeds over cold, bare red clay. He'd been given a scratchy wool blanket that might have once been white but was now a drab, uneven beige and carried Ragnar's signature unwashed aroma. Despite the stench, Pet pulled the blanket tightly around him as he rose on aching, blistered legs. He stepped out into dying sunlight, teeth chattering. The air was thick with the smell of campfires and countless iron pots full of black beans and salt pork.

The camp was oddly quiet. All around, men stood by their fires, their eyes turned toward Ragnar. He was kneeling over a fallen horse, helping a woman rise. Pet's sleep-clouded mind took a second to recognize her. It was Lin, the Sister of the Serpent who had split away from Shanna and him earlier. She looked as if she hadn't slept in days. Her fallen horse was still alive, but its jaws were foaming; its eyes gazed off in the distance with a dull, unfocused stare. It looked as if the beast had collapsed from exhaustion only seconds before Pet left the tent.

Lin looked up into Ragnar's bearded face. Her eyes were full of reverence as she said, "It's done. The fox entered the henhouse."

Ragnar nodded and looked over his shoulder toward one of his men.

"The hour is nigh," said Ragnar. "Tell Burke we can tarry no longer. The great day of His wrath is come; and who shall be able to stand against us?"

THE TUNNEL NADALA led them through was a tube nearly twenty feet in diameter. They had walked at least a mile, slogging through half a foot of icy water over slimy stone. Their way was lit by a small lantern Nadala carried.

"The humans who once ruled the world built this aqueduct to supply cities hundreds of miles from the lake," Metron said. Though no longer High Biologian, he still had a way of talking that made it seem that he was delivering a lecture. "Water once filled this pipe to the ceiling."

"I've always been skeptical of legends that humans built the dam," said Nadala. "You biologians approach knowledge on an abstract level only. We valkyries actually get out and touch the world. We've maintained the dam and kept its floodgates and pumps functioning since time immemorial. Scholars think of holding back a thirty-mile-long lake as a math problem. We warriors think of it as merely another aspect of our world that can be managed with muscle, sweat, and iron gears."

Graxen admired this aspect of Nadala. She was right. Biologians seldom solved problems because they never wearied of debating them. Valkyries were more practical-minded.

Soon they arrived at a pump station. Nadala produced a key that led them through a gate of welded steel bars. They passed through a long, tall tunnel with hundreds of pipes running overhead. Water dripped and drizzled from a hundred tiny leaks, producing staccato splashes that echoed through the concrete tunnel like drumbeats. The passage went on for many yards before ending at a platform with cement steps leading up to a set of double iron doors.

"Ah," said Metron. "I remember this well. The Thread Room lies directly above us."

Nadala handed the lantern to Graxen as she walked up the stairs. The twin doors were bound together with a heavy steel chain. The lock was a strange one—there was no slot for a key, only a dial with numbers upon it.

"We'll have to break it," Nadala whispered.

"No," said Metron. "I recall the combination."

His aged talons took the lock and spun the dial in precise turns. Seconds later, the lock clicked open.

"Sarelia didn't change it," he said, sounding relieved. "A good omen."

As the doors creaked open, Graxen thought he heard something behind them, near the leaky tunnel. A splashing sound, like footsteps.

"Did you...?"

"What?" asked Nadala.

"I thought I heard something," Graxen whispered, walking back down to the platform. The singing of the falling water, like countless fountains, was all he heard now.

"Perhaps it was a rat," said Metron.

"It's gone now, whatever it was," said Graxen.

Graxen climbed back up the stairs and pushed his way through a curtain of thick cloth to join Nadala and Metron in the Thread Room. They weren't far from the giant chalkboard, with its dense jotting of notes. Metron moved to better see the board. The room was lit with a series of lanterns. Graxen could read the board clearly from where he stood. His father studied the chalkboard and chuckled when he reached Vendevorex's name surrounded by questions marks.

"What's so funny?" whispered Nadala.

"I knew Vendevorex would vex her," said Metron. "The most famous sky-dragon in the kingdom and his origin an utter mystery. He came to Albekizan's court long after Sarelia and I had stopped speaking. I wrote her a letter concerning my theories about Vendevorex. I never sent it. Though I wrote it in the most professional voice I could manage, I feared she might read between the lines of the subject and find that I still loved her. At the time, it seemed as if it would only cause pain to send that missive."

"Whose pain?" a voice asked from across the room. Graxen looked behind him to discover the hunched form of the matriarch standing before a fluttering tapestry. She walked toward them, her cane clacking on the tiled floor.

"My pain?" the matriarch asked. "You should know the females of our species may endure limitless agony, biologian. If you've not spoken to me for nearly two decades, the weakness lies with you, not me."

"You're correct," Metron said. "You were always the stronger one."

"Not always," said the matriarch, now only a few yards away. "I gave in to your request not to destroy our great mistake." She cast Graxen a baleful gaze. Then she narrowed her eyes at Nadala. "Why are you in the presence of a tatterwing and a freak? Where are your armor and spear, valkyrie?"

Nadala bowed her head respectfully. "Matriarch, I've fallen in love with your son. I've admired him since the day he visited this isle. We've come to ask your permission to..." her voice trailed off. She took a deep breath, then raised her head and looked at the matriarch with bold eyes. "We seek permission to breed."

The matriarch scoffed. "You've gone mad, Nadala. Even if you were allowed to choose your seed-giver, you know you couldn't breed with this discolored freak."

"Of what importance is the color of his hide?" asked Nadala. "Why must all sky-dragons look so much alike?"

"Because physical variability leads to hatred," said the matriarch. "I've studied histories forbidden to you. I know what happens when different colors are allowed to spread within a race of intelligent beings. It leads to strife and warfare. I would spare our race these evils."

"You perpetuate these evils," said Nadala. "Why would we fear difference if we aren't taught to fear it?"

"Enough, valkyrie," the matriarch snapped. "It's not your position to decide the genetic make-up of our species. It's your job to kill intruders—a job you have failed miserably."

"Mother," said Graxen, "don't speak to Nadala this way. She only wants—"

"Yes!" the matriarch cried, lifting her cane and waving it at Graxen. "She *only wants*. She is poisoned by desire. Her hormones have addled her mind. I know too well the danger of *only wanting*."

"You're correct," said Metron. Graxen felt betrayed by the words, but Metron continued. "Our own chemistry can ruin our reason. Fortunately you've had two decades to free yourself from the biology of desire. Tonight, we can have the conversation our bodies prevented us from having so many years before. No dragon alive has studied the question of our genetic destiny more than you. However, as High Biologian, I was guardian of the true secret history of our race. I've come to persuade you that the age of guided genetics can now end. Everything the early biologians wanted to accomplish has been accomplished. We've flourished as a species without falling into the many genetic pits that could have doomed us. We needed many generations of careful guidance to avoid inbreeding and allow for the slow rise of mutations to give our shallow gene pool depth. Now, however, that guidance is crushing genetic variability. Graxen does possess visible mutations. Yet, despite his coloration, he has also shown speed and agility that is nearly unmatched in our race. He has excelled in scholarship despite the burden of constant abuse from his peers. Losing Graxen from the gene pool would be a tragedy."

The matriarch shook her head. "Our genetic threads were always contraindicated. I wouldn't have allowed Graxen to breed if he'd been born blue as the winter sky. It's my duty to keep the threads untangled. If not for the wisdom contained in this room, our species would have vanished from the Earth long ago."

"You can't know that," said Graxen.

"She *can* know that," said Metron in a scolding tone. "These threads guided us from almost certain extinction. Yet we're no longer the same fragile race we were when the first tapestries were sewn. Our species numbers in the tens of thousands. We can safely let go of the old ways and begin to experiment with new ways. Humans have endured eons without a guiding hand. There may be advantages to allowing individuals to choose their mates."

The matriarch grimaced, as if she'd just bit into something bitter. "Do you truly advocate the breeding practices of savages?"

"Humans have survived disasters we couldn't," said Metron. "Plagues, for instance. Dragons have been spared plagues due to our relative newness as a species. A thousand years is insufficient time for a microbe to have adapted to us as a carrier. What happens when that day comes? With all the females clustered together in the Nest, a single disease could wipe out our species overnight."

"We're spared plagues due to our superior breeding and fastidious hygienic practices," the matriarch said, in a tone that made it seem she was addressing a hatchling instead of the most learned sky-dragon in the kingdom. "Our isolation is a barrier to disease, not an opportunity."

"An intriguing hypothesis," said Metron. Then his eyes twinkled. He looked as if he'd just guided the matriarch onto the exact intellectual ledge he'd wanted her to stand upon. "Since we're rational creatures, we can test it. We can select a pool of candidates to live outside the Nest and the Colleges. The test subjects may settle where they please, and find mates as they please. A hundred members of each sex should provide a reasonable study group. Then, we will track their offspring for ten generations in a second Thread Room to analyze if the genetic health of their offspring improves or declines compared to the main population."

The matriarch tilted her head in such a way that it looked as if the idea had lodged in her brain and suddenly weighed down her left lobe.

"A second Thread Room?" she said, her voice almost dreamy. "I can think of many questions that such an experiment could answer."

"Nadala and I could be the anchor for such a population," said Graxen.

"No," the matriarch said, raising her fore-talon dismissively. "The control group must start with untainted candidates. Neither you nor Nadala would meet the criteria."

"I would hope, as designer of the experiment, that I would have some say in selecting the population," said Metron. "I will choose half the males and half the females without restriction; you shall select the other half."

"No. No, while I'm intrigued by your proposal, I fear you're overlooking a rather clear set of facts," said the matriarch. "You're a tatterwing. Your wings still stink of pus and scabs, and already you've forgotten your status? Your presence here is a crime punishable by death. Graxen, too, was told that if he returned he would face execution. It would be poor precedent for me to reverse that decision. And Nadala... my poor, deluded, hormone-poisoned Nadala... your sins are greater than either of these males. You're a traitor to the Nest. As such, your punishment will be far worse than either of these fools."

As the matriarch spoke, she punctuated her words with sharp, rapid taps of her cane against the tiles. The tapestries that lined the room bulged outward. Fifty valkyries poured into the chamber from unseen doors. Nadala sprang to place herself between Graxen and the guards. "Run back to the stairs," she hissed. "I'll hold them off as long as I can."

Graxen moved to her side. "I'll not abandon you."

"How romantic," said the matriarch. Then, to the valkyries, "Take them!"

A handful of the valkyries advanced, spears lowered. Things quickly became confused as the nearest valkyrie stumbled drunkenly. Spears clattered on the tiles as they slipped from trembling talons. One by one, the valkyries began to drop, unconscious. Graxen noted an acrid odor, like the smell of burning peanuts wafting through the room. A faint haze of blue smoke could be seen swirling as the valkyries continued to fall. Nadala suddenly swooned, her eyes rolling upward in their sockets. Graxen caught her before she hit the floor.

"W-what treachery is this, Metron?" the matriarch growled as she swayed unsteadily, reaching out one fore-talon to the blackboard to maintain her balance.

"I am not to blame for... oh. *Oh, no*," said Metron. "No! By the bones, he's played me for a fool! Why didn't I see his plan? I swear I didn't know he followed me!"

As Metron spoke, the last of the valkyries toppled. Then the matriarch, too, succumbed to the mysterious smoke. Only Metron and Graxen remained standing.

"What's happening?" Graxen cried out. "Who has followed us?"

The tapestry where they had entered was suddenly torn asunder. Bald human girls clad in leather armor danced into the room, brandishing black, wet blades. Metron moved as fast as his old body could manage to stand over the matriarch's fallen form. Graxen dragged Nadala to Metron's side, laying her carefully upon the floor, then taking a defensive stance next to his father as the group of girls surrounded them. Graxen took note of the tattoos on their shaved heads. These must be the Sisters of the Serpent, the cult that had attacked the palace.

The doorway to the stairs darkened. The black-scaled form of a sun-dragon squeezed through the too-tight opening, then stood erect in the much larger Thread Room, stretching his wings. Graxen was used to the company of Shandrazel, but this dragon seemed even larger, more menacing, as his black hide sucked in the light.

"Blasphet," said Metron, his voice cracking, on the verge of tears.

One of the girls darted forward. Graxen tried to stop her, but time felt distorted. The smoke that had felled the others slowed him. He couldn't reach the girl before she landed a savage kick in Metron's gut. The elderly tatterwing doubled over, falling to the floor.

"Your unworthy tongue may not speak the holy name!" the girl snarled.

"Greetings, old friend," Blasphet said, looking down at Metron's curled form. "For your own safety, I'd recommend use of my proper title."

"Murder God!" cried Metron, as his tears erupted.

* * *

RAGNAR STOOD ATOP a mountain of rusted rubble. His army stretched out around him in the thousands, a motley collection of slaves and farmers and mercenaries, most dressed in rags, many carrying only the crudest of weapons. Ragnar's voice was loud as thunder as he shouted, "The Lord is our light and our salvation! The serpents who've devoured our flesh shall stumble and fall! Though they raise their weapons against us, we shall not fear! The Lord shall give us strength to break their swords and shatter their shields. He shall delight in the desolation of our enemies!"

The army of men cheered, and Pet was certain that any element of surprise they might have possessed was lost. They were only half a mile from the eastern gate of Dragon Forge, hidden among the man-made hills of scrap. The debris blocked them from sight of the fort; he wondered if it would also swallow up the noise.

Pet, by his unearned reputation as a great archer, had been placed with a small contingent of men with longbows. The bows weren't the best weapon for attacking a sleeping city. If they fired blindly over the walls, their arrows would most likely lodge into rooftops or empty city streets, harming no one. When Ragnar's army poured through the gates, firing into the city would be as likely to injure a human as an earth-dragon. So, the archers had been told to hold back from the initial assault, to await further orders from one of Ragnar's closest companions, a white-bearded man everyone called Frost. Pet found himself disappointed not to be part of the main attack. He'd reached the moment in his life where he needed to know if he truly possessed the courage to fight. In the Free City, he'd been rescued by Ragnar and Kamon, then assumed the role of shouter of inspirational words. In actual combat, however, he'd lagged near the back, and had finished the battle without ever giving a dragon so much as a scratch.

Now that Ragnar had whipped his army into a frenzy, he gave the command for them to spread out to all four of the city gates. They divided into roughly even mobs and began flowing away through the ruins. They were a sad looking army; a few had shields, fewer still had helmets and breastplates. Many were armed with nothing more than clubs. The dragons inside the city had access to much better weapons and armor. Fortunately, earth-dragons kept roughly the same schedule as men, and most were asleep now.

As the archers waited, Pet climbed the rust heap. From his position, Pet could see the eastern gate in the distance. A half dozen earth-dragons stood guard. More accurately, a half dozen earth-dragons squatted near the wooden gate talking and passing around a ceramic jug from which they took long swigs. The night was bright, with a sky clear enough that the moon cast crisp shadows.

Suddenly, a score of those crisp shadows separated from the wall and rushed toward the guards. Men dressed in black cloaks pulled long knives that glinted as they slashed, swiftly and precisely. The earth-dragons silently vanished beneath the flapping black cloaks. For a moment, Pet was amazed by the efficiency of the attack; the way that six living beings had been brought to an instant, silent death. Unfortunately, seconds later, a howl reached his ears. One of the dragons had screamed in pain, a sharp, ear-splitting yelp that stopped in a wet gurgle. The sound had simply taken a few seconds to reach Pet.

Pet placed an arrow against his bowstring. The element of surprise was definitely gone now. These six might be the last easy kills of the night.

Ragnar apparently had become impatient with stealth anyway. His war cry reached Pet, an incoherent warble of rage that echoed from the city walls. Ragnar's nude form was easy to spot as he raced forward, outpacing the hordes that followed him, brandishing twin scimitars as he led the charge. The black-cloaked assassins darted aside as Ragnar bounded past them. The warrior-prophet let loose another primal scream. A single earth-dragon appeared, emerging from a door that opened in the only building Pet could see from his vantage point. Ragnar buried his scimitar into the beast's neck. The dragon fell, his head hanging by a thread of skin. Ragnar paused to kick the head free then leapt further into the city, beyond Pet's view, as hordes of men poured over the surrounding hills and flooded through the gates.

At the bottom of the rust heap, there was a flurry of voices. Frost was approaching. His close-cropped white beard and hair stood out in the night. Pet climbed down to receive his commands. In the distance, screams of agony drifted from Dragon Forge. It was impossible to tell if the sounds were human or dragon.

"Listen closely," Frost shouted. He had a deep voice; people said he'd once been a blacksmith, and despite his age he looked the part. He was pot-bellied and squat, but broad-shouldered, with thick arms and hands covered with white, shiny scars. "Since we got here, we've been working with the human gleaners. Some of their men are helping in the attack tonight, guiding us to the most valuable targets. Their wives and children have been taken to safety. Any living thing that remains in a two mile circle of Dragon Forge can be considered your enemy. The remaining gleaners are cowards. Now that the battle has started, most are probably preparing to flee the area. Our job is to see that they don't get away."

"We're going to capture the gleaners?" Pet asked.

"We're going to kill them," said Frost. "When we take Dragon Forge, the longer we hold it before Shandrazel learns of the attack, the better. Every day that passes before the sun-dragons arrive is a day that Burke will have to make us the finest weapons any army has ever wielded. The more gleaners we silence tonight, the longer we have before the counterattack takes place."

"I didn't sign up to kill humans," Pet said.

"Any true human is on our side tonight," Frost answered. "The cowards who denied us aren't men. They're animal scum; they serve us better dead than alive. Anyone you meet that isn't attacking the Forge with Ragnar is to be put to death. Any objections?"

"But, there are children—"

"There are no children tonight!" snapped Frost, with a vitriol that rivaled Ragnar at his best. "There are your brothers-at-arms, and there are vermin. Will you fight? Or will you be the first of the rats we put to death this evening?"

Pet felt hundreds of eyes turn toward him. He swallowed hard. The thing he was being asked to do possessed a cruel logic; indeed, it almost seemed a necessity. He let out a long, slow breath.

"I'll fight," Pet said. "Let's do this."

Frost snapped out orders, dividing the men into many small squads and barking out the areas they were to cleanse. Pet noticed that he wasn't being selected for any of the groups. In the end, there was only Frost, him, and ten other men. Frost eyed him coolly and said, "They say you're quite the archer. Tonight's your chance to prove it. Follow me."

Frost turned and ran away from the Free City. Pet and the others followed close behind. Soon, the clamor of the battle behind them faded. The rust mounds were eerily effective at swallowing up sounds. Suddenly, there was movement in the shadows before them. A band of tatterwings, outlaw sky-dragons, nearly thirty of them, were all moving away from the city, struggling beneath the weight of heavy sacks slung over their shoulders. Four of them strained to pull a cart laden with barrels.

"No survivors!" Frost shouted.

Instantly, Pet's fellow squad members let their arrows fly. The tatterwings spun around as some of their members let out agonized cries and toppled over. Pet drew his bow and took aim at a sky-dragon who was staring, dumbfounded, in their direction. His eyes had a drunken quality to them. Pet had never fired a bow at a living thing before, only at immobile targets. Fortunately, the drunken, dazed tatterwing was for all practical purposes immobile. Pet released the arrow and watched as it flew in a deadly line to bury itself in the tatterwing's belly. The dragon let out a grunt as he grabbed the arrow with both fore-talons. He took a few staggering steps, then toppled. His eyes were still open, staring straight at Pet.

Pet turned his face away and focused on placing another arrow onto the bowstring. His hands were shaking. By the time he'd readied for a second shot, his fellow archers had already unleashed arrow after arrow. There were no tatterwings left on their feet to target. Frost charged ahead, drawing a sword. The others followed, raining killing blows down upon the tatterwings that still breathed. Then they darted off into the night, in search of their next victims. Pet tarried at the scene a moment longer, looking at the contents of the cart. One of the barrels was already tapped. Pet unstopped the cork and was met with the eye-watering stench of goom, a liqueur distilled from cabbages and chilies, a favorite beverage of earth-dragons.

From some distance ahead, there were further screams—humans this time. Pet took a deep breath. He didn't need to try to catch up to Frost and his men. He could simply claim he'd gotten lost in the action. Apparently, Frost had been swept up sufficiently in the heat of battle that he was no longer keeping a close eye on Pet. He could just hide and wait out the night.

"Coward," he grumbled, addressing the word at himself. He'd accepted his mission. Gripping his bow more tightly, he ran toward the screams ahead.

Before he'd even gone twenty feet, he saw a form moving toward him. It looked human, coming toward him in sort of a limping half-run. The figure emerged from the shadows into the moonlight. It was a middle-aged man, dressed in a gleaner's rags. He had an arrow jutting from his right thigh. His eyes were wide with terror. Pet raised his bow and took careful aim. The man saw the movement and gave a yelp of despair. He turned, looking for some new direction to escape. Pet released the arrow. He was aiming for the man's torso. The arrow instead lodged in the gleaner's neck. The gleaner was knocked from his feet, landing on his back on the hard-packed earth. His hands feebly grabbed at the arrow Pet had fired. His breath came out of him in a series of rapid, wet clicks—*hic, hic, hic, hic, hic*.

Pet drew the sword he'd been given by Shanna. He inched his way toward the dying man. The gleaner's eyes were looking toward the moon above, blind to Pet's presence. Tears streamed down his cheeks. Pet punched his sword down with all his might into the man's left breast. The wet clicking sound in the man's throat fell silent.

Pet pulled the sword free and sheathed it, letting the cold night air dry the sweat that trickled down his face.

CHAPTER TWENTY-TWO

COGS IN A VAST MACHINE

ARIFIEL WAS POSTED in the central bell tower for the midnight watch. Her duty would be to ring the enormous bell if there were any hint of attack in the middle of the night—an unlikely event given the bright moonlight. Any males who attempted to fly to the island would be spotted instantly.

Guarding the central bell was an important task, but Arifiel regarded the duty as a demotion. Since the unhappy day her unit had failed to prevent Graxen from entering the Nest, she hadn't been assigned to any perimeter patrols. She'd had her chance at action, and she'd failed. Nadala and Sparrow hadn't returned to patrol either. Nadala had drawn a ceremonial guard assignment—a position that required her to be a living prop to enhance Zorasta's authority, but where she would likely never see true combat. Sparrow had fared worst of all—she was now doing administrative work in the armory, handing out weapons and armor to valkyries with duties more befitting warriors. Having been on two failed patrols, Sparrow would never again be trusted to defend the Nest.

Arifiel leaned on her long spear as she looked over the placid lake waters, so still they looked like ice. The windless night was utterly silent. Or was it? Arifiel stretched her neck out of the tower window. Had she heard someone cry out? She strained to hear the sound again. Had it been her imagination? Perhaps the call of some distant nightbird?

Just as she'd decided she'd heard nothing, a second cry came, right on the edge of hearing. But, it wasn't coming from outside the tower. She pulled her head back inside the window and went to the steps leading down and opened the door. As the door creaked open, she heard the noise yet again—possibly. Or had it just been the squeaking hinge?

Then, unmistakably, a voice, several of them, shouting, but far too distant to make out the words. What was happening? Were some of the valkyries fighting among themselves? She rose and took the bell rope in her hands. She paused. If she rang the alarm and woke the whole island simply because a squabble had broken out, she'd be branded as unworthy of even this simple duty. The bell was for genuine emergencies. She released the rope.

A movement outside caught her eye. From the lowest level, a valkyrie had taken to the air, and was now flying in an unsteady, wobbling path. All alcohol was forbidden to female sky-dragons, but the figure below was definitely impaired by something. Arifiel winced as the dragon's wings faltered and she fell to the bristling steel landscape. Arifiel couldn't see the spot where she hit, but it was almost certain the impact had been fatal. The Nest wasn't a pleasant place to fall.

Now the decision to ring the bell was easy. Arifiel turned, only to discover she was no longer alone in the tower. At the top of the stairs stood a human, a teenage female, holding a torch in one hand and a long, black blade in the other. The torch trailed a plume of blue smoke. Arifiel caught a whiff of the acrid fumes. Instantly, her vision blurred. Her legs weakened. Only by steadying herself with her spear did she remain standing. Instinctively, she clenched her jaws shut and held her breath. The girl smiled, an evil, satisfied grin that conveyed her belief she'd already won this battle. She thrust the torch forward, wreathing Arifiel in the thick fumes.

Arifiel toppled backward, releasing her spear from her fore-talons. Yet, as she fell backward through the open window, she grabbed the falling spear with her hind-talons, and used the momentum of her backward plummet to her advantage. As her torso fell over the window ledge, her legs flipped up. She kicked with her remaining strength, releasing the spear.

As she fell toward the jagged spires below, she felt a twinge of despair, not at her impending death, but because she fell in silence—she'd aimed her spear at the central bell in hopes of sounding the alarm, and missed. Her body was limp now, yet, as the wind rushed over her, fresh air was forced into her throat. Mere feet from the steel spikes beneath her, she spread her wings and turned her downward path into a sharp curve away from the tower. In seconds, she was out over the lake, well away from the paralyzing smoke, her strength returning. She wheeled about, eyeing the bell tower, devising a strategy to fly back inside, knock away her assailant, and reach for the bell rope. As she circled, she spotted other sky-dragons in the air, leaping from windows, rising from rooftops. A score of her sisters had escaped the fumes, and more were rising to safety with each second.

A large sky-dragon with a commanding voice shouted, "Valkyries! Gyre!"

Arifiel obeyed, as did the others. The gyre maneuver required the sky-dragons to gather closely around a central figure, maintaining flight paths where wing tips were separated only by inches. It was a formation adopted for rapid, in-flight commands from a high officer. Arifiel finally drew close enough to recognize the dragon who had shouted the order. It was Zorasta, the matriarch's ambassador. Did that mean Nadala was near?

By now, there were at least fifty dragons in the air. This meant that thousands were still inside the Nest, victims of the poisonous smoke. Who could be behind such an attack? Valkyries were trained to defend their home against male sky-dragons. Why would humans be attacking?

"These humans must be the same ones that attacked Shandrazel's palace," Zorasta shouted. "Sisters of the Serpent—they're servants of Blasphet."

Hearing that unholy name, Arifiel for the first time understood the extent of the danger. Servants of Blasphet wouldn't be content with capturing the Nest. They were here to kill every living creature.

By now, the guard patrols that kept watch over the perimeter of the lake had joined in the gyre. Arifiel was glad of their company. They were armed, ready for battle, unlike most of the other sky-dragons, who had been roused from sleep.

"We may have only minutes to act," Zorasta said. "We have to get back inside."

"They are armed with poisonous torches," someone said. "If we go back, we'll succumb to the fumes."

"Not if we act quickly," Arifiel said. "The humans can't know the layout of the Nest as we do. We can dive through windows holding our breath. We can only be inside for a minute, maybe less. But a minute is enough time to kill a human. We're valkyries!"

"That's the spirit!" shouted Zorasta. "And, as of now, it's our plan. Split up by your flock colors. Green flock, clear the northern rooms, yellow take the south, white the east, black to the west. If you have armor and a spear, take the lead. No more than three from each flock can enter a room at a time. Always leave someone at a window to pull you out if you succumb to the fumes. If you're unarmed, get down to the beach and get water into anything that will hold it. The torches are the real danger. Douse them, and we'll make short work of this enemy."

The white, black, and yellow flocks spun away in tight knots to perform their duties. Arifiel was a lifelong member of the green flock, the same flock as Zorasta.

Arifiel cast her gaze back toward the central tower. By now, they were a quarter mile away, but she could still see the light of the human's torch in the window—only now it had been joined by two others. How many valkyries still were sleeping, unaware of the danger?

Zorasta apparently had the same thought.

"Our first priority must be to take the central bell tower and awaken sleeping valkyries," she shouted. "Who was on guard there?"

"I was," said Arifiel.

"You abandoned your post?"

"I succumbed to the fumes and fell from the window," said Arifiel. "The rush of wind revived me."

"Then do your duty and get back in there!" Zorasta barked. She eyed two armed valkyries who circled near. "You and you! Aid her! Go!"

Arifiel felt fully recovered. She set her path toward the open windows of the tower, building speed. She could see she faced three human teenage girls—no true threat for a valkyrie. The space between her and her target narrowed. She attempted not to be distracted by the movements in the windows below, as she watched guards land on windowsills and peer into the interiors. Suddenly, Arifiel realized that if she succeeded in her mission, she was going to be condemning every dragon inside to death.

She slowed her flight, allowing the two dragons who followed to pull beside her.

"We can't ring the alarm!" she shouted.

"What?" the one to her right shouted back.

"If we ring the bell, the grates will close and seal the doors and windows. The Nest is designed to prevent an invasion from the outside. If the grates fall, we'll turn the fortress into a prison."

"By the bones!" the valkyrie to the left cried out. "I hadn't thought of this!"

As one, the three of them pulled up, allowing their paths to carry them over the top of the bell tower.

"We still need to get inside," the valkyrie beside her shouted. "I don't know why the humans would ring the bell, but we should make sure they don't. And, who knows? Perhaps some other valkyrie might sound the alarm by instinct, just as we nearly did."

"Agreed!" shouted Arifiel. "Follow me!"

Again they wheeled in a tight formation, darting back toward the open windows. Only now, to her horror, two of the three torches had fallen to the floor. There was a single sky-dragon standing below the bell rope, facing a lone human girl. The other two humans lay on the ground, gutted. With dazzling speed, the sky-dragon leapt up and kicked out with her sharp hind-talons, cutting a vicious slash across the throat of the remaining girl. She collapsed in agony, her torch and sword clattering on the floor.

They were now only a few dozen yards away from the open window. A shout rose in Arifiel's throat.

"Don't!"

But it was too late. The sky-dragon had already reached for the bell rope. Arifiel's shout was drowned by the peal of the magnificent iron bell. Arifiel whirled to the left of the tower, avoiding the window, as the night filled with the rumble of a thousand gears and chains kicking into motion. In half a moment, the fortress would be sealed, leaving all the dragons inside to the mercies of the Sisters of the Serpent.

She glanced back over her shoulder, to see if she could identify this lone valkyrie who had just unwittingly doomed her sisters. Her heart sank as a familiar face looked out the window toward her.

Sparrow.

THE BRUTE REWIRING of Jandra's brain had reached the peak of pain several minutes after the initial jolt, leaving her with the worst headache of her life, a skull-ripper that left her too weak to stand. Colorful explosions of light danced across her vision. Jandra had been unable to think during this time. She'd simply collapsed to her back and closed her eyes as she waited out the worst of it.

Jazz had been mostly quiet for the last few hours. Occasionally, Jandra thought she'd gone, but then she'd catch a whiff of cigarette smoke or hear a scratching sound a few feet away. Jandra willed one eye open. Jazz had produced a pad of paper and a pencil from somewhere, and crafted a granite park bench out of moon dust. She sat on the bench, making sketches as she studied Jandra. The stars above burned with unearthly clarity.

"You hang out with some very rude friends," Jazz said, aware that Jandra was awake.

Jandra licked her lips. "Wh-what have you done to them?"

"I'm just holding them for now. They seemed to have some pent-up aggression. A rather violent need to break things."

"They can't be happy that you've kidnapped me," Jandra said.

"There are more important goals in life than making people happy," said Jazz. "You feeling any better?"

"No."

"Really? Your nanites should be getting the swelling under control by now and boosting your endorphins to offset the pain. If you're feeling bad it might be because you want to feel bad."

"Why would I want to feel bad?"

"Low self-esteem. You were probably feeling pretty powerful before you met me."

"My self-esteem is fine, thank you," Jandra said. *Self-esteem?* It wasn't a concept that had been in her vocabulary before now. Her knowledge of it came from Jazz's brain blast. In addition to understanding the idea of self-esteem, she now knew what ice cream was, had a clear mental picture of an airplane, knew that penguins only lived in the southern hemisphere, and remembered that the first man on the moon had been Neil Armstrong on July 20, 1969. The new information in her brain seemed useless and trivial, devoid of the proper connections. It was like the loose pages from a million random books had been shoved into her head in no particular order. She suddenly knew how to make a coconut mojito despite not being certain what, exactly, a coconut was.

Jazz sketched her some more, then held the drawing up for Jandra to see.

"Like it?" she asked.

Jandra tilted her head. Surprisingly, the motion didn't cause her wrenching pain. The explosions of color had died off. The crisp white paper Jazz held showed a pencil sketch of Jandra as she lay in the moon dust, one arm over her head, one upon her breast, her hair spreading out in a dark yet radiant halo. She'd been sketched with her eyes closed. Her face looked peaceful; her lips seemed a little too full in the sketch, however.

"You'll forgive me if I'm not enthusiastic about being your model."

"I know. I probably seem like a monster to you. But I'm not a monster. I'm just a human being like you. I get lonely. I have worshippers, but not much in the way of friends. I think, with a few modifications, you and I can get along fine."

"You mean modifications to me, I presume," said Jandra, sitting up. She realized as she did so that Jazz was right. The worst of the pain was gone. There was only the memory of the pain still haunting her, causing her to move slowly and carefully as she stood up and wiped the dust from her clothing.

"You have more to gain from being changed than I do," said Jazz. "And, you've a lot to gain from being my friend. I've been sorting through your memories as you rested."

"You've been... you can read my mind?"

"Something like that. As my nanites mapped your brain connections they sent me back your existing data. You're a confused little girl. You've been raised by a talking lizard who didn't train you on how to handle human emotions. You're like Tarzan of the thirty-second century."

Jandra nodded. She hadn't known who Tarzan was when she first arrived on the moon. It felt wrong that she did now. But Jazz was right. Tarzan had been trapped between two worlds, neither civilized man nor jungle beast. Jandra sympathized.

"That Pet fellow was really coming on to you," said Jazz. "Turning him down for being a jerk is something I can respect. But you were also turning him down because you're afraid of your own sexuality. You really haven't had any girlfriends to talk about this stuff with. I can help with that."

"I didn't know you'd brought me up here to be psychoanalyzed." *Psychoanalyzed?* Was that really a word? A synapse fired and she suddenly knew that sometimes a cigar was just a cigar. She also knew that Bitterwood had been right when he'd pointed out that she dressed herself in dragon scales. She'd always subconsciously thought of herself as ugly for being scaleless, wingless, and tailless. She'd grown into a human woman's body without any preparation for thinking of it as a worthwhile thing to possess.

"Okay," said Jandra. "Maybe we don't have to be enemies. Maybe there are things I could learn from you. How to use my nanotech better, for one thing. You're obviously operating on a very different level than I am."

"That's the spirit," said Jazz.

"So, I'll stay and be your friend," said Jandra. "But only if you let Bitterwood, Hex, and Zeeky go."

"Hmm. A deal with the devil, huh? Well—" Jazz tilted her head, like a dog hearing some far-off sound.

"Oh great," she muttered.

"What?" asked Jandra.

"The central bell at the Nest just sounded," sighed Jazz. "This time it's not just some horny sky-dragon that's the problem." She shook her head and mumbled, mostly to herself, "Wish you hadn't done this, Blasphet. I sort of liked you."

Jazz stood up. The park bench crumbled back to dust. The pad of paper she carried disintegrated, leaving the graphite lines of the drawing hovering in the air. She reached out, wound the lines up into a little ball of thread, and shoved them into the pocket of her blue jeans. She flicked away the cigarette she'd been smoking. It cut a long glowing arc before her, which opened like an eyelid into twin rainbows framing a narrow slit of perfect nothingness.

"Follow me," said Jazz. "Let's give your friends something useful to do to work off their aggression."

AHEAD, THE CRIES of dying gleaners fell silent. Frost and his men had moved on. Pet trotted toward the direction he'd last heard them, hoping he might still catch up. The bright moon cut the junkscape surrounding him into spooky, surreal shadows. Pet felt lost and alone. He stared up at the white orb, trying to get his bearings. He wished Jandra were present. She was always so quick to tell him the right thing to do, even if he was always so slow in doing it. As he stood silently, he heard men's voices, and a woman crying. He hurried toward the sound.

"Hold her," a man gruffly commanded.

"Filthy gleaner scratched me," another said, his voice trailing off into nervous laughter.

The crying woman screamed, then her voice was cut short by a loud slap.

Pet ran around a junk hill and found three men holding down the woman. Her clothes were torn to shreds. Her face was dirty with rust, and blood was flowing from her nose and lips; she looked a few years older than Jandra. One of the three men was kneeling over her head, his knees pressing down on her shoulders, pinning her with his weight. A second man was fighting to pin down her pale, thin legs, which were kicking wildly. The third man watched with a leering grin, his fingers probing a set of long parallel scratches on his left cheek.

The scratched man giggled again. "Don't hit her so hard she blacks out. She won't learn her lesson if she's unconscious."

Pet drew up to his full height and marched forward. "What are you doing?" he shouted. "This isn't the mission. Let her go!"

Scratch-cheek giggled again. "Oh, it's the dragon-slayer. Funny how you disappeared at the first sign of danger."

"I've killed more men tonight than I have in years," Pet said in his best leadership voice. "Let her go and get back to your mission."

"We're just having a little fun," said the one at her feet. He'd finally managed to pin her legs down. The woman was crying hard now, barely able to inhale.

The one at her head said, "We're doing the mission. We'll kill her once we're done."

"Come on, dragon-slayer," said Scratch-cheek. "We'll give you first turn."

Pet placed an arrow against his bowstring and raised it, taking aim at Scratch-cheek.

"I can kill all three of you before you blink," he said, hoping they'd buy the bluff.

"Don't start believing your own lies, boy," said Scratch-cheek, still dabbing gently at his wounds. He seemed not the least bit afraid of Pet. "It's three of us against one of you."

Pet let the arrow fly. He imagined the shaft burying itself in Scratch-cheek's face. To his amazement, it did so, lopping off the man's middle finger before sinking into his skull just beneath the eye. Scratch-cheek dropped to his knees and fell over the crying woman, completely still. The two men who held her rose and drew their swords. Pet tried to pull another arrow from his quiver, but the men were charging him faster than he expected. Pet gave up on the arrow and drew his sword, raising it in time to parry a chop from the head-man. He jumped backward as the foot-man gave a rapid jab that terminated directly in the space his belly had occupied a half second before. Pet had no skills at actual combat, only stage combat, but instinct took over. He dodged and parried, drawing on his acrobatic training as the pair pressed their attack. Unfortunately, he could see no opening for a counterstrike.

A loud metallic *zang* rang out behind him, followed by a whistle as a razor-sharp disk big as a dinner plate flashed past his eyes. The head-man was suddenly headless. Pet's remaining opponent turned white as a ghost as he gazed at something behind Pet. Pet almost turned around to see why, but he was opportunistic enough to know he might never get a better chance to strike. He buried his sword into the right side of the man's ribcage, driving the blade in as deep as he could. The man staggered backward, a curse on his lips. Pet tried to free his sword but it was stuck, trapped by the man's ribs, and the hilt was twisted from his fingers as the man fell backward.

Ten feet away, Pet saw the gleaner woman kick herself free from the dead man who had fallen on her. She rose, clutching her torn clothes to her body. A black-haired woman no older than the gleaner leapt from the shadows with a sword and buried it in the woman's back. The gleaner fell lifeless to the dirt. Her assailant stared at Pet. She was dressed in black buckskin, nearly invisible in the shadows. A Sister of the Serpent? No. She didn't have any tattoos, and she still had hair, even eyebrows.

"Good job," said a voice behind Pet. Pet whirled around. The tall dark-skinned man stood behind him. He'd caught glimpses of this man earlier and knew his name was Burke. Burke was wearing a huge gauntlet that covered his left arm from shoulder to wrist. The gauntlet forced his arm to be held perfectly straight, and on his shoulder and back there was a tall cartridge full of the razor disks that had decapitated the first swordsman.

"Good job?" Pet asked. "Are you talking to me or her?"

"Both of you," said Burke. "Anza for fulfilling the mission. You for having the moral fiber to stand up to these thugs. What's your name, boy?"

"Pe—Bitterwood," Pet said. He cringed internally, wondering why he'd fallen back to the lie. There was something about this man's eyes, however, that made Pet feel especially ashamed of his true identity.

"Bitterwood? Oh! You're that fellow from the Free City. Are you Bant's son or something?"

"Bant?"

"Ah," said Burke. "You're just a nobody using his name."

"I prefer to think I'm somebody putting his name to better use than he is," said Pet. "I've met the real Bitterwood. He's not as heroic as you might think."

"I've fought beside the real Bitterwood," said Burke. "You're right. He's a psychopath. All he had going for him was his obsessive hatred of dragons. He wouldn't have been out here doing this clean-up work. Nothing would have stopped him from being inside Dragon Forge killing every dragon he laid eyes on."

"That's where I should be," said Pet. "I don't belong out here killing innocent people."

"Gleaners aren't innocent," said Burke. "They're a part of the infrastructure that has kept the sun-dragons in power for centuries. I don't like it either, but it helps to think that we're not simply killing people, we're breaking cogs in a vast machine of death and oppression."

Pet nodded. He felt tears welling in his eyes. "It makes sense. But I can't do it. It was bad enough to kill a grown man. I could never kill a woman or child."

"Then don't," said Burke. "Dragon Forge is back that way. It's where I'd be right now, except Ragnar thinks I'm too valuable to risk in the assault. If I die, capturing the foundry loses some of its strategic advantage."

Pet wiped his cheek, ashamed of his weakness. He desperately wanted to change the subject. "That's some fancy hardware," said Pet. "Are you going to build those for everyone?"

"This?" said Burke, running his hands along the gauntlet. "This is just a gadget I'm tuning for Big Chief. The disks are lethal at close range, and I can get off about thirty a minute if the damn thing doesn't jam, but after about fifteen yards the accuracy falls off at a laughable rate. No, when we get our hands on the forge, I have a much more fruitful item to mass produce."

"What?" Pet asked.

Burke reached for his thick leather belt, which was studded with countless tools in specialized pockets, from hammers to tweezers to wrenches to screwdrivers. He flipped open a large pouch on the side and produced two palm-sized flat ovals of polished steel with deep grooves cut into the edges. "These wheels aren't much to look at now," said Burke, "but a hundred of these things are going to kill more sun-dragons than if I built a thousand Big Chiefs."

Pet couldn't even imagine how that was possible. The wheels weren't sharp at all, and they didn't look heavy enough to do any real damage if you threw them at something. Still, he'd heard that Burke was a genius. Pet took it on faith that these wheels were important.

"Get to the forge," said Burke, walking over to the man Pet had stabbed. With a grunt, he pulled Pet's sword free. "The battle's still going on. Kill as many dragons as you can. Anza and I will be heading into the city come dawn. For now, we'll help clean up the remaining gleaners."

"Yes sir," said Pet.

"Before you run off, what's your real name, boy?"

"Petar Gondwell," he said. Feeling a sudden need for full disclosure, he said, "Pet."

"Don't get yourself killed tonight if you can help it," said Burke. "The world still needs a few men like you, with the courage to stand up to thugs and the moral fiber to at least feel some remorse at the thought of killing a fellow man. There aren't many like you left in the world."

Pet felt mildly disoriented; had the world truly turned so topsy-turvy that he was now being praised for his morality?

Burke tossed the sword toward Pet. An image quickly flashed through Pet's mind of the sword slicing off his fingers as he caught it, but then his years of practice as a juggler took over and he casually snatched it from the air by its hilt. He placed it in its scabbard and ran back toward Dragon Forge to discover who he was: a moral man, a coward, or just another cog in a vast machine.

CHAPTER TWENTY-THREE

CLICK CLICK CLANG

"INTERESTING," SAID BLASPHET, leaning close to Graxen. Unlike the dead-meat breath possessed by other sun-dragons, Blasphet's breath smelled almost medicinal, a not unpleasant mingling of camphor and cloves. "Your pupils are barely dilated, and your respiration is only mildly labored. The first time I used my paralyzing smoke on Metron, I drew a sample of his blood. I altered the formula to make him immune. It's fortunate he has no other relatives here. Apparently his blood kin share the resistance."

"Wh-why?" said Metron, still curled in a ball on the floor. "Why would you spare me?"

"I find your inner torments delightful," said Blasphet, turning from Graxen to address Metron. "Knowing that your old lusts have brought doom to your species must feel like a knife in your brain. Any brute could cause you physical agony. Only a god could flay you from the inside."

"Why do you hate him so?" asked Graxen. "Why would you attack the Nest? What grudge do you bear against sky-dragons?" The anger in the voice prompted the score of armed women who remained in the room to form a wall between Graxen and Blasphet. Graxen felt too lightheaded to overpower them. If he did defeat them, then what? Blasphet was twice Graxen's size and his claws were no doubt poisoned. All Graxen could do for now was stand over Nadala's unconscious form. If anyone approached, he would fight to his last breath to defend her.

From above, valkyries cried out in surprise and anger before their voices trailed into silence.

"This has nothing to do with grudges," said Blasphet. "Metron, as I built the Free City, you told me I used the gloss of philosophy to justify my cruelties. Your words haunted me during my recent imprisonment."

"I'm sorry," Metron whimpered.

"You need not apologize. You were correct. I've justified decades of murder by telling myself that it was an intellectual pursuit. I told myself that when all the secrets of death were unraveled, I would hold the key to unquenchable life. Now, you've guided me to a much simpler truth: I take pleasure in the suffering of others."

Blasphet placed his fore-talon on Metron's shoulder and lifted him, helping him stand once more. Metron showed no resistance; he would stand if Blasphet wished him to stand. His eyes were fixed on the floor in a look of utter defeat.

"There's a value in discovering oneself," said Blasphet. "The pleasure I feel in the suffering I cause is nearly sexual in nature. In retrospect, it seems obvious. Sex is pleasurable because it leads to the propagation of life. The procreative orgasm fills the body with bliss as it taps into a universal creative force. Yet, given the duality of this world, mustn't the universe possess a counterforce? An opposite yet equal climax that results when the energy of destruction is unleashed? Just listen to the screams above us."

Blasphet cocked his head to better hear the distant cries, his eyes wandering dreamily over the carpet of dead valkyries that covered the Thread Room.

"Never," he said, his voice trembling with excitement, "never have I felt more divine."

Graxen felt sickened by the Murder God's words. He wanted to leap at the monster and claw the look of serene satisfaction from his eyes. Yet, the second he moved, he knew the Sisters of the Serpent would slay both him and Nadala. He had to do something. But what?

The Murder God's reverie was broken by a commotion from the stairs that led up into the rest of the Nest. A Sister of the Serpent leapt down the stairs, panting loudly. She tripped on the wing of a slain valkyrie as she ran into the room, landing on her hands and knees. Breathless, she gasped out the words, "Valkyries. In the sky. Out of range."

"How many?" asked Blasphet.

"A hundred. Maybe more."

"I prepared for this," said Blasphet. "Smoke and knives were never sufficient to finish the task. This is why I had a crew capture the bell tower. Run there and tell them to ring the alarm. It's time for phase two."

But, before the girl could run back up the steps, the bells began to ring on their own. Graxen listened to the familiar sound of the gates and grates sliding into place, sealing the Nest. The machinery groaned and grumbled in every wall.

"My," said Blasphet. "That was fast."

"What evil are you working now?" Metron whispered.

"You sky-dragons always seem so confident you can outfly us sun-dragons. Smug, even," Blasphet said. "It's time we put that assumption to the test."

ARIFIEL CIRCLED THE bell-tower, shouting to Sparrow.

"Why isn't the smoke affecting you?" she cried out.

"I don't know," said Sparrow, sticking her neck out the gaps in the iron bars that had fallen to close the window. "It knocked out everyone else in my barracks but it only makes my eyes sting. I fought my way here to have you ring the alarm. Humans are attacking the Nest!"

"We know!" said Arifiel. "By ringing the bell, you've sealed the windows. You've trapped everyone inside!"

"Oh no!" Sparrow cried. "I didn't mean... I was only..."

"You only did what you were trained to do," said Arifiel. "I tried to ring the alarm myself—it's only because I failed that you've sealed the fortress instead of me. You have to get to the gear room. You must reverse the gates!"

Sparrow set her jaw in an expression of determination. "You can count on me," she said. Then, her eyes widened as she looked out over the lake.

"Sun-dragons!" she cried out, pointing with her fore-talon. "Are they coming to help?"

Arifiel looked toward the perimeter of the lake, as the dark shapes of a dozen sun-dragons flapped toward them. Perhaps they *were* here to help? A sun-dragon could rip open the iron gates that sealed the fortress with ease. But, in the moonlight, her keen eyes quickly spotted a strange detail. There was something on the backs of the dragons. Riders. Human riders.

"Go," Arifiel called to Sparrow. "Open the gates."

Sparrow gave a crisp salute and bounded down the steps. Arifiel flew back to Zorasta, who still held a position a half mile away from the Nest. She flew in a tight circle, surrounded by five or six remaining members of her flock.

"Sun-dragons!" Arifiel shouted.

"We see them," said Zorasta. "And their riders. This is more of Blasphet's handiwork, I wager. A clumsy gambit, at best."

"Clumsy?"

"If we were fighting on the ground, the sun-dragons would be a force to be feared. But we fight in the sky! We are valkyries! The air is our kingdom. We're swifter, more agile. Their size and power will be meaningless. We'll tear their wings and send them to inglorious deaths! We need not wait for others. Green flock, attack!"

Zorasta's brave words were matched by her speed and grace as she swiftly flew to the lead of the flock. She wore no armor, but some soldier had given her a spear. The flock fell into a V formation. There were nine valkyries in the charge, though only five had spears. Arifiel felt a sense of foreboding, though she knew that Zorasta was right. With their superior speed and maneuverability, the sky-dragons had little to fear.

Zorasta darted directly toward the lead sun-dragon, on a path that seemed as if it would lead to a nose-to-nose collision. It was a familiar tactic. At the last second, the flock would rise to avoid impact and then rake their spears along the larger dragon's wings. This maneuver had been drilled into them since they were old enough to lift a spear.

Spearless, Arifiel knew she would have to rake with her hind-claws—not as effective, yet still deadly. As the distance between her and the sun-dragons narrowed, she noticed that the great beasts all wore iron helmets. Atop each helmet was a nozzle attached to a long flexible tube leading back to the human rider who straddled the dragon's shoulders. The tubes seemed made of bovine intestine. Behind each rider was strapped a series of inflated sacks that looked like linked cow stomachs.

As Zorasta reached a distance of a hundred feet from the lead sun-dragon, with only seconds to go before she executed her attack, the woman riding the dragon squeezed a large bellows. Instantly, a jet of white flame shot from the dragon's helmet, changing night into day with its intensity. Zorasta screamed as the flames engulfed her. Arifiel veered left, dodging the burning stream. Zorasta fell toward the lake below, still aflame, leaving behind a black plume stinking of burnt feathers.

Before the flock could react, jets of flame shot out from the other sun-dragons and the sky was crisscrossed with a deadly white-hot web. Arifiel used all her strength to climb higher, above the killing zone. Below her she heard the screams of her sisters. Reaching a point where she felt she would no longer be in danger, she craned her neck downward. The sun-dragons and their riders continued to fly toward the Nest. None were harmed. In their wake, eight burning valkyries, writhing in agony, fell in spirals toward the distant water. Only Arifiel had escaped the initial assault.

Rage gripped her. No sun-dragon could ever fairly best a sky-dragon in aerial combat. They had won due to surprise and trickery. With a battle cry that caused all the riders to look upward, Arifiel pulled her wings tightly to her side and fell toward the hindmost dragon. She now knew what she faced. She had no trace of fear within her. The sky was the kingdom of the valkyrie. These invaders would pay the ultimate price for their trespass.

ONE IRONY OF the Nest, Sparrow realized, was that her own home stripped her of her greatest advantage over her assailants—she couldn't fly in the maze of rooms and stairways that led to the core of the island. There were a few halls long and wide enough to cover in flight, but none high enough that she could avoid the humans. They seemed to be everywhere she turned.

Fortunately, the humans mostly traveled alone or in pairs. Their mission wasn't to overpower the dragons—the paralyzing smoke had done this. They were instead methodically moving from room to room to slit the throats of unconscious dragons.

Sparrow had lost track of time since she had sounded the alarm. Five minutes? Ten? She'd killed six humans, not counting the three in the tower. The girls she fought always looked startled at seeing her move toward them so freely. This element of surprise no doubt protected her better than armor ever could.

Sparrow moved ever deeper into the Nest, toward the gear room. To her relief, she covered the last few floors without encountering resistance. Her relief turned to dread as the silence on these floors struck her. Had the humans already killed everyone?

She rounded the final corner and discovered a cluster of seven humans standing in her way. The girls looked up, their eyes wide as Sparrow rushed them. She buried her spear in the first human and released it, leaping over the falling body to clamp her toothy jaws tightly into the throat of the girl behind her. She pulled back as that human fell, beating her wings once and rising up so that she could kick out with her hind legs, gutting a third girl. The whirlwind of violence had lasted mere seconds, but now the element of surprise was gone. The remaining four rushed her, swinging their long knives, the black blades wet with poison. Sparrow skittered back down the hall, swinging her tail to trip the closest one. The girl proved too nimble—she leapt over Sparrow's tail and slashed with her knife. Sparrow dodged, but the girl still left a slender gash in Sparrow's shoulder. Sparrow bit her attacker in the face, feeling the girl's jawbone snap between her teeth.

Sparrow spat the girl away and danced backward, readying for further attack. The girl stumbled blindly, in obvious agony, falling against the woman behind her. Her knife clattered on the floor, spinning toward Sparrow's hind-talons. Sparrow lifted the knife and threw it with a kick, burying it to the hilt in the belly of a fifth girl. Now there were only two women left on their feet. They both edged back, knives held at the ready, warily watching for any opening.

Sparrow was now unarmed. Her left wing hung limp and lifeless. The tiny wound shouldn't be causing her to lose all feeling, should it? Yet with each heartbeat, her whole body grew increasingly weak.

"I've killed fourteen of your sisters tonight," she said, in the most threatening tone she could summon. "Which of you will be the fifteenth?"

She'd hoped the girls would run. Instead, they giggled and charged her, waving their knives wildly. They looked as if death was only a game to them. Sparrow knew she was little older than these women, but the time for playing games was forever gone. With a growl, she met their charge, sinking her teeth into the shoulder of the opponent to her left, burying the claws of her right fore-talon into the breast of the enemy to her right. Both humans stabbed her, driving their knives deep into her ribs. She felt no pain. She tightened her jaws, snapping the collarbone of the girl she held in her teeth. She felt the girl go limp with pain and release her grip on the blade.

With her fore-talon, Sparrow dug deeper into her final opponent's flesh, wriggling her claws past the cage of bone she found, probing for the lungs and heart. Streams of blood splashed on the floor beneath them as they whirled around, locked in a dance of death. The woman stubbornly refused to die, twisting her blade with all her remaining strength. Their eyes were locked. It was now a contest of will.

Sparrow fought for her home, her family, and her honor. She didn't know what drove the woman, and didn't care. At last, the woman's eyes clouded and her head slowly rolled to the side. Sparrow pushed her away. The woman slipped in the gore they stood in and fell roughly to the stone. Sparrow limped past her, steadying herself with her fore-talon against the wall. Dark specks danced all around her as she fell against the oak door, pushing it open with the full weight of her body. She staggered forward, the world narrowing into a dark tunnel. At the end of the tunnel was a large, steel bar, the master release for the fortress gates.

She reached out her fore-talon as she collapsed. Her bloody claw slipped on the steel. She fell to the floor, dying, uncertain if she'd pulled the lever or not. The world went perfectly dark. The only sound she could hear was her own heartbeat, which pounded in her ears like ceremonial drums.

And then, the drums stopped.

She was trapped inside herself, frozen, fading into the great unbroken silence.

Against that backdrop of oblivion came the *click, click, clang* of gears as the ancient machinery once more began to turn.

JANDRA STARED INTO the rainbow where Jazz had just vanished. Presumably, Jazz was now back on Earth, expecting Jandra to follow. Jandra looked around the unending gray desert. She could run. But to where? How long could she survive in this bleak and barren place, without hint of water or food?

"Ven," she sighed. "You can't know how badly I need to talk to you right now."

"We both know that isn't possible," a familiar voice said over her shoulder. "But perhaps I'll do?"

She turned around. Vendevorex once more stood before her, ghostly, translucent, the stars on the distant horizon shimmering in his golden eyes.

"You're back!" she said.

"I never left," Vendevorex said. "Or rather, this recording has never left. If you're seeing me now, it's no doubt because I reached my demise before we completed your training. I've attempted to anticipate your most likely questions about operation of the helmet and will answer them to the best of my ability."

"Well, for one thing, the helmet isn't a helmet any more," said Jandra.

Vendevorex's shade nodded. "It wouldn't need to be. You may have noticed it adapted its shape to fit your skull as you donned it. You could shape it into many different forms and have it retain its function. The Atlanteans call such devices Global Encephalous Nanite Interaction Engines—a GENIE."

Jandra glanced back at the rainbow. How long did she have before Jazz came back looking for her? And, what was Jazz doing to Hex and Bitterwood in her absence?

"Ven," she said, "I have a lot of questions, but let me start with the most urgent. Do you know how to lock the, uh, genie?"

"Of course," he said. "My skullcap and your tiara were always locked to avoid detection by others wielding Atlantean technology. I commanded the devices to unlock in the event of my demise, so that you could don my skullcap and, if you chose, pass on your tiara to an apprentice."

Jandra grimaced at the thought of this. She'd left the palace in a hurry; her tiara had been left sitting on her dresser. Anyone could grab it. Could anyone use it?

"Fine," she said. "So how do I relock them?"

"Simple," he said. "Here is the twenty-seven digit prime that will encrypt it to only respond to your thoughts."

Jandra listened to the number carefully. She repeated it internally, and could almost hear something in the back of her mind click shut. She repeated it once more and returned the device to the state it had been in when Jazz had last seen her. She didn't know what lay on the other side of the portal. She wasn't ready to spring this little surprise on the goddess until she knew where Hex and Bitterwood were.

"I wish we had more time to talk," she said, turning toward the rainbow. "But if I don't get back, she's probably going to come looking for me."

"We have all the time in the world," Vendevorex assured her, as she leapt toward the void.

BITTERWOOD STRAINED AGAINST his cocoon of thick kudzu. He was twenty feet above the ground, dangling upside down from the branches of a towering cottonwood; his struggles sent down a rain of leaves, but did nothing to loosen the grip of the vines.

Nearby, Hex was barely visible as a bulge beneath a thick carpet of green. His jaws were tightly wrapped by the clinging vines. The sun-dragon had made no noise for some time, but Bitterwood could tell from the rhythm of his breath that Hex was awake.

The artificial sky had, by now, transitioned to a false night, complete with stars. Mosquitoes crawled over Bitterwood's leathery face and the surrounding forest vibrated with the chorus of frogs and crickets. Against this cacophony, Bitterwood almost didn't hear the steps of the giant beast. Almost. In the end, his highly tuned ears knew that Trisky was approaching long before she came into sight, with Adam astride her.

Adam looked sorrowful. He obviously had something on his mind as he guided his mount beneath Bitterwood. He looked up and said softly, "I'm ashamed of you, Father."

Bitterwood said nothing.

"You desecrated the temple. You attacked the goddess and her angel without provocation. I'm captain of the long-wyrm riders. I've dedicated my life to serving the goddess. Why would you dishonor me so?"

Bitterwood blew away a mosquito that walked on his lips. He said, "I've spent the last twenty years believing you were dead. Perhaps it would have been best if you were. It would cause me less pain than to know you've devoted your life to this evil."

"Father," Adam said, struggling to maintain his composure. "I would slay any other man for uttering such blasphemy. The goddess is not evil. She spared you and the dragon."

"And what of the people of Big Lick? What of Zeeky and Jandra?"

"You cannot judge the actions of the goddess as good or evil," Adam said. "A storm brings rain and life to a parched land, yet may drown villages; its lightning may set fields aflame. Is a storm good or evil? The actions of the goddess are beyond the power of humans to judge."

Bitterwood closed his eyes.

"You've made your judgment," he said.

"Father, I implore you; repent your blasphemy and you'll be released unharmed. You may live out the remainder of your days here in paradise."

Bitterwood chuckled. "You live in a hole beneath the earth. How can this be paradise when you know that the stars above you are nothing but a lie?"

"Why do you think the world outside is any different?" Adam asked. "How can you know that the stars you look upon at night are real?"

Bitterwood didn't have an answer for this.

Adam continued: "You're a legend, Father. The dragons call you the Ghost Who Kills. Yet, you aren't a ghost. Does this make your struggle any less just? The dragons think of you as a force of nature, a supernatural being that slays without cause. Does this make you evil, Father? Or are you a good man because you've fought to make the world a better place?"

Bitterwood kept his eyes closed. He hoped Adam would go away. But he could still hear Trisky below, calmly munching on the grass.

Bitterwood sighed. "A lifetime of murder has corrupted me beyond redemption."

"If you believe this, why do it?"

Bitterwood opened his eyes. He looked down upon his son. Adam was a man now, yet still had a boyish softness to his eyes. There was an innocence within him, a hope and faith that the world was a good world guided by a watchful, benign power. There was a light inside him that had long since burned to ash within Bitterwood.

Bitterwood had never been called upon to justify his actions. If he owed anyone an explanation, it was his own son. "It is said that if a man's only tool is a hammer, then he will treat all the problems of the world as a nail."

"Why do you answer me in riddles, Father?"

"Hate was the only tool that remained after the dragons took everything else," Bitterwood said. "In a single day I lost my God, my family, my home, my hope. Hatred kept me warm in winter. Hatred slaked my dry throat in times of drought and fed me in times of famine. I would have died long ago if not for my dream of a world without dragons. Perhaps, in the end, all the evil I've done will lead to good when mankind rules this world once more."

"The goddess will never allow mankind dominion over the Earth," said Adam. "She says the race of man is unworthy. Listening to your words, watching your actions, I can't help but wonder if she's right."

Behind Adam, the air began to rip. Prisms of light opened to surround a black gate. A woman stepped through. She resembled the goddess statue on a human scale; tall but nothing unnatural save for the hue of her hair.

"Sorry to interrupt this heart-to-heart," the woman said. Bitterwood instantly recognized her voice as belonging to the goddess.

Adam threw himself to the ground.

"Oh, stand up and stop groveling," the goddess said, sounding mildly agitated. "It's starting to get old. I miss the days when guys your age couldn't take their eyes off my breasts. You don't know what I look like above my toenails."

"I'm not worthy to gaze upon you," Adam said.

"Worthy or not, I need you on your feet. Or on your butt, to be precise. Mount up."

Adam rose, still averting his eyes as he climbed back into his saddle.

"Here's the deal. I worked with the first matriarch to design the gene maps that would help her race slip out of the genetic noose it was caught in. But as we speak, Blasphet is attacking the Nest, trying to bring extinction to the entire species. He won't succeed, of course. He doesn't know about the sky-dragon population over in Tennessee or the big colony down in Cuba. Still, I'm a little pissed off that Blasphet's wrecking a thousand-year-old project that's one of my bigger success stories. So, Adam, I'm sending you and the other riders to stop him. I'm sending your dad along. Also, the big guy." She cocked her head toward Hex.

"You want me to fight for you?" Bitterwood asked.

"You've shown a lot of talent for breaking things. Go break Blasphet."

Bitterwood frowned. Was this a trick? Blasphet had long been one of the most difficult of Albek-izan's relatives to target. Normally, he would gladly accept an opportunity to face him. But not under these conditions.

"No," he said. "I didn't come here to serve you. I came here to find Zeeky."

"Sure," said the goddess. "So let's cut to the chase. Go kill Blasphet and I won't hurt Zeeky."

"How do I even know she's alive? Why did you send a replica to greet us?"

"I have her busy elsewhere right now," said the goddess. "She's not been hurt. For what it's worth, I like the kid. She's spunky. Reminds me of me when I was little."

Bitterwood ground his teeth as he thought the offer over. What did it matter if Blasphet was attacking the Nest now? Even if they were outside the mountain, the Nest would take several days to reach. This must be a trick.

The goddess waved her hands toward Hex. The vegetation around his jaws loosened.

"How about you?" she asked. "Think you can take out your uncle?"

"Where's Jandra?" Hex asked. With his head free, he strained to stand. The ground beneath him bulged as the full force of his muscles was brought to bear. In the end, the effort was futile. For every vine he snapped, two grew to replace them.

Suddenly, the rainbows behind the goddess rippled and a young woman stepped out. It looked like Jandra, though Bitterwood knew he couldn't trust his eyes. This one was even less authentic than the earlier one. She wore no helmet.

Jandra looked up into the tree, then glanced over to the vines that covered Hex.

"What have you done to them?" she demanded.

"They aren't hurt," the goddess said. "Merely detained. I've offered them a chance to go to the Nest to fight Blasphet. So far, they don't seem all that hot on the idea."

"I'll go," said Jandra.

"This is further evidence you aren't real," said Bitterwood. "Your eagerness to do her bidding shows that you're another doppelganger."

Jandra looked as if she had no idea what Bitterwood was talking about. "I have no idea what you're talking about," she said. "But, here's one thing I understand: Blasphet. He escaped from the dungeons right before I left. He's got a cult helping him, the Sisters of the Serpent, and one of them almost killed me. I'm finding there aren't a lot of easy moral choices in life. But this one's fairly simple. Anything that Blasphet wants to do, we should want to undo."

"What happened to your helmet?" Hex asked.

"I'll explain later. You coming?"

"Draw nearer," Hex said.

Jandra walked closer. Hex's nostrils flared as he sniffed her.

"She sweats," he announced, looking up at Bitterwood. "It's her."

Bitterwood nodded. A dragon's sense of smell rivaled that of a dog.

"I'll go," said Bitterwood. He didn't care much about doing the bidding of the goddess, but getting free of these vines was an improvement over his current state.

"And I," said Hex. "My uncle has tarnished my family's reputation even more than my father. Unlike Shandrazel, I'm not encumbered by any romantic ideas of law. I'll gladly gut the old monster."

"Swell," said the goddess. She snapped her fingers and the kudzu began to writhe. Bitterwood was spun downward and deposited on his feet. Hex rose as the vines lost their hold on him. He shook like a wet dog to free himself of the last of the clinging tendrils.

"If I'm going to face Blasphet, I'll require a weapon," said Bitterwood.

"Naturally," the goddess said. She reached up and grabbed a low hanging limb of the cottonwood. The branch snapped off in her hand. Before Bitterwood's eyes, the raw wood warped, the bark and leaves falling away as it straightened into a wooden bow six feet long. The goddess grimaced as she bent the bow into an arc and plucked a strand of her own hair. The hair wove and grew into a long silken cord that knotted itself around the ends. She tossed it to Bitterwood. He snatched it from the air and gave it a pull. It felt perfectly balanced, and was a good match for his strength. He looked up to find that the goddess had reconfigured the bark and remaining wood into a quiver of arrows, fletched with fresh green leaves.

She threw the quiver to him. "I've always believed in recycling," she said. "You'll be happy to know your equipment is 100% biodegradable."

Bitterwood wasn't happy to know this. He wasn't even certain what the word meant, though he felt it was similar enough to degradation that it must mean something unpleasant.

"Time's wasting," said the goddess. Another rainbow opened before her, the largest yet, wide enough for Hex to step through. "Go get him."

Jandra cast the goddess a stern look. "When we get back," she said. "I want to see Zeeky."

"We'll talk about it," the goddess said.

Bitterwood moved next to Jandra and Hex. He stared into the black rip in the center of the rainbow. A shudder passed through him as he gazed into the void.

He felt as if the void was gazing back.

CHAPTER TWENTY-FOUR

LONG SLOW fALL

"KILL THE GRAY one," Blasphet said, moving toward the stairs that lead up from the Thread Room. "Bring Metron up with us to watch the festivities. The attack of the sun-dragons should be well underway. The burning bodies of valkyries must be falling from the sky like stars."

As one the twenty women lowered their long knives and advanced toward Graxen. Graxen braced himself, running his eyes along the chain of attackers, searching for the weakest link. Unfortunately, the drugged smoke continued to play with his senses. It looked as if a rainbow had suddenly erupted in the air before him.

Then he slipped into madness. From thin air, a huge beast shot into the room. It was copper-colored, serpentine, and seemingly endless, studded with more limbs than Graxen could count. The serpent writhed, its body undulating as it trampled half of Blasphet's assassins beneath its claws.

The serpent hadn't come through alone. He was being ridden by a man in a white uniform, his eyes hidden behind a silver visor. The rider wielded a crossbow and coolly lowered it toward Blasphet. There was no way the rider could miss at such range. Yet as he pulled the trigger, one of the sisters leapt up and hit his arm. The shot went high, striking sparks on the ceiling above Blasphet's head. Blasphet winced as the bolt bounced against his skull. Then he quickly turned tail, slithering toward the door he'd entered.

With a back-handed slap, the rider knocked aside the girl who'd grabbed him. The copper serpent curved his head toward Blasphet, preparing to strike. The beast's eyes seemed unfocused in the smoky air. Suddenly, the serpent stumbled. The rider tumbled from his saddle as the serpent rolled to its side, succumbing to the poisoned torches.

Graxen's eyes were drawn by a motion to his left. He spun in time to find a tattooed girl attacking him. He thrust out his wing, knocking her knife away, then lunged forward, biting her throat with a quick snap of his jaws. He pulled back as she fell to her knees, clasping her neck with both hands.

Graxen coughed as he searched around the room for other attackers. The arrival of the giant serpent had caused so much confusion that no one was watching him. The atmosphere was increasingly difficult to see through. Some of the torches the assassins had carried had been knocked against the tapestries. The aged threads hissed as flames devoured them.

JANDRA PLUNGED INTO the rainbow gate, in pursuit of Hex and Bitterwood. In her previous journeys through underspace, she had exited the other side an instant after she entered. This time, something was different. She felt as if she were engulfed by the void, falling through a space that was not a space, a place disconnected from the normal world of up and down, back and forth. It was a place without light or sound. And in this nothingness, a familiar voice called her name.

Zeeky? she thought, before she stumbled back into reality. She was in a room full of smoke, with the dead bodies of sky-dragons underfoot. Bitterwood was helping Adam get free of Trisky's unconscious form. Hex had dropped to all fours, gasping for breath.

"J-jandra," he whispered, "the air..." before slumping to the ground.

"The smoke is poisoned," shouted a gray sky-dragon standing near a blackboard. The name "Vendevorex" was written on the board, the white chalk seeming to glow.

"You're Graxen, right?" Jandra asked. "Shandrazel's messenger?"

"Yes," he answered. "How did you get here? What is this rainbow?"

"I'll have to answer you later," Jandra said, fanning smoke away from her eyes. She reached into the pouch on her belt and threw thick handfuls of silver dust into the air. Despite the flames the air here was humid; she knew the Nest was located on an island. She commanded her tiny helpers to gather the water molecules in the air.

"Where's Blasphet?" Bitterwood asked Graxen.

Graxen pointed toward the stairs down. "He fled mere moments ago."

Now that the nanites had bonded to the water molecules, Jandra commanded a dozen small, localized showers to rain on all the torches and tapestries burning within the room. A second later the room went dark, with only a few red embers still visible. Content that the flames were extinguished, Jandra commanded the nanites to emit light. A soft white glow lit the nightmarish corpsescape.

"You must be Jandra," Graxen said. "Vendevorex's apprentice."

Jandra nodded. She looked back toward Bitterwood, but he was gone.

"Blasphet has sun-dragons attacking above," said Graxen. "We have to stop them!"

"If my father went after Blasphet, I must aid him," said Adam.

Before anyone could move, the rainbow rippled once more and a tall, silver-haired man stepped out. He was bare-chested, and sported long golden wings.

"Who?" Jandra and Graxen asked simultaneously.

"Gabriel," said the angel. "I'll take command. The goddess has explained the full situation. Blasphet's servants fan through the Nest, slaughtering valkyries. Adam, Jandra, since you cannot fly, it's your duty to stop them. The goddess is sending the remaining long-wyrm riders to other areas of the Nest to assist. Meanwhile, the valkyries are under assault from sun-dragons. Since only I can fly, I'll deal with them."

Graxen stepped up. "I can help."

"If you wish," said the angel. Without waiting to see if anyone would question his orders, Gabriel leapt over the dead bodies to the stairs, darting up them with superhuman speed. Adam followed as quickly as he could, drawing his sword.

Jandra knelt before Hex, placing her hands upon him to see if she could identify the poison that had claimed him. To her relief, he was still breathing. The smoke wasn't fatal.

"Aren't you coming?" Graxen asked.

"Not until I neutralize the poison," said Jandra. "He'll be a big help if I can revive him."

"If you possess Vendevorex's healing arts, please, save Nadala," Graxen said, bending low over the body of an unarmored valkyrie.

"I'll do what I can," said Jandra, as visions of molecules danced before her. She'd work better without any distractions. "She's safe with me. Go!"

She gave him a dismissive wave as she turned her concentration once more to Hex. Graxen ran up the stairs. The clicks of his claws were drowned out as unseen gears in the walls started to chatter and grind.

ARIFIEL AIMED HERSELF toward the sun-dragon that lagged behind the rest of the pack. She folded her wings and went into freefall, undulating like a snake swimming through water, racing toward her target. The tattooed woman astride the sun-dragon spotted her and pulled the reins to guide the dragon's head upward, but there was no way the gargantuan beast could move swiftly enough. Arifiel aimed for the dragon's left wing, a massive sheet of feathery flesh. As the dragon beat a down stroke, she extended her hind-talons. Her claws sunk into the hide with a satisfying jolt as she ripped long, parallel shreds from the wing. The sun-dragon listed, losing speed, its movement crossing the tipping point between flying and falling. Arifiel kicked, tearing one last shred as she pushed away. The sun-dragon craned its neck toward her. Arifiel caught the look of terror and confusion in its eyes.

Then, without warning, the dragon's rider gave one last squeeze of the bellows and a geyser of white flame shot toward her. Arifiel spun, pulling back from the worst of the flame, but cupfuls of the fluid splashed across her shoulders. She spasmed from the intense pain and found herself falling in the same path as the injured sun-dragon. She fought to regain control of her limbs, but each motion was utter agony as the liquid flame trickled across her scales.

The sun-dragon struck the water a hundred feet beneath her, creating a huge circle of waves. Cool droplets splashed against her face. A scream tore from her throat as she forced her injured shoulders to obey her will. She pulled from her dive, darting across the lake at neck-breaking speed.

She glanced up at the remaining sun-dragons. More valkyries charged them and the night again was lit with a web of flame. She needed to return to combat, no matter her injuries. She needed a weapon. She wished she could get back into the central tower to recover her spear. She wondered if Sparrow would ever make it to the control panel.

As she thought this, the island rumbled and the grates slowly rose. She tried to focus on her mission, ignoring the screams of the dying valkyries above her. Burnt feather-scales drifted through the air, filling the night with their stench. She flew only inches from the barbs and spear points that studded the Nest until she reached the tower. Through sheer will she beat her wings, shooting up the stony surface, until she found the bell room. She landed inside, avoiding the bodies of the girls that Sparrow had killed. Sparrow had made short work of them, certainly, and she'd apparently had no problem reaching the gear room. Arifiel could do no less. She retrieved her spear and steadied herself. She felt lightheaded. Blood streamed from the charred flesh of her shoulders. The battle sounded faint and distant compared to her labored breathing. She badly wanted to lie down to catch her breath.

"This isn't how you die," she whispered. "Go rip another of these interlopers from the sky!"

She leapt from the window. The spear in her hind-talons seemed made of lead. She climbed toward the cluster of sun-dragons. A cloud of valkyries swarmed them, darting and dodging through the jets of flame. Arifiel took heart as she saw a sun-dragon stumble in the air, spinning down in a deadly spiral to the rocky shore below. Another sun-dragon had lost its rider and was now covered in flames; the burning fluid in the bladders on its back had been punctured.

Arifiel felt that if she could only draw a deep breath, she'd be able to rise above the battle and once more attack with a dive. It would be her last dive ever, she felt certain, but at least she would not die alone.

Then, the spear in her hind-talons slipped from her grasp. The stars above her spun as her path tilted downward. She'd failed to reach her target. Her wings went limp. Below her was the Nest, with its vicious thorny surface. She vowed not to close her eyes. She would face death head on, without taking the comfort of a coward.

Below her, from an open balcony, she saw a human—a tall male, unlike the petite females who'd attacked her. She tried to steer her fall toward him. She could see that the spear she had dropped had already landed on this balcony; its tip was buried into a gap in the stone. If she could land on this human with equal force, her death wouldn't be in vain.

The man looked up at her with a placid smile as golden wings unfolded from his back. He leapt toward Arifiel. The distance between them closed in seconds. But instead of a violent collision, the man held out his arms and caught her, using his wings as a parachute to slow their fall. He hugged her against his muscular chest as he drifted back to the balcony. He placed her carefully upon her back against the cool stone.

"You've fought valiantly, valkyrie," he said, in a soothing, almost musical voice. "Rest now. Victory is at hand."

He once more spread his wings and shot skyward, drawing a sword from the scabbard on his belt. The blade glowed red, as if it had just been pulled from a forge, then burst into flame. The yellow fire glimmered against his golden wings as he hurtled toward the dragons high above.

GRAXEN WAS LOST in the maze of corridors. He found himself in a room where a human male dressed in a white uniform stood over the dying body of a tattooed woman. The man's eyes were hidden behind a visor, and his face was devoid of emotion. This wasn't the one the angel had called Adam. It must be another of the long-wyrm riders. A sky-dragon was slumped on the floor near him.

"I got here in time to save this one," the man reported.

Graxen nodded. He'd seen many horrors tonight, but as he'd passed through the fortress, he'd discovered more unconscious sky-dragons than dead ones. Hope wasn't lost. His species might yet survive Blasphet's assault. At the open window beyond the man, the night was aglow with white flames. He ran to it and looked up, trying to make sense of the chaos overhead. Bodies were falling from the heavens—sky-dragons, wreathed in fire. Graxen watched as the seven sun-dragons still in the air shot spouts of fire from their heads, frying the valkyries who bravely rushed to defend their home. One of the sun-dragons began to plummet, trailing a white-hot arc of flame. Above the falling dragon hovered Gabriel, burning bright as the sun. Gabriel was aflame—his clothes, his hair, even his skin was peeling away in the pillar of fire that engulfed him. Gabriel had obviously been the target of the dragons many times, but if the fire caused him any discomfort, Graxen couldn't tell it. The angel remained aloft on his metallic wings, fluidly wheeling through the air to target his next opponent.

Gabriel drew his sword back to strike a sun-dragon that barreled straight toward him. He landed a decisive blow, burying his sword to the hilt in the dragon's gaping mouth. Unfortunately, the great beast was slow to realize it was dead. The dragon closed its jaws tightly around the angel's shoulder. It carried Gabriel forward through sheer mass, traveling a hundred yards before its body shuddered with the spasms of death. The dragon started to fall but didn't release its death-bite on Gabriel. The angel was dragged from the air by the plummeting dragon, falling a quarter of a mile until they both vanished in the waters of the lake.

Graxen leapt from the window. There were fewer than twenty sky-dragons facing the remaining five sun-dragons. If the sun-dragons made it through this gauntlet, it wouldn't matter that Blasphet and his cult were in retreat. The sun-dragons could gut the Nest with fire if they weren't stopped. Blasphet could still have his victory.

Graxen scanned the shoreline for any sign of a weapon. He spotted a spear jutting upright on a nearby balcony. He swooped down and tried to grab it in mid-flight. Alas, its tip was buried so securely in the stone the jolt of tearing it loose also snatched it from his grasp. He heard it clatter against the balcony railing as he circled around to grab it once more. He landed on the railing and looked down, surprised to discover a valkyrie lying in the shadows.

"Arifiel?" he asked.

"Graxen?" she answered. Her voice trembled as if she were shivering.

"I need your spear, valkyrie," Graxen said, grabbing her weapon from where he'd dropped it. "I promise I'll make good use of it."

"Why are you here, G-Graxen?" Arifiel whispered. "Are you to b-blame for this?"

Graxen swallowed hard. Was he to blame? Had his foolish desires turned him into an instrument of death? He instinctively shied away from that line of thought. It could only lead to despair, and despair was a luxury he couldn't afford at the moment.

He removed the satchel he always carried from his shoulder. It would only weigh him down. It still held the beaded belt he'd intended to give to Nadala. It seemed as if the momentum of events would always conspire against him presenting her the gift. He tossed the bag to Arifiel's side.

"If you live and I do not," said Graxen, "give Nadala this bag, and tell her I loved her."

"L-love counts for nothing here," Arifiel said.

"Perhaps it counts for nothing anywhere," said Graxen, spreading his wings. "Tell her all the same."

He didn't wait for her answer.

With the spear in his hind-talons he climbed toward the conflict. He had seconds to study the aerial battlefield. The sun-dragons were relatively slow, but the jets of flame more than made up for that disadvantage. The flames could shoot out a hundred feet in the space of a second, and the five sun-dragons were swooping around in overlapping figure-eights. There was no part of the sky where a valkyrie could approach one dragon without being in the sight of another.

The sky above the sun-dragons was now thick with billowing clouds of gray smoke. Only the faintest hint of the moon peeked through the veil. Graxen flew wide of the combat, holding his breath against the stench as he rose through the dark cloud. Finally, he emerged into bright moonlight, far above the conflict below. He looked down to see the glow of the flame jets faintly visible through the clouds. He mentally mapped the flashes, calculating the speed and direction of each sun-dragon. When the moment was right, he released Arifiel's spear and went into a dive, beating his wings to fall faster than the spear. He angled his body so that he burst from the clouds well ahead of a dragon who would be heading directly for him. He spread his wings to slow his fall and make himself a better target. As expected, a jet of flame shot toward him, only to flicker out at least five yards away. He'd gauged the distance well.

As the flame died and the dragon flew closer, the tattooed girl astride the sun-dragon drew the bellows wide once more. Just then, the spear emerged from the cloud overhead. It landed in the back of her sun-dragon, sinking deep into the beast's spine, puncturing the half-empty bladder behind the rider. The dragon's wings went limp and a huge fireball grew on its back, a miniature volcano that exploded with a light brighter than the noon sun.

Amidst this blinding flash, Graxen closed his eyes and flew with all his power toward the location of his next target. His mental mapping was rewarded when he opened his eyes and found himself mere yards from the next rider. She had turned her face away from the fireball, shielding her eyes with a raised arm. She never saw him coming as he slammed into her, knocking her from her mount. Graxen halted his momentum by grabbing the loose reins as they flapped in the air. The sun-dragon turned his head at the tug. Graxen grabbed the bellows and squeezed at the exact moment the beast's head was perpendicular to its nearest neighbor. Suddenly, the wings of that sun-dragon were ablaze. Its rider let out a cry of alarm as the dragon tilted in the air and went into its death spiral.

Graxen jumped from the back of the sun-dragon he rode, holding the bellow handles in his hindclaws. The bellows tore loose, and Graxen beat his wings to put as much distance as possible between him and the conflagration that grew as the torn hoses sprayed burning liquid in all directions. The sun-dragon roared as it slipped into a long, slow fall.

In the space of seconds, there were only two sun-dragons left. Graxen wheeled, calculating his next attack, only to find that the valkyries had wasted no time in taking advantage of the defensive gaps in his wake. The remaining two dragons were torn apart in mid-air as valkyries swarmed over them. The wings of both dragons were reduced to tatters by the vengeful females, who let out a victorious war whoop as their much larger opponents dropped toward the water far below.

* * *

JANDRA FROWNED AS she studied the molecules of the airborne toxin that sedated Hex. The smoke was a mix of many chemicals, and she found it difficult to calculate which one she needed to break. Still, as she knelt beside Hex, monitoring his pulse, she felt that neutralizing the poison might not be necessary to wake him. His pulse and blood pressure were increasing as the residual smoke faded. The simplest antidote for the poison, it seemed, was fresh air.

She went to an unburned section of the tapestries that covered the walls. She ripped it down, intending to use it as a large fan to help circulate the air. She was surprised to discover an open door beyond. The cool breeze that carried into the room inspired her. She moved to the next tapestry and yanked it down.

"S-stop," a faint voice behind her commanded.

She looked back to discover that one of the valkyries was standing, her head swaying. The sky-dragon's eyes narrowed as they focused on the torn tapestry in Jandra's grasp.

"Intruder!" the dragon growled, anger giving strength to her still-raspy voice. "Defiler!"

"Wait," said Jandra. "I—"

Before she could say anything further, the valkyrie charged. Jandra dropped the tapestry and leapt sideways. The dragon landed where Jandra had stood, her teeth snapping empty air. The valkyrie wobbled on unsteady talons as she craned her neck to locate Jandra.

Jandra summoned twin balls of flames around her hands.

"I don't want to hurt you!" she shouted.

The valkyrie didn't share the sentiment. She pounced. Jandra again danced aside, only to trip on one of the fallen bodies. She hit the stone floor hard, wrecking her concentration. The flames around her fists vanished. She rolled to her back, sizing up her opponent, who had also stumbled upon landing. The mind-numbing drugs weren't entirely out of the valkyrie's system. There was no point in reasoning with her. Jandra clenched her jaw. This would be a stupid way to die, gutted by a dragon she'd come here to save. She'd killed so often in recent days, what was one more death?

Except, everyone else she'd killed had been attacking her with malice. This dragon was simply confused. Jandra willed herself invisible. She rose to her feet and moved to the side of the room as the valkyrie carefully probed the area where Jandra had last stood. Jandra remembered one of Vendevorex's favorite tricks. She cast more dust into the air and willed it to the opposite side of the room, where it coalesced into a double of herself. The valkyrie spun to face it.

"I'm not your enemy," Jandra said. The valkyrie twisted her body to see if someone was behind her. Jandra didn't know how to make her voice appear to come from her double. She had her duplicate hold out its arms. The movement drew the valkyrie's attention.

"I'm Jandra, daughter of Vendevorex, a loyal subject of Shandrazel. I've come to defend the Nest."

"What's happened?" the valkyrie asked, raising a fore-talon to stroke her brow. She looked ill as she gazed over the bodies of her fellow warriors. "How did everyone die? Why am I still alive?"

"Blasphet attacked," said Jandra. "He's using a smoke-borne poison that doesn't kill outright; he's sent his army of human servants to finish the job. I'm here to stop them. I'm not alone."

The sky-dragon's legs suddenly gave way and she fell to all fours. Jandra wondered if the smoke was taking effect once more.

"What have I done?" she whispered. "Metron was a tatterwing and still I led him in! How could I have been so blind?"

Jandra wasn't certain she understood what the sky-dragon was saying. How was Metron involved in this? She only knew she had never heard so much pain in a dragon's voice. The valkyrie closed her eyes to the horrors before her as she whispered, so faintly Jandra nearly couldn't hear, "Oh, Graxen. What have we done?"

CHAPTER TWENTY-FIVE

GIFTS OF MONSTERS

BLASPHET SQUEEZED HIS massive frame down the narrow staircase and into the larger room beyond. The dank darkness reminded him of his imprisonment in the dungeon. He'd had better lighting on his journey in; he'd been surrounded by an army of torch-wielding worshippers. Fortunately, years of dwelling beneath the earth had left Blasphet confident in his movements in darkness. The torches and lanterns in the room above dented the gloom below, allowing him to navigate back to the tunnel with all the dripping pipes. He stumbled as he reached the water, and the splash of his movements echoed up and down the passageway.

Soon he'd left even the faint light behind, but it didn't matter. The ancient corridor ran in a straight line. He stretched out his wings, feeling the enclosing walls, and used them for a guide as he pushed forward. He could hear nothing but the splash of his own talons above the splatter of the leaking pipes.

As he fled, Blasphet tried to make sense of what he'd witnessed. He'd been told that Vendevorex was dead. Perhaps it wasn't true? How else could an attacker have materialized from thin air? Blasphet knew that the so-called wizard's power was mostly illusion. Perhaps he was running from a trick of the light?

No, the crossbow bolt that had bounced against his head was real enough. Was there any other possible explanation? Blasphet stopped feeling his way down the tunnel as his mind snapped onto the most likely scenario. Vendevorex was dead, but what of the human he'd trained? The girl, Jandra? If Jandra had snuck into the room with an ally under the cover of invisibility, it could have looked as if they were stepping from thin air. Blasphet wasn't sure what sort of creature they'd been riding, but apparently the beast had enough reptilian physiology to fall to the smoke. Was he fleeing nothing more than a boy with a crossbow and a girl with a few trick mirrors?

Blasphet gazed back toward the Nest. Again and again his grandest designs were thwarted by the meddling of others. The Free City would have been a marvelous triumph if Albekizan hadn't interfered. Was he prepared to allow his latest scheme to be unraveled by a few youthful humans?

He shook his head. Fleeing such feeble opposition was simply… *ungodlike.*

Blasphet flicked away the ceramic caps that covered his poison-coated claws. As he slogged through the stagnant water back toward the dim and distant light, a voice, unseen in the gloom, whispered, "Where do you go, Murder God?"

Blasphet froze. The voice was human, male. Where had it come from? The falling water and the echoes in the tunnel made it difficult to pinpoint.

"Who's there?" he said. His voice echoed in the tunnel. No one answered. Blasphet slowly let out his breath. Perhaps he'd imagined the voice?

Just as he was certain he was alone, the voice once more spoke: "I am the screams of innocents crushed beneath the talons of your race. I am the shadow on the stone; I am the Ghost Who Kills. I come this day for you, Murder God."

"The Ghost Who... *Bitterwood*?" Blasphet asked, cocking his head. "The murderer of my brother?"

For a moment, only the water answered. Then a chill voice said, "You know my name."

"I don't know whether to curse you or thank you," said Blasphet.

Bitterwood gave no reply.

"I despised my brother," Blasphet continued. "I dreamed of his death. Yet, in the end, I loved the dream of killing him more than I wanted to actually watch him die. You succeeded where I failed, Ghost Who Kills. I'm in your debt."

Again, his words were met only by silence.

"Has my gratitude left you speechless?" Blasphet asked. He took a slow, careful step forward, drawing a yard closer to the dim light at the end of the passage. "We're much alike. We've transcended mere mortality: you, the avenging ghost; I, the god. We each tap a higher truth as our path to power—we know there is so much more to murder than simply ending a life."

Blasphet paused, allowing his words to sink in.

"Did you come here in search of an enemy only to discover an admirer? Reveal yourself, Bitterwood. I would look upon the man who rid the world of Albekizan."

At last, a reply came from the darkness. "Perhaps we aren't so different. In the end, only one small thing divides us."

Blasphet tilted his head, still unable to pinpoint the source of the voice. "And what would this small thing be?"

"I know where you are," Bitterwood answered.

The words were followed by the hiss of an arrow cutting the air. Blasphet grunted as the arrow sank into the wrist bone of his left wing. He sucked in his breath through clenched teeth as he spun to face the direction the attack had come from. The arrow had flown for mere seconds. Bitterwood wasn't so far away. He held his right fore-talon at the ready as he studied the darkness, glad he'd uncapped the poison. He thought he could discern a shape now, vaguely human, no more than twenty feet distant.

"You could have killed me with a single arrow," Blasphet said, attempting to keep his voice calm. "Yet you shot my brother three times. They pulled thirteen arrows from my nephew. You take the same pleasure from the suffering of your victims as I do. You drink fear like wine." Blasphet crouched down, the muscles in his legs coiling tightly as the nearby shadow emerged more clearly from the darkness. "I'm sorry to disappoint you. I'm a god. I shall not fear a ghost."

Blasphet lunged for the humanoid shadow. He thrust his poisoned claw before him, burying it dead center of his target. A rotten tree branch snapped beneath his grasp. He stumbled in the water, trying not to fall. When he found his balance once more, he was left standing with only a large piece of cloth in his hand. A human's cloak from the stink of it.

There was a splashing sound reverberating up and down the pipe. The echoes of his own attack?

Or was Bitterwood moving to better target him? Suddenly, he discovered that his left leg was numb. He toppled as he lost control of the limb. A dull pain throbbed through him as he discovered an arrow jutting from his hamstring. He hadn't even felt the arrow strike.

"Bitterwood," said Blasphet, swallowing hard. His saliva had a metallic flavor. "Killing me is a mistake! Legends say that you seek vengeance against the dragons who killed your family. Can't you see that I am an instrument to that end? Kill me, and you kill a single dragon. Spare me, and you guarantee the deaths of thousands."

Blasphet pushed with his uninjured wing to a sitting position against the tunnel wall. At least the next arrow wouldn't come from behind.

"No answer?" he asked. "My words intrigue you? We've killed so many, each acting alone. Think of what we could do as an alliance; ghost and god, holding the power of life and death over all."

There was a loud splash as something heavy dropped from the pipes above. Blasphet slithered his tail beneath the water as he saw the silhouette of a man rise, several dozen yards away. If Bitterwood got close enough, Blasphet would trip him with his tail and make one last strike.

Bitterwood was clearly defined now, a black outline against the distant light. He slowly walked closer. Blasphet braced himself to attack. Then, just beyond the range of Blasphet's tail, the shadow stopped. The Ghost Who Kills lifted his bow and took aim.

Blasphet opened his mouth to make one final appeal.

The bowstring rang out. Blasphet screeched as the arrow flashed into his open mouth, puncturing his cheek from the inside, pinning his head to the wall behind him. The agony of the arrow through his jaw muscle was astonishing. Was this white searing energy that filled him the same force that his victims had felt? If so, what a gift he had given them. As the pain washed through the recesses of his brain, it left in its wake a cleansing light that illuminated a simple, fundamental truth: it felt good to be alive. Only facing his end did Blasphet truly understand how much he cherished his existence.

It felt good to breathe. Each ragged gasp inflated his chest with damp air, bringing fresh oxygen to his hungry lungs. It felt good for his heart to beat, for the blood to race through his body with each pulse. Blasphet had long believed death to be a superior force to life. Life was merely a momentary act of resistance, while death was the ultimate champion. Ah, but what an act! What a glorious flickering moment!

Bitterwood stood before him, sword in hand.

"I won't be quick about this," he said.

Blasphet thought of the thirteen arrows that had been pulled from Bodiel. He recalled how the corpse of Dacorn had been found wedged into the crook of a tree, his tongue crudely hacked out. Blasphet's courage failed him. In one last hope of remaining the master of his own destiny, Blasphet sank the poisoned claws of his right fore-talon into his thigh. The deadening effect of the poison was swift.

Bitterwood pried his jaws open. Blasphet felt the touch of a blade against his tongue. He sighed as each heartbeat carried him away, further, further, to a place where even Bitterwood could not follow.

* * *

JANDRA STEPPED ASIDE as Hex staggered upright. The long-wyrm beside him was also stirring, but without Adam near she didn't know how well-behaved Trisky would be. Jandra took the tapestry she'd torn down a moment before and draped it over the long-wyrm. She covered the tapestry with silver dust and willed the fibers to reweave themselves. In seconds she'd created a makeshift straightjacket and muzzle for the long-wyrm. She'd apologize to Adam later if he objected to this treatment of his mount.

Hex stretched to fight off the effects of the poison. He winced as he smacked his head against the ceiling. Hex lowered his neck, his eyes wide open. He looked around the room. "What hit me?"

"Blasphet," said Jandra. "Poison gas. Bitterwood has gone off to catch him."

"Alone?" Hex asked.

"Yes," said Jandra.

"That's the last we'll see of Bitterwood, then," said Hex.

"I was thinking it would be the last we saw of Blasphet," said Jandra.

"Bitterwood is an impressive warrior for a human," said Hex. "But in Blasphet, he's met his match. My uncle didn't earn the title Murder God lightly."

"You sound oddly proud of this," said Jandra.

Hex shrugged. "Pride isn't the correct word. However, I do respect him. Like me, he lost his contest of succession. Yet he didn't fade from the world as I nearly did. Instead, he became a figure even more notorious than my father. History may long remember him after it has forgotten my father's name."

Jandra was bothered by Hex's confident tone. Had she been wrong in letting Bitterwood chase

Blasphet alone? On the other hand, how could she have stopped him?

She said, "Maybe we should..."

Her voice trailed off. There was something coming down the stairs. The chiming sound reminded her of Gabriel's wings. She drew back as a metallic skeleton stepped into the room. The steely bones were powered by a complex array of moist-looking bags that served as muscles. The machine possessed golden wings, though their color was dulled by a layer of soot. The skull's eyes were disturbingly human set in their lidless sockets.

"Don't be alarmed," the skeleton said. Its jaws moved, but the words seemed to come from somewhere within its rib cage. "It is I, Gabriel. The battle is won. The sun-dragons have been defeated; the poisoned torches have all been extinguished. The revived valkyries now search the Nest for any surviving assassins." Gabriel moved forward, toward the rainbow arc. As he moved, Jandra found her mind once more filling with memories not her own. She could recall building the synthetic creature before her, and a counterpart, the prophet Hezekiah.

Her borrowed memory merged with her genuine memory as she remembered where she'd heard the name Jasmine Robertson before. It had been the name given by Hezekiah as his creator when Vendevorex had interrogated him.

"In the Free City, I fought a man named Hezekiah," she said. "Are you the same sort of creature? He nearly killed me."

"I cannot be blamed for the actions of my brother," said Gabriel. "Jazz gave us life centuries ago. I was to bring worshipers to the fold of the goddess; Hezekiah was to spread the old faith, and denounce the goddess as the devil."

"Why would she want a competing religion?" Hex asked, puzzled.

"To keep humans divided," said Jandra, tapping into Jazz's memories. "To ensure that they would never unite to reclaim their former glory."

"Correct. Now, if you'll excuse me, I'm in need of new skin," said Gabriel. With a flash of golden wings, he jumped through the rainbow and was gone.

"Should we follow him?" Hex asked.

"Not yet," said Jandra. "The battle may be over, but the work isn't. There may be wounded dragons I can assist. One of us should go after Bitterwood. See if he needs any help with Blasphet."

"I need no one's help." Bitterwood grumbled as he stepped into the Thread Room once more. His clothes were covered in blood. He was carrying a big gray lump of torn meat in his left hand. Jandra's stomach turned and she looked away from the gory sight.

"What on earth are you carrying?" she asked, wrinkling her nose.

"Dinner," said Bitterwood. "I cut out his tongue."

"By the bones," Jandra said, unable to look at him. "Why would you do something so barbaric?"

"Tongues are easy meat," Bitterwood said. "No bones, no fur. A bit chewy, but I've developed an appetite for them."

Jandra remembered the shock she'd felt watching Hex devour a human's head. Somehow, realizing that Bitterwood ate the tongues of his victims seemed far more disturbing.

"You defeated Blasphet?" Hex asked.

"Yes. Yet another of your relatives. You and Shandrazel are the only blood kin of Albekizan remaining."

"Why are you taunting him?" Jandra snapped.

"Because you told me I couldn't kill him," said Bitterwood. "I'm going back to the cavern now. I'm going to rescue Zeeky."

"Wait and we'll come with you," said Jandra. "I have a surprise in store for the goddess when I see her again."

"I don't need either of you to help," Bitterwood said. "I've already killed one god today."

With this, Bitterwood stepped into the rainbow gate and vanished.

"Are all your friends this charming?" Hex asked.

"I'm not certain I have any friends," said Jandra. Her shoulders sagged. For all her powers, all her control over matter and light, the simplest human connections continued to elude her. Jazz's earlier accusation that she was only a confused and lonely little girl now lay heavy on her heart.

Hex's demeanor changed. His eyes softened as he reached out a fore-talon and placed it on her shoulder. "I hope I'm not being presumptuous in saying this, but I consider myself your friend. I haven't known you long, but I admire your bravery, your intelligence, and your decency. I said what I said in anger. Please understand: I don't trust Bitterwood. I believe he's deranged. But if you wish to go after him, I'll stand by your side."

Jandra nodded, feeling choked. She swallowed to regain control of her voice. "Thank you, Hex. I do need to go back; not to help him, but to help Zeeky. Jazz is too dangerous to—"

"Who's Jazz?" Hex asked.

"Oh. That's the real name of the goddess. Only, she's not a goddess. She's just a human like me, using many of the same tricks I use. She's just better at them. But I'm learning fast."

"Earlier, when the wyrm-rider knocked your helmet free, you seemed to lose your powers," said Hex. "I'd assumed you needed it to use your magic, but I see you no longer wear it."

"Actually, I still have it," Jandra said, lifting the hair at the back of her neck. "Jazz reconfigured it to make it less obvious. Which makes me think she's probably wearing something similar. It's called a genie. If we can take her genie away, Jazz will be powerless."

"If you plan to fight this goddess, you can count on my assistance."

"Thank you," she said, wrapping her fingers around Hex's talon and giving it a squeeze. "Before we go back, though, we should make sure we've done all we can do here. We need to make sure Adam's okay, then get him down here before I set his mount loose."

"If we're going to fight the goddess, should we be helping Adam?" Hex asked.

Jandra ran her fingers through her hair. "Good question. Adam hasn't done anything hostile toward us yet. My gut instinct is to treat him fairly for now. Who knows? Perhaps he'll turn out to be a friend after all."

BLASPHET OPENED HIS eyes. His body felt distant. Someone was standing before him, carrying a lantern, but his eyes wouldn't focus. His wing fell limp as the mysterious blurred shape pulled free the arrow that pierced it. The being then moved closer to his head. Blasphet could now see it was one of the sisters. Colobi?

She pulled free the arrow that pierced Blasphet's cheek. Blasphet slumped, and the woman caught his head on her shoulders.

"Your ruse worked, O Murder God," she said. "You trusted me with the knowledge that, should you ever face execution, you would simulate death by dosing yourself with your own poison. Your faith in me was not in vain. I found you in time to administer the antidote."

"Uuuuuhh," Blasphet groaned, feeling a haunting absence in his mouth.

"Bitterwood would have done far worse to you if he'd thought you were still alive," Colobi said. "You'll survive this, my Lord. I'll restore you to health. For now, we must flee. The invasion of the Nest wasn't completely successful. It's only a matter of time before the valkyries search these tunnels."

Blasphet nodded. He could barely feel his hind-talons as Colobi helped him rise. She handed him a valkyrie spear to use as a staff so that he could support himself on his injured hamstring. Colobi stayed beneath his wing as she guided him further down the dark tunnel. Together, they limped away from the Nest.

Blasphet's throat ached as his lungs sucked in the damp air. He could hear his heart pounding with the effort of motion, feel his pulse pressing against the back of his eyes. He'd never felt such misery. Every step reminded him he'd escaped the embrace of death to once more endure the agony of being alive.

Alive.

He chuckled at the thought. His tongueless laugh was an eerie sound that caused Colobi to shudder beneath his wing.

Alive.

Oh, Bitterwood, he mused, his first fully conscious thought since waking. *What a pathway to glory you have opened.*

* * *

AFTER HE LEFT Burke, Pet had run into a pair of earth-dragons fleeing Dragon Forge. Pet had killed them, but in the heat of battle he'd lost his bearings. After running more than a mile away from the fortress, he'd finally reoriented himself on a tall hill. Now, he raced through the maze of rusting ruins surrounding Dragon Forge toward the southern gate. A small canal ran along the southern road to the nearby river, the outflow of the fortress gutters and sewers. In the smoky moonlight, Pet couldn't help but notice that the water in the canal ran dark red.

The southern gate was wide open and undefended. If any earth-dragons wanted to escape via this route, Pet saw nothing to stop them. Hopefully, anyone fleeing the fort would run into Frost and his men. Pet ran through the gates and quickly discovered that escape simply hadn't been an option for most residents. Everywhere he looked, he saw slain earth-dragons. More than a few of Ragnar's men were among the dead as well. In the distance, toward the center of town, he could still hear the shouts of combat. He ran toward the noise, his bow at the ready.

At last, he reached the battle. Here at the heart of Dragon Forge, beside a large building belching smoke into the sky from its great chimney, the toughest warriors of the earth-dragons had rallied. A hundred heavily armored earth-dragons had circled, swinging battle axes that sent human limbs flying with each chop. The hundred dragons were better armed, better armored, and better trained than the men they faced. The only strategy of the humans was to charge the earth-dragons in waves. The dragons were killing five men for every dragon that fell, but the dragons were outnumbered ten to one. Pet climbed atop a rain barrel to see over the heads of his fellow humans and began to let his arrows fly into the center of the circled dragons. Amidst the chaotic action, he wasn't certain if his shots were finding any weak points in the dragons' armor, but still he fired. Through sheer overwhelming force the dragons were falling; one hundred became ninety, became eighty, became fifty, and at last a tipping point was passed. The bodies of the slain dragons became a mountain that the attackers had to climb to reach their remaining foes.

Rising atop this mountain of flesh was Ragnar, his beard and hair caked with gore, his body a network of cuts and gashes. He fought with twin scimitars, his eyes flashing with holy fury as he hacked at every dragon that climbed up the mound toward him. The dragons seemed to understand that killing him was their last hope of holding the city. They kept climbing up, and only the slipperiness of the slope and Ragnar's superior position were keeping him alive. Ragnar slashed savagely at two dragons who climbed before him, but seemed unaware of a third to his back. Pet drew his bow and took careful aim. The dragon was partially blocked by Ragnar. If he was off by inches, he'd kill the prophet instead of the dragon. He imagined the arrow sticking out of the dragon's throat, in the gap between its breast-plate and its helmet. He let the arrow fly.

He didn't even see it hit, but the dragon suddenly toppled backward. Ragnar was safe. Again and again, Pet placed the arrows in his quiver against the bowstring and imagined a dragon dying.

Moments later, his quiver was empty and the battle was over. The armored dragons who'd made the final stand were dead. Ragnar's men spread out, going from door to door, hunting for any dragons who might still be cowering within.

Ragnar fell to his knees atop the mountain of corpses. At first, Pet thought the hairy man was succumbing to his wounds. The prophet instead pressed his palms together and closed his eyes, giving thanks to his unseen Lord for the victory they had achieved this night.

Pet joined with a small band of warriors who kicked in the door of a nearby house and barged within. It was some sort of mess hall, with rows of tables and chairs that the warriors knocked over as they searched for more victims. The air took on the cabbage and chili stench of goom as someone smashed a barrel at the back of the room. Pet had never been able to stomach the stuff, so this was no great loss.

Pet found stairs leading down into a cellar. He discovered a small lantern next to the stairs, the wick showing only the barest blue flame. He let the wick out until it glowed brightly, then headed down the steps. He had a fantasy that he would find a well-stocked wine cellar below; sun-dragons were fond of wine, so perhaps earth-dragons kept it around as well. After the events of the night, Pet had a powerful thirst.

To his relief, he saw rows and rows of bottles. To his sorrow he saw they weren't wine, but mostly preserved foods. Unlike the omnivorous winged dragons, earth-dragons ate meat almost exclusively. The bottles were filled with foods Pet recognized: picked ham-hocks, brined eggs, and red sausages preserved in vinegar. He'd had this type of sausage before and liked them, but right now he had no appetite.

There were other things in bottles Pet didn't recognize, or at least hoped he didn't. Was this jar full

of brains? Were these pickled eye-balls? He moved
to the next row, still hoping there might be wine.

He paused before a bottle with contents that
caught his eye. Hands. Human hands. Female, to
judge from the size, though it was difficult to say.
The fingers were bloated and wrinkled by the pick-
ling brine. The flesh was a disturbing shade of pink,
colored by the red chilies that floated in the jar. His
stomach twisted into a knot. He was grateful he
hadn't eaten anything in several hours.

Then his eyes caught sight of another bottle full
of small lizards. Pet drew closer, in sickened fascination. He wasn't sure what kind of lizards these
were. They had heads like turtles, but their hands
were more like earth-dragons and... Pet suddenly
knew. The earth-dragons pickled and ate their own
young. Something inside him snapped.

Pet marched back up the cellar stairs, to go back
out among the gleaner mounds to hunt for survivors be they dragon or human. Burke was right.
Anyone who had aided the dragons was part of a
vast engine of death. In his old life as the pet of a
sun-dragon, he owed every luxury he'd ever
enjoyed to this system. Every silk pillow he'd slept
upon, every golden cup he'd drunk from, every
ivory comb he'd ever pulled through his locks—all
were the product of an economy of enslavement.
All the fine things he'd ever enjoyed, he now knew,
were the gifts of monsters.

CHAPTER TWENTY-SIX

YOU KNOW WHAT I HAVE DONE

THE DAMP, SMOKY, slaughter-scented air of the Nest gave way to warm floral breezes as Bitterwood stepped from the rainbow. The false sky overhead was still a nightscape dotted with stars and a moon. The light was bright enough to illuminate the footprints of the fallen angel that had preceded Bitterwood through the gate. He studied the shapes in the crushed grass; these weren't the prints of a living thing. The prints had hard, crisp edges that told him that what he'd glimpsed as the angel had vanished into the gate was true. Gabriel was a clockwork man, as Hezekiah had been.

Bitterwood followed the trail of bent blades, though he instinctively knew where they led—the temple. Gabriel only had a few minutes' lead. Bitterwood could tell from the trail that the machine man was limping, injured from battle. Bitterwood, on the other hand, felt energized after his murder of Blasphet. His fever dreams, his visions of Recanna, all the omens and portents suddenly seemed clear.

For twenty years, the hatred of dragons had given him reason to rise in the mornings. He'd been full of righteous anger at the thoughts of how dragons held power over the lives of men, power they'd used unjustly. Yet, what of the power of gods? He didn't know if his hatred could drive an arrow through the heart of the goddess. He was keen to find out.

He hoped his bruskness had been sufficient to dissuade Jandra from following him. If he died in pursuit of this task, it mattered little. He saw no reason for the girl to risk her life, however.

He caught up to Gabriel as the winged man climbed the steps of the temple. The angel was exposed for what he truly was, a mockery of a man made of steel bones and wet-clay muscles. Bitterwood dropped Blasphet's severed tongue the grass. From a hundred feet away, he took aim at Gabriel's skull and let his arrow fly.

Sound, however, flies more swiftly than arrows. Gabriel spun in response to the twang of Bitterwood's bow and swatted the arrow from its flight with skeletal fingers.

"Oh, it's you," Gabriel said. The angel drew his flaming sword from its scabbard. "I've known since you arrived you were an ungrateful guest. Put down your bow, human. You failed to kill me while my back was to you. You have no chance of victory now that I'm aware of your presence."

Bitterwood placed a second arrow against his bowstring and stepped forward. "I've just come from killing a god," he said. "An angel is no challenge."

Gabriel spread his legs into a fighting stance, holding his sword with both hands.

"Bant Bitterwood, you owe me gratitude, not anger. I saved the life of your son. He's grown into a valued servant of the goddess. It will cause him tremendous grief to know you died at my hands. For his sake, put down your bow."

Bitterwood continued to close the gap. Twenty feet away was close enough for him to feel the heat of the flaming sword against his cheeks. He knew what this being was capable of. He'd witnessed Hezekiah survive far worse injuries than anything his bow could inflict. The machine man's strength, even injured, was ten times his own. But he also knew one further thing that this angel didn't know—he'd watched Vendevorex disable Hezekiah in the Free City. He knew this creature's vulnerable spot.

He released the bow string. The arrow crossed the gap between man and angel in a time too fast to measure, yet the angel swung his sword swiftly enough to knock the arrow aside. He then raised the flaming weapon high overhead, and lunged. Bitterwood had anticipated this gambit. He charged forward with all his speed, coming in low under Gabriel's racing weapon, tackling the angel's torso with his full weight.

As with Hezekiah, it wasn't enough. Throwing himself against Gabriel was like throwing himself against stone. He found his footing and rose up, in the embrace of the angel, until his face was staring into Gabriel's steely skull. He could see his own eyes reflected in the angel's gleaming teeth. Gabriel calmly folded his arms around Bitterwood in a bear hug. Bitterwood reached around the machine man's back, feeling his way up the mechanical spine to the base of the neck. He smelled burnt hair from Gabriel's sword being so near his face; his ribs were on the verge of breaking. There was no way for him to draw a breath in the angel's death grip.

Bitterwood found the small, smooth orb that sat at the base of the angel's skull. He wrapped his fist around it and yanked as spots danced before his eyes. Suddenly, Gabriel dropped his sword. His clasped arms around Bitterwood didn't slacken, but they also didn't grow any tighter.

Bitterwood exhaled fully, creating tiny amounts of slack. He slipped down the angel's rib cage, twisting his shoulders to free himself. He staggered backward with a shiny silver marble in his hands. Vendevorex had called this sphere a homunculus—the machine soul that animated the artificial man. Gabriel was still now, save for a trio of wires that snaked from his back and floated toward Bitterwood like tentacles of a jellyfish. Bitterwood dived beneath these probes, reaching for Gabriel's flaming sword, which lay on the ground beside the angel's skeletal feet. He rose with the weapon and sliced upward through the wires, severing them. Instantly, they began to grow back.

Bitterwood ran away, down the lengths of the temple steps. He didn't know the range of the wires, but it couldn't be infinite. Or perhaps it could. They might seek out the homunculus wherever it went. Bitterwood stopped, having put several yards between himself and the wires. He laid the silver orb upon the polished steps of the temple. Then, he placed the flaming sword upon it. He stepped back, hoping that the wires would melt away before they could reach the orb. Instead, the homunculus suddenly popped like a kernel of corn, violently enough to throw the sword into the air. Tiny fragments of shrapnel tinked against the stone. A steel splinter buried itself deeply in Bitterwood's cheek, barely an inch below his left eye. He dug the sliver out with his ragged nails, then wiped the wound with the back of his hand. He allowed himself a deep, calming breath, though it sent needles of pain through his bruised ribcage.

He retrieved the flaming sword from where it had landed. It had burned a circle around it in the grass, though the ground and vegetation were too moist to allow the flames to spread far. He carried it at arm's length, unable to even look directly at the white-hot weapon. He hoped that placing it back in Gabriel's scabbard would squelch the weapon. Yet, as he wished that the weapon wasn't so hot, the weapon responded. The white searing flame faded to the intensity of a torch. Bitterwood no longer felt as if his shirt sleeve on the verge of catching fire. He stared at the now manageable flame and wondered if it could grow dimmer still. It did, lowering its intensity until only the barest halo of faint orange flame danced around it, and Bitterwood could no longer feel its heat on his face. With a thought, he willed it to brighten again.

He allowed himself a rare grin as the sword obeyed his unspoken command. He went to Gabriel's paralyzed form and placed the sword back into its scabbard, then fastened the scabbard to his own belt.

He cast a glance back to Blasphet's severed tongue. At least he now knew how he was going to cook it.

BITTERWOOD LEFT THE flaming temple. For an hour, he'd shouted in the place, calling the goddess down. He'd burned her statue and set fire to the walls to no avail. She hadn't come for him.

Very well. His true purpose in returning, he reminded himself, wasn't to kill angels and goddesses, but to rescue Zeeky. He walked away from the conflagration of the once sacred place. With the angel slain and the temple on fire, Bitterwood saw no further need for subtlety. "Zeeky!" he shouted. "Zeeky, where are you?"

He listened to the night jungle, to the chirping of frogs and the buzzing of insects, to the agitated cries of birds and monkeys as they chattered about the scorched earth Bitterwood had left in his wake. For all he knew, Zeeky could be crying out for him and he couldn't hear her beneath this cacophony.

JANDRA LET THE prime number that locked her helmet run through her mind once more. She and Hex were in the Thread Room, looking at the rainbow gate. They had already sent Adam and Trisky through, and the other long-wyrm riders had returned through the gates they had entered.

The situation at the Nest wasn't good, but there was little more she could do. The matriarch had recovered from the anesthetic smoke and taken command once more. She'd ordered Graxen and Nadala taken away in chains, and Jandra didn't feel she had enough of an understanding of the situation to protest this decision.

Jandra had spent much of the night healing injured valkyries. She'd also been waiting for news of Blasphet—the valkyries who searched the tunnels hadn't yet found his body. But, Jandra couldn't believe he wasn't dead. She'd seen his severed tongue, after all, and for all of Bitterwood's flaws he wasn't a liar. If he said he'd killed Blasphet, he had. Could he possibly have done something so awful to the body it could never be found? It was best not to think about it.

Besides, she had other things to focus on. She suspected that Jazz would know almost instantly that her helmet was locked once they were together. The genies communicated at radio frequencies—with Jazz a hundred miles away and a mile beneath the earth, and Jandra in a room beneath the surface of a lake, she was reasonably confident that Jazz couldn't listen in to her conversation with Hex right now.

"You know, this isn't your fight," she said. "You've never even met Zeeky. I have a score to settle with Jazz, but you don't need to get yourself killed on my account."

"On the contrary," said Hex. "I feel that confronting this Jazz is required if my beliefs mean anything to me at all. I've spent much of my life developing my philosophy. I believe that all law is ultimately a shackle, and that all kings are ultimately tyrants. If I don't trust power to a king, how can I rest knowing that Jazz wields even greater power? I told you earlier that I don't believe we must be the puppets of fate. This would-be goddess imagines herself as a puppet master. It's my duty as a warrior-philosopher to cut her strings."

"Warrior-philosopher? Is that what you are?"

"My last official title was assistant librarian," Hex said. "Confronting a god as an assistant librarian is a risky undertaking; a warrior-philosopher, however, is suited for the task."

Jandra smiled. She appreciated Hex's dry humor. She handed Hex a silver ring that she'd created from the dust in her pouch. It was scaled to fit his talons; on her, it would have been a bracelet.

"Wear this," she said. "It might come in handy."

"What does it do?" Hex asked.

"You've seen me turn invisible. I do it with the aid of the silver dust. It fills the air and configures itself into a billion tiny mirrors that carefully guide the light around me. I've taken that dust and shaped it into this ring with a preprogrammed command to form an invisibility sphere around you. Unfortunately, I can't make the sphere big enough to cover you if your wings are fully outstretched. The illusion falls apart once you get much past a twenty-foot diameter. Too many gaps in the integrated mirrors. So, it won't work if you're flying, or fighting all out. But it might help you hide, or ambush someone as long as you stay compact. Keep your wings and tail tucked in, don't stretch your neck too far, and no one will be able to see you."

"How do I activate it?"

"I'm keeping it simple," she said. "All it needs is a good jolt of kinetic energy. Just hit it against something hard and part of the ring will flake off and form the field. There's only enough dust in the ring to work a half dozen times, so use it wisely."

"Thank you," said Hex, sliding the ring on. "Though, I confess, stealth and invisibility aren't my style."

"Not your warrior style," said Jandra. "But it may come in handy for a moment of philosophy. Jazz can probably see straight through the illusion, but maybe not. Here's what I do know about her: despite all her seeming power, she's only human. She's no doubt enhanced herself physically; she can probably heal from grievous wounds almost instantly. Mentally, she seems to think she has the right to do anything she wants because the world owes her. She claims to have saved the world from environmental catastrophe."

"Do you think she did?"

"No. I think like most people she wants to believe her presence makes the world a better place. She pushed a bunch of her memories into my head that

I think are supposed to make me sympathize with her. For instance, I have this memory of her when she was only a teenager; she's crouching on a beach covered with oil, cradling a dying seagull. I can feel her sorrow, her genuine longing to keep this from ever happening again. Two years later, she was the mastermind behind the bombing of an oil refinery. She killed nine people and triggered economic turmoil that ruined the lives of millions. She's given me this as one of her *good* memories, one of the things she's *most* proud of. She wants me to see that while her methods may be harsh and violent, she's always striving for the greater good."

"Just as my father justified war in the name of peace, and oppression in the name of order," said Hex. "If there's one thing I've learned about life, it's that those with the most passionate convictions can justify the most savage cruelties."

"I don't know that I agree with you," said Jandra. "You're passionate about your beliefs, but it hasn't left you bloodthirsty and ruthless like Jazz. Or like Bitterwood, now that I think about it. You're a living contradiction to your own assertion."

"If there's a second thing I've learned about life, it's that any truth I can sum up in a single sentence is almost certainly going to snap once I place the weight of reality upon it."

"One thing I've learned from these new memories is not to be intimidated by Jazz anymore. She may be powerful and smart, she's not omnipotent or omniscient. She's just a woman with a human brain in a human skull. Not to be gruesome, but I've seen what you can do to a human skull. We stand a chance if we get close enough. I believe we can beat her."

"Well then," said Hex, moving toward the gate. "The time has come to once more test a belief against reality." He leapt, vanishing into nothingness.

As he did so, the rainbow seemed to vibrate, and the air around it shimmered with countless tiny prisms that faded as quickly as they'd formed. Yet in that brief flash, Jandra was certain that she'd once more heard her name spoken by Zeeky. Bracing herself, Jandra stepped into the rainbow...

... AND NOW THE void was endless. Rather than emerging from the other side, Jandra was adrift in darkness and silence. She couldn't breathe; she couldn't feel her heart beating within her. The disembodied sensation felt the way she imagined death must feel. And yet... she wasn't dead. She was thinking. What was happening to her?

She tried to summon fire around her hands to break the darkness, but she couldn't feel her hands. She wasn't certain she even had hands anymore. It was as if all that was physical about her had been stripped away and she was left as only a mind.

"Jandra," a voice whispered.

"Zeeky?" she asked, despite lacking a throat or mouth to form the words.

"Follow my voice," said Zeeky. As she spoke, the darkness split and a sliver of light formed. Jandra wanted to move toward the light, but didn't know how. She had no limbs to push herself with. Panic seized her. The presence of a way out of this void and her inability to reach it left her feeling trapped.

Then, hands that were not hands pressed against her, or the idea of her, and pushed.

JANDRA LANDED HARD on a concrete floor in a gray, windowless room. The presence of gravity felt both reassuring and confining. She was pinned to the cold, hard surface by the weight of her body. The light here was dim, but after her encounter with the void even this faint illumination felt like daggers stabbing her eyes. She threw her arm across her face to block the light. She took long, slow breaths, welcoming the air across her lips after her brief encounter with airless, lipless nothingness.

Something wet, cold, and circular pressed against her forehead. Jandra moved her hand to see what it was and found her fingers touching the snout of some kind of animal. She opened her eyes and looked up into the face of a pig, its hide mottled black and white. The pig looked down at her with an expression that resembled concern.

She'd never actually met Zeeky's pig, but her porcine examiner seemed to fit the bill.

"Poocher?" she asked.

"Yes."

It took her half a second to realize it hadn't been the pig who answered. She sat up and discovered a girl standing in the center of the room. She was dressed in a white robe; her golden hair was washed and braided. She stood before a glass orb the size of a man's fist, which floated in the air seemingly without support. The girl's eyes were fixed upon the orb in an almost hypnotic gaze.

"Zeeky!" Jandra cried. "Are you okay?"

"Yes," said Zeeky, not taking her eyes off the orb. Her tone made it sound as if Jandra's voice was an unwelcome distraction.

She rose, looking once more around the room. Jandra somehow recognized it though she'd never been here before. It was a cell built by Jazz, accessible only via an underspace gate. She had a faint memory of building it.

"How did I get here?" Jandra asked. "Did you guide me here somehow?"

"Yes," Zeeky said again, tersely.

Jandra walked over to her and placed her hand on Zeeky's shoulder.

"Is something wrong?"

Zeeky turned away from the orb. Tears welled in her eyes as she said, with a trembling voice, "Everything is wrong! I don't know what to do!"

"What's happening?" Jandra said, squatting down to Zeeky's level. "What's the problem?"

"My family and my neighbors are still inside," Zeeky said, wiping her cheeks. "I can hear them; we've been talking. But they've been in there too long. It's changing them. They've forgotten what their bodies looked like. They say they don't want to come out. They say it's like heaven in there."

"Heaven isn't what I experienced," said Jandra.

"It wasn't what they first experienced either," said Zeeky, running her fingers along the glass orb. "They said it was more like being dead. They're spirits without bodies. It terrified them at first. But, slowly, they found out that the place responded to their thoughts. It became what they wanted it to become. They imagined heaven, and it became heaven. Now they want me to go inside with them."

"Could you?" Jandra asked. "Does this crystal ball have that power?" She looked into the transparent sphere, but saw nothing but the distorted image of Poocher on the other side.

"Jazz left it here for me. She says there's a tiny slice of underspace forever opened at its heart, but I can't reach it while it's sealed in the globe. The globe isn't really glass... it's some sort of energy that that looks like glass. Nothing in this world can ever break it."

"How do you know that?"

"The villagers told me. They're telling me so many things. I don't understand half of what they're saying. Freed of their bodies, existing as pure thought, they're beginning to know everything... but they're forgetting what it was to be human."

"Jazz told me she wanted to stay inside underspace because it would make her omniscient," said Jandra. "Perhaps she was right."

"Jazz can't be allowed inside," said Zeeky. "They don't want her there. Jazz is a bad person."

"I know."

"They say I should go with them to escape her," said Zeeky. "But, I don't want to. I don't want to live without a body. I want to stay in this world with Poocher. I want to see Jeremiah again. I just want things back like they were." A tear traced down her cheek as she spoke. Her lower lip trembled.

Jandra wrapped her arms around Zeeky and pressed her wet cheek against her own. "It's okay," she whispered. "I won't let anything happen to you."

"How touching," said a woman's voice behind her.

Suddenly, the room smelled of cigarettes.

BITTERWOOD HAD COME once more to the shores of the island. He walked its perimeter, trying to find something he could use as a boat. He came at last to a broad beach of black sand. In the distance, he could see a second island. Perhaps Zeeky was there. His search of the temple island had certainly proven unproductive.

Bitterwood looked up as he heard the rustling of leaves in the forest behind him. The greenery parted as the copper-colored heads of three long-wyrms pushed through onto the beach. Adam rode the wyrm that led the way. Behind him were two riders Bitterwood had never seen.

Adam's voice shook with outrage as he spoke. "The temple is destroyed! Gabriel is dead! One of your arrows was discovered near his remains. What have you done, father?"

"You know what I have done," said Bitterwood.

"The goddess possesses infinite grace," Adam said. "She may forgive any insult if you approach her with a repentant heart. Throw down your bow, father. Surrender yourself. She may yet show you mercy."

"I do not desire mercy," said Bitterwood. "I have slain her angel. Is this the act of a repentant heart? Let Ashera show herself if my actions anger her. I want very much to see her; I still have arrows in my quiver. Let her test her power against me."

"Blasphemer!" shouted the rider to Adam's left.

"Calm yourself, Palt," said Adam.

"No!" he cried. "He speaks of arrows. *We* are the arrows in the quiver of the goddess! We are the missiles of her wrath! Let us fly, Adam. We shall strike this heretic down!"

Adam looked toward Bitterwood once more. "Father, if you've any love of life, you will drop your bow. Do not make us kill you."

Bitterwood lifted his bow and calmly drew an arrow. He took aim, dead center of Adam's chest.

"I have no love of anything," he said. "Kill me if you can."

CHAPTER TWENTY-SEVEN

BAD WOMAN

J ANDRA SPUN AROUND.

"You've locked the helmet," Jazz said, taking a drag on her cigarette. "Interesting."

"I didn't enjoy being your doll," said Jandra.

"Then we won't be having tea with Mr. Teddy?" Jazz said, her voice mocking Jandra's accent. "Fine. You still need me, Jandra. Those memories I gave you won't be of much use without me to guide you through them. And I kept a lot of the good stuff to myself. Wouldn't you like to learn to open the underspace gates? Wouldn't you like to tap into a thousand years of experience and wisdom without the tedium of actually having to trudge through all those centuries? Swear your loyalty to me, Jandra, and I'll help you become a goddess."

Jandra guided Zeeky behind her. Poocher came up next to her knees, grunting as he stared at Jazz.

"Godhood doesn't hold much attraction for me," Jandra said. "I'm having a tough enough time learning to be human."

Jazz rolled her eyes. "You're such a drama queen. Fine. You don't want to be my friend. But, we don't have to be enemies, either." Jazz stepped aside as a glowing rainbow opened in the air behind her.

"Here's the door," she said. "It leads back to Shandrazel's palace, your old stomping grounds. Get out and don't bother me again."

Jandra looked at the gate. It would be so easy just to grab Zeeky and leap for it. But, escaping Jazz wouldn't solve anything. If escape were all she wanted, she wouldn't have come back from the Nest.

Then, to her surprise, Poocher charged toward the rainbow and leapt in. Zeeky ran past her, grabbing her hand. In Zeeky's other hand, she cradled the crystal ball. "Hurry!" shouted Zeeky, dragging her toward the gate.

Seeing a look of shock flash across Jazz's face, Jandra decided to trust Zeeky. She leapt once more into the place that was not a place.

THE LONG-WYRMS RIDDEN by Palt and Adam lunged toward Bitterwood and the third rider took aim with his crossbow. Bitterwood stepped aside as the man fired. The bolt whizzed through the air behind him. Bitterwood shifted his aim from Adam to Palt's charging serpent. The creatures were more a threat than the riders. He let his arrow fly, targeting the long-wyrm's left eye. The creature jerked, its legs twitching fitfully. Black sand flew as the long-wyrm crashed and Palt fell from his saddle. By now, Trisky was only a yard away, opening her maw wide. Without dropping his bow, Bitterwood drew Gabriel's sword, willing it to flare into white brilliance. He tossed the sword down Trisky's gullet and jumped away from her charge at the last possible instant. As momentum carried Trisky past him, he reached out and grabbed Adam's leg. With a violent tug, he tore his son from the saddle.

As Adam landed hard in the sand, the third long-wyrm rider reloaded. Before he could take aim, Bitterwood drew another arrow. He saw the skittish look in the long-wyrm's eyes. He released the bowstring and the man toppled from his saddle, an arrow jutting from his heart. The long-wyrm panicked as his rider fell, turning in a nearly perfect arc and darting once more into the forest.

Trisky's head was beneath the surface of the lake now. Water boiled up around her, white steam rising into the air. Her body was wracked with spasms as Bitterwood vaulted over her. He looked toward the first wyrm he'd killed. The rider was back on his feet, his sword drawn. Bitterwood fired his bow once more and the man fell to his knees on the black sand, a confused look on his face. Then his body sagged, and he fell to his side.

Bitterwood let out a long, slow breath. There was only one foe left. By now, Adam would be recovering from his abrupt dismount. Bitterwood clenched his jaws, contemplating the unpleasant task before him.

JANDRA EXPECTED TO land in the familiar rooms of the palace. Instead, she emerged from the rainbow back in the clearing where Bitterwood and Hex had been held captive by the vines. The same place she'd departed from to reach the Nest.

"What?" she asked. "How did we—"

"I don't know how to open a gate into underspace," Zeeky said, still pulling on her hand. "But once you're in the warp, the villagers can push you out anywhere a gate has ever been opened. I don't understand how they do it, but it works; it's how I got you to find me. I couldn't leave Jazz's prison, though, because I couldn't reach a gate."

"But we're still on Jazz's island," said Jandra. "If you wanted to escape, the palace would have been further from her grasp."

"This is where the villagers say we should be," said Zeeky. "This is where your friend will be."

"Do tell," said Jazz, now standing in the clearing before them, a rainbow closing behind her. "So, you *can* talk to your family inside. You've been holding out on me."

"I'll never help you!" Zeeky screamed. "You're a bad woman!"

"Oh, screw this," said Jazz. Lightning wreathed both her hands as she lifted them. "I'm through playing nice. You'll do what I tell you, girl, once I get rid of your would-be protector."

Jandra suddenly felt as if millions of tiny hooks dug into her skin. She gasped as the hooks began to tug, ripping molecule from molecule. In seconds she would be torn apart, shredded to her component atoms by Jazz's nanites.

She lifted up her hands and watched her fingernails fly off into the breeze, carried by flecks of silver dust.

BITTERWOOD DROPPED HIS bow as his son climbed onto Trisky's corpse. Adam had his crossbow loaded. His visor had been knocked loose when Bitterwood had thrown him to the sand. His eyes burned with rage as he screamed, "Why are you doing this? What can you possibly gain by defying the goddess?"

Bitterwood asked, "What can you gain from obeying her?"

"I owe everything to the goddess! My mother was gone. You abandoned me! If she hadn't showed me her divine mercy, I'd have died as an infant."

"Everyone dies eventually," said Bitterwood.

Adam growled as he took aim. "I'm weary of your mockery. To be smiled upon by the goddess is like being smiled upon by the sun. There is no better joy than to serve her."

"Huh," said Bitterwood. "It's been a long time since joy motivated me. But I remember it. I remember the last time I felt happiness. You were there."

"What do you mean?" Adam asked, still staring down the shaft of the bolt.

"Back in Christdale. I had two daughters by your mother, Recanna. You were my first son. I loved my daughters. I was happy. But the first time I ever held you in my arms, I felt something greater than happiness. You were my hope and my future, Adam. I could see myself in you. I looked forward to teaching you as you grew: how to fish, how to hunt, how to plow. I wanted to teach you everything I knew."

"And what have you taught me now? Blasphemy? Hatred? Revenge?"

"This wasn't what I planned to teach you. I used to think of Christdale as Eden, even though times weren't always easy. We were farmers working fields full of stones. Most years, we didn't get enough rain. Other years, we lost the crops to storms and floods. Yet we endured as a community. We shared our food. We worked together to feed the children and care for the aged. I wish you could have grown up there. Then the dragons came. They ruined everything. I thought they'd killed you."

"Earlier, you said you wished they'd killed me," said Adam, lowering the crossbow.

Bitterwood nodded. "I was angry when I spoke those words."

"You're always angry!" Adam snarled. "You've been hostile since the moment we met!"

"I know. I also know I could have killed you just now," said Bitterwood. "You were my first target."

"You had me in your sites. Why didn't you fire?"

Bitterwood sighed. "I almost died not long ago. I think I caught a glimpse of heaven. I don't know. It may all have been a dream. Still, your mother was there. When I cross over to the other side, if there is another side, I don't want to tell her I was the man who killed you."

"I've already been assured of my place in heaven," said Adam, aiming the crossbow once more. He stared down the length of the weapon to look Bitterwood in the eyes. "Why shouldn't I kill you?"

"I can't think of any reason you shouldn't pull that trigger," said Bitterwood. "If you spare me, I'm going to kill your goddess, or die trying. I'm the antithesis of everything you hold as good in this world."

"You're nothing like the man I used to dream about, the great dragon-slayer."

"I'm not the man I used to dream about either," said Bitterwood. "But today I found out something I didn't know about myself. Something that makes me think I might yet have a hope of heaven."

"Go on," said Adam.

"In twenty years, I've never changed my mind about a target. I've only aimed at what I hated, and I've always let the arrow fly. For twenty years, I thought that hate was the only thing left in my heart. But, Adam, even though time and fate have left us on opposing sides, I don't hate you. You're brave, you're reverent, you're merciful; you're everything I failed to be. One day something's going to kill you, son... but it won't be me."

Adam stared at his father. He let out his breath, and lowered his crossbow.

"Despite all you've done, I don't hate you either," said Adam.

"What about the fact I still plan to kill your goddess?"

"You only risk your own life. If you seek out the goddess, she'll surely destroy you."

Bitterwood leaned over and picked up his bow.

"No man lives forever," he said.

JANDRA'S BATTLE WITH the goddess unfolded on a microscopic level. She imagined her skin was a sheet of iron, too hard for the tiny machines to penetrate. She focused the nanites that swam within her blood, to resist the invading molecules and repair the damage as quickly as Jazz inflicted it.

"Ah, you're a little more advanced at this than I thought," Jazz said as she flicked away the butt of her cigarette. "I figured you'd be reduced to dust in five seconds. Maybe you'll hold out for a few minutes. But all it's going to take is one stray thought to distract you, girl. Then your epidermis will peel away. Your hair will fall from disintegrating follicles. You'll be able to watch it all because your eyelids will be vapor. Panic will set in, and before you know it, poof, you'll be nothing but a pink cloud, drifting off in the breeze. Kind of a lovely image, if you think about it."

As if the warning of a distraction made it so, Jandra's attention was captured by a shrill squealing sound. It was the cry of an enraged pig. Poocher charged up behind Jazz, a furious one-hundred-pound torpedo of black and white fur. For half a second, Jandra's mind lingered on the sight. Instantly her skin began to crack and flake. Poocher plowed into Jazz, clipping her at the knees. The tiny hooks that tore at Jandra vanished as the goddess's feet flew into the air.

Jazz landed on her back, shouting out a string of obscenities.

Jandra took the brief second of respite to repair the skin that Jazz had torn away. Then, she summoned twin balls of Vengeance of the Ancestors around her fists.

Jazz sat up, rubbing the back of her head. "Ow," she said.

Jandra threw the fireballs. The raging plasma crackled toward the goddess. As the flaming orbs reached her they fell apart, transforming into a cloud of rose petals that fluttered down onto Jazz's lap.

"Come on, Jandra," Jazz taunted. "The pig did better than that."

Poocher now stood next to Zeeky. Jazz glared at him.

"You know, I've been vegetarian for a thousand years. But I always did love the smell of bacon."

The petals in her lap rose in a small tornado, coalescing into a ball of red flame once more. Jazz gave the glowing orb a slap and it raced toward the pig. Poocher darted aside, but the orb seemed to suddenly possess intelligence. It turned, pursuing the pig. Poocher squealed and darted off into the underbrush.

Zeeky charged toward Jazz with her left fist clenched. She still cradled the crystal ball in her right hand. She shouted, "Don't you dare hurt Poocher!"

"He started it," Jazz said, kicking out, catching Zeeky straight in her gut. Zeeky flew backward from the force of the blow, landing breathless on the grass. She curled up in pain, yet never released the orb.

As Jazz climbed back to her feet, Jandra concentrated. She could sense the radio waves Jazz was emitting to command her nanites. They were the same sort of waves her own genie emitted. She couldn't understand the signals Jazz was transmitting, but a mental map formed in her mind pinpointing the origin of the radio waves. Unlike Jandra's genie, Jazz wasn't using an external device. Her genie was buried in her torso, below her rib cage, right where her heart should have been.

Jazz brushed back her hair and grinned. "Been a while since anything's got my adrenaline flowing like this," she said. "My combat skills are a little rusty, maybe. Now it's time to show you an attack that always works!"

Jandra braced herself for the next assault of nanites. Instead, Jazz sprinted across the ten-foot gap that separated them, drawing her arm back. She swung with a loud grunt, her fist hammering into Jandra's chin. Stars exploded in front of Jandra's eyes as she fell backward. Her brain felt like it rattled in her skull as she hit the ground. Jazz landed on her, delivering another punch to Jandra's left brow. Jandra's vision doubled. She felt herself fading out of consciousness as Jazz ran her fingers behind Jandra's neck, feeling for the genie that clung to her skin there.

"Since you've locked this, there's no way to take this off your spine without ripping your clothes off," Jazz said, giggling. "Hope that doesn't offend your sense of modesty. I'm not normally this aggressive, but, girl, you were asking for it."

Jandra arched her back in pain as Jazz peeled the metal away from her skin. The genie resisted as if it had a mind of its own, stimulating Jandra with a mild shock that jolted her back into full consciousness. She remembered the important thing she'd learned just before Jazz had punched her. And, she remembered Zeeky's words: *This is where your friend will be.*

"Hex!" she shouted, grabbing Jazz's wrist. "It's inside her! Near her heart!"

Jazz looked up to see who Jandra was shouting at. Thirty feet away, the air exploded into a thousand shards of silver. Hex materialized from the center of his invisible hiding place, his open jaws shooting toward the goddess.

"Motherf—" Jazz said before Hex clamped his teeth down on her ribs and tore her away from Jandra's chest. He whipped Jazz back and forth in his jaws like a cat shaking a mouse.

Seconds later, Jazz's entire body erupted in flame. Hex spat her out, jerking back, his teeth smoking, black burn marks on the roof of his mouth. Jazz landed on the grass, on her hands and knees, shaking her head as if she was dizzy. The vegetation beneath her withered and charred; she radiated more heat than a furious bonfire.

"I can't figure out why y'all don't like me," Jazz said. She chuckled as she found her footing once more. "Most people think I'm pretty hot."

Jandra raised her hand to shield her face from the inferno. She scooted backward, still on the ground. The goddess roared into an even brighter heat. Jandra's hair curled and singed. The soles of her boots were smoking. Her hand fell on Zeeky's ankle. Zeeky was still curled up from the blow she'd taken.

Hex growled as he shook off the pain of having his mouth catch fire. He lunged toward the goddess. She lifted a hand toward him without even looking, and suddenly Hex's head was once more enwreathed in flame. With a howl of agony Hex shot skyward as fast as his wings could carry him. An instant later, there was a loud splash. Apparently, they weren't that far from the lake.

Jandra willed her nanites to fly around her. Heat was only another form of light; if she could form a shield of invisibility, she could form a shield to deflect heat. She rose to her feet, grabbing Zeeky as she stood, hugging her to her chest and backing away from the goddess. Her shield was working; she could breathe again without the air searing her lungs.

"You don't know what you're facing, girl," Jazz said, taking a step toward Jandra. Jazz grinned and Jandra jumped backward, wary of her next move. "You thought just because we use the same technology that you were my equal? You have all the artistry of a kindergartener with a box of crayons. I'm Michelangelo! I'm Da Vinci! You stand no—"

Suddenly, there was an arrow jutting from Jazz's left temple. The bright green leaves that fletched it curled and blackened as the wood burst into flame. Jazz looked annoyed as she reached up and plucked the burning stick free. She closed the hole into her brain with a touch of her fingers.

"That was unpleasant," she grumbled, looking in the direction from which the arrow had flown. Suddenly, a second arrow whizzed from the brush. Jazz raised her hand and it crumbled to ash in mid-flight. A third arrow flew, then a fourth. Jazz turned her full attention to the missiles, crisping them before they reached her. Jandra noticed that, despite her powers, Jazz possessed at least one human weakness—she only focused on one thing at a time. If she could somehow distract Jazz... Jandra put Zeeky down, eyeing the fist-sized crystal globe still in her grasp.

"Can I use this?" she asked, placing her hand upon it.

Zeeky handed her the ball.

To have been made of energy, it was quite heavy. It easily weighed as much as if had been crafted of iron, at least thirty pounds. Jandra reared back and shouted, "Bitterwood! You have to hit her heart!"

Jazz looked toward the shout. Jandra flung the globe with all the strength her genie-tuned muscles could muster. Whatever the ball was made from, it proved immune to the flames and flew straight and true. It collided with Jazz's mouth in a lip-splitting smack.

Jazz staggered backward, bringing her hands to her mouth, looking dazed. Jandra reached out with her nanites and grabbed the kudzu vines behind the goddess. The vines darted out to tangle Jazz's feet. They quickly crisped to cinders, but not before Jazz stumbled. She landed on her butt, hard, then rolled to her hands and knees. Jandra ran to retrieve the crystal globe, intending to fling it again.

Before she could reach it, Bitterwood burst from the branches of a tree above the goddess. His clothes were dripping wet. He plummeted toward her fiery form, both hands clasped around the hilt of Gabriel's sword. The weapon glowed even more brightly than the goddess as he buried it in her back, driving her down. He used his momentum to leap away, dropping and rolling as he hit the moist grass to extinguish the fires that had erupted on his now-dry clothes.

Jandra tried to look at Jazz, but it was impossible. It was like looking into the sun. The ground beneath the goddess boiled and her glowing form melted into it. Slowly, the light dimmed. Jandra walked over to the hole in the ground. All that was left at the bottom was the burning sword lodged into a heart-shaped piece of silver metal. Blackened bones lay scattered around the pit. The soil had been turned to glass by the heat.

Bitterwood leaned over the edge of the pit and reached in with blistered fingers to grab the hilt. Instantly, the white-hot blaze dimmed to a dull cherry glow. Jandra blinked, trying to clear her vision.

The leaves in the trees stirred as Hex flew overhead. He swooped down to land, dropping Poocher from his hind talons. The pig was uninjured, but sopping wet. Hex's face was charred, with one eye swollen shut. Here and there, a gash of pink tissue peeked through his blackened scales. His tongue was covered with blisters. He lisped through missing teeth as he asked, "Ish she dead?"

Bitterwood lifted the sword and looked at the silver heart on the end. The fire hadn't melted it, but it was split by a jagged crack where the blade had pierced it.

"If she isn't," Jandra said, "we've certainly broken her heart."

Zeeky ran from Jandra's side to give Poocher a hug.

"I saw Trisky dead on the beach," Hex said, giving Bitterwood a stern look with his one open eye. "What happened to Adam?"

Bitterwood shrugged. "We've agreed to disagree."

High above, the sky began to fragment and drift down as a silvery snow, leaving the rock behind it exposed. The jungle grew hauntingly quiet. Bitterwood dropped the sword back into the pit.

"I don't sense any radio waves," Jandra said. "I think she's really dead. What should we do with her heart?"

"We should bury it, with the sword still in place so it will never heal," said Bitterwood. "Then I want to eat my dinner in peace and get some sleep. I've killed enough gods for one day."

CHAPTER TWENTY-EIGHT

ZING!

S HANDRAZEL STUDIED THE map of the world inlaid on the Peace Hall floor. This was his father's world—a world forged with violence. All his life, Shandrazel had considered his father's ruthlessness an antiquated relic from a less enlightened time. Violence had been necessary once, perhaps, to tame a savage world, but dragons now had centuries of civilization during which more enlightened concepts could take root. Ideas such as justice stemming not from the concept that might makes right, but in the belief that all intelligent beings are inherently equal.

Now, he found that all his high and fanciful thoughts were nothing more than soap bubbles: ephemeral, beautiful, and doomed as they brushed against jagged reality.

Word of the massacre at Dragon Forge had reached him quickly. It was said that the rebels had tried to slow the news by slaughtering innocents for miles around, but those deaths had been for naught. A valkyrie from the Nest had been sent to Dragon Forge in the aftermath of Blasphet's invasion to warn them that the Murder God was still on the loose. She'd discovered the killing fields around Dragon Forge. The humans had tried to bring her down, but, of course, their arrows couldn't reach her. She'd journeyed on to the palace to report what she'd found.

Shandrazel looked up from the map as Androkom entered the hall. The High Biologian looked grim. "When Charkon learns of this, he'll demand swift action. This rebellion must be crushed if you are to prevent a civil war, Sire. After the Blasphet debacle, any further show of weakness will cause your fellow sun-dragons to turn against you. The Commonwealth will shatter."

"Agreed," said Shandrazel. "Summon everyone."

"Everyone, sire?" Androkom asked.

"Gather the aerial guard. Dispatch them to the far reaches of the Commonwealth. The sun-dragons who control their various abodes are bound by a pact of mutual defense. Gather them at Dragon Forge within three days. These humans were offered a chance at peace. They've chosen war instead. It is time mankind is reminded that sun-dragons are the undisputed masters of war. We must strangle this rebellion in its cradle before it can grow any further."

"Of course, sire," said Androkom. "Overwhelming force is the swiftest path to returning security and order."

Shandrazel nodded. "Before you go, send Charkon in. I owe it to him to deliver the news personally. If I'd allowed him to return, perhaps his leadership could have prevented this."

"We can't know that, sire."

"I know," Shandrazel said, looking up to the tapestry of his father devouring the army of humans. "It haunts me just the same."

THE AIR OF Dragon Forge stank of smoke and death. Pet stared at the thick black smoke that rose from the third chimney. Immediately following the fall of the city, Burke had taken control of the three central furnaces. Two were now dedicated solely to the production of weaponry. The third had become a crematorium, and it was this furnace that provided most of the oily black soot that drifted down onto the town. There wasn't enough time or manpower to bury the dead. Burke had reluctantly cut his production capacity by a third due to the fear of disease. He'd seen the plagues that followed in the aftermath of slaughter. Clearing the dead and all their attendant gore from the water supplies and sewage was the task of half the available men. Burke had said there was no point in creating weapons if all his soldiers were dropping dead from fevers.

Pet turned his attention from the furnace back to the wall of wood before him. Pet had been placed with a team of men tasked with closing the gates of Dragon Forge. It was difficult, backbreaking labor. Digging a trench to free a gate whose bottom edge was buried in centuries of dirt required the use of muscles Pet hadn't known he possessed. He found himself working alongside men with faces rough as leather from years laboring in the sun. Their hands were thick, callused masses immune to blisters and splinters. They were tough men of the earth who worked stoically, uncomplaining of the cold. Pet wanted to grumble about the pain of his broken nose, or the way his legs were still chapped from the ride, or his fingers still raw from the bowstring, but he held his tongue. These men wouldn't be a sympathetic audience.

It was their second day of labor. Pet joined the rest of the crew in putting their shoulders to the gate and pushing. The legs of a hundred men strained against hinges long locked by rust. Burke had given the foreman a special oil to penetrate the rust and release the gates, but if it had had any effect, Pet couldn't tell. They may as well have been pushing a stone wall.

At last the foreman shouted for the men to stop. Pet collapsed to the dirt, certain that all their efforts had been for nothing. But, as he rested, he watched the foreman at the far edge of the gate measuring scrapes in the ground with a length of ribbon.

"That's five inches!" he shouted.

The men around Pet grumbled, but Pet rolled to his back and thrust his fists into the air, feeling triumphant. Five inches was much further than no distance at all.

"Only twenty feet to go," the foreman said.

After a short rest where Pet shared a drink from a bucket of soot-flecked water, the men once more put their shoulders to the gate.

"Push!" the foreman shouted.

Pet strained with all his might, feeling as if the bones in his legs might snap. The gate groaned as the hinges loosened further. The wall of wood crept another inch, then gained speed for nearly a foot before grinding to a halt once more, cutting into the hard-packed earth. The door was sagging as it swung. There was more digging to do.

Pet passed beyond all exhaustion as a long day gave way to a long night. He'd hoped that when darkness came they would be allowed to sleep, but word was that Burke had given the decree that the gates must be closed before dawn. The men chattered among themselves. Was an attack imminent? How many more hours would they have before the dragons tried to retake the forge?

The night sky was black as tar. The foundry smoke and the thick clouds blotted out all traces of the moon. A chill drizzle began to fall over Dragon Forge, turning the ground to mud. Pet's teeth chattered even as his body sweated. At some point he was given a wheelbarrow. He couldn't even recall who'd charged him with the duty. He mindlessly set to work carting away the mounds of earth that others broke free with picks and shovels. Pet dumped the heavy, damp dirt at the base of one of the rust mounds. He coughed from the effort. His head felt full of rust and dust and burnt bone ash. The mucus he wiped from his lips onto his once fine shirt was pink, not from blood, but from the red clay grime that clung to him.

In the moonless, starless night, he lost all track of time. He felt as if he were only dreaming; trapped in a nightmare where he struggled through the darkness, soaked by rain and sweat, pushing heavy heaps to and fro for reasons he could no longer remember.

"Okay men," the foreman shouted at last. "Dawn is only an hour away. Get your shoulders into the gate. Move it. Now!"

Pet dropped his wheelbarrow where he stood. He slogged through the now ankle-deep mud to take his position.

"Push!"

Pet fell instantly. The mud gave no traction. He clawed his way upright again, digging his broken nails into the grain of the ancient, weathered wood. The gate was built of logs thicker than his torso, bound by iron bands with rivets as big as his fist. He pressed both hands against one of these rivets and burrowed down into the mud with his feet, seeking purchase.

"Push!"

Everyone was groaning now. The mud slurped and sucked as men dug their feet into it, churning it into an ever-worsening muck.

And yet, the very mud that made their movements so frustrating was proving to be an aid. The gate slowly began to swing, no longer obstructed by every little rock or bulge in the packed earth that had halted it earlier. The damp ground gave way to the mass of the gate, and the more the gate moved, the easier it was to push.

Then, the gate ground to a halt once more. Tears welled in Pet's eyes.

"Move!" he shouted, straining with every last ounce of will within him. "Damn you, move!"

The gate didn't budge.

Slowly he realized that the men around him were standing back from the gate, looking up in amazement. Pet staggered away from the logs, his legs trembling.

The gate was closed.

The gate had stopped moving because it had met its matching neighbor for the first time in centuries, the two pieces fitting together as neatly and nicely as a man could want.

Pet dropped to his knees in the mud.

He wiped a tear from his cheek as the men around him began to cheer.

He'd heard men cheer like this before. They'd cheered him like this in the shadow of Albekizan's castle, when he claimed to be Bitterwood, claimed that he would lead humanity to a new era.

Those unearned cheers had tortured his sleep ever since.

In this cold and damp predawn hour, the cheers weren't directed at him. He'd not led a single man on this project. He hadn't given them a vision to rally around, or even said an encouraging word to his fellow laborers.

No one would sing a song about his labors today. No one would ever weave it into a tapestry, or write it in a book. Yet he felt as if this were the first truly worthwhile thing he'd ever done in his life.

PET COUGHED HIMSELF awake. He sat up, feeling as if his lungs were being scoured by the cold air and ever-present smoke. He was in a large room that had been converted into a makeshift barracks and slept on the floor with scores of fellow soldiers, all curled beneath tattered blankets. The far end of the room possessed a roaring fireplace, but any heat the fire put out was sliced apart by icy drafts that cut through the room from innumerable gaps in the walls.

Pet rose on stiff legs and carefully stepped across his sleeping brethren to reach the main door. He wondered what this room had once been that it was so shabbily constructed. He opened the door and found a familiar figure in the street beyond. It was Burke, carrying a large wooden box slung over his back. His daughter followed close behind, a large bundle wrapped in burlap held in both arms.

"Ah," said Burke, his head turning toward the sound of the opening door. "If it isn't Bitterwood himself."

"I told you it isn't," Pet said.

"You look like hell, Pet," Burke said over the rims of his spectacles. "I could still tell that was a silk shirt when I met you. Now it looks like something I wouldn't let my dog sleep on."

Pet looked down at his torn and mud-caked clothing. Burke and his daughter gleamed in comparison. Anza looked especially immaculate, dressed in soft buckskin, her jet-black braid showing not a single stray hair. If there was a bathtub somewhere in this hellish city, she must have taken possession of it.

"I've been working," said Pet. "Helped close the eastern gate."

"Good," said Burke. "That will slow the earth-dragons."

"I know," said Pet. "But, I have to admit, I'm worried. What good is having a gate when the sun-dragons can attack from above?"

"Follow me. I'll show you what's going to be our wall in the sky." Burke pulled the heavy case off his shoulder and handed it to Pet. "Carry this," he said, then walked off briskly, with a confident stride.

Pet hurried to draw beside Burke once more.

"A wall in the sky?" he asked.

"Patience," said Burke. "You're going to be the first to see it. Cold tonight, isn't it? I think we may see snow. Maybe not today, but tomorrow. I feel it in my knees."

"It feels warmer out here than it did in the barracks," said Pet.

"Ah, yes. The wench house. Not exactly a palace, is it?"

"Wench house?"

"It actually has a more derogatory name that I choose not to use in front of my daughter. Tell me,

Pet, can you spot the difference between male and female earth-dragons?"

"Not really."

"Neither can they, most of the time. Their sex organs are hidden away in a cloaca. Until they're about ten, all earth-dragons are raised on the assumption that they're male, because the species has a gender imbalance of almost ten to one. The vast majority are male, and it's not until the females go into their first heat that their true sex is discovered. Despite their rarity, the earth-dragons don't exactly treat their females like royalty. They're locked away in the wench house during their fertile period where they're brutally used by the males until they produce a clutch of eggs. Each female lays over a thousand eggs, then is essentially done. She won't be fertile again for another seven years. She goes back to the normal duties and lifestyle of a male, even taking part in the brutalization of those poor souls in the wench house, though, of course, they aren't capable of fertilizing anything."

"That's horrible," Pet said.

"Is it? It's easy to judge earth-dragons," said Burke, leading Pet up a steep staircase to the top of the wall that surrounded the city. "They reproduce through violence. They eat their own babies. Most of them are dumb as dirt. It makes killing them feel less like murder, doesn't it?"

"I suppose," said Pet.

"You don't sound convinced," said Burke as they walked along the wall. He gave the guards silent nods of greeting.

"I'm sorry," said Pet. "I'm not feeling up to contemplating deep moral questions right now."

"War isn't the time for that," said Burke. "Morality becomes what you carry in your gut."

Burke stopped, surveying the surrounding land-scape.

"Give me the box," he said.

Pet handed him the heavy case and watched as Burke nimbly flipped clasps and slipped open hidden compartments. The box transformed into a tripod and stand for a large owl figurine with giant glass eyes. Burke leaned over to stare into a small window at the back of the owl's head, fiddling with knobs on the owl's wings. Anza waited a short distance away, her arms crossed, her hands tucked into her armpits.

Pet looked at her and gave a wink. "Cold enough for you?" he asked.

She glared back at him. Pet wasn't surprised his charm was failing, given the ratty state he was in.

Burke said, "Anza doesn't speak."

"Oh," said Pet. "Is she deaf?"

"No. She hears better than my dog. She's just not said a word her whole life."

"Oh," said Pet.

"It hasn't held her back. Anza has other ways of getting her point across." Burke adjusted one more knob and said, "Ah, there we are. I've tied a ribbon in a tree down the north road, almost exactly one thousand yards distant. A thousand yards is a sig-nificant number. Do you know why?"

"Why?" asked Pet.

"Because sun-dragons rarely fly above 700 yards. Sky-dragons usually cruise even lower. It takes a lot of energy to fly. There's a safety element from being well above the landscape, but there's a trade-off in the energy it takes to get up there."

"That's still pretty high," said Pet. "Almost half a mile."

"More significantly," said Burke, "it's about twice as high as most arrows reach. A strong man and a good bow might get 500 yards' range. It's nothing to laugh at, but it means that dragons always command the high ground in war. They can drop anything they can carry on us, and we can't stop them. They might not have accuracy on their side, but they don't need it. They can fly a thousand passes over this fortress, confident that not even one arrow can reach them. If only one in a hundred of the war darts they drop kills someone, what does it matter? They'll whittle us down. If we take shelter in buildings, they drop flaming oil, or send in the earth-dragons while we're cowering. It's how they destroyed Conyers, and that town was much better prepared than Dragon Forge. We had food stocked, plentiful water, and bows in the hands of every man. Yet we were slaughtered by the thousands, and only three sun-dragons failed to return from that war."

Burke cast his gaze toward Anza. Pet looked back to find she'd unwrapped the bundle she'd carried. Propped on the wall in front of her were three bows. At least, they looked something like bows. They were shorter than a longbow, only four feet tall, and crafted from freshly forged steel instead of wood. At the tips of the bows were the grooved oval disks Burke had showed Pet when they first met. They served as pulleys and were strung with a thin, braided, metallic cable.

Anza grabbed one of the bows and took an arrow from the quiver on the wall. Burke pointed toward a distant tree that was almost invisible in the darkness. Anza drew the bow, her well-defined muscles bulging as she first pulled the string, then slackening as the pulleys held the force of the bow while she aimed.

She opened her fingers and the arrow simply vanished. The bowstring snapped back into place with a loud, musical *zing!*

Burke leaned over to look in the owl.

"Ooooh," he said, sounding sorry. "Close. You hit the limb, but missed the ribbon."

Anza frowned.

"Take a shot, Pet," Burke said.

Pet lifted one of the bows. It wasn't as heavy as it looked. The metal wasn't pure steel, apparently, but an alloy with something lighter. He placed the arrow against the cable and was surprised by the resistance of the first few inches of the draw. Then, suddenly, the remainder of the pull was effortless. He held the bow at full draw without any strain at all.

He aimed at what he assumed was the target tree. He couldn't see where Anza's arrow had hit, and definitely didn't see a ribbon. He released the arrow and was startled by the speed it launched into the air.

Burke clucked his tongue a few seconds later.

"You missed the whole damn tree," he said. "Shot over it, in fact."

"I can barely see it," said Pet.

Burke bent up from the owl, stretching his back. "Neither can I without mechanical assistance. Anza can be grateful not to have inherited my family's eyes."

"Her mother must have good eyes then," said Pet.

"I wouldn't know," said Burke.

"Why wouldn't you know?" Pet asked. Immediately, he regretted asking the question. Burke's relationship with his wife was none of his business.

Burke didn't seem offended by the question. He scratched the gray streaks of his hair, looking thoughtful. "After Conyers fell, I found good reason not to think of humans as any better than dragons. The survivors of the battle, the refugees, did terrible things. We'd gathered from distant villages, drawn together by Bitterwood's tale of injustice. He believed if we would all put aside our differences and stand together, we could change the world. We'll never know if he was right. We never did put aside our differences. We were squabbling among ourselves before the dragons came. After they left, the squabbles turned to bloodshed. They call it the Lost Year. For twelve months, there was no peace or safety as man turned on man in an orgy of reprisals, pillaging, and rape."

"Oh," said Pet. He wasn't quite sure how this answered his question about Anza's mother, but it seemed like something that Burke needed to get off his chest. "I'm sorry," he said.

"The only time I saw Anza's mother was in the ten minutes my tribe took to burn her village" Burke said. "Two of my brothers raped her. I didn't stop them. It was a bad, lawless time, a world turned upside-down."

Pet didn't know what to say.

"Somehow, knowing that my own blood was capable of such atrocities made me feel as if Conyers had been doomed from the start. What's the point of fighting monsters if we ourselves could be so inhuman? How much history have you learned, Pet? What do you know of the time before dragons?"

"I didn't know there *was* a time before dragons," said Pet. "I mean, I know a little of the *Ballad of Belpantheron*, where the dragons defeated the angels, but I assume that's only fairy tale."

Burke shook his head, as if he was sorry to hear these words. "A thousand years ago, there were no dragons. I know this because I am a descendent of the Cherokee, the true natives of this land. We had already had our land stolen from us once, by men. When these men lost it to dragons, my tribe vowed to remember the true history of the world. We called ourselves the Anudahdeesdee—the Memory. We remembered not only our history, but the history of all nations before the time of dragons."

"Is this how you know how to make all these things? These bows? This owl?"

"Over time, we lost much of our knowledge," said Burke. "Some men say our memories were a curse. Anyone who knew the great secrets, such as how to make gunpowder, always met misfortune, as if some evil spirit was out to destroy the memory of these things. I've only inherited a handful of secrets: an education in alloys and engineering that's but a shadow of the knowledge mankind once possessed."

"But why are these things secret?" asked Pet. "Why didn't your people share them with the world? Maybe men could have done more to free themselves from the dragons."

"Perhaps. But, having watched my brothers turn into savages, I've despaired that men would only use the knowledge to hurt each other. The only good to have come out of my stand at Conyers was Anza."

Pet looked at Anza. She looked back at him with an unflinching gaze. He had the impression she'd heard this story before, and didn't enjoy hearing it.

"If you didn't know her mother, how did she come to live with you?"

"As things calmed, our tribe resumed trading with villages we'd made war with only weeks before. Rumors came that the woman my brothers raped was pregnant. My brothers made jokes about it. Months later, I learned that the woman had died in labor, but her baby girl had survived."

Burke looked at his feet as he relayed his story. Behind him, Pet heard the *zing!* of the wheeled bow as Anza took another shot at the distant ribbon.

"I knew... I knew as a half-breed, a child of rape with her mother dead, the girl would be raised as nothing more than a slave. I had no children. The only woman I ever loved died at Conyers. So, I left the Anudahdeesdee forever. I stole Anza from her cradle in the dead of night. I fled north, until I reached a place where no one knew my name. I ran as far from war and death and memory as I possibly could."

Zing! Anza let another arrow fly. The silence that followed was deafening. Burke looked out into the darkness with weary eyes. He sighed.

"In the end, I couldn't escape. I, of all people, should have known you cannot outrun the past."

Zing! Anza's fourth arrow flew out into the night. Seconds later, she let out a triumphant grunt.

Burke leaned over to look into his owl.

"That's my girl!" he said. "Right into the ribbon!"

Anza sat the bow down, looking satisfied and smug.

"I assume she'll be leading the archers," Pet said.

"You assume wrong," said Burke. "She's the only one in this fort qualified to copilot Big Chief."

"Big Chief?"

"My giant."

"Your giant what?" asked Pet.

"Patience," said Burke. "You'll see it soon enough. For now, though, I do need someone to lead the archers. It's taken me three days to make three bows, but now we've got the process worked out and the machinery geared up. Tomorrow we'll have another dozen. The day after, fifty. I'm going to let you drill and train the men, Pet."

"Me? I'm not the best shot in the world."

"No, but you're a man who knows who the enemy is. Until someone rediscovers the formula for gunpowder, these are the most dangerous weapons any man will put his hands on. I want them aimed at dragons, not other men."

Pet bit his lip, afraid to say the thought that instantly flashed through his mind.

"What?" Burke asked, reading the unasked question in Pet's face.

"You seemed willing to aim your weapons at your fellow men the other night. You had no problem with killing the gleaners."

"We weren't killing them because we hated them; we were killing them out of strategic necessity."

"They wound up dead all the same," said Pet.

Burke reached out and put his hand on Pet's shoulder. "The fact you feel this way makes me trust you all the more. I knew what you were made of the second you stepped to the defense of that poor gleaner. I told you, morality comes from the gut. I think you've got the guts to stand on this wall when the dragons come and, more importantly, after the dragons fall."

Pet wasn't certain that Burke had the right man. However, Burke was a genius and Pet wasn't, so his gut said to trust the man's judgment. He gave Burke a nod of acceptance, and then pulled another arrow from the quiver. He gave Anza the most charming smile his chapped lips could manage before taking aim once more at the distant tree.

"I'll split your arrow before the night's out," he said. She smirked.

He never even hit the branch. But he did eventually hit the tree.

CHAPTER TWENTY-NINE

AT DAWN, AS THE DRAGONS CAME

THE FOLLOWING DAY, Pet joined Burke in the task of auditioning archers. There were three thousand men inside the fort, but finding fifty with eyes sharp enough to meet Burke's criteria proved challenging. Burke had sent Anza out to a rust heap about 700 yards away. She stood atop it, holding a dinner plate over her head. A large letter was painted on the plate. The plate was nearly a foot tall, but Pet could only see the letter as a smudge. He was glad Burke was apparently satisfied enough with his performance the night before that he wasn't being asked to read the letter.

After they'd tested a hundred men and found only two with sufficiently sharp eyes, Pet said, "Burke, I know you're a lot smarter than I am. But, isn't this test tougher than it needs to be? We're fighting dragons, not dinner plates."

"True," said Burke. "But your arrows are going to be mere specks at killing range. While dragons are big targets, they only have a few body areas where a single arrow is going to knock them from the sky. If you can't see where your arrow's going, you can't adjust your aim."

Pet nodded. "Makes sense."

Another candidate stepped up, a young man, boyish except for a wispy blond mustache. He was five feet tall at most, but looked wiry and tough. Pet felt there was something eerily familiar about the boy. The youth gave Burke a crisp salute.

"What's your name, son?" Burke asked.

"Vance," the young man answered.

"Where you from?"

"Stony Ford, sir."

"Never heard of it. That one of the towns where Ragnar gave his 'join or die' speech?"

"No, sir," said Vance. "It's down the river a spell. My brother and I heard about the rebellion and came to take a stand, sir."

Burke pointed toward Anza in the distance. "You see my daughter out there?"

Vance shielded his eyes from the sun. "Yes, sir."

"What's she holding above her head?"

"Looks like a plate, sir."

Burke gave an approving nod. "And do you see something painted on the plate?"

"Yes, sir. Some kind of marking."

"Good. It's a letter. Can you tell me which letter?"

The boy shook his head. Burke looked disappointed.

The boy said, apologetically, "I don't know one letter from another. But it looks like this." The boy traced a serpentine shape in the air.

Burke smiled. "That's an 'S,' boy. And you're an archer now."

The boy gave a wide smile.

"You won't regret it, sir. Me and my brother were the best shots for miles around."

"Excellent. Where's your brother? What's his name? Let's get him to the front of the line."

Vance looked solemn as he reported, "His name was Vinton, and he's dead, sir. Vinton was charged with killing the disloyal gleaners the night we took the fort. We found him dead from an arrow shot. The two fellows he was running with were also killed. One had his head sliced clean off."

Pet felt a chill run down his spine. Now he knew why the boy looked familiar. The rapist with the scratched cheek was a ringer for this boy if you added five years and thirty pounds.

"Sorry to hear it," Burke said. "I'm sure Vinton was a good man."

"Yes, sir," said Vance. "One of the best."

Burke gave a nod toward the ladder leading down the wall. "Go down and join the others. You'll be given a bow. Later, we'll start target practice. Welcome to the sky-wall."

Vance couldn't stop smiling as he climbed down the ladder.

Pet felt the need to say something about the boy's brother.

"Don't say anything," Burke said, reading Pet's mind.

"But…"

"But the past is past. As of now, Vance is your brother-at-arms. What happened before this moment is of no importance."

Pet knew that Burke was right, but he couldn't keep the scene from replaying in his mind. What could he have done differently? Would the world have been better if he'd just turned his back? If a dragon made it through the sky-wall, would he be haunted by the knowledge that Vinton might have fired the arrow that would have killed that dragon? He barely paid attention to the next candidate Burke tested. He was only broken out of his reverie by a sudden outcry from the eastern gate.

"Dragons!" someone was shouting.

"Four days," Burke sighed. "So much for my fantasy of doing this with a well-trained army."

THE DRAGONS WEREN'T attacking, not yet. Instead, they gathered at a large field a mile downriver. Pet listened quietly as spies reported back to Ragnar, Burke, and the other leaders. Pet, as commander of the archers, was now privy to these meetings.

The lead spy, it turned out, was Shanna, the woman who'd rescued Pet from the dungeon. She hadn't taken part in the raid on the Nest, but she had learned from her contacts that Blasphet had failed in his attempt at genocide. Only a handful of the sisters had managed to escape in the aftermath, but Shanna was confident there would be no valkyries joining in the attack on Dragon Forge. Blasphet hadn't been found; the matriarch wasn't letting anyone leave the Nest until his threat was neutralized.

Shanna was now dressed much more modestly than she had been as a servant of Blasphet. She was wearing the gray, non-descript clothing of a human slave. She hadn't shaved her head in a week and already her scalp tattoos were vanishing beneath a haze of dark hair.

Burke listened impassively as the numbers were reported. Nearly ten thousand well-armed earth-dragons, with at least five hundred cavalry mounted on the backs of great-lizards. The earth-dragons had catapults and ballistae. There were also a thousand humans among the dragons, slaves working to assemble the tents, dig latrines, unload the supply wagons, and staff the mess tents.

"The supply wagons are the most dangerous thing we face," Burke said. "If Shandrazel has any management skills at all, his army has access to all the food in the world. We have all the food inside the walls of Dragon Forge, which will last us, if we're careful, a month."

"I'm not eating those pickled earth-dragon babies," said Pet.

"If a man gets hungry enough, he'll eat anything," said Burke.

"The Lord sent ravens to feed his prophet Elijah," said Ragnar. "We shall have no want of provisions."

Burke gave Ragnar a sideways glance and returned to questioning the spies. The next number that caught Pet's attention was the figure of two hundred sun-dragons. He thought back to his former mistress, Chakthalla. She'd loved him like he was her child and had never mistreated him, but he remembered how intimidating she could be with her sheer size and power. Even as she had showered words of praise upon him, he'd never been completely unaware of the fact that those words came from a mouth that could have snapped him in two. As of this meeting, Burke's manufacturing team had produced only thirty-six bows. Apparently, Burke had brought coils of cable from his tavern to use for the bowstrings, but those spools were now emptied. He'd assembled a machine to make new cable, but the process was a difficult one to calibrate, and the earliest batches were producing cables that were too brittle. If the dragons attacked soon, thirty-six sky-wall archers against two hundred sun-dragons wasn't a promising ratio.

"How long will it be before the dragons finish assembling their army and decide to attack?" Pet asked.

Shanna shook her head. "We haven't heard. Some say that Shandrazel is awaiting more troops from the southern provinces."

"That's good and bad," said Burke. "Good if we have more time—it would take at least a week for all those troops to arrive. But it's bad if we wind up facing three times as many dragons."

"However, it's also said that Shandrazel is being prodded by Charkon to invade tomorrow at dawn," said Shanna. "Charkon believes they have all the troops they need to take back the fortress."

"Charkon is probably right," said Burke. "But only because he doesn't know about our surprises."

"Surprises?" Pet asked, noting the plural. "Do we have something other than the wheel-bows?"

Burke nodded. "There's Big Chief. I carted in most of his parts, and the team has him just about assembled. He's mostly a psychological weapon. Earth-dragons aren't terribly bright. They get confused and frightened easily by things they've never encountered before."

Before Pet could ask further questions, Shanna stepped in with her own answer about surprises. "Our time with Blasphet has proven fruitful. We've learned how to make oil that, when burned, produces a smoke that paralyzes dragons. Unfortunately, it works best in a confined space. Also it requires a fungus that grows on peanuts, and Blasphet used most of his stockpile invading the Nest. I've had people producing a supply for us ever since I learned the secret, but we only have a few barrels. Still, if any dragons make it inside Dragon Forge, we can ignite the bonfires and spike them with the poison. We can put half the invaders to sleep if the wind is in our favor."

"That sounds useful," Pet said.

Shanna nodded. "That's only part of the knowledge we've stolen from Blasphet. If we knew for certain that the attack was tomorrow, we could make life unpleasant for the invaders. There's a tasteless, odorless mineral salt we can add to their breakfast that will produce diarrhea and vomiting three hours after its ingested. It doesn't kill dragons, but it can make them wish they were dead."

Ragnar spoke. "Tell your spies to poison tomorrow's breakfast, Shanna. The Lord has revealed to me the attack will take place at dawn. Our ultimate weapon, of course, is the guiding hand of God."

Burke took his spectacles from his nose and wiped them with his shirt. He said, in a thoughtful tone, "Not that I don't trust the Lord's word, but I'd like some insurance. Shanna, you've been good at gathering rumors. If we really want this attack to take place at dawn, I need you to spread one."

"Do we want this attack to take place at dawn?" Pet asked. "Half my men don't have weapons. We've had barely any training at all. We aren't ready!"

Burke placed the spectacles back on his face as he nodded. "It's true, we aren't. But, right now, Shandrazel's army is as small as it's ever going to be. We'll be better armed and better trained a week from now, but we aren't going to have anymore men. Shandrazel, on the other hand, might have doubled his army in that time. If he attacks tomorrow and finds half his army shitting themselves and the first wave of sun-dragons slain by our sky-wall, we'll have achieved an important psychological victory. Shandrazel will no longer have the confidence of other dragons. If we're lucky, his army will abandon him."

"What if we're not lucky?"

Burke shrugged.

Ragnar smiled. "We need not trust in luck. The Lord is on our side."

Pet sighed. "Fine. I just wish I had more time for my men to practice."

Burke grinned grimly. "As you pointed out, we're not fighting dinner plates. Your men have a target forty feet across to shoot at. It's like hitting a barn wall."

"A barn wall moving straight overhead and dropping darts on us. Still, I'm not arguing. Your reasons for wanting the attack tomorrow make sense."

"So what rumor do you want me to start?" Shanna asked.

"Say that we're unprepared. Say we're outnumbered five to one already."

"That's a cutting a mighty fine line between a rumor and actual intelligence," said Shanna.

Burke nodded. "Most of all, make sure the dragons know that a man named Kanati is in here. It's vital that Charkon hears that name."

"Why Charkon?" Pet asked. "He already wants to attack tomorrow."

"Yes. But he's a good soldier and will wait until Shandrazel gives the word. Once Charkon hears the name Kanati, he'll stop taking orders from Shandrazel and start giving them. He'll make this attack happen no matter what Shandrazel wants."

"Why?" Pet asked. "Who's Kanati?"

"I am, or used to be," said Burke. "And since you've met Charkon, you might have noticed he's one ugly son-of-a-bitch."

"That scar," said Pet, shuddering. "Half his face is practically gone."

"I only wish I'd swung hard enough to cut through to the other half," said Burke.

AT DAWN, AS the dragons came, snow began to fall. During the night, Burke had fine-tuned the cable-making machine. Now Pet had bows in the hands of three-score men, and nearly three dozen arrows for each of them. Delicate snowflakes settled gently on the filthy gray-brown blanket Pet had turned into a cape. All around him, his men stood in silence as the sun crept over the horizon. The rust heaps and scraggly trees cast long, dark shadows over the faint film of white snow on the ground.

The rising sun tinted the shroud of low clouds subtle shades of pink. In all, it was a serene winter landscape, a picture of peace, save for the hordes of dull green dragons pouring over the distant hills and charging the walls of Dragon Forge.

Pet cast his eyes skyward. The earth-dragons weren't his concern. A different squad of archers, armed with traditional bows, would be responsible for seeing that the earth-dragons didn't reach the walls. His duty was to scan the clouds for the first signs of sun-dragons. Slowly, one by one, their dark ruby forms emerged from the shrouding snowfall.

There were at least seventy in the initial wave, coming in at a height of five hundred yards, all carrying large buckets in their hind claws. The buckets would be full of iron darts. The dragons wouldn't even bother to aim, Pet knew. They need simply dump their cargo above the town and fill the winter sky with something much more deadly than snow. The men on the walls would either be killed, or forced into shelter, leaving the earth-dragons free to storm the gates and overwhelm the city. It was a time-honored strategy of the dragons, one that had crushed human uprisings for centuries.

As the dragons neared, Pet ran the back of his hand along his scratchy mustache. The mineral oil Burke used to lubricate the wheel-bows had thoroughly coated his fingers by now. It smelled faintly of pine.

"Aim!" Pet shouted. He drew a bead on an approaching sun-dragon. His lifelong familiarity with the beasts allowed him to judge their true distance against the trackless sky. He knew the dragons could see his men and their bows; they'd lose all element of surprise the second the first arrows flew. He had to wait until he was certain they would be in range.

He held his aim a few seconds, then a few seconds more, calculating the dragons' speed. Pet targeted the empty sky, aiming at the spot where the dragon would be when the arrow reached it, then shouted, "Fire!"

Arrows flash upward like frozen shards of light. The snapping steel bowstrings made the wall sound as if a large harpsichord were being stroked by a giant—*zing, zing, zang, zing, zang!* For an instant, Pet worried he'd overshot his target, until the sun-dragon dropped his bucket. The crimson beast doubled over, clutching the arrow in its gut. A half dozen of its brethren performed similar aerial contortions before they began to plummet from the sky. The dragons that followed veered and wheeled away as the seven struck in the initial volley fell. Keeping his eyes on the sky, Pet paid no attention to where the bodies landed. He'd already drawn another arrow.

"Aim!" he shouted.

Behind him, there was a powerful WHANG as a catapult Burke had salvaged from the dragon armory sent a shower of shrapnel skyward. Its target wasn't the sun-dragons, but the advancing army of earth-dragons who flowed toward the fort like a living river.

While some of the sun-dragons were pulling back in confusion, a full score continued to advance. Pet took a calming breath, making certain of his aim, then cried out, "Fire!"

Zing, zing, zang, zing, zang!

This time, ten dragons felt the bite of the arrows, some falling in gentle arcs, some in dizzying cartwheels, and a few simply plunging straight toward Earth. One smashed into the ground outside the wall not twenty feet away from Pet. The vibration of the impact ran up his legs. A rust heap crashed with a noise like a band of drummers falling down stairs as one of the dying beasts smacked into it.

By now, the remaining dragons were near the wall. One by one, they tilted their buckets, and a black rain of darts fell toward the men.

"Shields!" Pet shouted. In unison, all the men along the wall lifted the wooden disks propped before them, ducking their heads as they crouched. The thick oak shields were banded with broad strips of steel. Seconds later, the darts struck, and the entire wall rang out with a clatter and chatter as a thousand tiny, deadly knives buried themselves in the wood. Men started screaming seconds later. Pet looked up. A few of the braver sun-dragons had swooped down, snatched up men from the wall, and lifted them skyward. Pet tossed his dart-studded shield aside and drew his bow once more.

"Fire at will!" he shouted, knowing there was no longer any hope of unified action. Dragons were everywhere. A score of sun-dragons remained high overhead, but their darts would now be striking their own forces if they dropped them, for at least as many of the sun-dragons had broken ranks and were attacking the bowmen on the walls directly. Below, the river of earth-dragons spread out in waves as they reached the walls. From every direction, there was shouting and confusion. Pet tried to put it from his mind.

It wasn't courage that welled up within him at this moment. Instead, it was something far less passionate and far colder. He became deaf to the cries of his fellow men. He was undistracted by the bodies of sun-dragons falling from the sky around him and turning to red, meaty smears as they crashed into the snow. He gave no thought to his own life or safety. He simply became mindless, his body moving with a cool, machine-like efficiency.

The sole purpose of his life was to place an arrow in his bow, aim, fire. Again and again he followed this action, without a thought in his mind. Find a hole in the sky where a dragon would be, fire. Find another hole, fire. One by one, his victims fell. The sky was so thick with the bodies of dragons, it was nearly impossible to miss. If his arrow flew past one dragon, it would strike a second behind it.

Pet lost all sense of time. He maintained this trancelike state until he reached to the quiver on his back and found his fingers closing on empty air. Suddenly, the calm emptiness in him was broken and his thoughts came crashing back. His heart leapt into his throat. He consciously became aware of how empty the sky above suddenly seemed.

He cast his gaze down the wall, then toward the men on the other walls. He could tell their ranks had been thinned by the initial assault. In the city below, blood once again ran in the gutters. A wooden building near the center of town had been completely crushed beneath the remnants of a sun-dragon, and at least two more of the huge corpses blocked the streets. Yet there were no living dragons within the walls, not even an earth-dragon. Looking down, Pet surveyed a field of fallen green bodies. Many of those still surviving were crawling away on all fours, violently vomiting. The poisoned breakfast was taking hold! Despite this, there were still so many. Ten thousand earth-dragons, the spies had said. Were there even ten thousand arrows in Dragon Forge?

Turning his eyes skyward, he took comfort in the nearly empty palette of white. In the distance, he saw over two dozen sun-dragons in retreat, racing back toward their camp. Still, the aerial assault wasn't completely over. One last dragon swooped down from the covering clouds and raced toward Dragon Forge, its dart bucket still in its claws.

Pet lowered his eyes back to the wall and began to run, spotting the body of a fallen archer ten yards away, near the eastern gate. He saw fresh arrows in the slain man's quiver. Pet snatched up a handful of missiles and turned to find his target.

The sun-dragon he'd spotted was heading on a path toward Pet. Pet calmly drew a bead and let his arrow fly. He watched with great satisfaction as the arrow buried itself deep in the beast's breast, a shot that almost certainly pierced the heart. The dragon's eyes rolled upwards and its whole body went limp. It transformed instantly from a thing of grace in the air into a half-ton bag of falling meat.

For a second, it seemed as if the dragon were hurtling straight toward Pet, carried by momentum and gravity on a deadly path, but the dragon was actually coming down at a slight angle to his side. For a sickening second, Pet imagined the body of the dragon smashing into the gate he'd worked so hard to close, its corpse transformed into a swift and heavy battering ram.

Then, he no longer imagined it. He watched it, unfolding with an unnerving déjà vu, as the corpse rammed at high speed into the thick wood. The mass and speed of the dragon were such that the body didn't so much crash as splash. A rain of dark gore shot in all directions as a thunderous crack split the gate. The wood tore from the hinges as the ancient logs snapped like sticks.

Pet found himself frozen, unable to think, as a hundred earth-dragons sprang against the ruptured gate, forcing it wider. Seconds later they charged into the city, with cries of victory shrieking from their turtle-like beaks.

Pet fumbled to place another arrow against the string. The calmness that had filled him so completely was now gone, replaced by the trembling certainty that he'd just doomed the city.

Then, a strange thing happened. A few of the dragons stumbled and fell, and others tumbled and tripped over them. Others who avoided colliding with fellow soldiers began to weave in drunken circles. A thick, oily smoke drifted through the city streets as Shanna and the men she commanded poured buckets of blue oil onto bonfires. Ragnar's men surged from the doorways of the buildings, bringing a swift end to these drunken dragons. Yet for every dragon they slew, two more poured through the gate. Not all seemed affected by the smoke. Perhaps the open air didn't allow the poison to spread evenly through the city, or perhaps the thick-headed earth-dragons possessed members of their race who simply were too dumb to be poisoned.

Whatever the cause, Ragnar's men soon found themselves being pushed back toward the open city square.

Chaos was again spreading along the walls. Some archers began firing into the city, while others aimed outside the walls. Pet looked up and found the dark shapes of sun-dragons once more on the horizon. It was time to bring order to the chaos.

"Sky-wall!" he shouted, running up and down the walls. "Sky-wall, man your positions! Grab whatever arrows you can find and get ready for the next wave! Hurry!"

To his amazement, the men obeyed. He eyed the distant dragons. There were fewer than twenty. Where were the rest? If Shanna was right, there should still be over a hundred. Was this all that was left of the sun-dragons who would obey Shandrazel? Was the psychological element of the sky-wall working as Burke had predicted?

Behind him, he heard a loud, mechanical whistle. Breaking his own order to watch the sky, he looked toward the courtyard. A cloud of steam shot into the air as the whistle sounded once more. There was a loud clattering like the wheels of a thousand wagons. Into the courtyard rolled a human figure twenty-feet tall. It was a man made of iron, with buckskin-wrapped legs set on giant rolling treads as long as it was tall that propelled it forward with a rapid lurching gait. The giant had an angry, demonic, iron visage, and a headdress hanging down his back made from red and blue dragon feathers. The giant man brandished a long iron war club as it advanced and let loose another shriek of steam.

"Ah," said Pet. "So that's Big Chief."

Burke the Machinist sat in the area where the giant's crotch should be, in a wire cage that protected him from most blows but allowed him a wide field of vision. He was operating a series of wheels and levers that controlled Big Chief's treads, while Anza sat in a similar cage at the giant's throat, pulling levers that controlled the giant's arms. Its left arm swung the war-club, easily seven feet long and as thick as a fence post. A lone earth-dragon stood near Big Chief, staring up, its turtle-mouth agape. The giant club came down on the stunned dragon like a sledgehammer on a watermelon.

The huge iron boiler on the treads behind Big Chief whistled in the aftermath, belching steam, giving the giant life by powering the chains and pulleys that drove it. Anza flipped a switch and flames shot out Big Chief's eyes as she turned his head toward a crowd of earth-dragons pushing toward the square. The mouth of the demonic face opened and let fly a dozen of the razor disks that Pet had seen demonstrated in the initial invasion. The green hides of the earth-dragons suddenly sported horrid red stripes.

As a wave, the earth-dragons turned and ran, leaving behind only a few stragglers.

No, not stragglers.

Warriors. The earth-dragons left behind wore gleaming armor and carried broad axes that cut a swathe through the humans around them. Pet recognized the dragon at the center of this band, and knew that Burke was in for a fight.

"Charkon," he whispered.

The *zings* of the sky-wall bows rang out and he turned away. He had his own job to do. The rest was up to Burke.

CHAPTER THIRTY

STOMACH FOR BRUTALITY

BIG CHIEF LURCHED and shuddered as Burke shifted into second gear and rolled into the square. The mob of earth-dragons all turned toward the noise as he pulled the steam whistle. Their beaks dropped in astonishment as flames shot from the giant machine's eyes. At his back, the falling snow sizzled as it vaporized against the boiler. Anza released a round of the razor disks; the ratchets and springs firing in sequence sounded like music. There were probably five hundred earth-dragons in the square—at least half of them turned tail and ran as Big Chief lumbered forward on its treads. Even though most of the components for the steam giant had been assembled over the years in his basement back at the tavern, until this moment he'd worried that building Big Chief had been a foolish waste of time and resources. But as the earth-dragons stampeded, he felt his devotion to the machine had been worthwhile. The fact that darts weren't raining down on everyone in sight told him the sky-wall bows had worked as well. It looked as if they'd survived the initial assault. Now all they had to do was clean up stragglers, clear the streets of dragon corpses, and prepare for the inevitable siege.

In his confidence, Burke didn't notice the human head hurtling through the air toward him until it clanged against the wire cage and splattered him with blood. The jolt of adrenaline that surged through him completely changed his view of the battle. Yes, most earth-dragons were running from the square. But so, too, were many of Ragnar's men. Was Big Chief frightening them as well? Or was something worse hidden in the square behind the crush of bodies?

A second head flew up in the air, then a third, a fourth, a fifth, until it looked like a demented juggling act. The crowd between himself and the source of the flying heads parted as men fled. At last he had a good view of the problem.

"Charkon," he muttered.

The earth-dragon leader and his five bodyguards advanced in a tight circle, protecting each other's backs, spinning through the human warriors like a giant killing wheel. Their axes slashed out, cutting down anything in their path. Burke found himself in grudging admiration of the choreography and teamwork the six warriors displayed. They were fighting with years of experience, the finest weapons and armor the dragons had ever produced, and sheer superhuman power. Earth-dragon muscles grew denser as they aged. Charkon was twenty years stronger than when they'd last met. Burke was twenty years older.

And Burke had spent those twenty years designing this machine for exactly this moment.

"Okay Anza," Burke said. "Chew them."

The giant tilted its head and Burke listened with great satisfaction to the precise clockwork *click zzizz, click zzizz* as the razor disks shot from their cartridge. Anza handled the disk shooter better than he'd ever managed. Each one sliced through the air straight toward its target, a testament to Burke's precision craftsmanship and Anza's steady aim. Unfortunately, Charkon's elite armor proved to be of an even superior craftsmanship. The disks snapped and ricocheted from his breast plate in a shower of sparks. The wildly careering shards cut into the human warriors nearby, biting into bone.

Anza stopped firing. Burke could tell from the clanking of chains that she was resetting the war club to strike. Burke shifted gears and spun the guide wheel to swing Big Chief into a better attack position. The ancient, hard-packed earth of Dragon Forge was the perfect surface for Big Chief. Not even the snow was slowing it down.

Charkon gazed up at the approaching giant. Suddenly, the elder dragon broke ranks with his fellows and leapt forward. Anza swung the war club. Charkon raised his massive shield and took the blow. The shudder of the impact knocked Burke's spectacles free. He caught them against his chest. Slipping them back on, he found that Charkon's shield had been shattered by the blow—but Charkon himself seemed unharmed.

Charkon tossed the fragments of his shield aside before Anza could raise the club again. Dropping his axe, Charkon grabbed the iron club in his gauntleted claws. He twisted the weapon with all his strength, grunting loudly. Big Chief's arm groaned and creaked from the stress. The wrist joint exploded as Charkon tore the weapon free.

Shrapnel rattled off the mesh cage surrounding Burke. Big Chief's arm fell limp, the shoulder ratchets completely stripped.

"Kanati!" Charkon screamed, his voice given a metallic, cymbal-like quality by his helmet. He retrieved his axe and brandished it with both hands, launching into a charge. The arc of the swinging axe would slice directly into Big Chief's crotch. Burke was fairly certain that the wire mesh wasn't going to offer much protection. Then, to the surprise of both Burke and Charkon, Big Chief's left arm swung down and struck Charkon on the blind side of his helmet, knocking him from his feet with a loud *whang!* Charkon hit the ground hard as his dented helmet bounced away.

Big Chief, unfortunately, took the blow as badly as Charkon. Burke struggled to keep the giant upright as vibrations tested every bolt in the machine. Shrill whistles of steam cried out at his back as the boiler sprung numerous tiny leaks. Above, Anza ground gears as she tried to command the arm to rise once more, before Charkon could get back on his feet. The arm lifted barely a yard before freezing. Burke winced as cables throughout Big Chief's arm snapped.

Charkon rolled to his belly, looking dazed. Burke saw one last chance. He jammed Big Chief to maximum speed and steered straight toward Charkon, hoping to crush him beneath the treads.

Charkon rose to his knees, facing the giant as it rolled toward him. His thick claws reached out to retrieve his fallen axe. He threw the goreencrusted weapon parallel to the ground, the blade spinning in an uneven orbit, until it buried itself between the tread and the grooved wheels it rolled on. With a jolt, Big Chief's left leg ground to a halt. Burke kicked the right leg out of gear before they toppled.

Behind Charkon, Burke noticed that Ragnar was now leading the fight against the remaining earth-dragons. Ragnar almost flew as he leapt up, swinging his scimitars with such force they bit easily into his foes' seemingly invincible armor. When the earth-dragons returned the attack, Ragnar, naked and nimble, simply hopped away from their blows.

Burke sighed. He'd lived his life dedicated to the premise that preparation and inventiveness were of greater value than blind faith and naked savagery. Why did he believe anything at all when the world seemed intent on proving him wrong almost daily?

Burke was snapped from his philosophical musing as Charkon climbed onto the treads and stepped toward the wire cage. Burke was strapped into a leather harness, barely able to move. His little bubble of safety was now his death chamber.

"Kanati!" Charkon growled as he sank his claws into the mesh. "You should have learned your lesson twenty years ago!"

With a grunt, he tore the mesh aside.

"Humans are weak!" Charkon shouted, reaching in to take Burke by the throat. "Dragons are strong!"

To prove his point, Charkon yanked Burke from the remnants of the cage, snapping the leather straps that held Burke in position. Burke was certain his right thighbone fractured as it pulled free of the harness. However, since his whole leg was completely numb, he wouldn't know until he put weight on it.

"This feeble rebellion was a fool's dream!" Charkon snarled. His single eye was full of scorn.

"They said the man who took my eye was clever! But a clever man would have stayed in hiding! A clever man would know there isn't a chance mankind will ever best the dragons!"

Above, there was the rattling sound of a harness being unfastened. Burke struggled with both hands to try to open Charkon's claws even a fraction of an inch, so he could breathe.

Charkon chuckled and squeezed even tighter.

"Go on, clever man," he taunted. "Give me one reason mankind has for hope!"

Burke twisted his chin upward as he heard the creak of the cage door swinging open above. The movement of his chin created a tiny passageway for air. His words escaped in a barely audible whisper: "*We... don't... eat... our... young!*"

Anza dropped from the sky, her sword extended. The tip landed atop Charkon's skull with her full weight driving it. The sharpest blade Burke had ever crafted lanced into Charkon's head, sinking to the hilt. Anza somersaulted away, landing on her feet. If Burke knew anything about earth-dragon anatomy, the tip of her sword was now resting in the center of Charkon's liver. The earth-dragon's eye rolled up in its socket and his grip slackened.

Burke dropped to the ground, remaining on his feet for a full three seconds before he toppled over in agony. *Ah, yes. Right femur, definitely broken.* He hit the ground hard, blood speckling the white snow before him. His spectacles landed nearby with the unpleasant tinkle made by dancing shards of broken glass.

He could no longer see anything but blurs beyond the length of his arm. Ragnar's men were cheering. From people shouting back and forth, he surmised that the last of the earth-dragons had been slain, and Shandrazel's army was in full retreat. Mankind had won this day. Perhaps, if his internal bleeding didn't finish him off, he'd give out a cheer of his own when he woke up.

For now, he settled on allowing the ghost of a grin to flicker across his lips. He closed his eyes as the sound of cheering faded. He was only barely aware of Anza's hands on his face, increasingly lost to all sensation but the cool and gentle kisses of snow flakes melting on his cheeks.

JANDRA CLUNG TIGHTLY as Hex glided across the snowscape. The winter storm had stopped midday, leaving the world draped with a blanket of white. It was such a peaceful scene, it almost made her forget they were flying toward a war zone.

After they'd made the long trek through the underground to escape Jazz's kingdom, she'd convinced Hex to return to the Nest. Bitterwood had refused to accompany them. He'd remained behind with Zeeky and Jeremiah, saying the children should not be left to face the world alone, despite Zeeky's insistence that she wasn't alone... her parents still spoke to her through the crystal ball.

Upon returning to the Nest, they'd learned of the invasion of Dragon Forge, and of Shandrazel's plan to retake the fort. Now they were heading for the town, or, rather, for Shandrazel's encampment.

Jandra felt introspective. The world below her seemed sculpted from cotton, a soft world with soft edges. The only unpleasant thing about the scene was the stench—even unseen in the distance, the foundries of Dragon Forge filled the air with their fumes.

"Bodies are being burnt," Hex said as he smelled the smoke. "I expect we'll find that Shandrazel has already retaken the forge."

Jandra suspected that's what they'd find as well.

"That will be one less problem to worry about then," said Jandra. "When I left the palace, I had three big worries: who took Vendevorex's corpse, where could I find Bitterwood and Zeeky, and what was Blasphet up to?"

"Now you know the answers to two out of three of these. This isn't so bad."

"But I still have two missing bodies to worry about. Since they didn't find Blasphet's body, I think the Sisters of the Serpent must have taken it. Are they planning to worship his corpse?"

"I don't know much about religions, but could even humans be so irrational as to worship a mutilated corpse?"

"Maybe. And since Ven's body vanished around the same time that Blasphet's worshipers were freeing him, I can't help but think there's some connection. Since we never did learn the location of Blasphet's temple, that's going to be the second item on my list of problems to tackle after we make sure this Dragon Forge situation is under control."

"What's the first item?"

"My old tiara," said Jandra. "It's still sitting unguarded and unlocked back in the palace. I'd hate for it to wind up in the wrong hands."

"We won't tarry long at Dragon Forge," said Hex. "Shandrazel may not be a warrior by nature, but he's certainly smart enough to squash a human uprising on his own."

Jandra frowned. Something about Hex's tone made it seem like he felt that humans were naturally less intelligent than dragons. "Don't underestimate mankind. One thing that Jazz's implanted memories have shown me is that men didn't wind up in subservience to dragons overnight. Humans might have ruled the world if Jazz hadn't been actively working to cripple them. If she hadn't killed everyone who knew how to make gunpowder, for instance, the world would no doubt look very different."

"What's gunpowder?" Hex asked.

Jandra furrowed her brow at the question. She was frequently beset by these moments of cryptomnesia. Odd bits of knowledge flashed through her awareness as her brain endeavored to catalogue Jazz's forced memories.

"I'm not sure," she said, as Hex flapped his wings to lift them higher. The winter wind bit into her bare cheeks. The cold helped pull her back into here and now; she had fallen too easily into daydreams since Jazz had altered her mind. "It's so frustrating. It's like parts of my brain aren't talking to each other. I know that Jazz thought that gunpowder was dangerous, and spent centuries killing any human who knew how to make it. I have another memory of what it looks like and the chemical formulation. But these memories are just hanging there, disconnected. I'm not even certain what a gun is, or why you'd want to powder one! I have no idea if it would change the world or not."

Hex's shoulders stiffened ever so slightly as Jandra spoke. She'd grown quite sensitive to his reactions as she'd ridden him. She could sense his emotions in the subtle movements of his muscles beneath her thighs.

"What?" she asked.

Hex started to speak, then stopped.

"What?" she asked again.

"If an individual is nothing more than the sum of their memories, what will happen if Jazz's memories ever fully take root within you? Will you become her?"

"That's crazy," Jandra said. "I still have my own memories. I'm still Vendevorex's daughter first and foremost. I'm not going to forget that."

"But you aren't Vendevorex's daughter, not in truth," said Hex. "How can you trust your memories when the central memory of your life is so…" Hex paused, searching for the right word, "… so *edited*."

"That's a very diplomatic way of putting it," said Jandra. "I know the truth, but I choose not to dwell on it. I know that Vendevorex killed my true family, though Jazz thought that I might still have a surviving brother. But I'm making the choice to remember the good things I got from Ven: self-sufficiency, discipline, and compassion. So, yes, I suppose I am editing my memories."

"Perhaps," said Hex, "in the end, it's not what we remember that defines us, but what we willingly forget."

"Spoken like a true warrior-philosopher," said Jandra.

On the horizon, the town of Dragon Forge was a dark blot on the white landscape. The chimneys belched black plumes toward the gray clouds. The ground for hundreds of yards around the city was dark brown instead of snowy-white. Mounds of rusted metal were stacked around the city, along with other unidentifiable heaps. As they drew closer, a jolt of realization ran through her. Some of these heaps were the corpses of sun-dragons.

"By the bones," she whispered.

"I see it as well," Hex said. "What could have caused such slaughter?"

Jandra's finely tuned eyes focused in on the town walls and the forms moving along them. *Humans.* Dragon Forge was still under rebel control.

A fountain of anger bubbled up inside her. It was true that humans had suffered horribly under Albekizan. When Albekizan had launched his campaign of genocide, she'd been swept up with a passionate desire to fight for humanity. But didn't these people know Albekizan was dead? Shandrazel was intent on bringing peace and fairness to mankind. Why were these fools ruining the best hope of true justice this kingdom had ever known?

"It looks like humans are on the walls," Hex said a few seconds later. Jandra was surprised to realize that her vision was better than his now. Sundragons had eyes that were the envy of eagles.

"I see them," she said. "It looks like they have bows. We should veer away."

"No worry," said Hex, climbing slightly higher. "We're well above the range of arrows."

They closed in swiftly on the city. The little snow remaining on the ground was tinted pink with blood. Her eyes were drawn from the gore toward a strange contraption standing in the center of town. Some sort of machine, built to roughly resemble a man.

"I'm thinking we've just missed a fight," said Hex.

"Yes," said Jandra. "It looks to me as if the rebels beat back an attack of sun-dragons."

"How is that possible?" Hex asked, sounding genuinely puzzled. "Shandrazel may not have a warrior's heart, but I can't believe he couldn't command his forces competently enough to retake the city."

"The facts speak for themselves," she said as they drew ever closer to the fort. "Humans are still in control of the city, and the only dragons I see are dead ones."

Before Hex could mount an argument, a volley of arrows rose into the air from the fortress walls. Hex didn't react. Either he didn't see them, or wasn't afraid of them. But Jandra's mind quickly calculated the paths of the arrows and realized Hex was wrong about their reach.

"Watch out!" she shouted, leaning down, extending her arm. Hex veered sharply to the left, out of the path of most of the deadly missiles. Jandra was thrown from his back by the evasive action. She paid no attention to the distant ground. Instead she extended the nanite cloud that surrounded her to disassemble the arrows as they drew close. In seconds, she'd transformed the deadly wall of arrows to a cloud of dust.

Hex's hind-talons clamped around her waist as he wheeled back to catch her.

"I see the tents of the dragon army in the distance," Hex said, racing away from Dragon Forge. "Let's take the long way around to reach them."

"Yes," said Jandra. "Let's."

PRUDENTLY, JANDRA TURNED herself and Hex invisible as they descended into Shandrazel's camp. The camp had been transformed into a mobile hospital. Jandra had never seen so many wounded dragons. While Dragon Forge had been a flurry of activity, with men laboring to clear corpses from the streets and repair the broken eastern gate, Shandrazel's camp was subdued and silent.

Hex landed and Jandra remained seated on his back. She was uneasy. There was no reason to think that Shandrazel would be angry with her over the human rebellion, but she was worried what other dragons might think. She'd always felt like an outsider growing up in the palace. Here among all this suffering caused by men, she felt that sense of isolation grow.

Hex pushed aside the flap of Shandrazel's tent. The tent was palatial, an acre or more of canvas propped up by thick poles cut from the tallest pines. Though it was still early afternoon, the space was lit by hundreds of lanterns. Shandrazel was alone in the tent, sitting near the center, perched atop a mound of golden cushions. His cheeks were wet with tears. His bloodshot eyes looked haunted as he looked up.

"Who's there?" he asked hoarsely. "I gave orders that I wasn't to be disturbed."

"Remove the invisibility," Hex said.

Jandra released the dust around them. She hopped from Hex's back onto the long, broad crimson rugs that covered the ground. The muffled crunch of dry leaves came from beneath the rugs as she walked.

Shandrazel looked up, staring at them as if he wasn't positive they were real.

"Hexilizan?" he whispered.

"Brother," Hex said. "What has transpired?"

"We lost," said Shandrazel. "Charkon was so impatient. I wanted to wait for more forces. He convinced me that we had enough troops, and that the longer we waited, the better prepared the rebels would be."

"How many troops did you have?" Hex asked.

"Ten thousand earth-dragons, two hundred sun-dragons. Nearly half that number is dead or wounded. Thousands more lie incapacitated in their tents, the victims of some unknown digestive illness that swept the camp."

"I can't believe things went so badly," said Hex. "How many did we face?"

"Our spies said there were only a few thousand rebels. But they possessed a new bow that reached higher than any weapon we've ever seen. There are also reports of some monstrous armored giant. The earth-dragons claim he's fifty feet tall, and has eyes of fire. I sent my troops into slaughter, Hex."

Shandrazel sounded on the verge of tears.

Jandra stepped up. "What happened to the peace talks? Where's Pet? Maybe he can talk to the rebels and—"

"Pet proved disloyal," Shandrazel said, cutting her off. "There's evidence he conspired with Blasphet. He's now a fugitive."

"You can't be serious," she said. "Pet? Working with Blasphet? On what? His nails? Nobody knows Pet better than I do. It's absurd to think he'd help the Murder God. What really happened?"

"It isn't important at the moment," said Shandrazel.

"It's important to me," said Jandra.

"We have a much more pressing crisis," said Shandrazel. "The humans still hold Dragon Forge. Many of the surviving sun-dragons have deserted. If we don't retake the town, it won't be a human rebellion I face, but a rebellion of my own race."

"It was your goal to be the king who brought an end to kings," said Hex. "It looks as if you'll see your dreams come true."

"Do not taunt me, brother," Shandrazel growled. "I wanted to launch a new world order! I didn't intend to unleash anarchy throughout the Commonwealth!"

"Anarchy need not be a bad thing," Hex said. "Indeed, it may—"

"Silence," Shandrazel said, raising up onto his hind-talons and spreading his wings wide to make himself look more intimidating. "I have no stomach for your juvenile philosophies."

"Fine," Hex said, coolly. "Then do you have the stomach for brutality? Because that's the only choice remaining to you. The humans repelled a direct assault with bows and a mechanical giant. But they still occupy only one small patch of earth, while you have the resources of the world to draw upon. You can starve the humans if you want a victory."

"That could take months," said Shandrazel.

"If it's a quick victory you desire, you now know the range of the new bows. I wager it's less than the range of your catapults. Shower the town with balls of flaming pitch."

"That would burn Dragon Forge to cinders!"

"You would destroy the town," agreed Hex, "but you would kill the rebels and command the ground Dragon Forge stands upon. You would look very kingly as you magnificently spend our father's treasure to rebuild the forge."

Shandrazel stroked the underside of his jaws with his fore-talon as he contemplated Hex's advice.

Jandra felt it was time to intervene. "Excuse me," she said. "But before you destroy the town and kill everyone in it, have you thought about talking with these people? They're rebelling because of the actions of Albekizan. Maybe they just don't know that you want to give them a better deal."

"It's too late for negotiation," said Shandrazel. "I didn't choose to start this war. Men spilt the first blood."

"They probably think Albekizan spilt the first blood at the Free City," said Jandra. "Let me go inside as your ambassador. I'll talk to the leader. Find out his demands."

Shandrazel took his head. "My spies say the leader is a survivor of the Free City named Ragnar. He's a religious fanatic who would rather die than make peace with dragons. His only demand, from what I'm told, is that all dragons be slain. You can see why I've no interest in accommodating him."

"If what you say is true and I can't convince this Ragnar to make peace, then you won't have to kill thousands to stop this rebellion," she said. "It sounds as if one person might be enough."

"Yes," Shandrazel said, perking up. "Yes, if you killed Ragnar, the others would break. It's only his charisma that holds their army together. If you kill him, victory is assured."

"I didn't volunteer to be your assassin," said Jandra. "I'm going in to talk. After I speak to him, I'll give thought to the appropriate actions."

"Do it," said Shandrazel. "I give you full authority to undertake this mission."

"Shall I fly you there?" Hex asked.

"No," said Jandra, fading into invisibility. "I'm in the mood for a little walk."

CHAPTER THIRTY-ONE

REVELATIONS

THE SNOW CRUNCHED beneath Jandra's boots as she hiked toward the fortress. The day was at its end. Long shadows painted the ground, and the dark clouds beyond Dragon Forge were tinted red. Here among the gleaner mounds, the winter evening was silent and peaceful. As she'd walked toward the fortress, she'd built dozens of hopeful scenarios in her mind, plausible, logical ways that this siege could end without further blood being spilled.

As she walked past the gleaner mound, she spotted the corpse of an earth-dragon. His body was riddled with arrows. His eyes were frozen open in death. From the scrapes in the mud behind him, she surmised he had crawled hundreds of yards in an attempt to escape the assault on Dragon Forge and return to Shandrazel's camp before finally succumbing to his wounds.

Her optimism that further violence could be avoided was suddenly rattled. Earth-dragons wouldn't soon forget this infamous day. Could she blame them? They'd want revenge. Would evicting the rebels from Dragon Forge be enough to calm them? Earth-dragons were such alien, stoic beings, it was hard to say. Perhaps there was still hope of peace, despite the atrocities committed by the humans.

She walked past the dead earth-dragon and found herself in the presence of another corpse only a dozen yards away. Her stomach tightened as she recognized that this twisted thing before her had once been a sun-dragon, like Hex or Shandrazel. The great beast had hit the ground so hard its body was half buried in the red clay. Only a single crimson wing, largely intact and jutting into the air like a sail, instantly identified the hill of flesh before her as a member of the royal race.

She knew, in her gut, that all hope of a peaceful solution was gone. Albekizan had launched genocide over the death of his son, Bodiel. Today, countless sons, brothers, and fathers had been slaughtered by rebel bows. The sun-dragons would now be a race of Albekizans. Human blood would be spilled throughout the kingdom if swift justice wasn't visited upon the rebels.

She bit her lower lip, knowing what she had to do. She'd undertaken this mission as a diplomat. Shandrazel wanted her to be his assassin. Could she bring an end to this madness by killing, or at least capturing, Ragnar?

"Oh, Ven," she sighed. "What would you do if you were asked to be an assassin?"

Of course, she knew his answer. Vendevorex had confessed to her that he'd served as Albekizan's assassin multiple times. Indeed, he'd killed her own family at Albekizan's orders, simply to demonstrate his power. Her life story proved that when asked to be an assassin, Vendevorex had answered, *As you wish, sire.*

It was strange to think of Vendevorex as a killer. He'd always been so kind to her. Indeed, she'd never seen Vendevorex show cruelty toward anyone. Though perhaps the most powerful dragon in the kingdom, he hadn't abused his abilities. He never acted in anger, nor had she ever known him to hold a grudge. When Vendevorex had decided to use his powers to kill, he made the decision based on logic, and only acted when he felt that resorting to violence would serve some greater good.

She could almost hear his counsel now. "Killing one man might spare the lives of tens of thousands if a wider war breaks out."

By the time she reached the eastern gate, she'd convinced herself. She was no longer here as a diplomat. Invisibly, she approached the bloodied wood of the eastern gate. The giant wooden structure looked as if it had been knocked flat, then hastily rebuilt. The ground had been trampled into a gory muck that sucked at her boots. The stench of vomit hung heavy in the air, making her eyes water.

Standing ankle-deep in the dark mire, the air full of death, she remembered how she'd stood on the oily beach, cradling the dying seagull. Killing for the greater good wouldn't be murder. Only, they weren't her hands that held the seagull, were they? *And it hadn't been her decision.* Those memories belonged to Jazz. She shook her head to try to push back the alien thoughts.

She touched the wood of the gate, impregnating it with her nanites. She allowed a few seconds for the tiny machines to slip between the molecules, then willed a hole to appear. A rough rectangle five feet high and two feet wide crumbled to sawdust. She ducked to step inside the gate and glanced back at the mound of pulverized wood, like a puzzle formed of a million impossibly tiny pieces. She could see in her mind's eye how all these pieces had fit together only seconds before. With a nod, the sawdust rose and swirled as her nanites lifted it on magnetic pulses. In seconds, the hole began to close. A moment later, the door was restored, as if she had never touched it.

Shandrazel's camp had been silent as a morgue. Even with the sun down, Dragon Forge was noisy. Men shouted back and forth, hammers struck metal, and dozens of carts rolled toward a central furnace, all loaded with the bodies of earth-dragons. The stink inside was even worse than outside, as the aroma of two thousand unbathed men mixed with the other odors.

She wasn't certain how best to locate Ragnar. She'd met him briefly in the Free City—he'd been the naked, wild-eyed prophet Pet credited with saving his life. She'd instantly disliked him. He manifested every unpleasant trait the dragons attributed to humans. He'd been dirty, irrational, and brutish. How had such a man bested an army of dragons?

Then she heard a familiar voice from above. She looked up. The wall here was thirty feet high. She couldn't see who was talking, but was certain she knew the speaker.

"Pet!" she shouted out, losing all caution. Could he really be part of this rebellion?

Some of the men in the street glanced in the direction of her voice. Seeing nothing due to her aura of invisibility, they turned away.

A soldier in a tattered cloak leaned over the wall, staring down where she stood. This man's face was misshapen, his nose bent and broken, his scabby brow knotty and bruised. His chin and cheeks were covered in a scraggly beard. Her heart sank. It wasn't Pet.

The stranger asked, "Jandra?" He pushed the hood of his cloak back, revealing a head full of golden hair, greasy and matted. His face was smudged by mud and blood and soot. Yet, as torchlight caught his eyes, she saw they were the same blue as a sky-dragon's scales. She only knew one man with such breathtaking eyes.

"Pet?" she asked.

"It's me," he answered. He dropped his voice to a whisper. "What are you doing here?"

"That's what I was going to ask you!"

"I'm fighting to free mankind from dragons," he said. He disappeared back over the wall. She heard him say, "Take over up here, Vance." An instant later, Pet reappeared at a nearby ladder. He slid down the ladder rails in a fluid move that reminded Jandra of the first time she'd met him, when he'd performed as an acrobat.

"When did you get all militant?" Jandra asked. Pet approached with such confidence she wondered if he could see her.

"Since Shandrazel started torturing helpless women," he said, now speaking to the empty air a few feet to her left. "Since he outlawed all weapons for humans, then threw me in the dungeon as a traitor for standing up to him."

"Torturing women?"

"Yes. The Sister of the Serpent we captured."

"What was the point?" she asked, confused. "She had no tongue. What could she have told him?"

"I don't think there was a point," said Pet. He turned his body a bit more, and was now speaking directly toward her unseen face, barely five feet away. "I think he's in over his head and doesn't know what he's doing. He's drawing on the lessons his father taught him: the real power of a king lies in the force and fear he commands."

Jandra shivered at these words, remembering how Shandrazel had been energized by the thought of her serving as an assassin. Was she now part of the fear he commanded? And if Shandrazel had fallen back on the lessons his father had taught him, was she any different? She was drawing on Vendevorex's moral choices to guide her this evening.

"You never answered my question," said Pet. "Why are you here?"

"I've come... on a mission of diplomacy. I need to talk to Ragnar."

"I can take you to him," said Pet. "But I don't think he's interested in diplomacy. Neither am I, to be honest."

"I need to at least try," she said.

"If diplomacy means surrendering Dragon Forge, forget it," said Pet. "We've paid for this fort with blood. We won't give it up."

"Not even if it means more blood shed?"

"We've made our stand," said Pet. "Every man here would give his life to keep this town in human hands."

"You might get that chance," she said. "Shandrazel's talking about burning this city to the ground. And, from what I'm told, it sounds as if Shandrazel's army might have lost their first attack due to bad luck. He says some sort of illness swept his army just after the attack began. Can you count on a mysterious illness a second time?"

Pet crossed his arms, looking stone-faced. He answered, in a cold tone. "We don't rely on luck.

Ragnar says the Lord is on our side. So far, he's been right."

"You used to be so scornful of prophets," she said. "How can you be part of this?"

"I'm not the man I used to be," Pet said.

"Look, this is getting us nowhere. Just take me to Ragnar. I should at least hear what he has to say. Maybe he can make a believer out of me."

"Maybe," said Pet. Then he paused again. He was now close enough that she could smell him. His scent didn't trigger the same erotic response it had the last time she'd been near him. Her senses were now more under control, for one thing, and he smelled especially ripe, for another.

Despite this, a small chill raced through her as she met his gaze. Before, when she'd looked into his eyes, though they had been beautiful as gemstones, they'd been empty; vacant windows into a vacant soul. The only emotion she'd ever seen inside him was lust. Now, his eyes were lit with something else—a hardness, a seriousness that told her Pet no longer desired her. He'd surrendered his life to a larger cause.

"Shandrazel hasn't sent you here to do something dumb, has he? You're not here to kill Ragnar, are you?"

Jandra froze. Pet couldn't see her face though he was less than an arm's length away. Was there something in her tone that tipped him off? Or had war simply left him with a greater degree of caution than he'd once possessed?

"I told you I'm here to talk," she said.

"Good. Because you'd be dead in a heartbeat if you tried anything."

Jandra was incredulous. Pet couldn't possibly be threatening her, could he? "Why?" she asked, scornfully. "His God would strike me down?"

"No." Pet's open hand darted out. He clumsily struck her shoulder, rapidly ran his fingers down her arm to grab her bicep, and growled, "I would."

"Unhand me," she hissed. His grip was solid; his rough and jagged nails were piercing the sheer fabric that covered her arms. "Or I'll unhand you. You've seen what my powers can do to human flesh."

He relaxed his grip, but still held her. They stood, unmoving, for several long moments. Pet stared at where he knew her eyes must be. She turned her gaze away. At last, he released her.

"As long as we have an understanding," he said. "You can follow me."

JANDRA DROPPED HER invisibility as Pet led her into the house at the end of the street. She hoped Pet would take it as a sign of goodwill. Plus, it could prove useful not to have anyone else in the room know she could turn invisible.

The wooden house was modest and plain. The place felt claustrophobic compared to the abodes of sun-dragons or sky-dragons. They entered a kitchen dominated by a large table built of roughly finished pine, with stripes of black grime caked into its oily surface. A bushel basket of onions sat on the table and, from the smell, a fair number of the onions were rotting. Pet opened the kitchen door into a room with a fireplace. The heat washed over her in a wave.

Ragnar sat on a wooden chair by the fire. There was a woman sitting on his lap, her clothes in a state of disarray. The woman looked toward the door; her eyes were hard and indignant at the intrusion. A serpentine tattoo was faintly visible under the short dark hair that covered her scalp. A Sister of the Serpent? Jandra tensed. Shandrazel had said Pet was working with Blasphet.

Ragnar sneered as he caught sight of Jandra, his eyes wandering in disdain over her fine clothes and careful grooming. They had never been formally introduced. The last time he had seen her, in the Free City, she'd been disguised as a peasant.

"Who's this?" Ragnar demanded of Pet. "Why do you disturb my counsel with Shanna?"

"Sorry," said Pet. "This seems important. Apparently Shandrazel wants to talk."

"I'm Jandra Dragonsdaughter," Jandra said, with a respectful bow. "I'm here to speak for Shandrazel."

Ragnar's face slackened. He stared at Jandra as if she were a ghost. It wasn't the reaction Jandra expected. After an awkward moment of silence, she decided to proceed. "Shandrazel intends to take back Dragon Forge. Your most valuable weapon in the recent battle, your improved bows, will no longer have the element of surprise. The illness that swept his forces was a chance occurrence. You faced an army unfit to fight. When the dragons attempt to take this city again, you'll face certain death."

Ragnar didn't say anything in response to her words. He continued to stare, his expression unfathomable.

Mildly rattled by the possibility that Ragnar was, in fact, a madman, Jandra tried once more to appeal to reason. "There's still a chance that bloodshed can be avoided. I was at the Free City. I'm sympathetic to the cause of human liberty. Shandrazel, too, is a proponent of greater human freedom. Tell me your demands for the surrender of this city, and I'll carry them back to Shandrazel."

Ragnar's face took on a gray pallor as he looked down at the floor. He said, quietly, "I almost killed you as an infant, you know."

Jandra cocked her head, perplexed. Was this just insane babble?

"What?"

"When you were a baby. A sky-dragon killed all my family save one, my infant sister. Later, he attempted to return her to me. But I knew she'd already been corrupted. I tried to kill you. To this day, I'm not certain what saved you. One moment I held a rock, preparing to smash your skull. Then I was struck unconscious by an unseen enemy. When I woke, you were gone. I was never certain of your fate."

Jandra's forehead wrinkled in confusion as she stared at the nude man. His body was crisscrossed by a hundred scrapes and cuts, his hair hung around his face in tangles. There were clumps of horrible things in his beard that she didn't want identified. This was the leader of the rebels? He was so obviously insane, she couldn't believe anyone had ever listened to him.

"Wait a minute," Pet said. "Are you saying Jandra is your sister?"

"Once," said Ragnar. "Before the dragons stole her and infected her spirit. I've heard rumors over the years of a girl named Jandra being raised in the palace. She had the same name as my sister—I had blurted out her name to the dragon who'd stolen her. The powers attributed to the king's wizard, Vendevorex, were the same as those the sky-dragon displayed that night—command of fire and ice, and the power of invisibility. These are powers of the devil."

Jandra felt the hair rising on the back of her neck, at least where it wasn't clamped down by her genie.

"My powers have nothing to do with the devil," she said defensively.

"Perhaps you believe this," Ragnar sighed. "I regret that I couldn't spare you such corruption, sister. The fact that you come here as a representative of dragons rather than standing for your own race is proof that you're beyond redemption."

Jandra felt like the room was spinning. Vendevorex had never told her of a brother—but, he'd never told her anything about her origins until she'd discovered it by chance. And the goddess had said an older brother had survived.

"She does kind of look like you," Shanna said, looking back and forth between the two. "Same color eyes. The lips are similar. The hair color's pretty close."

Jandra shuddered. She didn't look anything like Ragnar. Yes, they had a few superficial similarities. But it was impossible that she could be related to this brutish lunatic.

"If this is some kind of trick," she said, "it's not a very good one. Pet, what did you tell him about me?"

"I never mentioned you," said Pet.

"Can you prove this?" Jandra asked Ragnar. "Do you have any evidence that I'm your sister?"

"None," said Ragnar. "I lost everything that night. When I returned to the site of the fire, everything was burned, even the stones of the walls."

Jandra nodded. Vengeance of the Ancestors burned stone. How could he know this if he wasn't telling the truth?

"That night I made a vow to the Lord," said Ragnar. "I would never again cut my hair or wear clothes as long as dragons had the freedom to kill humans without consequence. I gave myself over as an instrument of God, allowing Him to guide me to this great day. Go and tell your master there will be no surrender. Tell them we will slaughter any dragon who comes near this place."

Jandra knew what Shandrazel would want if she went back with these terms. He would want Ragnar dead.

But what if Ragnar really was her brother?

She needed to get back outside, into the cool air. She needed time to think.

"I'll tell him," she said. "I should go."

"Wait," said Pet, grabbing her by the arm. "I want to come with you. I need to talk to Shandrazel."

"What?" she said. "Why? Shandrazel thinks you're a traitor. He'll kill you on sight."

"We both know you could protect me," he said.

"What can you possibly hope to accomplish?"

"I spent weeks listening to Shandrazel talk about his dreams for peace. I know what he wants more than anyone in this room. Make no mistake: I'm willing to die to keep Dragon Forge in the hands of humans. I'm not going there to compromise. But I think I know what I can say to him that will change his mind about retaking the city. If he believes half the words he's said, he'll listen to me."

"You cannot speak to that serpent," said Ragnar. "I forbid it!"

"I take my orders from Burke," said Pet. "He's the one who made me commander of the sky-wall team. If you have a problem, go talk to him."

"Talk to me about what?" a faint voice asked as a chill breeze swept through the room. Jandra looked into the kitchen. In the doorway, there was a man sitting in a strange contraption that was half-chair, half-wagon. His right leg jutted straight out before him, immobilized by steel rods. His eyes were red, as if he'd been crying, and he was squinting, as if he couldn't see well. His wheeled chair was being pushed by a woman only a little older than Jandra. She was tall, dressed in dark buckskin. She stared at Jandra with an unnerving directness, like a cat watching a bird.

"Burke," Pet said. "This is Jandra. She's a representative of Shandrazel. The dragons want to talk."

"I bet they do," Burke said through clenched teeth. He was obviously in horrible pain.

"I know Shandrazel personally," Pet said. "I want to talk to him. I don't think there's anyone in this fort better qualified to give him our demands."

"We have no demands!" Ragnar shouted, waving his fist at Pet. "We have victory! We have Dragon Forge! Let him send his armies against us! We shall crush them! As the days pass, the forge will provide our armies with better weapons, better armor, and machines of war the likes of which no dragon has ever seen! The end days of Revelations are upon us. When next we march from this fortress, it will be to drive the dragons into the sea!"

Burke closed his eyes and rubbed the bridge of his nose as Ragnar ranted. He seemed to be thinking over Pet's proposal rather than listening to the prophet.

"Ragnar's right," Burke said, at last. He sounded quite rational. "We have no demands. The dragons are only willing to talk because they're scared."

Jandra found herself worried that she'd given these people false hope. Shandrazel wasn't truly interested in talking, either. But, perhaps if Pet could talk to him? Maybe Pet really did know Shandrazel well enough to persuade him to return to a path of peace.

Jandra walked over to Burke. The woman behind Burke lowered her hands to the hilt of her sword.

"Sir, you sound like a rational man. You look like you're in pain. I can heal your leg with my magic if you let Pet go talk to Shandrazel. I can use my powers on all the wounded here in Dragon Forge if that will help avoid further bloodshed."

"Magic?" Burke answered with a sneer. "Girl, I'm the last person you should talk to about magic. I know who you are. You're that girl Vendevorex raised. He was either a pawn of the Atlanteans, or a pawn of the goddess. In either case, if you've been raised by him, you're no friend of mankind."

"I'm nobody's pawn," said Jandra. "If you know about the goddess, you may be interested in learning that she's dead. Bitterwood killed her with one of her own weapons."

Burke raised an eyebrow. "Do tell. Bitterwood? He's still alive?"

"Yes."

"Huh," Burke said. He shifted in his chair as he contemplated this news. He winced at this minor movement. "You know, girl, if you'd told me anyone else had killed the goddess, I'd tell you you'd been tricked. My ancestors fought that high-tech witch many times, and thought she was dead more than once. But if I've ever met anyone up to the task of killing her, it was Bant."

"So, I'm not a pawn," said Jandra.

"Not *her* pawn," said Burke. "But, if you possess Atlantean technology and aren't staying in this fort to fight for the freedom of mankind, then you're a pawn of the dragons. From what I know of Vendevorex, he had access to machines I can only dream about. If you possess a tenth of his knowledge, you have the power to change the world. Technology was mankind's greatest competitive advantage in the Darwinian struggle for survival. If the goddess hadn't crippled mankind, the dragons never could have risen to where they are today. If we still had gunpowder, the last dragon would have vanished ages ago. If you possess advanced technology, why aren't you sharing it? Why do you allow your fellow men to grub around in the dirt to survive, rather than helping us rise once more to our rightful role as masters of this world?"

Jandra frowned. Burke was trying to make her feel guilty, but his use of the phrase *masters of this world* made her wonder if Jazz had been right. Maybe mankind couldn't be trusted with the power she commanded.

"I don't need you to heal my leg, Jandra," Burke said, his bloodshot eyes burning into her. "If you want to use your 'magic,' heal the world. Lift mankind back to the top of the food chain."

Jandra sighed. This was more than she could think about at the moment, and didn't seem to address the immediate crisis at hand. "There's no reason dragons and men can't share this world. We're intelligent beings. We can talk this out. Let Pet come back with me."

Pet nodded in agreement. "Let me take my best shot."

Burke sat quietly, looking past Pet and Jandra toward the fireplace in the next room. He looked tired.

"Go," he said at last. "I guess it can't hurt to hear what the big lizard has to say."

As THEY LEFT the house, Pet lingered until Jandra had stepped into the street. Then he turned and fixed his eyes on Shanna. He'd worked many years on the ability to communicate his innermost desires to women with a single glance. Unspoken words passed between them. He held his hand open, as if to catch something.

Shanna understood. She moved to the table where she'd placed her belt. She loosened the sheath that held her poisoned dagger. She tossed the sheathed weapon toward Pet, who snatched it from the air, then spun smoothly on his heel to follow Jandra. He stuffed the dagger into the back of his pants, beneath his filthy cloak. Jandra wouldn't be the only one this night in command of an unseen power.

CHAPTER THIRTY-TWO

THAT STRANGE LAND TO WHICH WE MUST JOURNEY

JANDRA AND PET walked through the snow-covered night in uncomfortable silence. She found it difficult to look at him; his once fine face was now ruined. She knew she could heal him; he must also know this. But he hadn't asked her to restore his looks. Somehow, in this most serious of times, it struck her as an insufferably trivial subject to bring up.

A driving wind cut down from the north. Pale patches of moonlight dappled the ground as the sky churned. Countless gaps in the breaking clouds opened and just as quickly closed.

In the end, it was Pet who spoke first. "I don't think you look all that much like Ragnar."

He said the words in an almost comforting tone, as if he sensed that the matter was weighing heavy upon her.

"I don't either, but it's not impossible that he's my brother," she said. "I guess I could use my powers to learn the truth. Compare our cells and find out how closely they match. But what if it's true? What then?"

"What do you mean?"

"I mean, I used to dream of having a human family. I saw the way that Ruth and Eve were so close. I envied the intimate bond they had as sisters. The way they knew that they were bound by blood to the best friend they would ever have. So what if Ragnar is my brother? I can't possibly feel that same connection. It's pretty obvious he loathes me. If I want the companionship of an irrational, dragon-hating fanatic, I can go hang out with Bitterwood."

Pet laughed. "Killing Albekizan didn't mellow him?"

"Did you know he eats the tongues of dragons?" Jandra asked. "I mean, he was preaching to me about how I shouldn't trust sun-dragons because they eat people, and then he cuts out Blasphet's tongue and eats it for dinner!"

"Wait, Blasphet? He killed Blasphet?"

"Oh, right. There's a lot to fill you in on. And, just looking at your face, I'm guessing you have a lot to tell me."

Pet cut her a glance that wasn't exactly angry, but it let her know she'd crossed a line. He said, "If Ragnar is your brother, at least you can find out your family history. You don't even know your family name. You might still have cousins out there, aunts and uncles and grandparents. You never know."

"How about you, Pet?" Jandra asked. "You've never mentioned your family."

He shrugged. "I'm a thoroughbred. I know my lineage. I know who sired me, and the mother I came out of. I know I have five half-brothers, six half-sisters, and two full-blood sisters. But dragon favorites don't really have family lives. I went to live with Chakthalla when I was five. She thought young humans were cute, in the same way you might think a puppy is cute."

"Oh," said Jandra. She'd known this, of course. Many dragons over the years had assumed she was Vendevorex's pet. She'd never really understood before how Pet and she shared such a common experience of being raised by dragons rather than humans.

"I'm not the most introspective person in the world," Pet said. "But looking back, when I think about all the women I seduced, I feel really bad. I used my finely bred looks and Chakthalla's wealth to earn the affection of tavern wenches."

"From the way you bragged about it, I thought you saw that as sort of a privilege."

"That was an element of it," said Pet. "On a deeper level, I was seducing women because it made me feel human. I craved human companionship. Chakthalla would never have allowed me true love, or life-long mating. As long as I was still her faithful pet and could breed with other pets, she didn't care about my trysts. All my little conquests were a substitute for a love I could never experience."

Jandra felt an unexpected sympathy well up within her at these words.

"Perhaps you should try introspection more often," she said. "It suits you."

"Until now, when I've looked inside myself, I've found nothing there," he said. "I was so empty, Jandra. But, fighting at Dragon Forge, I feel as if something has filled me. The human bond I could never find sleeping with the village women—I feel it, at last, with my fellow men. I would gladly give my life to save anyone in that fortress."

"Even Ragnar?"

"Especially Ragnar," said Pet. "He's the will that drives our army. And Burke… Burke is the brains."

"And what are you?"

"I'm just a soldier," said Pet. "And it suits me."

"Well, now you're an ambassador," she said. "Let's hope you're up to that role as well."

Pet said nothing as the clouds above continued to roil.

INVISIBLY, JANDRA LED Pet toward Shandrazel's tent. There were angry shouts coming from inside. Was that Hex's voice?

Jandra pushed aside the tent flap. The interior of the vast room was cold, but still a welcome sanctuary from the winter wind. As she dropped her invisibility, the two sun-dragons at the center of the room looked toward her. Shandrazel looked unhappy.

"Have I interrupted something?" she asked.

"Nothing important," said Hex.

"It's nothing important only because my brother believes that *nothing* is important," said Shandrazel. "He advocates letting the world spin into chaos. He's willing to enumerate the faults of the world, but unwilling to do a thing to fix them."

Hex calmly said, "I've long maintained that anyone who thinks they have the right to fix the world is doomed to failure by their own arrogance."

Shandrazel dismissively waved his fore-talon, as if trying to clear the air of such a preposterous utterance. "This discussion has ended. I see you've brought back a fellow human, Jandra. Do you plan to introduce our unexpected guest?"

Pet pulled back the hood of his cloak, revealing his face.

Shandrazel's eyes widened.

"I need no introduction, sire," Pet said.

"How... how did you get here?" Shandrazel asked. "Are you fighting for the rebels?"

"I am," said Pet.

"I knew you weren't at the talks seeking genuine peace," Shandrazel said. "All along, you were—"

"No," Pet interrupted. "No, when I was at the talks, no man in that room had more faith in your promises than I did. I believed your fine words, Shandrazel. I believed your philosophical arguments, and I trusted that you had nothing but the best interests of mankind at heart."

"I still do!" Shandrazel said. "I will still be the king who brings an end to kings. I will be the dragon who brings an end to human slavery and inequality."

"You say that while commanding an army where the menial labor is performed by slaves."

"I would have no need of an army if you humans hadn't launched a war!" Shandrazel snapped, spittle spraying from his jaws. "The nearby river runs red with the blood of dragons you've slaughtered. How can there be peace in the aftermath of such an atrocity? There can be no peace until there is justice. You humans have left me with no choice but to crush your rebellion, and return Dragon Forge to the earth-dragons."

In contrast to Shandrazel's temper, Pet sounded very calm. "If the earth-dragons need a new city to build a new foundry, let them have the Free City. It was designed by dragons. It should house dragons."

"Don't be absurd," Shandrazel said, his voice trembling. "Dragon Forge is the historic home of the earth-dragons. They won't—"

"I'm told that Dragon Forge was built by men long ago," said Pet. "If it's history that drives your decisions, then you will support mankind's claim to the town."

Shandrazel narrowed his eyes. "You've stolen the city by violence."

"Yes," said Pet. "And dragons rule this world by force. We can argue endlessly about which act of violence spawned which act of revenge. Back in the palace, however, you said something profound. You told me that history had ended. You declared the dawn of a new age. Do you still believe those words?"

"What are you talking about?"

"If you must declare an end to history, a stopping point for old grudges, let it be today. Take your armies home and allow Dragon Forge to remain in human hands. Show us that history has ended, and that you're willing to open a new age of peace. Show us that your fine words actually mean something."

Jandra held her breath as she watched Shandrazel's eyes. She couldn't begin to fathom the thoughts racing through them. Hex, meanwhile, was standing nearby with his wings folded to his side, with a look of something approaching amusement.

Shandrazel let out his breath slowly. He said, "Pet, you're a fugitive. With a single shout, I can summon my guards and have you bound in chains once more."

"This is a fine threat to direct at a man who's come to talk," said Hex. "I can tell you learned diplomacy from our father."

"No," said Shandrazel. "Father would have already killed this man. Pet, you may freely leave here. Tell your fellow men in the city that there will be no further negotiations. Your position is unacceptable. Dragon Forge must be liberated. Humans took the fort in a single night. I will give you a single night to flee. Come the dawn, we shall retake Dragon Forge and slay everyone we find within its walls. Reinforcements have arrived through the day. You humans no longer enjoy the element of surprise. You shall fall."

"You'll let us abandon the fort?" Pet asked. "You wouldn't hunt us down?"

"No," said Shandrazel. "Anyone who flees and leaves behind their weapons will be spared."

"But if we take weapons?"

"There's no corner of my kingdom where you can hide."

"So, it's a kingdom again? Not a Commonwealth?"

"I misspoke," said Shandrazel. "Our old patterns of thought die hard, I fear."

Pet scratched his beard, as if he was thinking over Shandrazel's offer.

He looked toward Jandra. His shoulders sagged. His eyes looked mournful as he said, "I'm sorry."

"For what?"

Pet answered her by swinging his fist toward her. Her enhanced eyes tracked his hand as it approached her face. The knuckles were cracked, and caked with red clay. She recalled the first time he'd stroked her cheek with his soft and gentle fingers, back when they'd first met, at Chakthalla's castle.

Then stars exploded throughout the room as the force of the blow knocked her from her feet.

She landed on the carpet, blood filling her mouth, unable to form a coherent thought. Her vision seemed softened by a veil as her head flopped toward a flurry of motion. A giant red blur lanced toward the brown-gray blob that was Pet. The red blur snapped its jaws around the human shape. Pet cried out in unintelligible agony.

Her vision cleared slightly as she tried to rise, but couldn't. Pet had a black blade in his hand, and was lifting it again and again and driving it deep into Shandrazel's snout. Shandrazel whipped his head and Pet went flying through the air, crashing into one of the tent poles with a back-snapping crunch. The light flickered as the lanterns that hung from the tent poles danced wildly.

A large red shape loomed over her, blotting out everything else in the room. Hex. She felt a sense of relief as the warrior-philosopher slipped his fore-talon under her back and lifted her. He rolled her over and pinned her hips to the ground beneath the tremendous weight of his hind-talons.

"What?" she mumbled through bloodied lips, not understanding what was happening.

She felt as if daggers were being driven into her neck as Hex dug his claws beneath the genie that clung there. With a jerk, he snatched the device away with a violence that tore away chunks of her hair and ripped her gown from neck to hip. The pain was unreal. The metal pulled from contact with her spine felt like her soul being ripped from her body.

Then, the weight of Hex's hind-talons lifted.

She rolled over, still groggy, still confused by what was happening. Had Pet actually punched her? She sat up, feeling her teeth loose on the left side of her jaw. It certainly seemed as if it had really happened.

She coughed as a stream of blood trickled down her throat. She wiped pink spittle from her chin.

She stared up from the red smear to see Shandrazel collapsed on the scarlet carpets, staring at her with cloudy, pain-filled eyes. Blood poured from stab wounds in his snout. A black dagger still jutted from just behind his nostrils. She crawled toward him and pulled the dagger free. Shandrazel shuddered with pain. The blade still dripped with venom.

She placed her fingers on his snout, intending to heal him. Only... She suddenly felt deaf, blind, and numb. She could see him clearly; she could hear his dying gasps, she could feel his hot blood trickling across her fingers. Still, something was wrong.

She felt the chill air touching her naked spine. She reached to touch the back of her neck and found nothing there but a sore patch from where her hair was missing.

She turned, and saw Hex standing behind her with the genie in his claws. She'd never seen it in this configuration. It looked like a long, thin, silver ribbon with a three-fingered claw at the top that had cradled the back of her skull.

"Hex, what?" she asked.

"If you had this, you would heal him," he said.

"Yes!" she said, standing up. "*Yes!* Why do you want him to die? He's your brother!"

"I'm not helping him die," said Hex. "I'm helping him reach his destiny. He wished to be the king who brought an end to kings. When he takes his last breath, the age of kings draws to an end."

"But—"

"Listen," said Hex. "His armies will disperse. The sun-dragons will return to their abodes and resume squabbling over local matters. The earth-dragons will be free to pursue their own destinies, no longer mere pawns in the game of kings. It's for the greater good that my brother must die."

"Who gave you the right to decide the greater good?" Jandra shouted. "This isn't like you, Hex."

"Have you failed to take seriously a single word I've said?" Hex asked. "I was willing to slay a goddess because I didn't trust any individual to possess that much power. My brother didn't have the power of a god, but he did possess the power of a king. It had already corrupted him. It's an act of mercy that he passes from this world now, before he ever understands what a brutish dictator he was becoming."

"Give me back the genie, Hex," said Jandra. "It won't do you any good. It's locked. No one can use it but me."

"I don't want to use it. I don't want anyone to use it. If I knew how to destroy it, I would."

"You've fought by my side. You know my heart. You know I haven't abused my power. Give me the genie."

"I know you have a mind that's been altered by the goddess. Perhaps you could resist the temptation of power. But what if she's changed you? What if you're becoming her?"

"Hex, I know my own mind."

"And I know mine," he said. He pulled the silver ring of invisibility she'd given him from his talon. He tossed it toward her. It landed next to her feet. "Take this. It will let you pass safely from this camp. You've confided in me your inner struggle, Jandra, torn between your role as a human and your role as the daughter of a dragon. Leave here and embrace your destiny as a human. It may not be such a bad thing."

Jandra held the poison dagger. Hex seemed so confident, so powerful.

She glanced at Pet. He was propped against the tent pole, eyes closed. She couldn't tell if he was alive or dead. She might face the same fate if she attacked. The poison wouldn't act quickly enough to kill Hex instantly. But what choice did she have? If she could get even a single finger on the genie, she could end this nonsense.

She lunged toward Hex, gritting her teeth, driving the dagger forward with both hands.

She never reached him. He kicked out with his hind-talon, catching her torso, the force of the blow knocking the dagger from her grasp. She was thrown across the room, landing against the tent wall, the world again an incomprehensible jumble of light and dark.

She rubbed her eyes to clear her vision. When she opened them, Hex was gone. Outside, she heard the beating of his mighty wings as he rose into the night.

She stood on trembling legs. Her ribs felt as if they might be broken. She staggered toward Shandrazel. He was no longer breathing.

She stumbled toward Pet, dropping to her knees before him. His eyes flickered open.

"Why?" she demanded, as tears streamed down her cheeks. "Why did you do this?"

"I lived... as a p-pet," he whispered. "I... w-wanted to d-die... as... as..."

His eyes fluttered shut.

Jandra brought her hands to her mouth, trying to silence the sobs that burst from deep within her.

GRAXEN SHIVERED AS he was pushed onto the balcony railing. His fore-talons were chained together to prevent flight. His hind-talons were hobbled by a short length of chain that reduced his movements to uncomfortable hops. He looked down onto the jagged shores of the Nest and the moonlit waters beyond. The balcony was full of valkyries, all armed with spears. They fixed their hard eyes upon him.

He'd been kept in an unlit cell since the night of Blasphet's invasion. He wasn't certain how many days had passed. He stoically met the judgmental gaze of the valkyries. He'd brought great tragedy to the Nest. He could expect only the harshest of fates.

The valkyries parted as a second prisoner was brought forth. His heart fluttered as he recognized this sky-dragon, though her head was hung low and her shoulders were bent beneath the weight of the chains that bound her.

"Nadala!" he cried out.

She glanced toward him, her eyes full of shame. Her handlers lifted her to the balcony and forced her to stand beside Graxen.

For several long minutes, Graxen and Nadala stood in silence, unable to look at each other.

Finally, the quiet was broken by the clicking of a cane on stone. Graxen looked up to see the familiar form of the matriarch. The withered sky-dragon hobbled forward, glaring at her discolored son.

"Eight hundred seventy-three," said the matriarch. "That is the number of valkyries dead due to your dishonorable lusts."

Nadala jerked, as if the number were a physical blow.

The matriarch sighed. "You came asking for freedom from the Thread Room. You wanted a different future for sky-dragons. Many of the tapestries were destroyed by fire or smoke. So, you'll get your wish. Those valkyries whose threadlines have been lost will be released from the breeding guidance of the Nest. Future matriarchs will monitor these unguided pairings; it will take many generations to determine if the choice I'm making is a wise one. It will be the duty of some future matriarch as to how to respond should our race find itself failing. It is, however, my duty to decide your fates."

Graxen lowered his head. He knew her decision before she spoke it. They would not be the first dragons to plunge to their deaths on the sharp steel spikes below.

"You're both to be banished," the matriarch said.

A murmur ran through the valkyries.

Graxen looked up, uncertain he believed the words.

"Traditionally, I would send you forth as tatter-wings," the matriarch continued. "But fate has already distorted your bodies with malformed scales. It's for the best that your wings remain intact. You must fly west, beyond the cursed mountains, that you may not contaminate our species further. You'll have two days' grace. After this, any dragon you encounter will be duty bound to kill you."

"But," Nadala said, her voice hoarse, as if she'd spent many days crying. "But you said in the Thread Room we would be put to death. We've caused so much harm. How can you spare us?"

The matriarch shook her head.

"Blasphet and his cult took so many of your sisters, Nadala," said the matriarch. "This island has seen enough death."

Graxen was confused. Was this a trick? The matriarch seemed incapable of mercy. Yet, there was no trick apparent as two valkyries approached and released them from the chains that bound them. The iron links rattled as the valkyries carried them away.

"Fly now," said the matriarch, turning. "Darken these shores with your shadows no longer."

As she said this, the valkyries who'd unchained them gave them harsh shoves. Graxen toppled toward the spikes below. His limbs were numb from confinement. He felt weak; he'd been given no food during his entire imprisonment. Yet, he instinctively spread his wings. The wind caught his feather-scales, and he pulled from his descent.

Nadala continued to fall. His heart raced as she drew ever closer to the spikes. Then, at last, she opened her wings and veered away from death by impalement, following him out across the lake.

Beyond the water's edge, Graxen landed in the bare branches of a tall tree. The perch swayed as Nadala joined him. She looked forlorn.

"She should have killed us," she whispered.

Graxen took her fore-talon into his own.

"Would our deaths have undone the tragedy?" he asked softly. "I'm surprised by her decision, but my mother is right. There's been enough death. We've been given the chance to live."

"We've been banished," said Nadala. "I'll never again see my sisters. I'll never again see my home. Nothing lies before us but the unknown."

"Not only the unknown," said Graxen. "We have each other."

Nadala met his eyes, looking lost.

"Graxen, why did we do such an insane thing? Why did we throw all caution to the wind? Is that love? Is it love that rips the world asunder? If so, I no longer know if I want any part of it. We're banished to journey beyond the mountains. It's for the best if we do not make this journey together."

Graxen shook his head. "I don't know. You may be right. I haven't made the clearest decisions since I met you."

"If love strips us of reason, maybe the old ways were correct," said Nadala. "Perhaps love can only lead to ruin. The first matriarchs were wise to remove it from the breeding process."

"Perhaps," said Graxen. "When I first visited the Nest, I was driven from its shores hungry and thirsty, without hint of hospitality. You followed me, gave me food. That's still a cherished memory; it gives me hope for the essential goodness of the world. Isn't that love as well?"

"That wasn't love, Graxen," she said. "That was only... only kindness."

"Then perhaps kindness will be enough to sustain us as we journey over the mountains," he said. "If you'll accept my kindness, I pledge to do all I can to help you survive in that strange land to which we must journey."

Nadala let her fore-talon drop from his grasp. She looked down to the forest floor. A chilly winter breeze stirred the fringes on her neck. She shivered, looking lost in thought. She glanced back in the direction of the Nest. Suddenly, her body stiffened.

Graxen followed her gaze and found a squad of valkyries coming toward them. Some were wearing armor and carrying spears. Graxen and Nadala were naked—perhaps they could outfly them. Unfortunately, they were also half-starved, with bodies and wills weakened by days chained in solitary cells. These valkyries were no doubt at the peak of health.

Except, as they drew nearer, it became obvious that the lead valkyrie was injured. Arifiel led the squad, unarmored, her shoulders covered in bandages. She flew slowly, in obvious pain, yet the other valkyries controlled their speed to stay behind her.

The valkyries reached them and Arifiel landed in the same tree that Graxen and Nadala rested in. The other valkyries found perches in neighboring trees. Graxen looked around, expecting to find icy, hostile stares. Yet, instead of scorn, these valkyries had a different emotion in their eyes. Graxen was hard-pressed to interpret it. He noted that Arifiel wasn't the only one among them who wore bandages. Several had bare, raw spots on their wings where feather-scales had been burned away.

"Nadala. Graxen," said Arifiel. "The matriarch doesn't know of my mission here. You've been sent into the world unarmed, without food, without even a blanket to shelter you from the cold at night. We've come to rectify this."

Arifiel nodded toward a nearby valkyrie who tossed her spear toward them. Nadala caught it. Seconds later, she caught a helmet thrown her way, and one of the valkyries began to unbuckle her armor.

"Graxen," said Arifiel. "You left a bag in my care. I've come to return it."

Again she nodded toward one of the valkyries, this one carrying his satchel. It bulged, stuffed to the point where its leather seams looked as if they might rip open. The valkyrie tossed the bag to Graxen. In his weakened state, he was nearly knocked from his perch when he caught it.

"There's food," said Arifiel. "Dried fish, dried fruit. A wool blanket and flint and steel to start a fire."

Nadala slipped on the helmet and caught the armor that was tossed to her by the valkyrie who'd stripped.

"Why are you doing this?" Nadala asked.

Arifiel looked around the band of warriors. "Every one of us fought against the sun-dragons; every one of us faced their flames. We will carry the scars for the rest of our lives."

"And we are the cause of those scars," said Nadala, her voice cracking. Tears rolled down her cheeks. "We betrayed you! I betrayed you! I'm the greatest shame of the valkyries!"

"Sister!" Arifiel snapped, sounding angry. "You didn't give us our scars. Blasphet and his minions caused this suffering. Not one among us views you as our shame. Indeed, we view you as our greatest hope."

Nadala sniffled. "What?"

"We all witnessed Graxen in combat. He was fearless and cunning; the shame of the valkyries would have been if his virtues were allowed to pass from our species. We have plain evidence that the system we were prepared to give our lives to defend was a flawed one."

"But—"

"We must leave you now," said Arifiel. "Buckle up your armor. Keep your spear sharp. I don't know what dangers await you in the lands beyond the mountains. But before I part, give me your vow: whatever foes you may face, never surrender. If you find yourself facing an army of sun-dragons, face them as a warrior born. Teach them what it means to challenge a valkyrie!"

Nadala swallowed hard. "I so vow," she said softly.

Arifiel gave some unseen signal to her fellows, and with a single movement they all leapt into the air. They spiraled upward, a flurry of dragons, then turned as one and soared toward the Nest.

Graxen stood quietly, watching the sky as Nadala buckled on her armor. Graxen slung the satchel over his shoulder, the limb swaying as the weight shifted. He dug his fore-talon in beneath the blanket and found the oily parchment wrapping the dried fish. There was something under the parchment that had an odd texture. He pulled the fish from his bag, then dug his claws back in as he realized what it was that he'd felt.

"I… When I went to the coast, I found this," he said, pulling the beaded belt from his satchel. He held it toward her. She took it and unrolled it, looking confused.

"It's a belt," he said. "It's probably not the best time to give it to you, I fear."

"It's lovely," she said.

"It reminded me of you," he said.

She fastened the belt around her waist. It fit as if it had been made for her. She sniffled again and said, "Now that we have supplies, it does make sense for us to journey together. It sounds as if there's only a single blanket to share."

"I could give you the bag," he said.

"Keep the bag. Just share your kindness."

Graxen nodded. He held out the dried fish toward her.

"I'm not hungry at the moment," she said. She raised her fore-talon to the gray teardrop scale on her cheek and wiped away the moisture that lingered there. "We have miles to journey before we reach our new world."

The branch shuddered as Nadala leapt.

"Try to keep up," she called back, rising into the pristine winter blue.

* * *

THE MATRIARCH CLOSED the door behind her. A soft talon reached out to touch her shoulder. She turned, and allowed herself to fall into Metron's embrace. It was as comforting as she remembered.

"I did what you asked me to do," she whispered. "I never could deny you."

"You made the right choice," Metron answered. "The books of our lives have reached their final chapter. But the story of Graxen and Nadala is just beginning, Sarelia."

The matriarch sighed. "It's been many years since I've been called by my true name. It's been so long since anyone has known me as anything other than my title. They've forgotten the dragon underneath; perhaps I'd forgotten as well."

Metron slid his cheek along hers. She trembled at its smoothness.

"I'll always be with you to help you remember," Metron whispered. "I know you, Sarelia. You're still the wise and wonderful dragon I met those long years ago; I love you still."

The matriarch nodded as her cane slipped from her talon. As long as Metron held her, she had all the strength she needed to stand.

JANDRA PULLED PET'S tattered cloak more tightly around her as she approached the gates of Dragon Forge. The ring of invisibility sat on her wrist like a bracelet. She'd not used it on her journey. She'd walked from Shandrazel's tent boldly, never looking back, and no guard had challenged her. She'd been at the edge of the encampment before she'd heard the shouts behind her as the bodies were discovered. She'd made it to the shelter of the forest shadows soon after.

Only as she reached the gleaner mounds had she'd glanced over her shoulder. She was certain she could hear the distant beating of wings. The sun-dragons were abandoning the camp in droves, dark shapes in a dark sky. Jandra didn't know what the dawn would bring when the earth-dragons found their sun-dragon masters absent. Nor, for that matter, did she know the fate of the human slaves. Hex would have his victory, it seemed. An age of anarchy was upon them.

Or, perhaps, the age of a new order.

She reached the gates and looked up, shouting, "Let me in!"

A young man looked over the wall at her.

"That's Pet's cloak," he said. "Who are you?"

"I'm Jandra," she said. "Pet's dead. Shandrazel killed him. But Pet killed Shandrazel as well."

"Oh my gosh!" the boy said. "Pet's dead? Oh my gosh!"

"What's your name?" Jandra called out.

"Vance, ma'am," he answered.

"Will you open the gate?"

"No, ma'am," he said. He threw down a rope ladder. "You'll have to climb up."

As Jandra climbed, Vance said, "I've heard your voice before. You're the girl who called out to Pet earlier. He seemed mighty excited you were here."

Jandra reached the top of the wall. She looked around the tortured landscape.

"I still can't believe you beat back the dragons," she said.

"I'm kinda surprised myself," said Vance. Jandra noticed how short Vance was; he was barely up to her chin. He was also slightly older than his voice let on, judging from his wispy mustache. "Pet really kept us together up here on the walls.

He was a good man, ma'am. I'm sorry to hear he's dead."

She nodded. "I have to speak to Burke," she said. "Pet said he was the brains of the rebellion."

"Yes, ma'am," said Vance. "He made our bows, and he built that giant."

"Good," said Jandra. "Then I may have some information that will interest him."

Vance ordered a man nearly twice his age and girth to watch his post. He led Jandra down into the fortress. She coughed as the full force of the sooty smoke hit her. Now that her nanites were no longer protecting her lungs, she felt especially vulnerable. She wished she could at least seal up the open back of her gown. Even beneath the cloak, her spine felt cold and exposed.

Vance led her through filthy streets toward the central foundry. The doors of the great factory were wide open. The sound of hammers on anvils rang through the air. Jandra raised her hands to shield her eyes as a cauldron of white-hot molten metal was poured into a form.

Vance led Jandra to a small office. He pointed toward a chair and said, "Wait here."

Jandra remained standing as Vance tapped on the door beyond the office. He looked back apologetically as several long moments passed. Finally, the door creaked open. The woman who'd been dressed in buckskins earlier was now dressed in a cotton nightgown and carrying an unsheathed sword. Jandra's eyes were still highly tuned; apparently some of the physical changes the helmet had made were permanent. She noted the razor-sharp edge of the blade. It was the sharpest thing she'd ever seen.

The raven-haired woman glared at Vance. Then she cast her gaze at Jandra. Her expression softened as she saw the blood staining Pet's cloak.

She gave Jandra a slight nod, and waved her inside.

The room beyond was pitch-black. Jandra stood still inside the door as the woman struck a match. Seconds later, a lantern fluttered to life. Burke the Machinist lay in his bed, looking still as death.

The woman sheathed her sword and touched Burke on the shoulder. Burke's eyes slowly opened. He stared up at his daughter, and then turned his head toward Jandra. He, too, nodded slowly as he saw Pet's bloodstained cloak.

"Shandrazel gave his answer, then," he whispered.

"Shandrazel is dead," said Jandra. "Pet killed him, as he killed Pet."

Burke rested his head back on the pillow. "That doesn't end this. But it buys us time. We might win this thing yet."

He turned back to Jandra. "We could win it tomorrow if you'd share your so-called magic."

"It's gone," said Jandra. "Stolen by a dragon."

"Oh," said Burke, sounding weary. "Well, we're screwed, I guess."

"No," said Jandra. "The dragon won't be able to use the technology. Only I can use it. Pet said you were the brains behind this rebellion. I need your help to get my tools back."

Burke sat up, intrigued. "I've always had an appreciation for tools. If we get them back, will you share your secrets? Will you help me bring an end to the Dragon Age?"

"I'll help even before we get it back," she said. She took a deep breath, searching her soul, trying to decide if she should speak the words that had echoed in her mind on her journey here. Whatever remained of the goddess within her grumbled at the thought of revealing the secret. The part of her that was the daughter of a dragon also rebelled, knowing that her words might bring death to all dragons.

But the part of her that was human knew it was her duty to speak.

"How can you help if you're powerless, girl?" Burke asked.

Jandra narrowed her eyes, and spoke in a firm, calm tone: "I know how to make gunpowder."

DRAGONS

ON THEIR SPECIES AND LINEAGE

SUN-DRAGONS

Sun-dragons are the lords of the realm. They are huge beasts with forty-foot wingspans and jaws that can bite a man in half. Sun-dragons are adorned with crimson scales with touches of orange and yellow that give them a fiery appearance. Wispy feathers near their snout give the illusion that they breathe smoke. They are gifted with natural weaponry of tooth and claw, but are intelligent tool users who often use spears and other missiles to enhance their already formidable combat skills. Politically, sun-dragons are organized under a powerful king who, by right, owns all the property in the kingdom. A close network of other sun-dragons, usually related to the king, manage individual areas within the kingdom. Sun-dragons of note are:

ALBEKIZAN (Deceased)

The king of the dragons for 68 years, Albekizan conquered dozens of small feudal states to create the current kingdom. He perished at the hands of Bitterwood.

BODIEL (Deceased)

Albekizan's youngest son, known for his courage and cunning. Bitterwood assassinated him during a contest of succession, leading Albekizan to launch a campaign of genocide against humans.

SHANDRAZEL

Albekizan's heir, known for his intellect and integrity. As the new king, Shandrazel intends to use his power to reform the old, authoritarian ways of ruling and bring about a new age of self-governance and enlightenment.

HEXILIZAN

Shandrazel's older brother. He lost his contest of succession and has been castrated and banished to a lifetime of service to the biologians. His years of servitude have left Hexilizan with political leanings far more radical than even Shandrazel's.

BLASPHET

Known as the Murder God, Blasphet is legendary as the most wicked dragon ever to have flown over the earth. Albekizan's brother, Blasphet was the architect of the Free City, a giant death trap where humanity was to meet its end. He was captured by

Shandrazel following the battle of the Free City and sentenced to life in the dungeon.

SKY-DRAGONS

Half the size of sun-dragons, sky-dragons are a race devoted to scholarship. The culture and history of the dragons are protected by a group of sky-dragons known as biologians, who are part priest, part librarian, and part scientist. Sky-dragons have blue scales and golden eyes. Sky dragons practice strict segregation of the sexes. The female sky-dragons all live on and island known as the Nest, where they are defended by the fierce female warriors known as the valkyries. Sky-dragons of note are:

VENDEVOREX (Deceased)
The king's wizard, also known as Master of the Invisible. He perished fighting to prevent the slaughter of mankind at the Free City.

METRON (Banished)
The former High Biologian, Metron is over a century old and was famed for his wisdom and scholarship before he was manipulated into aiding Blasphet in betraying the royal family.

ANDROKOM
A young biologian with a reputation for arrogance, Androkom was promoted to the position of High Biologian following Metron's banishment.

GRAXEN

A freak with scales of gray instead of blue, Graxen now serves as messenger to Shandrazel.

SARELIA, THE MATRIARCH

Leader of the female sky-dragons, the matriarch is charged with guiding the genetic destiny of the sky-dragon race.

ZORASTA

A valkyrie commander pressed into service as the matriarch's diplomat.

NADALA, ARIFIEL, AND SPARROW

A trio of valkyries whose fates become entangled with that of Graxen. Sparrow in noteworthy for being the niece of Metron.

EARTH-DRAGONS

Wingless creatures, earth-dragons are humanoids with turtle-beaked faces and broad, heavy bodies. Seldom more than five and a half feet tall, earth-dragons are twice as strong as men, though also twice as slow. It's nearly impossible to spot the differences between a male and female earth-dragon. The king's armies are composed mostly of earth-dragons. Few can truly be said to be of note. The one exception would be:

CHARKON

The boss of Dragon Forge, Charkon is an old veteran who served Albekizan in battle and now lives his life dedicated to keeping the king's foundries producing weapons and armor. Charkon is unusually wise and well-spoken for an earth-dragon, and is legendary for his strength and toughness.

HUMANS

THE LESSER SPECIES

The bottom rung of the dragon society, humans exist as slaves, serfs, pets, and prey. While some humans have proven to be as smart as dragons, humans have never successfully shrugged off the chains of dragon rule. For the most part, they live in villages with little daily interaction with dragons, and are left alone as long as they pay their taxes. Human society is highly fragmented and tribal, organized around competing prophets who are constantly waging small wars against one another. A lucky few humans have escaped the squalor of the human villages and have been adopted as pets by dragons. Humans of note are:

BITTERWOOD
A legendary dragon-slayer.

JANDRA
A girl raised by the wizard-dragon Vendevorex who has been trained in many of his arcane arts.

PET
A dashing and handsome purebred human, Pet was the loyal companion of the sun-dragon Chakthalla. A skilled actor, he pretended to be Bitterwood in order to save his home village, and is still dealing with the ramifications of being regarded as a great dragon-slayer.

ZEEKY
A run-away girl with a mysterious power over animals. She is devoted to her pet pig Poocher.

KAMON
An aged prophet who teaches men should be subservient to dragons until the savior arrives.

RAGNAR
A young firebrand prophet who teaches that men should struggle against dragons at every chance.

BURKE THE MACHINIST
Proprietor of Burke's Tavern, Burke is well-known for his inventiveness.

ANZA
Burke's mute daughter, trained since the age of five in the warrior's arts.

ACKNOWLEDGEMENTS

THE ACKNOWLEDGEMENTS FOR *Bitterwood* were tricky because that novel had been written in several drafts, chapters from the various versions having been read by dozens, if not hundreds, of fellow authors who gave me feedback. For *Dragonforge*, thanking the people who laid eyes on the early drafts is a much more manageable task. My early chapters were read by my biweekly critique group of Abigail Ferrance-Wu, Paul Paolicelli, Alex Wilson, William Ferris, Suanne Warr, Jud Nirenberg, and Mike Jasper. The first (and only) person to see the complete original draft was Joy Marchand, one of the finest writers I've ever read. The complete second draft was read by a handful of wise readers drawn from volunteers from *Codexwriters.com*. Cathy Bollinger and Laurel Alberdine did top-level work as wise readers on *Bitterwood*, and proved invaluable again on *Dragonforge*. Guy Stewart, Oliver Dale, and Ada Brown signed on as wise readers who hadn't read the first book, and all provided useful insights that helped me make

Dragonforge more user friendly to readers unfamiliar with the *Bitterwood* storyline. The third draft was read by my friends Jeremy Cavin and Cheryl Morgan, and I've been brainstorming with them (as well as Cathy Bollinger) on the possible plot threads for the book that will follow *Dragonforge*. The only other people to have read *Dragonforge* as I write this are the folks at Solaris, with a special nod going to Christian Dunn and Alethea Kontis. I also owe a debt of gratitude to Mark Newton for emailing me the breathtaking cover by Michael Komarck at a pivotal moment in the first draft. Seeing the cover art inspired events that flavored the very creepy interaction between Jazz and Jandra, and the book is richer because of it.

I SHOULD ALSO mention Solaris editor George Mann, since my conversation with him at Readercon inspired the clockwork chess-monkey at Burke's Tavern. Dragon Age fans will want to track down the *Solaris Book of New Fantasy* George edited since it contains a short story detailing the first encounter between Vendevorex and Jandra, a story that has ramifications in both *Bitterwood* and *Dragonforge*.

SPEAKING OF READERCON, I owe a big debt of thanks to the various cons I've attended in recent years. Each con is the work of dozens, and in some cases, hundreds of individuals, too many to name, so I'll have to thank the cons themselves: Dragoncon, Stellarcon, World Fantasy, Readercon,

Trinoc*con, StellarCon, RavenCon and ConCarolinas. I've had a great time at all of these cons and look forward to attending them again. If you're a fantasy fan who hasn't been to con, google one of the above and go! Geeks of the world, unite!

ZEEKY'S ABILITY TO "talk" to animals is based on the work of a scientist, Temple Grandin, who wrote a book called *Animals in Translation* that is a masterwork on understanding the minds of animals. I also owe a debt to the late Stephen Jay Gould, whose writings on evolution sparked my imagination on the creation of biologically plausible dragons.

I ALSO OWE thanks to my family and friends, who have been very patient with me these last few months as my personal time was increasingly devoured by dragons. I owe a debt as well to all my co-workers who've put up with me as I spend less time at my old job and more time dedicated to novel writing. And a special thanks goes to my agent, Nadia Cornier, for helping guide me through the twists and turns of contracts both foreign and domestic.

THERE IS ANOTHER group of people who also is owed a great deal of gratitude for the existence of *Dragonforge*, namely the legions of people who went out and picked up copies of *Bitterwood*. If you are one of these people, thank you. If you are one of these people who then went on to mention

Bitterwood in your blog or in an Amazon review, keep reading—your name (or at least your screen name) might be in the following list.

Thanks go to Laughing Lion, Michael and Angela Goodwin, Bob A. Reiss, Rick Fisher, William Howe, S. Pendergrass, Anthony McPherson, Nancy Fulda, A.J. Myers, Cyronic, *Deathray* Magazine, Eric Brown, and *SciFiNow* magazine. Authors E.E. Knight and John Marco both gave the book big boosts by mentioning it on their blogs. Fellow NC fantasy author Lisa Shearin has helped me sell many copies by not only mentioning *Bitterwood* on her blog, but appearing at joint signing sessions with me at various Barnes and Nobles in the area.

Gail Z. Martin, Aiden Moher, Isaac the Master of Weirdness, Bill Bittner, Craig Morgan, Otterevil-reads, J.G. Thomas, Lynne (Kaijugirl), Judy H in NC, John Joseph Adams, Rick Novy, Babies Stole My Dingo, Tony Frazier, Eric James Stone, Andrew Wheeler, Aliette de Bodard, Mur Lafferty, Pat Esden, Helena Bell, and J Diggy aka Norton G, all have talked about the book to some degree or another on their blogs, as have many others that I'm no doubt skipping over since I'm missing them in the roughly 2,500 hits I get when I google, "James Maxey Bitterwood." All blog mentions are appreciated (even the negative reviews are helpful— I made structural changes to *Dragonforge* to address what I felt were fair criticisms of the time-skipping approach of *Bitterwood*). I can't wrap up this list without giving special thanks to Robert Thompson (*fantasybookcritic.blogspot.com*) and

Angela (*SciFiChick.com*) who gave the *Bitterwood* a big boost with early, well-thought-out reviews on their respective forums.

READER FEEDBACK IS always welcome. The questions people ask me about my stories often spark my imagination. If there are further adventures in the Dragon Age beyond the current trilogy, they will no doubt be shaped by the commentary I get on *Dragonforge*. Cathy Bollinger (her third mention, if you're counting) asked after reading *Bitterwood* why we didn't meet any female sky-dragons. Pondering that question produced the Graxen/Nadala plotline that frames the events of *Dragonforge*. So, drop me a line if you have any questions or comments. I currently blog at *jamesmaxey.blogspot.com* and *bitterwoodnovel.blogspot.com*. There are also threads about my books at *solarisbooks.com* that I routinely check. Hope I see you there.

James Maxey
February 2008

ABOUT THE AUTHOR

JAMES MAXEY LIVES in Hillsborough, NC, USA. After graduating from the Odyssey Fantasy Writers' Workshop and Orson Scott Card's Writer's Boot Camp, James broke into the publishing world in 2002 when he won a Phobos Award for his short story, "Empire of Dreams and Miracles." Phobos Books later published James's debut novel, the cult classic superhero tale *Nobody Gets the Girl*. His short stories have since appeared in *Asimov's* and numerous anthologies. For a listing of his currently available stories, and frequent rants about circus freaks, comic books, and angels, visit James on the web at *jamesmaxey.blogspot.com*.

The first novel of the Dragon Age

ISBN: 978-1-84416-487-5

It is a time when powerful dragons reign supreme and humans are forced to work as slaves, to support the tyrannical ruler King Albekizan. However, there is one name whispered amongst the dragons that strikes fear into their very hearts and minds: Bitterwood. The dragon hunter is about to return.

www.solarisbooks.com

Book one of the Chronicles of the Necromancer

ISBN: 978-1-84416-468-4

The world of Prince Martris Drayke is thrown into sudden chaos and disorder when his brother murders their father and seizes the throne. Cast out, Martris and a small band of trusted friends are forced to flee to a neighbouring kingdom to plot their retaliation. But if the living are arrayed against him, Martris must call on a different set of allies: the ranks of the dead...

www.solarisbooks.com

 SOLARIS FANTASY